TRIGGER WARNINGS

A Fool's Bargain is a dark romance urban fantasy with heavy themes. Reader discretion is advised as this book contains:

Alcohol Consumption

Breath Play

Cannibalism

Child Abuse (remembered)

Childbirth

Consensual Dubious Consent

Death

Death of a Parent (off-page)

Description of a Violent Death

Fear Play

Fire and Arson

Foster Care

Home Invasion

Mask Play (mentioned)

Mentions of (off-page) Sexual Assault and Harrassment

Mentions of an Eating Disorder

Mentions of Drug Use (off-page)

Mentions of Self-Harm

Mentions of Suicidal Ideation

Physical Assault

Post Traumatic Stress Disorder

Primal Play

Scars

Sexually Explicit Discussions and Scenes

Torture

To the souls who wander where light dares not go,
May you find power in the darkness,
and pleasure in the pain.

PART ONE: THE CITY

CHAPTER 1

River

Heavy traffic echoes off the near barren apartment as if the bustling streets below ran straight through these thinning walls. Emergency sirens blare ostentatiously through the wet paper bag equivalent of drywall and stucco. The sounds filter in and swirl around me, the only forms of life outside my tired breathing. Reminding me that I am, in fact, conscious. Unfortunately.

A 'newly' renovated kitchen sits quaintly to my right. The only signs of its pesky existence are the low whirring of electricity pulsing through the air. Cold seeps through my clothes from the icy tiles below, chilling my exhausted muscles. A painful yet welcomed reminder.

I'm barely able to fight the sagging of my eyelids as they flutter closed, my head dipping down every few seconds. Panic erupts over my senses as I jolt awake from each doze, returning me to the view to my left.

It's the same city I've called home for the last decade but with a new view. Atlanta wasn't new to me at all. She's been my home for almost as long as my hometown. I've grown up more here than I was ever allowed to back home. I am forever grateful to her.

The overcrowded city exists in the same hustle and bustle of any major city. Malls, overcrowded roads caused by underfunded public transportation, and (some would say) too many restaurants. Every street lamp has the same wattage, equidistant apart. A Chinese takeout restaurant located in a shopping center with a grocery store.

Out of all the cities I could have chosen, there's always been something calling me here. Ten years ago, I packed what little I had to my name and shipped myself off to college in the hopes of a better life. A fresh start. That the stark difference between here and there was enough to make me forget what lay waste behind me.

I ran from my birthplace in search of something, whatever it was, that called to me beyond the town limits. Something unknown that beckoned to me. Whispering to me through the forests. Making me run as far as the eye could see.

I never looked back. Never regretted taking flight.

There's always been something excitingly unsettling about a new start. No matter how big or small or if you've done it a million times.

The overwhelming exhaustion that now courses through every muscle is a blaring reminder of that. The sheer determination that roared through me to make something better for myself.

I wanted this. I remind myself. *Deserve this.*

Taking this job. Furthering my career. Doing the things I'm good at, in an area that I adore so much. Infinitely more than that wretched town where all my worst nightmares still reside.

I wanted to celebrate this milestone with Nancy, my childhood best friend. Even if that meant paying for her flights here. Even if it meant bringing the smell of that wretched man into my brand new home. No matter that it's attached to the only person I've ever loved outside of my older brother.

No matter that she doesn't know that the man she claims to love is a monster. No matter that ever since her mother got sick, she's been the worst, most abhorrent version of herself. No matter that she's taking it out on me.

No. No matter.

In her absence now, in the wake of silence, I revel in the reality of it all. That everything I've worked so hard for, for so long, is now coming true.

It all seems so surreal. I want to pinch myself, thinking it'll all disappear when I wake. Waiting to be filled with disappointment. But as my thumb and pointer finger pull at the skin on my arm, hard, I internalize a yelp. A smile washes over me.

A warm lull washes over my hunched body, eyelids slipping lower and lower. No amount of willpower I will ever possess can stop the gentle cradle of sleep.

Warm white sheets draped over a muscular body lying beside me. Tiny dust particles float around aimlessly in the morning light that streams in through the uncovered window. A brilliant blue sky hung overhead, just outside the enclosed room. Abstract wall art hung on each wall, reminiscent of an art gallery more so than a bedroom.

This felt like no other dream I had encountered before. There was something innately real about this place. Familiar. Comfortable. Safe. All emotions I couldn't understand.

Bare, tan skin peeks out from under the duvet, glowing under the soft yellow light of the morning. Inhale. Exhale. Soft snores of REM sleep. Ruffled black hair starkly contrasted against the whites and yellows of its surroundings.

Inhale. Exhale. Peace.

Inhale. Exhale. Fondness.

Inhale. Exhale. Forever.

A smile that I can only explain as content laces its way over my face. The figure's tousled hair ruffles further as they turn their toned, naked body. Toward me. As if they had known I was there this whole time.

A near-silent moan escaped their throat. Toned arms extended to the sky in a stretch, seconds before encapsulating my body in an embrace.

Deep brown eyes peer warmly into mine. So deep I could have gotten lost in them if I stared a moment longer. Paired with those puffy eyes was a long, straight nose, full cheeks, and pink lips. The man's face was slender, free of facial hair and blemishes outside of the tiny scar on the bridge of his nose. Thick eyebrows knitted together as a puzzled look passed over his gorgeous face.

Déjà vu eclipses my senses. I'd been here before or I'd known him in another lifetime. I wasn't sure which one it was. A knot in my stomach tightens as the familiarity creeps over me.

A smile pulls at the corners of my mouth. Contentment warmed my cold, aching heart. If I lived here for the rest of my life, I'd die happy. Washed with the softness of a loving embrace.

The stranger's softened features accentuate his beauty. One that comes so naturally to him, even subconsciously. Subtle lines form when a grin passes over his lips, a reaction that reaches his eyes. Ones that I continue to get lost in.

The world around us is eerily silent. Not even the uncanny quiet could sour the hand-shaking anxiety that coursed through my veins. The same way energy drinks used to in high school.

Long, slender fingers reach out from under the plush comforter that adorns both of our bodies. Gently touching my cheek. He lets out a low, smooth hum as if surprised his hand didn't pass right through me. A thumb strokes my skin, his smooth hands are kind and fragile in the same way his eyes depict sincerity.

"River, wake up." He says in a voice that rumbled through my very existence. One filled with deep emotions that I didn't dare begin to explore. The gruffness of the tone is abrasive but welcomed against my bones as they reverberated with the echoes. He was a force to be reckoned with, I just knew it.

"What?" I asked abruptly. Panic settles into my core. There was something so endearingly comfortable here that I didn't want to let go of. "I don't want to go."

"We'll meet again soon, my angel." He says. Angel. No one in the history of forever has called me 'angel'. I'm not getting into heaven, let alone be an angel. But the name sounds so perfect on his lips. His tongue. He can call me anything, anytime.

His image and the environment around him faded out just as quickly as they had appeared. Before I had time to say goodbye.

My eyes snap open as a gasp sends cold air shooting through my lungs. At the eyes staring back at me. Not the ones of the dream man I had grown so fond of, but those of someone far more familiar.

"River, I-" Nancy begins, her piercing blue eyes filled with concern first, then relief.

"I'm up, I'm up." I grumble, pushing her away from me.

"Thank god." She sighs. "I thought you had crossed the rainbow bridge on me." Her southern-twang-filled words rattle through my near-empty head.

The words of the dream man echo off the walls of my soul. *We'll meet again soon, my angel.*

"You think I'm going to heaven?" I chuckle, rubbing my dry eyes. Delirious humor elicits a dry laugh out of Nancy. But it's not enough to pull me from the high I'm still feeling from my dream.

"Not a chance." She confirms.

"Agreed," I smirk.

"Must have been sleeping well. You're drooling like a sixteen-year-old pug." She mocks, pointing to the pool of saliva in the corner of my mouth. I wipe it away with the sleeve of my shirt. She extends a hand to help me stand, my knees, elbows, and wrists crack like a very old, unused glowstick.

"I needed that nap," I admit, a smile unwavering from my tired face.

"Must have been a good dream." She says. I hum in agreement. "Did you dream of Brad Pitt?" She teases.

"I don't think anyone's dreamt about Brad Pitt since the mid-2000s, Nance."

"I do!"

"Then you're the only one." I counter. She laughs, but the light doesn't reach her eyes. "I don't know who he was, but he was very scrumptious looking." I take the time to twist my spine into a contortionist's position to crack the stiffness away.

"Never seen him before?" She asks, busying herself with

unboxing the bag of African food she had brought up.

"Never, and I would remember a face like his," I reply, approaching the kitchen island.

Jollof rice and fufu overtake the stale air, wafting from the containers being gently placed on the marble-colored laminate countertop. A new wave of hunger overtakes me. My mouth waters as if I hadn't eaten a solid meal in a year.

A light, curious hum escapes from Nancy.

"So, Riv." She states, settling down in one of the bar chairs. I follow suit, sitting next to her. I begin feeling the weight of the entire day slipping from my shoulders into my legs. Resting my arm on the counter to prop up a head that feels as though it weighs a thousand pounds, I poke at my food lackadaisically. "Are you excited?" She asks.

"Hm?" I ask in return.

"You're starting a new job. With people who don't know you. People who didn't watch you go through puberty and were repulsed by your rendition of the worm at junior prom." I chuckle into my bite of food. "I'm envious."

"No one told you to do the dead worm in front of Jason Crawford." I responded. She gives me a light shove with her palm.

"Bitch, you know what I mean." Her eyes carry a veil of jealousy that I've never seen before.

"I haven't lived around those hillbillies in a decade, Nance." I counter. "I'm almost certain none of them remember me. Or care to think about the shit they put me through. Why should I give them more kindness than they ever gave me?"

She hums again, this time less enthusiastically. She would never say it, but she hates me for abandoning her. Ever since the day she found out I was leaving; she's been cold to me. Physical distance or not, the fact that I even planned to leave our hometown drove a wedge so deep between us that the scar tissue from that wound would never heal. And after ten years, I'm all but given up on who we used to be.

It was always my dream to move out of the middle of

bumfuck nowhere. The big city's always called to me, but that town was never my home. I've found more pieces of myself in the journey to get to where I am now than I ever had before.

What I never understood was why she didn't go with me. What stopped her from at least venturing off to college to explore herself? Get some outside perspective before making the hard and fast decision to stay home and marry the first man that asked.

The worst man that could have ever asked.

"If you hate it there so much, just move in with me." I suggest. A glance around the one-bedroom apartment doesn't offer much room for the invitation, either. My words ring hollow through the silence settling between us. Almost like I didn't believe the offer, either.

"You know I can't." She whispers as her head falls forward into her chest. "You know I can't leave Mama." I nod, unable to understand what possesses her to be so faithful to a woman that caused her endless amounts of suffering.

"Yeah." I sigh, not wanting to fight about it anymore.

"I know you don't get it, Riv., but she's all I have." The comment stings sour in my mouth. Rotten words hit their mark.

I once considered the same of her. She used to be all I had. The only piece of grace that I clung to. No matter how hard and fast I ran from things that I couldn't stomach, couldn't explain, I always found comfort in Nancy. She was calm, maternal.

She was my friend when nobody else would even acknowledge my presence. When the world failed me time and time again, she was the rock I clung to. For the majority of our childhood, she's been the only guiding light. She was all I ever had. Now, she's just bitter. And things are different now.

Somehow, the air around us feels heavier than it's ever been. A looming darkness shrouds over our shoulders. The kitchen around us is sparsely lit with the dim yellow coming from under the counter. Hardly granting enough light to see the disdain on Nancy's face.

"You're all I ever had, Nance." I whisper, almost to myself. So low I wasn't sure she even heard me as my chest bore a weight of twenty years of unspoken words.

"Yeah, well, you left me. Didn't you? You left me like your brother left you." She snips.

"Asher didn't leave on purpose." I snap. My eyes and nose sting with threatened tears, ones I wouldn't dare bear to her. To anyone. "Besides, we were supposed to go together."

"I couldn't leave. We both always knew that."

And I did. Deep down, I had always known that I was always destined to leave, and she was destined to stay.

Her mom had always been excessively controlling, neglectful, and incredibly emotionally abusive. And we all found out the hard way that CPS will never be concerned about upper middle-class white kids with influential parents who could lie their way into a snake-charming tournament and win.

She fell sick last year with an illness that the doctors haven't been able to diagnose. And ever since, Nancy has acted like Sharon could do no wrong. Has *never* done wrong. Nancy waits on her hand and foot. Having to beg to be 'allowed' out of the house, to eat, to watch TV. Sharon always feigns some excuse or heartache that always convinces Nancy to be at her beck and call.

I've personally been counting down the days until that old hag kicks the bucket like the ass she is. If there is a God or two out there, I like to think they've got a sense of justice. Or humor. Whichever comes first to them.

Nancy thinks I'm a horrible person for thinking that this undiagnosable disease isn't the perfect example of karma. But maybe I would feel the same way if I loved my parents in the same Stockholm Syndrome way she does. Maybe I would have turned out different if I had parents that loved me.

Though, love isn't what her parents showed her either. Just an expansive future full of lavish things, an unrelenting influence over common folk, and an eating disorder.

Nancy's parents divorced shortly after we graduated high school. We were four hours into our road trip to the Outer Banks when Sharon called Nancy sobbing, as if she weren't the one who had served Todd the divorce papers on their finest, whitest China.

Todd retired early from the State and moved down to the Florida Keys, free to eat greasy food until his heart gives out. He calls Nancy on her birthday and sends her a check at Christmas, but past that he's almost no contact. The grape vine says that he has a girlfriend younger than his own daughter. Though, no one's proven it, and no one cares enough to go looking into it.

Nancy puts a lot of blame on her dad for her parents' failed marriage. Which I completely agree with to an extent, but if you're going to hate your shitty parents, you should take off the rose-tinted glasses and see the whole picture.

Which she hasn't done yet.

Sharon doesn't have much longer if we're all being honest with ourselves. And once she passes, Nancy will be free to live out her life as she seems fit. With a sizable inheritance and unburdened by the need to be her mother's favorite only child. And a man child she's taken as her betrothed.

I used to worry that she wouldn't know what to do with her new-found freedom when it finds her. That she'll go down dark paths that are so hard to walk back from. Paths that I ran down to escape the ever approaching darkness, only to slide into deeper waters.

But I think my time worrying about her is coming to a close. That her and I are too different now. She's remained the same meek teenager whose spine is made of dry sand, and I've grown enough to see that she has no intentions of changing.

My heart aches for the friendship, the girlhood we shared. The good memories that are all muddled with mourning for a loss that can never be repaired.

"Are you listening to me?" Nancy asks, snapping her

fingers in front of my face. My eyes snap up from where they had unfocused somewhere in the marbling of the countertop. Guilt racks over me as she scolds me with her mother's glare.

"I know you don't like her, but with you gone, she's all I have. Brian stepped up when you left us all alone."

I put the lid back on my to-go container, setting my fork on the counter with a metallic *dink*. "Convenient that he didn't have the balls to step up when I was around. If he loved you so much." I snark under my breath.

"You smothered me. He was intimidated."

Intimidated my ass. If she knew what he was capable of, she'd . . . She's just as wretched as he is.

"First I smother you, then I abandon you. Which is it?" I ask, louder than originally intended. Mentally cursing the enemies for neighbors I'm collecting.

"Why is it so hard for you to believe that you're both?" She asks, slamming a hand onto the counter.

"You can't make me the villain in your story."

"Watch me."

"You hate me. You hate your mom. You hate your fiancé. Are you just going to paint yourself a victim?" I snap.

"I *am* a victim." She demands. "And I don't hate anyone but you."

"I hope you know that this hell you say you're living in is of your own making."

Nancy pauses, her breath audibly catching in her throat. A shaky hand rises to her throat, clasping around the shitty heart necklace Sharon had given her as a Christmas gift last year. The witch couldn't be bothered to part with any expensive, nice jewelry from her own collection.

"Just promise me you'll come back once she-" Her voice cuts out with a harsh swallow. "Please. Just be there for me."

"No." I say without hesitation. Tears threaten to overflow my sleepy eyes. "I will not be both the bad guy and your shoulder to cry on. When you pick one, then we'll talk."

I glance over at the clock through a watery yawn.

Midnight. "I'm going to bed." I declare.

She nods. I slide out of my chair and onto my aching feet, scooping up my still warm take-out box and shoving it in the fridge.

I meander into the bedroom where a mattress lay on the floor covered in a baby blue fitted sheet and an undetermined amount of haphazardly dispersed blankets. One of which is a quilt I had made two or so years ago as a matching set with Nancy. The bright yellow of the stars stand out against the wine tones of the rest of the background. A secondary pile of boxes sits in front of the closet that contain all semblances of my wardrobe.

"Good night." I say, waving her off as I slip into the bathroom and close the door gently. To allow myself to release the heaviness in my chest without her prying eyes.

With a flick of the light switch, the big fluorescent bulbs above the mirror flash on, nearly blinding me. Their harshness is a stark contrast to the dimly lit rooms – apartment – that preceded them. The person staring back seems so foreign to me. Not an ounce of familiarity registers me as me as I take in how tired I look. These last few weeks have been excruciating and grueling.

Between job interviews, resignations, packing, and moving, it was almost too much. I was barely surviving. I wasn't eating or remembering to eat more than one meal near bedtime. I regularly forgot to take my medication. I am just ready to have some sense of normalcy back to my daily life.

When I was searching for a new apartment, I wanted something closer to work that I wouldn't have to potentially drive 2 hours to go 10 miles. Or bike. I don't want to be sweaty every day. This place isn't cheap, it's in the city for God's sake, but it checked enough boxes to be the only apartment I put in an application for.

I pride myself on how well I've done for myself, considering where I came from and all that's happened to me. I got a full ride to college, worked two jobs to provide for myself the life I knew I deserved, and now I'm here. I'm one step closer to being where I want my life to be. Though, I don't really know where it is that I truly want to be.

The universe has a gentle, guiding hand on my back. I follow where she leads. And it's all led me here. I may not always know why, but I know it will always work out.

I can breathe a sigh of relief for being comfortable. I'm proud of myself. It's been ten years since I got out, and I've built my own little empire from the ground up with no one there to guide me.

And everyone wished me harm.

A sigh of relief washes over me as if I'm, for the first time in my whole life, exactly where I need to be. Where I should be. I take the extra moment to revel in the thought that the universe is aligning its stars just for me.

Rubbing cold water over my face, the iciness tingles. I drink in how alive I feel. After changing into pajamas, my eyelids begin to retain some of the weight that they had earlier during my nap.

Flicking off the light, I prepare for my trek to the bed, unable to see mere inches in front of my face. I slide under the covers, ready to relinquish any consciousness that I possess.

A faint instrumental melody wanders through the wall directly behind my head. The soft, unfamiliar beat is a quiet, upbeat tempo. It immediately puts a smile on my tired face. Occasionally, the music would stop and rewind, or the faint tapping of a keyboard would interrupt the music, but only briefly.

I could listen to the music forever.

CHAPTER 2

Leon

Great. New neighbors. Just when I thought today couldn't get any better, either.

First, dinner with my *lovely* parents. A dinner I'd been dreading since last year.

Now, my finally quiet apartment is suddenly being filled with the sounds of furniture scuffing floors, arguing, and heavy breathing. I once had hopes of enjoying the peace and quiet of an empty adjourning apartment for longer than a week.

But sadly the universe always has other plans.

The previous tenant was a certified freak. A guy who liked sex so loud the paper walls couldn't contain him. He didn't care who he brought home, just so long as they could make him scream at all hours.

The ones before that were an unhappy couple on the brink of a divorce on any day that ended with 'y'.

And the one before that was an old guy who liked to watch football with the TV volume on a thousand, act as standing referee, commentator, and spectator. Plus, he would conveniently forget to wear his hearing aids. Regularly.

I had held the door for the two ladies moving boxes as big as they were on rented hand trucks, hoping and praying to a God I don't believe in that they weren't going to my floor, but they were.

They always are.

The two women argued amongst themselves about

topics I chose to remain not privy to. One of them was taller, long blonde hair and big blue eyes that you could see from outer space. The other was shorter, with honey red hair and hazel eyes that were soft and inviting as they peered into the depths of my soul.

The second one was the only one who bothered to say 'thank you' for holding the door. Her voice a crisp defiance against her friend's nasally one. No hint of southern drawl.

The second one looked too kind, too sweet. Too many stars hung in the constellations of the green flecked throughout the almost golden brown eyes. She was undoubtedly beautiful, ethereal.

I forced myself to look away from her. Forced myself to forget about her existence instantly. For I knew she was more than the universe would allow a bastard like me to have. Even if all of the stars in the galaxies aligned, I'd be nothing of interest to her.

Dwelling on it wouldn't make it come true. No amount of wishing and wanting could bring to life a fantasy that I know I'm not destined for.

Walking into my apartment, my eyes fell upon the pile of laundry that I've been avoiding, the dishes scattered in the sink, the crumbs on the tile. Disdain courses through me.

It's been a rough few weeks. My mental health had been at its lowest leading up to my birthday dinner with disinterested parents. So bad that I had neglected simple things that hadn't been an issue before.

But now, it was over. I was another year closer to thirty. My parents still didn't acknowledge my career successes since it's not what they had once wanted me to do. They had always wanted me to follow in their footsteps. Go into their line of work, but it was never something I had been interested in. Music was always my passion, and that was never good enough for them, I suppose.

I set the soju they got me as an attempt at a birthday present in the fridge to chill indefinitely. I'd like a good reason to celebrate other than another cursed trip around the sun.

And new neighbors certainly weren't anything to cheer for. Especially not with my string of luck.

The image of the hazel eyed girl with freckled cheeks keeps creeping into my mind. Thoughts of her swam in my head like swans on a crisp, blue lake. Circling and dancing upon the water. Every time I push the image of her back, she comes to me. A smile graced on her full, pink lips. Mischief in her enchanting eyes.

Ring, Ring.

My phone chimes from its resting place on the island. I jog to retrieve it, though I'm not expecting it to be anyone but spam. Glancing at the caller ID, a shred of happiness slides through me.

"Happy birthday!" Grandma sings into the receiver of Uncle Ricky's phone, following it closely with the full birthday song. "Happy birthday, grandson."

"Thank you," I reply, grinning hard enough to hurt the muscles in my cheeks.

"Did you do anything special?" She asks, her voice cracking around the tears she refused to acknowledge. Her only grandson, quickly approaching thirty. The little boy she helped raise, a full-fledged adult.

"If you consider dinner with Mom and Dad special, then yes." I retorted, eliciting a laugh out of her.

"They still in the business?" She asks somberly.

"Unfortunately. And still upset that I didn't follow suit."

"Typical." She huffs, "Still single?" She asked.

She knew the answer. "Of course. That'll never change."

"It will. I just hope to see it."

"Don't get all depressing on my birthday." I crack.

"Give me a granddaughter and I will reconsider."

"Fair." I chuckle, the thought of that red haired woman on the other side of the thinning wall careens into my mind again. I stamp down the thoughts as quickly as they come. "Isn't it past your bedtime?"

"Isn't it past yours?" She counters sharply.

"Absolutely. Every year I get closer and closer to that knee replacement we talked about and a Tempur-Pedic mattress." She cackles at my jokes. "Did Uncle Ricky convince you to call?"

"He thought it would be better than a letter. I disagreed and sent you one anyway. Do you even check your mail?"

"Yes, I check my mail. Do you not get my letters back?"

"I'm just making sure you aren't forgetting about this old hag." She snorts.

"I'd never forget about you." I smile, one that reaches my eyes for the first time in a long time. "I'll have to take a trip out to see you soon. If you'll have me."

"You better bring a girlfriend with you." She snips.

"Noted." I chuckle.

Meandering into my bedroom, in the silence that lingers, the faintest of hums drift in from the other side of the wall. Ones that sound as crisp and clean as the autumn wind.

"Get some rest, grandson." She orders. We say our brief good-byes before the call ends, and I'm left listening to the music tumbling into my ears.

If I can hear her, then she most certainly could have heard me talking. Another smile settles on my face at the idea of her, one I'm not as quick to toss out, but I do eventually.

I toss it out because I know I don't deserve it. I throw away any semblance of hope I have in regard to her. Not even allowing her to live in my memories. It's too dangerous. She's too pretty.

CHAPTER 3

River

A dim room, lit only by a handful of candles in mason jars strewn about the room, flashes into view before coming into clear focus.

A spacious bedroom with floor to ceiling windows that overlooked a city that refuses to sleep. Lights of varying colors and saturations flicker down below. Ants running their farms completely unaware of their onlookers.

The flames dance about, contained to their little glass houses. Each one unmarked and nestled on top of a hard surface, illuminating two shadows. One stationary figure and one approaching. The stationary figure makes no move to turn and look at the approaching one and no sense of fear washes over me as I realize that I am the still being I was once staring at.

As the movement stops, I allow myself to peer at the person, taller than me and amorphous through a layer of baggy clothing. Turning feels like slow motion combined with the worst case of head spins right up until the moment my eyes meet his.

The deep brown familiarity rattles the Déjà vu yet again. Before I can speak, his hand finds the back of my neck, pulling me into a kiss.

A kiss as deep as his eyes are brown and as passionate as someone who's missed you for a thousand lifetimes. Supple lips caress mine in a desperate need for more.

Strong hands and fingers intertwine their way through my hair and body, a reassuring force that I don't fight. My heart swells like I've finally loosened a breath I had been holding my entire life. An oasis appearing after a twenty-year drought, awaking an unquenchable thirst within me that I fight to hide.

I sense that my desperation, my longing, will be met with playful mockery. That's the last thing I want to encounter when all I want to do is feel the soft lines of this man's face for all of eternity. With one last peck, he pulls away from me with a smirk on his reddened lips.

"I missed you." He coos, creases forming around his eyes from a hearty chuckle. A familiar, gruff voice washing over me in a sweeping caress.

I make no move to reply, only to smile at him, his deep voice reverberating throughout my body. "What? You didn't miss me?" He asks, quickly turning his smirk to a playful pout.

I stumble over my words. Unable to form coherent syllables let alone sentences. This only furthers his giggling and relinquishes any signs of pouting he had previously shown.

"I missed you, too." I utter, unsure how I could possibly miss someone I've only ever met in a dream once before. But somehow I feel as though I've known all my life.

The familiarity of him envelops me as his arms roam across my body. Strong hands that once were smooth, now have calluses. Those puffy eyes are now full of clarity. A commanding presence before me, and I am almost willing to give myself over to him.

Perplexed at the likelihood that the same dream guy that I drooled over before is somehow back, and even dreamier than ever.

"Good. I was worried you stopped loving me there for a second." He retorts with a scrunch of his nose.

"I could never." I say, watching the sparkle in his eyes grow under the compliment.

Do I love him? I don't even know him. I can't possibly love someone I don't know. But here he stands, a perfect image of everything I have ever wanted to encounter in someone. I feel compelled to love him. Drawn to the love I see in his opulent eyes. Those dimpled smiles.

"How was work?" I ask, trying to gauge any semblance of who he could be. He doesn't look like anyone I've ever met.

"*Eh, it was work. Same old, same old.*" *He scoffs playfully with a Cheshire grin.*

I raise an eyebrow at him as he moves himself to sit on the bed, dragging my willing body with him to stand in between his legs. He rests his head on my chest with his ear right above my heart. "*I forget how fast your heart beats when you're near me.*"

"*What?*" *I gasp, trying to pull away but failing against his iron grip.*

"*You can't hide how I affect you.*" *He chuckles as my heart quickens as if on command.* "*I've always wanted to record it. Bottle it up so I don't forget that you're real.*"

"*You forget I'm real?*" *I ask, throwing a similar level of pout at him that he threw at me earlier.*

He rolls his pretty eyes and flashes me a brilliant, pearly smile. Butterflies swarm in full force, swirling around my stomach like a school of fish.

"*Only once or twice.*" *He teases, a genuine playfulness flickers in his eyes.*

Mirrored within them, my reflection peers back at me, completely foreign yet entirely recognizable. Somehow, seeing myself through someone else's eyes, someone who would swear I could do no wrong, changes everything about how I view myself.

I scoff, rolling my eyes and half-heartedly attempting to escape his grip around my waist. A bubbly giggle escapes my lips as his arms clasp around my midsection and his fists become filled with grasps of my shirt. My gaze wanders from his incredibly soft features and out the window, once again mesmerized at the consistency of the city below.

I wonder if this is what real love is meant to feel like.

Not the puppy-love you experience in childhood. Or the speed love that comes with your late teens and early twenties. Is love really this slow?

*Unhurried interactions of people who are **really** in love. The whole world could crumble around me right now and the only thing I find it in me to care about is how delicately this man is looking at me. The curvature of his smile and how his inset eyes* *couldn't paint him more gently. How his features make him look so menacing until he's staring directly into my soul the same way I imagine Johnny looked at June.*

Everything felt pure and sentimental. His casual unseriousness will forever be locked away in my memory as a living portrait of something I wish to remember for as long as my soul walks this earth. Even after I wake and all of this will dissipate, I want to remember the way I felt here. The softness and comfort of someone who is so deeply and madly in love with me is something that I want to hold on to.

Even if I know it isn't real.

Especially since I know I'll never experience what it feels like to be truly loved.

"Do you think we're lovers in every lifetime?" I ask softly into the top of his head. His velvety hair tickling my nose as the sweet smell of rosewood and sage linger on my senses.

"Absolutely." He mumbles into my chest without an ounce of hesitation. "Do you think you could love me if we were strangers again?" His hands leave my waist and find my chin, pulling my attention back to him.

"Absolutely." I reply, feeling unprompted tears swell in my eyes, like this was our goodbye. "I- I love you beyond words."

"And I love you beyond all earthly constraints, angel." He coos, hands exploring my body, under my shirt. Callused hands roaming the expanse of my skin. "I love you more than the moon loves the stars. More than anything in this life and the next." He lifts my shirt and plants an open mouth kiss on my sternum. "I'll love you even if I'm nothing but a shell of a man. When I think I'm at my lowest, you lift me from that infernal darkness."

His breath is warm over my exposed midriff.

I don't know this man.

I don't know him. But I know that I feel at peace here. A little apartment in the sky, in my dreams. Dreams that were once cursed with nightmares, now hold a love I refuse to back down from. A lover I must return to.

I command myself not to cry, to push back any negativity

bubbling deep down at the idea of losing my dream lover. It's just a dream. He's not even real. Nothing about this scenario is real, but it feels painful. If I screamed, I'm almost certain that it would break the windows with the volume.

He's right in front of me and he loves me, and I don't want to leave, but something's calling me to.

And as if in the blink of an eye, I'm surrounded by darkness. Not a fiber of hair or linen floating around for me to grab onto. Nothing left of the love I feel certain I'm undeserving of, but so desperately want to cling on to.

Moisture stains my face. My eyes flutter open, revealing the first glimpses of an orange sunrise. Warmth leaking from the empty spot beside me, though Nancy is nowhere to be found. Running water sounds from the bathroom to my left along with the faintest sounds of music.

I listen intently, trying to discern if the music's Nancy's or if it's my new neighbors. But once my brain registers the song, I know it's Nancy. A wave of relief washes over my sweaty brow, a smile on my dry lips. They went to bed.

Good.

Swinging my legs off the bed and sitting up, I pull my stiff body off the mattress. Wincing at the pops and cracks that erupt from each joint. The plush rug under my bare feet offers little support.

Changing into something other than my pajamas that have clearly seen better days, I do what little I can to get ready with the bathroom occupied and the door locked. Nancy's never locked the bathroom door when I'm around. Weird.

I check the time, nearly six thirty.

Striding swiftly over to the bathroom door, I knock loudly three times. "Come on, Nance! I don't want you to be late."

"I got time, you old bitch." She croons from closer to the door than I anticipate.

"This isn't the airport back home. They have more than two terminals." I counter, lacing a sense of urgency into my plea. "If you don't move your ass, I'm making you take a taxi."

"Fuck you!" She snaps. When I don't reply, she says. "Fine, I'm coming."

The water and music quickly cease to exist, sending a quiet plea to my neighbor for forgiveness for being so obnoxious. There's a mad scuttle behind the door before she exits. Sopping wet hair stuck limply to her head, freshly brushed.

"Do you think I'll have time to grab a bite to eat?" She asks, throwing what little belongings she had into her backpack.

"You can eat after you go through security.." I reply, my tone of that of a scorned lover.

"I was hoping you'd pay."

Assuming I would pay. So her transaction history doesn't show she bought anything. To hide her eating from her mother. Or fiancé. Or both.

She strides by me, wearing excessively baggy clothes. A light blue pocket tee and sweatpants. Not at all like her usual style, but I guess what her usual is now isn't the girl I knew growing up. She slings a backpack over her shoulder without so much as a glance in my direction. I throw on a pair of running shoes and follow her determined strut toward the door.

We exit into the hallway, and I lock the door behind us as Nancy calls the elevator. Baby talking to it in hopes that'll make it show up sooner. The cream colored walls are dimly lit by half working overhead lights. Chris Boyle, the property manager that gave me my original tour of the place, said the bulbs are on backorder and that they'll be replaced soon. Given the state of the rest of the facility, I find that hard to believe.

Right as I join her at the elevator, someone exits their apartment one door down. A tall, muscular figure fumbling with his keys. He pays no attention to us, to me, but I can't look away from him. I'd seen people come and go very sparsely in this place. Even at a distance, I could tell that he didn't belong here.

He's at least six two with toned, broad shoulders. A baseball cap sits low to cover the eyes gazing down at his phone. A black, nylon windbreaker and baggy, acid wash jeans are paired with white Nikes.

His attention flashes to me – us – quickly. I quickly busy myself with finding the intricacies of the tiled floor beneath my feet. Nancy doesn't even notice. I can't be sure if it was my imagination or not, but I think a breathy chuckle escaped from his direction.

This elevator couldn't get here fast enough.

"You know, Riv. I think the elevator doesn't want me to leave." Nancy snickers, still *somehow* unaware of our guest. "If I wasn't so exhausted, I'd take the stares."

"Ditto." I comment, sneaking another glance at the stranger and meeting his smirking face. I hastily glance at Nancy. She's oblivious to the heat blooming in my cheeks, but the stranger absolutely is not.

Ding.

"Oh, thank god." She sighs. I do the same internally.

The metal doors slide open, allowing the three of us to file in. Nancy first, then me, then the strikingly handsome stranger. The air in the claustrophobic box becomes liquid filling my lungs. An increasing need to scratch my nails along my neck overtakes me as I try to find something, anything to do with my hands. To avoid the gaze of this man. To avoid it all entirely.

Once the doors close and we begin our descent to the lobby, the guy stuffs his phone in his pocket. I hadn't noticed my eyes were watching his every move, but they were.

Are.

And suddenly he was looking at me.

My heart convulses inside my chest at the sight.

Deep, dark chocolate brown eyes anchor me to the

ground hurdling closer. A mischievous swirl of the cosmos peaks through the halos that the overhead light casts.

Oh, God.

Every speck of dust, the reflective light, seems to bend to his mercy. My knees almost do the same. He's so otherworldly beautiful. It's almost criminal. Even the air around us seems to swirl in his favor. Dancing to him to grasp at his scent just to send it my way. His gaze holds me still, and I'm certain that once he lets me go, I'll crumble to the Earth. Collapse where I stand.

And then I see it.

The scar on the bridge of his nose. The thick, bushy eyebrows as black as the night sky. Matching hair peeking out from under his hat. And those eyes.

Those eyes that know me. Know my deepest, inner most desires. All of my nightmares. Hopes. Dreams. They hold them all. There was nowhere to hide in those eyes. Utterly exposed, as if I were standing naked before him.

Part of me wished I were. A part that I struggled to push deep, deep down within me. A need that coursed through my veins as if it were exactly the cure for whatever ails me.

Large, veiny hands flex and curl, his eyes never once releasing me from their vice grip. I can only see what he wants me to see in my periphery. But all I could see were those damn eyes. Ones that I would recognize anywhere. Those that held me captive.

He gives me the faintest smile and I'm certain the world could collapse around me, and I wouldn't notice. He redirects his gaze elsewhere. Dropping me completely.

Blush rushes to my cheeks rapidly. My eyes find my shoes, lungs beg for deeper breaths of air. I reach into myself, pulling out all the logical pieces of this 3D chess game. Trying to figure out if I'm being brash.

I have to be. There's no way. It's not possible.

The elevator dings on the first floor. He's the first one out, shoes squeak under the damp tile. I follow suit with Nancy hot on my heels. Curiosity getting the better of her.

I expect the handsome stranger to run for the hills, as far away from the maniac on the elevator as he can possibly get. But he doesn't. I find him holding the lobby door open for us as we trail behind. Our hands brush gently as I lose my grip on the door handle as he lets go. Leaning in quickly to save me from being beaten with the heavy metal, he grasps my fingers in his.

The spark sends a shock to my heart. All I can do is smile and say, "Thank you."

"You're welcome." He replies, his voice gruff yet comforting. He flashes me another captivating smile, all the air escaping my aching lungs once more.

He nods his goodbye seconds before he turns on his heels and waltzes away with a grace I've never seen before. Thankfully, Nancy and I go the opposite way.

I don't think my heart could have taken another moment of whoever he was.

As soon as he's out of earshot, Nancy grips my elbow and asks, "What the *fuck* was that?!" I let out a shaky breath, unable to comprehend what the fuck that even was. "What's got you quiet?!"

"That's the guy from my dream." I say, baffled.

"Wait, are you for real?" She asks skeptically as we traverse the parking lot to my '09 Corolla that's seen better days. I hum in some form of agreement. "The scrumptious one?"

"Yeah." Is all the words my lungs could stand to say.

"You've got to be joking." She pushes, releasing me from her firm grip only once we've reached the car, both piling inside.

"No, I swear. That's him."

"How can you be so sure?" She asks as I maneuver out of the parking lot and to the exit. "How do you even remember a dream that vividly?"

We sit at the stop sign, behind a 2020 BMW X6 with

heavily tinted windows. The driver's side window was rolled down against the warm August morning air.

"There's not a snowball's chance in hell that I could forget a face like that." I say, focusing on the hand drumming casually on the car door in front of us. A slipped glance up had me seeing stars.

"You should have said something sooner! I would have killed to have checked him out." She dishes. Handsome stranger shakes his head, like he can hear our very *private* conversation from all the way up there.

"Shut up!" I shush her, trying to calm the wave of nerves from my flushed skin. "He's right in front of us."

"Are you kidding me?!" She straightens in her seat.

I laugh, sneaking one more glance at him before he gets the opportunity to merge into traffic. His shoulders bounce with laughter. He speeds off in the opposite direction and my body physically relaxes.

"Tell. Me. Everything." She demands.

CHAPTER 4

Leon

"You're late, Mr. Kang." Larisa, the receptionist, drones. Not bothering to look up from her computer screen. Thick rimmed glasses glimmer reflections of whatever she was browsing on the internet in her down time.

Mr. Kang. My father's legacy.

I internally scoff.

"Good morning to you too, Ms. Galloway." I say, biting my tongue at the formalities. She's a nice woman. I've never had any problems with her in the past, but she loves calling me *Mr. Kang.*

I can't stand it.

Behind me stood an expansive, brilliant white hallway filled with modern art of all flavors, and sculptures of various abstractness. In front of me lies a corridor to the elevators, and to my right lies marketing and social media offices.

The fifteen floors between this one and the one I'm aiming for consist of different meeting rooms, recording and mixing rooms, and offices decorated to match the futuristic vibes of the outside and main lobby. The higher your office is the more money you make, the better the view.

Which is why I don't mind the extra hike I have to make on the rare occasion when the elevators are out of service. It reminds me that I've worked for my spot in the clouds. Despite my not so squeaky clean reputation.

But the sight of the spotless stainless steel doors that stare me down elicits an avalanche in my gut. All I see, outside of my reflection, is the apparition of someone that's been unnecessarily stuck in my head.

Honey red hair framed her heart-shaped face so angelically. It took more willpower than I'd care to admit to not reach out and brush my finger down her cheek. Square glasses framed her almond shaped eyes, golden in color. Right underneath her left eyebrow, almost completely covered by her glasses sits a nearly faded scar. Crimson blush erupted over her plump cheeks in a silent fluster when our eyes met.

I pretended not to notice. In hopes of seeing it – her – again. Selfishly, I know. I'm undeserving of someone so breathtakingly beautiful, but I can't stay away from her. Even now, the vision of her is so clearly etched into my mind, it would take hell freezing over to forget the way her eyes dance like crystal clear waters.

The elevator dings on the top floor. The polished metal door opens into a wall of windows in front and on the left, conference rooms, offices, and recording booths with a hallway in between the two. At the end of the long hallway is a large, lavish studio. My studio.

The thick, plush carpet caves gently underneath my shoes as I break into a brisk walk. Anxiety and worry creeps over me finally. *I'm late.* I'm never fucking late.

Late and anxious. I'd hate to have that be my first impression. Without my hardened exterior, the mask that keeps my vulnerability at bay, I risk bearing my bleeding heart for all to see. And I'd prefer to be someone unapproachable than exposed.

Being constantly surrounded by artists whose whole personality is their fame and their looks grates on my own sense of self-worth. I wouldn't consider myself arrogant in the god's-gift-to-creation way that most of the people I work with do. But the constant squabbling of who's the hottest, sexiest, is all but enough to drive anyone mad.

When I decided to pursue music, I didn't think I would be scrutinized like them. I thought I could stay in my studio, day in and day out without any inkling of having to dress up for award shows, go to parties, be public property.

I don't date like I know I should, could. Like how my parents and grandma want. Like I want. Having this celebrity status that I despise hanging over my head does me no favors either. The pressures that come with trying to hide part of who I am from someone almost always ruins any form of trust that could be built. Either they don't want to have anything to do with a celebrity, or I can see the greed in their eyes almost immediately.

My parents are still holding out hope that I will settle down. Find myself a wife, have two kids. Buy a house with a crisp, white picket fence in a suburb in a good school district. Not because they desperately want to be grandparents. No, but because that's just what people do by the time they're thirty.

When they were my age, they were both busy with their careers and neglecting their only son. Putting their jobs and aspirations before the well-being and needs of their child. They want me to assume that role. The same one that left me emotionally stunted as a kid.

Have a baby because that's what you do. Who cares if you want to wait for someone you actually love to have them with. Or if you have goals that you want to achieve before you bring another human into the world. Or if you never actually want them at all.

You're always on someone else's timeline. Everyone has an opinion about when, where, how, with whom you do everything with. Everyone's entitled to their opinion on everyone else's life.

That's not to say my parents never loved each other. Or they don't love me. No. They love and care for each other more than anyone I know. Their relationship is very strong and healthy, and it's one I'd love to have for myself. They were high school sweethearts. They just never wanted children, but like anyone with traditional values, they didn't have a choice but to keep me.

Push me off onto my grandma. I love that old woman.

Walking into my dimly lit studio, two figures greet me from within, having already taken their seats in front of the mixing board. A tall figure looming in the glow of the computer light turns to face me as the door clicks closed.

"There's my favorite producer! It's about damn time." He grumbles, slapping his palm on my shoulder.

"Sorry, man." I replied. Isaac Graves, another famously talented music producer from LA. He'd personally escorted his newest incoming artist across the country to collaborate on his debut album. I turn my attention to the young man sitting in my comfy and expensive office chair, tapping away on my keyboard. "Hey, Trey. Nice to finally meet you."

He spins around to greet me with a big grin on his face and that youthful twinkle in his eye. "What's up, Leon?!" He asks, holding out his hand for a handshake. "Thanks so much for working with me, man. I have big plans for this album."

"Yeah, I can't wait to hear your vision." I reply, trying to remain as professional as I can, but I'm already exacerbated by the niceties. He seems like a nice kid, and I want to like him. But it seems like I'm wholly preoccupied.

It was nearing midnight when I forced the two men out of my studio with promises of returning tomorrow to finish the work we had started. I pack up my things, making the trek to my car with a new-found pep in my step.

I wanted to get home and write down some song ideas. Separating work from my creative liberties at home, allowing those inner most thoughts spill out where no one can see or hear them. The works I keep on my personal hard drive aren't ones I ever intend for anyone but myself to listen to. It leaves me too vulnerable, those songs. I can't stomach the idea of them ever coming to light. To be under public scrutiny.

Stepping out of my car into the warm humidity, the wind sweeps hair around my face and into my eyes. Whistling in my ear, tinnitus whispering its painful symphonies.

Pounding footsteps echo into the night, against the pavement as I attempt to escape the brewing storm. Lightning crackles over the navy sky, counting down the remaining seconds before the flood gates open.

Cracked tiles line the lobby foyer, squeaking underneath my soles and echoing through the desolate room. Buzzing lights flicker in rhythm with the oncoming downpour.

I make my way through the narrow hallway and down the half-flight of stairs to the mailroom. Grasping my box key in between my fingers, metallic jingling rings around me with each step. Down the adjacent hallway, there's a noise coming from the laundry room. Only spooked for half a second, I quickly remind myself that it's just another tennant and not an ax murderer and what other people do in the middle of the night is truly none of my business.

The smell of mildewing clothes and grime coats the inside of my nose. The barely lit space is a perfect atmosphere for an A-list horror movie. Almost immediately regretting coming down here at this hour, but it's too late to turn back now. I've most definitely alerted the monsters. All the hair on my body stands up at attention, senses heightened and on high alert.

With the handful of unimportant envelopes and the poly-mailer package from my grandmother, I turn on my heels. Ready to leave with my life in tact. Ready to escape the creepy basement space. With my head down, I open the poly-mailer from my grandmother.

The plastic gives way easily, the contents stop me dead in my tracks. A palm-sized, intricately carved wooden box. The detailed markings are beautiful and delicate. Dovetail joinery and engraved initials 'KS' on the bottom indicative of its previous owner. A handwritten note to accompany it, a full page of beautiful cursive writing.

My Dearest Grandson,

Happy Birthday, Leon. You have accomplished so much in the twenty-nine years (thirty if you're counting Korean years like you should be) that you have graced this Earth.

Do you remember when you were fifteen and we went to Natural Bridge in Virginia? Oh, what a long drive that was, but it was so beautiful. So worth the headache of lugging your angsty teenage self around.

I had always dreamed of going, but I never had anyone to go with and I never got to go before your grandfather died. I don't know how you found out it was on my bucket list, but you did. And you thought I wouldn't notice that you insisted we go, not because you really wanted to, but because I did.

Do you remember that young girl who found your wallet? You talked about her the whole way home. I think that was the first time you'd ever expressed having a crush on someone and I knew it broke your heart to not be able to find her again.

I know you'll make some beautiful woman very happy.

Nothing would make me happier than if you took my wedding and engagement set to give to your future bride. Even if she doesn't come for another ten years, or tomorrow, I want you to have mine and your grandfather's rings.

I have missed your grandfather more and more every day since his passing. I can't believe it's been almost twenty years without him. I thought for sure we'd be the old married couple with a billion grandkids over every weekend. But life doesn't always work out the way we expect it to, does it?

Enough sadness.

I'm sending you all my love. I hope you cherish the time you have in this world, Leon. You never know how long you have. With those you love, and yourself.

All my love, Grandma

My eyes sting with tears I unexpectedly have to hold back. Shaky fingers delicately open the wooden box, the box my grandfather made for my grandmother's engagement ring. And inside lay a bed of velvet and a satin ribbon, holding the brilliant gold rings into place. The metal sparkles like new, clearly freshly cleaned and unworn in quite some time. The teardrop diamond is encompassed by four smaller ones on either side, growing smaller the further down the band they go. Paired with it are two matching gold wedding bands with *'Forever is just the beginning'* engraved on the inside of both bands.

Suddenly the weight of the entire world is on my chest.

Tears stain my vision as I hold in my hands the last thing my grandma ever wanted to part with. The things she swore she would take to her grave. One of the last pieces of my grandpa that survived. The only thing she got back from the police.

In my stupor, my blurred vision, I bump into something.

Looking up through the moisture in my eyes, I can make out a barely human shape. Blinking away the tears, the emotion that resided within them. A soft, freckled face with the most apologetic look comes into view.

Eyebrows turned upward. Tiny lines form between them. Mouth opened in surprise and matched confusion. An empty mesh laundry bag in one hand, a silver phone with a purple transparent case in the other. Baby pink pointed acrylic nails grip both items with white knuckles.

"I'm so sorry!" She apologizes profusely, holding her hands up. A voice as angelic as the morning sun, the way it echoes throughout my brain, the space around me. Being this close, citrus and hibiscus wafts around me, replacing the rancid mildew. The shitty lighting creates a halo in her almond eyes.

It's her.

"Don't be sorry, angel." I reply, basking in the ease of tension from her shoulders. *Angel.* It just slipped my tongue, but it fits her so well.

A grateful yet bashful smile plays at the corner of pink lips. Not expecting to see anyone, the baggy shirt falling off her shoulder, almost hiding her shorts. Bare legs shine in the dim light, leaving little to the imagination of their curvature and expanse. I quickly recenter my gaze to her face, her eyes. She watches with blushed cheeks as my eyes roam over her body.

"My friend always says I need to stop being such a hazardous pedestrian." She rambles shyly, putting her phone into her other hand, tucking her hair behind her ear.

In the transition, her fingers haphazardly turn her phone on, revealing a lock screen that's just as sugary as she is. A yellow, heart shaped bubble wand that's emitting a rainbow bubble. "Again, sorry." She reiterates, cheeks deepening with a crimson blush.

"Again, don't be." I tease, flashing her a toothy grin.

My eyes are desperate to trace the outline of her body. The way her oversized shirt falls over her shoulders and down her bare chest. The shortness of her green shorts, how perfect her legs are. How my hands want to explore the vast expanse of her. Her button nose is flushed with the same crimson as her cheeks. Up close, her eyes are even more magnificent. The outer irises are lined with an earthy green that quickly fade into gold and hazel.

She's intoxicatingly beautiful, like a Renaissance painting in the Louvre. A marble statue carved with perfect precision and accuracy, hidden in the very back of the British Museum, where no one can appreciate her beauty. She so clearly belongs in more exquisite spaces.

"You're just saying that to be nice." She gripes, her eyes falling on the still open engagement ring box. "Those are gorgeous." She breathes in the tiniest gasp.

"Oh, um. Thank you. They're-"

"She's very lucky."

"They're my grandparents'." I say, suddenly shy. In the silence we share, her eyes never falter from my own, but there's a heaviness that wasn't there before. Something I can't quite place. "Shall we?" I asked, gesturing towards the stairs, the way we were both going. She nods, quickly scampering up with me trailing behind her.

"I'm River, by the way." She says, spinning on her heels to face me. I quickly wipe whatever dumb grin has settled there off my face. Hopefully before she notices. She walks backwards down the hallway with ease, empty hand extended.

"Leon." I reply, placing my hand into hers. Soaking in how well fitted our hands are together. "A pleasure." My palm's a little sweaty and I desperately want to hide it, but I can't bring myself to let go of her just yet.

"Likewise." She says, her nails scraping my palm as she drops my hand gently and quickly. Once we reach the elevators, I lean around her to press the call button. The metal door creaks open automatically the moment I reach around her to hit the call button. We step on, standing much closer now than this morning. "Have you lived here long?" She asks, doe eyes on me, waiting for a response.

"About seven years." I say, unable to take my eyes off her. "You?" Confusion flashes across her pretty face, quickly replaced with squinty eyed giggles. *Shit.* I'm such a fucking idiot.

"Oh, yeah. Same apartment my whole life. You don't know me?" She retorts, trying to hide her laughter.

"Remind me again, were you the guy who liked loud, kinky sex or the old man watching football?" I counter.

Without missing a beat, she grins and says, "Definitely loud, kinky sex." That sparkle illuminating her eyes again.

"Good to know."

"Is it now?" She asks warily, eyeing the now closed ring box still in my hand. "I can give you a few pointers, if you want." An open invitation floats in her eyes. Backlit with vulnerability.

The elevator dings, opening its doors to let us out. Silencing my rampant thoughts. Snapping her out of her devilish look. I motion for her to step out and I follow a pace behind her. We walk together down the hallway in tense silence. The only sounds are the shuffling of our shoes on the tile. My mind races over our brief conversation. The mesmerizing words that fell from her perfect lips heated my blood, causing my heart to race.

Once we reach her door, she pulls her keys out before turning to me, a solemn smile on her face. "Nice meeting you, Leon." She says sweetly, no hint of the sultry woman from before existing in the words she utters. The sound of my name on her lips is enough to send me into orbit.

"You too, angel." I reply, forcing down the urge to pin her to the wall where we stand.

"My name's not 'angel'." She teases.

"I know." I retort with a wink. "If you need anything, just let me know, *River*." Her eyes brighten as she looks down at her shoes to avoid my eye contact for just a moment.

"Thank you. I will." She replies, turning the door handle and slipping halfway inside before turning back to me and saying, "If you ever want those pointers, my offer still stands."

"I just might take you up on that." I tease, stuffing my free hand in my pocket. "Good night, angel."

"Good night, Leon." She says.

I watch her smile, her sparkling eyes, the silhouette of her body before she slips into her apartment, latching the door closed. The faint click of the deadbolt releases me from her magnetic grip, leaving me with my own filthy thoughts. All I can think about is how I have to write a song about her. And touch myself to the thought of her.

CHAPTER 5

River

I couldn't breathe. Couldn't feel the air in my lungs as they nearly collapsed inside of my chest. The way my knees wanted to buckle from the grip he had on me until the moment my door shut. Leaving him standing in the hallway while I collected every morsel of self-respect I contained.

I had another hour and a half before I could go downstairs to collect my laundry, and I fear that I will be unable to move from where I stand just inside my entryway. My feet suddenly glued to this particular spot on the floor.

Get it together, Riv. You've flirted before, this is nothing more than all those times you'd flirted with random strangers in bars. He's a random stranger.

But he's not a stranger. His name is Leon. A name that felt so buttery smooth on my tongue, the way it slid from my lips with ease.

Okay, that might be all I know about him, but he doesn't feel like a stranger. In fact, it feels like I've known him since the beginning of time. Since I was little. Since the Big Bang.

Enough. That's enough of this. I don't need to get involved with anyone right now. Especially not him.

Though, it would be so easy to slip into something casual with him. I could find myself wrapped around his voice, feel it rumble inside of my chest, feel him all around me.

But I know that someone as gorgeous as him isn't in the cards for someone like me. I know that I'm just the weird girl next door who's terrible at flirting and has grandma hobbies.

I know I'm not someone that people like him go for. I do just fine without working myself up to chase someone I know will never fall for me. But there's just something about this one that I can't shake. Something that refuses to release me from its filthy grip.

He has to have a girlfriend anyway. He had the rings and that fancy handcrafted box. Even more romantic that they're his grandparents'. She's one lucky girl for sure.

I'd be lying if I said I wasn't even just a tiny bit jealous. Not that I ever stood a chance with him, or that he would like me in a million years. But after that dream, this infatuation felt heightened. The fall feels a million times worse somehow.

It was almost two in the morning before my head hit the pillow, the pile of clean laundry now taking asylum on my couch. Exhaustion racked my entire body with a vengeance. I relished in the idea of sleep, tiredness compounded from the days before.

The faintest hums of music wafts in from the wall behind my head once again. Barely audible and different from the night prior, but its origin's still the same. A face and a name to go with a lullaby, all my own. A small, uncontrollable smile laces its way across my tired face as my eyes flutter closed.

If I can't have Real Leon, then may Dream Leon visit me for the rest of my days.

Skylar invited me out to brunch to celebrate the new job and to catch up since she was in town this weekend. I was hesitant to go at first, but I hadn't seen her since our college graduation party at her favorite brewery. I figure it would do my soul some good to get out of the still disheveled apartment and get some fresh air. We talk on the phone occasionally and I see all her posts on social media, but it'd be nice to finally sit down and chat in person with her for the first time in six years.

Outside of Nancy, Skylar has been one of my closest

friends, if not the closest. And with the way Nancy's acting, I'd venture to say Skylar is winning in something that shouldn't even be a god damn competition in the first place.

My freshman year of college, Skylar was my roommate. We quickly hit it off and soon became as thick as thieves. We requested to live together year after year until we graduated. We had always joked about how we'd be roommates after college, too. But she got her dream job out of state, only coming back to Georgia occasionally to visit.

The more I thought about it, the more excited I grew. So, I did what anyone invited to brunch in the middle of August does. Dress comfortably, but stunningly.

Brunch is for hot bitches.

As I make my way down to the lobby, the sheer sight of the elevator gives me butterflies. A massive swarm laying siege in my abdomen. One that I now wish to avoid, but the heels I chose don't offer me hardly any support for scaling down ten flights of stairs. So I climb onto the creaking metal box, forcing down any and all emotion that dares to bubble up to the surface. Into the deepest, darkest depths of my psyche where all my repressed trauma lives.

I exit into the lobby, tingling fingers and rapid heartbeat to accompany the eyes on the floor. Skirting around everyone who looked right through me, nearly bumping into someone with a coffee in their hand as I do so. The stranger reaches their free hand up to steady me when I course correct. A firm grip on my shoulder.

"Whoa," A familiar voice sounds, causing my head to snap up to the person holding me at arm's length. "Where are you running off to, angel?" The question is jovial and light, stilling the anxiety thrumming through me.

"Wouldn't you like to know." I say with less confidence than I had intended. Staring directly into those deep brown eyes that could hold a galaxy inside of them.

"That's kind of why I asked, isn't it." Leon retorts with a smirk. "You look nice."

Heat rises to my cheeks at the compliment. "Thank you." I say, painfully aware of the tan hand still gripping my shoulder. "You do as well." I nod to his outfit, one that I would describe as the 'old money' style. Slacks, a white dress shirt with the sleeves rolled up to reveal his forearms, loafers, and an expensive looking watch.

"Thanks." He mumbles, becoming shy himself. Averting his eyes from my watchful gaze as I drink in the very essence of him. He drops his hand, and it feels as though I'd done something wrong. Said something I shouldn't have. "So, where are you off to in such a hurry?" He asks again.

Pushing all those negative thoughts and emotions aside, I say, "Meeting a friend for brunch." It takes more willpower than I'd like to admit not to divulge him with the minute details. To not tell him who Skylar is and why she's so important to me. Or how I had to dig this sundress from the depths of my bins for this occasion only. Or how I'd consider cancelling if he asked me to hang out instead.

"Well, then I won't hold you and make you late." He says with a half-smirk, sipping his coffee. The hand that once grounded me is now stuffed in his pocket.

"Wise choice." I tease half-heartedly, coming up empty with anything else to say.

"See you around, River."

"Yeah, see you around." I reply, a little saddened by the choice of my government name over the nickname he had given me. I watch briefly as he strides past me and onto the elevator that was just opening again. Almost like he commanded everything to his will. Like he commanded me.

I got to the restaurant a few minutes before Skylar. Racked with nerves I couldn't quite place. Grabbing us a table and putting in an appetizer that I knew we'll both like, I wait for her to show. But the only thing on my mind is Leon. Fuck, why can't I stop thinking about him?

After about ten minutes, Skylar waltzes in like she owns the joint. Clad in a sage green romper and wedge heels, her chin-length, curly black hair frame her small oval face. Sliding into the booth across from me, a giant black Coach bag first and then herself. We exchange greetings and pleasantries.

"There's my sunshine girl! It's so good to see you after all this time!" She squeals excitedly. "I have so much to catch you up on!" The waiter makes his rounds, taking our beverage and entrée orders before leaving us alone once again.

The restaurant was slowly filling with patrons, chatter rising in volume as people had similar meetings to ours. Old friends catching up, gossiping about their latest drama. Family outings create their own problems.

Skylar recounts the last few years of her life. How she's going on her sixth year at her company and that she still loves her job. How she just bought a house with her fiancé. I congratulate her on the engagement, since it was the newest event that I hadn't heard of. She pauses her steamrolled conversation, a hefty grin on her dark lips.

"That's why I asked you here." She smirks, reaching into her bag. "I wanted to tell you the good news in person."

"What?" I ask with a raised eyebrow.

"But-" she interrupts. "I have a question first." She slides a box across the table, a dusty lavender keepsake box with a gold ribbon around the center. Gently pulling off the ribbon, I open the box. The underside of the lid read 'Will you be my bridesmaid?' in bold calligraphy. In the box was a metal lavender water bottle engraved with my first initial.

"Yes! Of course, I'll be your bridesmaid! It'd be an honor." I gush, picking up the cup to examine it more closely.

"I remembered that you hate your last name, so I didn't bother adding it. And it's your favorite color." She rambles, fidgeting with her hands.

"Thank you so much. I love it, but you didn't have to get me a gift to convince me to be in your wedding party."

"Yeah, well, I'd hoped it would sweeten the deal when

I told you that Dana and I are eloping in October. And I want you there. We're having a big family and friends reception the following Sunday, but the ceremony is just us, the officiant and one close person. And I wanted you there with me. Just like we had always schemed." Tears well in her almost black eyes.

"October's still a couple of months away. I think that's plenty of time to make arrangements." I say, wiping the tears from my own eyes.

"You know I couldn't do this without you." She says voice barely above a whisper. Like she's holding back a flood behind her lashes.

"I don't know how we can stand living so far apart."

"Me either. I wish we were closer." She almost says something else, but the waiter brings over our food and drinks. We both drop the sap, quickly delving into our latest gossip, where I regale her about my Nancy drama and my latest crush.

CHAPTER 6

Leon

I caught all of four hours of sleep the night after our second encounter with her dressed like the walking depiction of beauty. Staying up late to capture my every waking thought, how the light reflected from her golden eyes, how it feels as though I know her from somewhere. Projecting anything and everything I felt onto music that will never see the light of day. Surviving on so little sleep, I was almost late once again.

And I may be in the business of being an asshole, but I'm not a late asshole. Twice in one week would have sent me spiraling. However, I couldn't exactly shake this – whatever this is – feeling that's all-consuming for this ethereal woman. A near goddess walking amongst the mortal realms.

It'd been nearly impossible to focus on anything but her. My waking thoughts are consumed by the scent of her hair, the twinkle in her eye, the color in her cheeks. How I spend entirely too much time staring off into nothingness with thoughts of her swirling cataclysmically in my head. The unholy filth that sends me spiraling into oblivion.

The thought of her, in all facets, drives me mad.

Each night, like clockwork, at about eleven thirty, she pleasures herself. The obscene, yet muffled moans that drift through the paper-thin walls almost instantly make me antsy, thirsty. I'd spent years drowning out the sounds from the other side of that wall. But I hadn't noticed that I now am a trained bloodhound, keened in on her slightest moves.

It only took me a couple of nights to catch on to the

pattern. But now it's been two weeks.

Sometimes she uses a toy, sometimes her fingers. But her reactions are always the same. Spending a few minutes finding the perfect rhythm before the sparks fly behind her blurry eyes. Her voice rises the closer she gets to release.

And most of the time, I'm right there with her. My hand strokes up and down my aching cock as I listen to her gentle moans through the paper-thin walls I once hated so much. Barely audible hitches in her whimpers as I picture her hands sliding into those scandalous shorts. Desperate to replace hers with my fingers, feel her wetness as I circle her clit in a way that would have her screaming my name.

Legs splayed out over her bed sheets, revealing her throbbing pussy. One hand in my hair, the other gripping the comforter like it's the one thing keeping her grounded. I won't come up for air until I know she won't be able to walk for a week. Until her legs shake so violently with overstimulation that she's begging me to stop. Until tears stream down her beautiful, helpless face.

Maybe I've lost sleep because I'm picturing all the ways I'd fuck her if I ever got the chance to. If whatever deity's up there allowed me one sliver of an opportunity to bury my head deep within those luscious thighs, I'd give her a high that she'd crave until the end of time. Because I know if I got a taste of that sweet nectar, I'd never give it up.

I'd thought about all the ways, the positions, the spectacle that I'd make of her. Just for me. *God.* The idea of sharing her with anyone else enrages me beyond comparison. Blood boils under my skin any time I picture someone else loving her, touching her, pleasing her, pleasuring her. She's mine. I can feel it in the depths of my soul, my bones. She's meant for me. Convincing her of that may take a little longer than I'd like.

Last night was a particularly loud night for her. Her pleasure seemed to carry over tenfold. The once near whispers were suddenly full, hearty moans. I came so hard I saw stars.

Which is why I can barely stand to look at her now.

I stare as she innocently brings in two reusable bags full of groceries in another sundress. I want to hike it up and fuck her right there against her car. My car. The wall. In the elevator. In her apartment. In mine. On every surface imaginable.

The September heat does nothing to help or hide the bulge in my pants. The warm wind feels more like an oven than refreshing. I contemplate for a second whether or not I should turn the other way, and ignore her and the internal turmoil. Pretend I don't have these thoughts and feelings about her.

But I can't.

I'm so drawn to her it hurts more to watch her walk away than it does to be embarrassed by my boner.

I jog as close to her as I can get without looking stupid and sounding stupider. Once I'm within range, I casually stroll up beside her, narrowly avoiding the potted plants on the sidewalk.

"Let me help you with those." I offer, reaching to take the bag closest to me from her. She jumps at the first sound of my voice.

"Jesus Christ, you scared the piss out of me!" She whirls around, clutching one hand to her chest in an attempt to still her erratic heart rate.

"Apologies." I say with a half-smirk. "I thought you'd want some help." I extend my hand out for the bag once more, but she shies away.

"I got it." She mumbles and continues walking. The scrape of her sandals echoes against the walls of the building.

"Clearly. But let me help. For scaring you." I offer, lackadaisically holding my arm extended toward her. She looks down at my hand, an inquiring look on her gorgeous face. An eyebrow raises as her gaze lifts.

"What are my chances of denying you the pleasure and you accepting the answer?" She asks, the corners of her mouth fighting hard to remain stoic. A light breeze trickles around us, wafting her honey-red hair around her face.

"I'm not in the business of being denied." I say almost instantly. Possessed by a man who has no fear, nothing to lose. She hums, taking in my words. Completely unphased by the demanding nature. Contemplating how she's going to respond with mischief twinkling in her golden eyes.

"What do you want in return then?" She asks, sliding the handles of her bags into my hands. I hook a finger around her palm, drawing it close to my chest. Surprise darts across her face, a look that she fights desperately to hide.

"Not a thing, angel." I tease, fighting the urge to push my luck. To test the waters between us with a kiss, a taste of her that would ruin my sweet tooth.

"Chivalry's only dead if you're not attractive." She says nonchalantly, fidgeting with her fingers after I let her go. We slip into the slightly cooler lobby of the complex, and our departure is fast approaching.

"I enjoy being a gentleman to a pretty lady."

Blush riddles her cheeks and nose, eyes dropping to the floor as if it suddenly became the most interesting thing she'd ever encountered. Her slender fingers slam into the call button before I have a chance to reach for it. As the elevator ticks down from the top floor, a figure appears in my peripheral vision.

Chris Boyle, the general property manager and general creep. His specialties consist of being weird and gross with no breaks.

The first time I ever met him, there was something off with him that I couldn't place. But after seven years, you hear stories and see things that you can't explain.

And I won't let him get anywhere near River. I would kill him where he stands before I let him hurt her.

"Hey, Leon!" He says, strolling towards us. Calculating each move the three of us could make in this 3D game of chess we're about to play, I snake my free arm around River's waist. Protectively. Oh, so possessively.

Her body is rigid against me, unsure what to do or how to feel about it. The scent of her encapsulates me, fingers digging slightly into her flesh. Her eyes scream at me, begging for an explanation, anything to gain her bearings.

Every curve, hill, and valley of her body presses against my own. I'm left fighting for my sanity once again. Focusing all my concentration, what's left of it, on being the face of this operation. To do what calls to me in my blood.

"Just go with it, angel." I whisper to her before pressing my lips to the shell of her ear. Without thinking. My heart stops dead in its tracks at my actions, but I refuse to let it show on my face. Instead, I replaced whatever could have bloomed there with a smug smirk. "Hey, Chris. How's it going?"

He's barely five six. Long white hair down to his shoulders. A round, mundane face devoid of any life. Hollow eyes and pale, greasy skin. He looks perpetually sick.

Couldn't miss him even if I wanted to.

"Never better, man." He stops in his tracks the moment he spots River. Eyes roaming up and down her body. Reveling in the curves of her. In a way that only I was allowed to. Blood pounds in my ears as his eyes linger a second longer on her lower half. "A *pleasure* to see you again, Miss River. What are you doing with a guy like this?" He asks like he knows about my past.

"She's my girlfriend." I defend. Her body tenses tenfold under the weight of my words. The implication, and expectations, for her to play this new role. Quietly, she slips her arm around my waist, grabbing a fistful of the back of my shirt.

Play along, angel.

"Is that so?" Chris asks, completely ignoring me. Eyes focused solely on River trained on her like a hawk on its prey. Her throat bobs, but she braves through it. No other sign of her discomfort.

"Not that you ever had a chance." She retorts, pride coursing through my veins at her words. A wicked smile creeps across my face, one that I don't bother hiding. My thumb rubs the bare skin of her arm, gently praising her efforts.

"Is that a way for a lady to talk?"

"Is that any way to talk to a lady?" I ask, niceties quickly vanishing from my system. Tightening my grip on her waist, laying claim to what's mine.

"I didn't know you were into fucking anything other than a common whore. Why was I to assume otherwise?" He snickers, stuffing his sausage fingers into his pockets. "Though, you've never said any of them were your girlfriend, so congratulations, whore. You're officially a world-class slut."

"I'd recommend you shut your fucking mouth, Boyle." I growl through clenched teeth. Snow white knuckles wrap around the canvas bags in my free hand.

"Or what? You're all talk. I don't know why people say you're so menacing. You probably couldn't land a hit if I stood still and let you." He cackles, eyes tainted as he taunts me. I lunged for him, moving to drop the bags and let go of River. But she stops me, pulling me back to her.

"Don't give him the satisfaction, babe." She whispers, barely loud enough to hear over the rage coursing through my veins. "He's just trying to rile you up." Her gentle touch on my chest stills me enough to focus on her words, her pleading eyes.

"Shame. Letting your *girlfriend* call the shots. Even she knows you'd lose." He quips, turning his attention to her now that she's standing closer to him than I ever wanted her to be. Closer than I ever should have *let* him get to her. "Don't waste your time on this guy with a stick up his ass. Let me show you a good time, doll." I scoff, unable to hide my sheer disgust.

"You couldn't please me in your wildest of wet dreams." She counters, turning on her heels toward me, the elevator that was reopening, pulling me away from Boyle. I follow without contest, without another word from any of us until she and I are safely in the elevator. She drops my arm, the absence of her immediately waning my mood.

The silence grows between us. I'm desperate to reach out and breach the force field forming around her. Arms crossed, hardened concentration on her face as she stares at the totes I'm still carrying. She doesn't dare ask for them back.

My fingertips sting from where they once caressed her supple skin, softer than anything I could imagine. An aching body longing to hold her close. My muscles scream for her to come back to me, let me wrap my arms around her.

The door slides closed with a muffled thud.

"What the ever-loving fuck was that?" She seethes, pissed as hell with darkened eyes. I knew what she meant.

"He's a creep. I didn't want him making a move on you."

"And you somehow have the authority to make those kinds of decisions for me? Do you think that I need saving? That you get to kiss me and touch me whenever you want just because you think someone's going to *hit on me*?"

Her words ooze with a deep-seated anger that freezes me where I stand. Fists clenching and unclenching at her sides. Chest heaving with each measured breath. Even now, when all that distaste is angled at me, I want nothing more than to comfort her. Apologize for crossing that boundary. But I can't bring myself to open my mouth. To say those words. Because I don't mean them.

I meant that kiss. I meant those soothing caresses. I meant those threats. I meant it when I vowed that she's mine, even if no one but myself heard. That I would kill anyone that gets between her and me. Anyone who tries to hurt her. I meant *every fucking word.*

"Don't undermine me, Leon. I'm not someone you need to save." She grumbles, the muscles in her jaw tensing.

"I wasn't undermining you." I growl sternly. "Chris is a sleazy guy. You would have spent the rest of your life trying to avoid him."

"You don't know me. You don't know the hell I've lived. A persistent slimeball is child's play." She says. "You don't get to make decisions for me."

The doors open and she storms out, toward her apartment. I follow a pace behind her, heart pounding in my chest. Spinning around toward me, her skirt twirling around her legs, she holds her hands out for her bags.

"I can bring them in if-"

"Just give me my bags, Leon. I'm too tired for this."

"River, I'm not asking." I say firmly. "If you're tired, then I'll bring them in."

"You're so full of self-righteous bullshit." She sneers, turning away and unlocking her door. Walking inside and leaving the door wide open for me to follow.

Across the threshold, I stood in a mirrored apartment to my own. A desolate entryway, barren and messy kitchen with bins strewn about. A half-assembled coffee table in between a hand-me-down couch that looks like it hasn't seen a good day since 1984. Peeking through the one doorway into what I assumed was her bedroom was a messy, unmade bed with at least five pillows and handmade quilts strewn about.

There is life leaking out from all of the bins, the barely decorated space, the place she should find the most comfort in. A sewing machine sits on the floor beside a clear bin labeled *'fabric'*, a roll of whatever the inner part of a quilt is called propped against an opposite corner, almost as tall as she is. Baking ware scattered throughout the kitchen, clean but lacking a home. A small collapsible crate filled with sketchbooks, painting, and drawing supplies. A small silver laptop opened but asleep perched on the counter. Next to it, is a cherry red stand mixer. The fridge is decorated with magnets from different states and attractions.

It was an attempt to piece together her life. One that she hadn't wished for me to see so disheveled. Something like shame fills her eyes as my gaze wanders around the room.

"You can set them on the counter and go." She nearly whispers, arms folded over her chest.

"Do you want some help with unpacking?" I offer.

"No."

"I don't mind."

"I do. I'm fine." She insists through clenched teeth. "Go."

The very essence of my being screams at me, rejecting

the will I throw into each movement as I turn away from her and toward the door. My heart lingered in the space I once stood, now walking away from.

I can't explain it, the pull she has on me. The sway her words hold and the uncontested power she possesses. I see the outline of her silhouette behind my eyes, the pain in those golden eyes. The hollowness that shines amongst the makeshift home.

But I force myself to keep walking. Even when the click of the door sounds as loud as a gunshot right to the heart.

CHAPTER 7

River

I want to hate him.

No. I don't. I want to not like how his body felt against mine. Or the electricity that sparked from his skin. I want to hate the way he was protective of me, even when I shot him down. Even after everything I said, he was as unwavering as the ocean's tide.

Between my repressed feelings, the numbness in my bones, and the still unpacked boxes, I'd lost all motivation to seize the day. Productivity completely evades me as I stand frozen in my kitchen. Surrounded by the pit of despair that I'm actively falling through.

My chest bears the weight of a thousand elephants crushing my ribs. Punctured lungs screaming for air. For my body to move. For my brain to stop screaming *'whore'* and *'slut'* like those words had ever hurt me before. For the world to be quiet for just a moment as the tears stain my skin, leaving trails from my cheeks to my breasts. Only interrupted by the cotton dress that feels so constricting it's cutting the circulation off in all the places it touches.

My fingers, hands, work frantically to release myself from the confines of my clothes. Balling up the once soft and delicate fabric into a wad of itchy gauze to be tossed into the deepest corners of this too-small apartment. The walls are ever closing in.

Standing naked, save for my underwear, in the middle of my kitchen, I catch a glimpse of my distorted shape in the reflection of the stainless steel fridge. The lumps and divots of my heavily flawed skin, love handles, small boobs, and larger stomach. Scarred and stained, both natural and manmade. Heavy freckles line the expanse of my skin. The scars that litter my stomach, my thighs. Red and purple. Pink and white. What others regard as a temple, a vessel for souls, my tomb.

It's an image so repulsive that I can't bear to look at it for a single second longer.

I hadn't spoken to Leon in a week. Mostly because I was avoiding him at every turn. Every corner, he's somehow always there. I don't know if he's looking for me or if our schedules have now suddenly aligned. Either way, I have made it my life's mission to not speak to him.

Not until I can look into those brown eyes and not see the man who loved me so feverishly in my dreams. Not until the man that stood before me in this fucking apartment with so much agony shimmering in his eyes is gone.

It's not the words that Boyle said. The half-assed names he'd called me. How Leon's lips felt against my skin, even though I had detested their lusciousness. Or the Knight-In-Shining-Armor act that Leon had put on. For my safety, he claimed. It had all been water off my back. I've been called far worse. Always been able to take care of myself.

But it was pity that shone in Leon's eyes.

He could see each shredded piece of myself, all of the broken parts of me lay open and bare in front of him. Somehow seeing right through all of my shields, my walls that I'd built to stop Peeping Toms like him. It's like he waltzed right in like the gates were wide open for him. He looked at me, all of me. And he *pitied* me.

God, the look in his big, doe eyes nearly brought me to my knees. Like everything I'd worked for, fought for, and accomplished meant nothing. Suddenly, I was eleven years old again. My world collapsed around me, and there wasn't a thing

I could do to stop it.

The world around me turned icy, frozen air piercing my overexerted lungs. Like I was screaming for him to stay. To change his mind. To not listen to the lies I asked of him. The only words screaming into the void of my head as I stared at the spot Leon stood just before he left.

Shaky hands grasped at nothing at my sides. Silently wishing, begging, that he would stay. That he would wipe that fucking look off his face and just stay with me. To stop looking so closely at the disarray of the person I try so desperately to hide and just see me.

Though, I'm not sure how he'd separate the two. I am the mess. The mess is me. I am the squalor that I swim in.

I was right all along. He'd never be able to look at me – the real me – and see past the condemned hole that once held my heart, my soul. No matter how many times I look in the mirror and tell myself that I am worthy of love and compassion, I will never be anything more than a quick fix. Then the hookup you never tell your friends about.

I'm not worthy of someone like Leon. Who'd selflessly put his pride and reputation aside to protect me from someone he deems dangerous. And I had thrown that back in my face. I'd spewed vile bullshit at him because I felt too exposed. Because he saw too much of the real me and could see that he was disgusted with me. He didn't deserve that. No matter how undeserving I was – am – of his kindness.

A couple more days pass before I can summon the courage to speak with him. To apologize for my misconduct. To mend the bridge I had set fire to. I didn't have to go out of my way to seek him out. It wasn't hard to find him lingering in the hallway this morning. Exactly where he'd been for the last nine days. Silently waiting. For me. Giving me the space I clearly needed.

He's propped himself up against the wall between our apartments. One foot on the baseboard, phone in one hand, other in his pocket. Dressed in baggy jeans and an oversized shirt and matching sneakers.

My hands clam up, sliding against the metal of the door handle. My heart is pounding erratically in my chest. The world spins. I could wait it out. Wait him out. He usually moves on within ten minutes, giving me the time to run down the stairs and leave before he even notices.

But I'm not running away today. I'm not hiding from him. Not even as I stand in the almost decorated and unpacked apartment. Virtually no evidence of the girl I was nine days ago. The one that fell apart so violently. Who couldn't see any light behind her own eyes and had almost no willpower in her body to keep going.

Through the peephole, I see the distorted figure retch his head toward my door as I turn the handle, quickly dropping my vantage point. Stepping over the threshold, my eyes find him instantly.

I forgot how calming he is. How soothed my soul feels just at the sight of him. His presence eases the pounding in my chest. I couldn't forget how beautiful he is, though.

He makes no moves other than his eyes roaming my body. Not in the way they once had checked out my tight-fitting dress, but one of concern. Big doe eyes even wider as he assesses me. For what, I don't know.

"Good morning." I say meekly.

Pushing himself off the wall, he strides over to me. Still eyeing me cautiously. "Are you okay?" He asks, forgoing the open greeting I had given him. "I haven't seen you in-"

"I'm okay." I say, a bashful smile sliding over my lips.

"Oh." He says, stunned. "Good. I was going to give you to the end of the week before I hunted you down. To apologize." His hands were shoved deep in his pockets while we waited for the elevator.

"What for?" I ask, studying his otherworldly handsome face. "I'm the one who's sorry for acting like a Grade A asshole."

"Then we can both be sorry. For handling it poorly."

He compromises. A relieved smile eclipses his full, pink lips. And the same wave of relief washes over me like that was the easiest makeup I've ever encountered. "I'm sorry for crossing your boundaries." He adds gently.

I want to tell him not to be sorry for something that I wasn't ever mad at in the first place. To tell him that he's already a saint for being so civilized about this. But I don't. I can't. All words escape me as we cram into the elevator with four strangers, causing us to squish together. His chest pressed against my back.

The bystanders are a nosy audience. Eyes pinning me to him, to heighten the anxiety already stewing in my blood.

I reach a hand behind me, searching stealthily for him. Fingers find denim, the front of his pants. I tapped his leg twice. A second passes, and his face doesn't change, but his warm fingers circle mine. Give them a single, reassuring squeeze.

He leans over the opposite shoulder and whispers against my ear, "Is this your way of accepting my apology?" His words are barely a ghost against my skin. Confidence oozes from his lips, and I can hear the smirk that resides in them. I don't dare turn to look at him. Don't dare indulge myself in the sultriness of his voice.

Before I have a chance to answer, his other hand grabs my waist, pulling me closer to him. Closer than I even knew possible. Close enough to feel the bulge in his pants.

My breath hitches in my throat at the touch, the hardness I feel against my back, the commanding presence. If I didn't trust my words before, I definitely don't now.

"Act natural, angel. We have an audience." He grovels. Acting natural is not something I'm going to feasibly achieve with his hands on me, his cock pressing into me, the way he's talking to me.

Angel. He keeps calling me that. And I keep loving it.

We reach the lobby. Our onlookers pile out before us. His hands release me gently. Nothing coating his face but a hint of mischief. Once the last of the audience has exited, he ushers me out by my elbow.

"What was that?" I ask when we're far enough from anyone else that they couldn't possibly hear us. My throat bobs under the pressure of him all around me.

"What?" He asks with a knowing smirk.

"You keep calling me 'angel'." I say with a raised eyebrow. Not daring to address the bulge in his pants, even still. His motives behind pulling me closer. Or the raging thoughts swirling in my mind.

"We're still fake dating. Might as well play the part." He chuckles, mostly to himself. A devilish grin laced over his lips, as if he knew exactly what power he holds over me. As if he could see right through all of those walls and mental shields I'd built back up just to see how putty I am in his hands.

"I don't think a single person heard you call me that." I say sheepishly. Lacking all the suave that I had hoped my words would carry.

"They weren't meant to." He replies with a smirk and a wink in my direction. Heat floods my cheeks as the tease, butterflies exploding in my abdomen like a dormant volcano erupting for the first time in centuries.

Stunned. Out of words.

I have nothing to say to that. Flustered beyond measure.

"I'll see you after work, *angel.*" He says with a tainted smirk on his lips Stopping just short of my red Corolla that I hadn't noticed he had escorted me to. With a brief wave, he left me to walk in the opposite direction, toward his car.

"Yeah, see you later, babe." I mumble, unsure if he even heard me or not.

One thing I hate about a new job is being the new kid on the block. I don't know who the two faced snake is. Who the food thief is. Who the weird kid that you don't know why everyone hates them until you're knee deep in drama and crazy bullshit that you then realize why everyone despises them is.

But I'm just the new girl. I get called 'New Girl' more than I do my real name. I'm not entirely convinced that anyone here knows my name or if they care to.

Not that I really care about any of them. None of them have shown me anything but superficial niceties that I wouldn't want in anyone I'd be close with anyway.

One of the ladies in reception did warn me about Mark. That he would be back from vacation today. If I knew what was good for me, I wouldn't bother even saying hello to him. But I don't know Mark from a hole in the wall.

But I fucked up.

I said hello.

And I watched him sink his teeth into a new obsession.

CHAPTER 8

Leon

I had never felt such a roller coaster of emotions. From terror to elation to concern. All emotions hit me at once, like an oncoming train barreling straight for me.

But she was fine, unharmed. Smiling, even. Her essence illuminated a part of my soul that had dimmed the moment she forced me out of her apartment. From the pain she carried in her eyes at the state of her living space.

I was no judge, no juror, no executioner. Nothing about the dismay that she stood inside of scared me, ushered me away from the woman I was so unrelentingly drawn to. But what I saw was not who I expected her to be.

And I realized that I had put too many expectations on her. She was right. *I didn't know her.* Didn't know anything about her before stepping into her home and piecing together remnants of the person she clung to. Of the material objects that were like clues to a riddle. Pretending to know her and actually knowing are two vastly different oceans, and I was crossing the wrong one. I was on a voyage into a land that was filled with expectations, developed civilizations, and charted territories.

But that's not where I needed to go. Not when what I was desperately searching for was on the other side of the world. Not when I let slip the grasp of reality for a siren's vision. I had to course correct before it was too late. Before I lost her completely into the void that was attempting to swallow my ship. To save us from drowning before we could even reach shore.

I will go to the ends of the Earth, the moon, the stars, and all the galaxies to find out exactly who she is before I let these bering straits collapse my vessels into nothingness. To sink into the deepest crevices of the ocean for monsters to make their castles.

That part scares me. Not her or anything that she could possibly have done or undone. Not the kintsugi-ed parts of herself that she'd laid bare for me. Nothing of who she *could* be. But how feverishly I'm willing to fight to find her, around any obstacle. Any dangerous, winding turn that could cause her harm, I'm willing to throw myself blinding into it first.

My blind faith terrifies me.

I knew demons were resting, sleeping behind those golden eyes. The ones that so easily scan the room, you'd barely notice their constant rotation. Eyes that watched for even the smallest change in someone's demeanor. Ones that I hadn't realized held a world's worth of pain until she stared at me with *hatred* behind them.

Her nose splotchy with repressed tears, fists clenched at her sides. She had seen whatever emotion I had thrown at her unintentionally as an attack on her character.

So I'd given her the space she wanted, needed. And I'll spend the rest of my time with her making it up to her. To prove that I am worthy of being in her presence. Worthy of her grace.

Even though I am not.

I can never pretend to be anything more than living on borrowed time. She is a gift that I do not deserve. A goddess amongst humans, sparing me a second glance. Another chance at sanctuary. She is the embodiment of everything I could only wish to possess. I have money. I could have anyone in this world that I so wished. I know that. But I do not have *her*. And she is who I want.

She is who I desire beyond my wildest comprehension. Who keeps me awake in the dead of night with unholy thoughts. Who, by all standards, shouldn't even want to look in my direction if she saw what everyone knew me to be. A vile troglodyte only concerned about himself and never about the sanctity of others. Only ever looking out for myself. Doing whatever it takes to make sure I get it.

That I'm a coward. Whore. Player. Abuser.

The only thing I ever claim to be is a damn good shot.

I had never once cared about what others thought about me or called me. No matter how painful the words were meant to sting. They never bothered me the way that they should have. Never stuck to me, until recently. All those despicable things spewed at me with hatred and condemnation had all been nothing to me.

Until the things they said started holding weight.

Until I was face to face with the one person who could break me into a million little pieces with those same vile accusations. When all of those words, the sticks and stones they'd thrown at me, finally hit their mark.

For most of my life, it was just my grandmother that got me through those tough times. Supporting me and being proud to call me her grandson. She was the reason I didn't bother listening to anyone's opinions of me. I never cared because the only person who believed in me saw the good in me through the shitstorm.

And if it wasn't my grandma, it was Elio, my best friend since kindergarten. He was the greatest friend I've ever had. But life's cruel. Life takes away the things and the people that mean most to you. That lifts you when you can't stand on your own. I'd stopped caring about anything since Elio.

But now, all the shitty things that's ever been said about me comes crashing down like an avalanche. They ring truer than anything I've ever known about myself.

Suddenly, the person I see in the mirror each day is someone I no longer recognize. There is no confidence, no smugness, nothing of the man I once was. Not a single shred of him left for me to even ponder where he went.

I've never felt more worthless than I do right now. Believing everything anyone has ever said about me. Hoping to distance River from that person everyone thinks I am. To prove to her that I'm capable of being exactly who she needs me to be. That who I am is enough for her.

That she'll never have to worry about some of those rumors being true, because I'll have debunked them before she even knows about that public side of me.

If she doesn't already know.

CHAPTER 9

River

It's been a couple of weeks since I apologized to Leon. Since he insisted that we were both even since we were both sorry. Every day since he's walked me to my car in the mornings and we chat.

Usually about nothing in particular. Nothing deeper than work, hobbies, or plans. But things are easy with him. Things are as easy as they ever could be. So easy that it feels like I've known him my whole life. Like we didn't just meet less than two months ago.

I still haven't told him about the music. I can hear the lovely melodies drifting through my bedroom walls like a ritualistic nighttime symphony. How beautiful the music is. I want to ask him to share the playlist, and to tell me what artists he's listening to. I can always hear him singing along, but I've never been able to make out enough words to search for them.

Receiving a personally curated playlist from Leon would make my life.

I doubt he knows I can hear it, though. I'm terrified that if I tell him I can hear it, he'll stop.

I enjoy being around him greatly. I can't imagine not seeing him constantly. Hearing his voice, chatting about nothing and occasionally pretending we're dating if we happen to walk by a security camera that he claims Boyle checks often. I don't know if he's being truthful or not, but I've decided that I like this ruse we're playing.

He hasn't tried to kiss me again. Nor does he become physical when we're roleplaying. The occasional shoulder touch, and even rarer that we hold hands. While our conversations are never deep, I usually chalk it up to the limited time we have together. Hardly ever encountering each other after work or on the weekends.

We always gravitate toward one another, though. Like we're our own solar system, inevitable to be near one another.

I enjoy our almost daily chats. But I think I enjoy his presence, even in the silence, more. Something I might never admit out loud.

This week, though, I hadn't seen him outside. Hadn't heard a peep from him at all. There has been radio silence all week. I haven't seen or heard any movement in his apartment in days. I thought maybe he was out of town, but since our plans are something we usually talk about, I thought to rule that out.

Then, I thought maybe he was avoiding me. That he was so sick and tired of my mundaneness that he couldn't stand the sight of me for a moment longer. But our last interaction, last Friday, was good. Great even. Or so I thought.

Or maybe he's dead. Maybe he went and died on me without coming to haunt me to let me know. What kind of neighbor would that be? Just sitting, rotting, in the adjoining room. The whole time I think he's mad at me or hates my guts.

All were plausible theories until I heard some coughing today. Oh, God. Why didn't I think about the possibility that he might be sick? What kind of neighbor – friend – am I for not going to check on him? Make him some soup? I don't even know how to make soup. I bake. I don't cook. Can I go *buy* him some soup? Heat it up? Would that suffice?

No. That's fucking stupid.

This is all fucking stupid.

Should I just leave him alone? Should I go see if he's okay? If he's sick, he probably doesn't want visitors. Definitely doesn't want to see me, right?

But what if I make it look like I was coming over anyway? Bring him some cookies or something to just test the waters. He can take the cookies and tell me to fuck off while he takes my baked goods back inside.

That's a good plan, right? Make some cookies. Simple enough. I have extra dough from earlier this week when I made my coworker a cookie cake for her birthday. I had actually made extra just for Leon, but he never showed. So I gave them to the birthday woman as an extra gift, even though I was heartbroken that I couldn't share my creation with Leon.

Get yourself together, River. You're losing it.

Should I get dressed up? No, then he'll definitely know something's wrong. I need to look as normal as possible.

How the hell do people look normal when in severe distress and panic? Why the hell am I panicking again? Oh, right. Because I have a massive *fucking* crush on a man who I have manifested from a dream. My larger-than-life crush on a stupid fucking man who probably doesn't even want to give me the time of day most days.

I'm making mountains out of motherfucking molehills. He's practically a stranger. Giggling and kicking my feet over a guy I don't know. About to walk into a complete fucking stranger's apartment.

Well, he's not a complete stranger at this point, but he might as well be. He might as well be Jack the Ripper with as little as I know about him.

Do I play it off as something casual?

If I play it too well, then he'll think he's just an afterthought, right? But if I make it obvious, then he'll know that I have a crush on him. I can't have a man knowing I have a massive crush.

Slow down, girlfriend. The world isn't ending.

Well, it is ending, but there's nothing I can do about that.

If this goes poorly, I can just eat the cookies. Be anxious and alone in my own apartment, no need to get someone else involved in this idiotic mess.

Fuck. I'm such a goddamn mess.

I feel more like three opossums in a trench coat than a living, breathing, functioning adult.

After a few deep and measured breaths, the walls stop closing, stop swallowing me up whole. White knuckling the kitchen counter with my head hung over the sink. Cold air swirls around the flowing cold water easing my heightened anxiety.

I'm going to vomit.

No, no vomit, just anxiety. There's nothing on my stomach that would make its way up anyway. Grabbing a ginger ale from the near barren fridge, the light illuminates the kitchen in a soft white hue. A cold fog rolls to the floor, chilling my legs. The crack of the can rings out through the room, reminding me of the magnitude of quiet that the apartment carries.

Eight hundred square feet. Still carries no sense of home. No amount of artwork, fake plants (because I can't keep anything alive), Lego sets, and books have made this space my own.

Everything here is mine. A new set of cream sheets and an olive-green quilt I finished two years ago don't even begin to scratch the surface of making this space the one I want to call my home.

I've unpacked. Finally. Except, I don't have enough stuff to fill the space in the maximalist way I have always dreamed of. My pink kitchenware, heart-shaped bowls, and cherry red stand mixer seem almost out of place against the sanitarium white of the walls. White string lights hang from command strips encircling the living room. Yellow towels and bathmats bring artificial sunlight into the ensuite bathroom.

There is no joy here. No sense of belonging. It's all just *stuff.* Stuff that I love, mind you. Things that have become a part of who I am. My most treasured items that survived the moving purge. But even my love for these items can make this place love me back.

I've spent the last ten years trying to create a life that I can be proud of. The only thing being in foster care for six years taught me was to trust no one and to never put roots down. Never unpack your duffle, don't put up posters, and don't open up for anyone under any circumstances. Much like a dandelion swept up by the wind, I've got nowhere to call my own.

Even before foster care, my biological parents weren't much better. They'd spend the last dollar they had on drugs and cigarettes rather than food and clothes for their *mistake.*

There were always the threats. The one's Mama and Daddy would scream at me after they'd get a phone call from the school that CPS was called because of whatever reason it was at that time. The verbal ass chewings I would get. I half wanted CPS to come and take me away. Take me to a better place.

CPS came and went. Many times. And one time I went with them. But that better place never came.

The oven timer dings, snapping me out of my dissociative spiral. Back to the fresh smell of cookies, anxiety returning in full swing. I take the pan out of the oven and perform some minor quality control. Before I step into the throws of this situation.

Once both the cookies and I have had ample time to cool, I grab an extra Tupperware from the cabinet above the fridge, arranging the thick chocolate chip cookies into a pretty formation. As pretty as I can with shaky hands.

I attempt to fix my hair in the reflection of the fridge. Deem myself as middle of the road as possible. Not too put together, not too messy. Grabbing the box, what little dignity and confidence I have left before I head towards my door. March myself over the threshold and down the hallway to Leon's apartment.

Knock, knock, knock.

No turning back now.

My heart pounds against my chest benevolently, like

I've never spoken to him a day in my life. I can't lift my eyes from the floor, hoping that he won't answer the door. Hoping that I don't have to see his stupidly gorgeous face.

Fucking hell.

I don't have shoes on. Just mismatched socks, one pink and one purple.

I'm a quarter of a millisecond away from turning around. Walk right back to my apartment, embarrassed. When the door cracks open, revealing a disheveled Leon, completely wrapped in a hoodie and four blankets. His nose is beet red. The usual stoic look is replaced with one of tiredness accentuated by the dark circles under his half-closed eyes.

He looks like hell.

"Oh my god, are you okay?" I blurt out, completely losing any and all sense of self-consciousness about my appearance. His tired features soften, smiling at my obvious concern.

He sniffles. "I've looked and felt better." He states. Turning away, coughing loudly, then turning back to me with an apologetic smile on his face.

"I'd have to agree." I chuckle nervously, my stomach somersaulting as worry befalls upon me. "May I come in?"

"What are you? A vampire?" He asks, voice strained.

"Are you into that?" I ask with a raised eyebrow.

He chuckles. "Eh, I don't think I'd be a good meal for you right now. I'd probably taste the way a drugstore smells."

"You're right. That sounds disgusting." I reply with a light laugh. "I wanted to make sure you were okay, though. I hadn't seen you all week."

"You're always welcome to come inside, angel." He says smoothly, making a swarm of butterflies appear in my abdomen. "I don't want you to get sick, though."

"I'll be okay." I lie. Knowing full well if he's contagious, then I'll probably end up dying on the bathroom floor by the end of next week. That my immune system has been fucked since I got mono in the seventh grade from making out with

Isla Ramirez.

"Do you want to come in, then?" He asks.

"The vampire would like that very much." I joke, nodding. Opening the door fully, stepping aside to invite me in. Making a grandiose gesture. Hesitantly, I ponder what it is that I want to get out of going into his space.

Why not just leave the cookies and move on? Why put my health at risk? Why won't my feet turn around? Retreat to safety. To places he can't see and hasn't seen in weeks.

But my feet decide for me. My head screams at how wrong this is. It's oh, so wrong. But the deepest reaches of my pathetic, dampened soul scream to be near him. To calm this wave of worry and anxiety that can only be settled in his presence.

I cross the threshold, an appreciative smile on my face. Cold fingers steel gripping the plastic container carrying the only way I know how to show affection, appreciation.

Upon first glance, I notice that his apartment is as clean as if someone never lived here.

No wonder he was repulsed. That he couldn't stand the sight of the disarray before him when he stood in my kitchen.

A gold and glass console table sits behind the door to the left. On top is a gold ceramic dish with keys and a black leather wallet. A smaller matching bowl for coins sits at a strategic angle. Shoes line the floor under the table. Sneakers, slides, and loafers. A hanger on the back of the door holds a single jacket and a navy blue windbreaker.

An oversized, gray couch sits under the window facing the TV. A warm, wood-toned coffee table is nestled close enough to the couch to be easily accessible. Thick matching curtains frame the windows. Various flora litter a plant stand that sits in direct light.

Various medications and boxes of tissues are scattered across the island. The only signs of disarray as far as I can see. No dishes clutter the sink, no crumbs on the floor, nothing to show any signs of life outside of the mini drug store that was on display.

He wasn't joking when he said he'd taste like one.

Looking through the doorway to his bedroom, which butted directly against where my bedroom wall is, the foot of a bed was visible with unmade white sheets and duvet. A small desk – that matches the console table – sits against the wall with a computer and hunks of what look like music production equipment.

The place smelled like fresh laundry and lavender.

"I brought you some cookies." I say, holding out my hand in his direction. His eyes flit to the container, pouty lips curl with confusion. Passing the cookies to him, I study his expression closely as he delicately plucks the top off. Long fingers dive around a cookie, selecting one from its package to bring to his lips. He takes a bite, eyes widening in delight.

"Where did you get these?" He asks before he takes another, larger, bite. I chuckle at his enthusiasm. Constellations forming in his still tired eyes, shimmering similarly to a quote from my favorite author, Florence Cromwell.

There will be a day when I sit across from you,
And I won't remember a time without you.
Your laugh similar to a breeze on the summer's eve,
Welcomed and embraced.
Twinkling eyes that are my own constellation,
I connect the stars that swim in your irises.
Your smile bests the sun,
Outshining in every way.

And as I'm standing across from him, those words could not ring truer. His smile, laugh, and voice all a sense of familiarity, like they were made to ease the roaring seas inside of me. As if we'd done this a million times.

Outside of his presence in my dreams, I know I don't know him. I know that he does not exist elsewhere in my life prior to almost two months ago. All of these things I know.

But I can't shake the familiarity of him.

I remember that dream better than most memories. How vividly it stands in my mind. How petrified I was to find out he was real and just as beautiful if not more so. How anxious I was to speak to him properly when we collided in the mailroom. But no matter the ailment, terror, unease, his presence lulls it. Decimating it all to a calm I still can't understand.

Yet, we seem to always gravitate towards one another. Like the universe is shuffling our lives closer and closer to each other. How all conversations, interactions, have been so natural. Even when I'm a walking embarrassment.

"I made them from scratch." I reply, fiddling with the hem of my shirt as he ushers us over to the couch. He takes the seat closest to the window. I take the one farthest from him.

"Really?" He asks, almost skeptically. I nod sheepishly. He collects a second cookie from the box and places the rest on the coffee table.

"Are they good?" I ask, recoiling from the question. I'd feared they wouldn't live up to his standards. That my baking was actually terrible and everyone around me is just being nice.

His flabbergasted look says otherwise.

"Good? No. Heaven sent? Absolutely."

"Heaven sent?" I ask with a raised eyebrow.

"Much like you."

Oh, I think I'm going to be lightheaded.

A blush coats over every inch of my face. All of the air is stolen from my lungs, squeezing them so tightly. Fingertips grow instantly numb and cold, almost deadly cold. My eyes find comfort in the pattern in the fabric between us.

"Don't get shy on me now, angel." He coos, though not nearly as seductive through a stuffy nose.

The words still hit their mark. In my chest.

In between my legs.

CHAPTER 10

Leon

She's the absolute cutest covered in blush. I can imagine how intoxicating she'll look covered in my cum. I don't care how sick and tired I am, I'd take any and all opportunities to bend her over any surface in this apartment. Have my way with her until the only name in her head is my own.

There's a need building inside of me that I can't ignore any longer. Roiling deep within me. Demanding to be set free. Unleashed.

Adjusting in my seat to hide my now aching cock, my eyes never leave her. Hers never meet mine.

"You know," I say, willing her gaze to part with their spot on the cushion in between us. Golden eyes encapsulated by thick, red heat look up at me from behind her thick red eyelashes, and I can only imagine her looking at me like that with those perfect pink lips wrapped around my cock.

"What do I know?" She asks when I take too long to complete my sentence. Too busy wet daydreaming.

"You really didn't have to make cookies just for me." I say, chickening out of whatever filthy things that were about to fall from my lips.

She breathes a chuckle, shoulders relaxing. "It was no trouble really. Being called 'heaven sent' certainly made up for the vampire comment earlier, though." She jokes. "But if the cookies will make your sickness go away, then I'll be back again tomorrow with more."

"Good thing the doctor ordered a *healthy* dose of

antibiotics, sunshine, and baked goods made by a pretty lady. So it looks like you've got two of those things covered. I'm feeling better already."

A blaze erupts across her self-conscious gaze. Her eyes refuse to falter from my own. A silent understanding that my demanded attention never be broken. "You sound like Skylar. She calls me her sunshine girl." She says with an eye roll, clearly avoiding my blatant flirting.

"Well, she's definitely on to something." I reply with a smirk. I reach for the cookies, picking a third out of the container. Smiling at her smugly as I sink my teeth into it.

I've always had a sweet tooth.

"Don't make yourself sick." She scolds, leaning back against the corner of the couch.

"Already sick, angel. Can't make it worse."

"You absolutely can." She counters, squinting her eyes at my defiance. "And I won't sit here and watch you do it."

I hum contemplatively. Thinking how easily I can twist her words to filth. How I'd truly love nothing more than to make her *watch* as I pound into her from behind in front of the bathroom mirror. Those delicately manicured fingers white knuckling the counter for dear life.

Get it together, Leon.

Snapping myself out of my trance once again, I ask. "Is Skylar the one who helped you move in?" In an attempt to stifle the burning need growing deep within me.

"No, that was Nancy. Skylar is the one I met for brunch." She says like there was no mistaking the two.

"Oh, yeah. I never got a chance to ask you how it went."

She smiles sweetly, and says, "It went well! I don't get to see her often, so it was nice to catch up. She asked me to be her bridesmaid and witness to her elopement!" A tiny squeal escapes her throat. "She and Dana are flying back in at the end of October. Then, we're hiking through Stone Mountain on that Saturday to the peak that they stopped at on their first date. And finally, they're having a backyard reception in Dana's parent's backyard out in Forsythe on Sunday."

"Sounds like you're a very busy woman."

"Eh, it's only for a weekend. Though, I'm not looking forward to Debbie, Skylar's mom, asking me if I'm still single. I don't think I can take her trying to set me up with her son again."

"But you're not single." I say, packing bass into my voice. Commanding her to sit up just a little bit straighter.

"Oh, right." She says. "I didn't realize our scheming would spill over into my real life." The sound of disappointment, embarrassment, rings sharply throughout the room.

"We can call off the relationship if you don't want to keep doing this." I offer as calmly as I could muster. Her eyes grow to the size of saucers.

"No!" She clears her throat. "No. I don't see the need to be dramatic." I don't stop the smile from spreading across my increasingly tired face.

"Our agreement is there for any situation you need to get out of. Or into. I am at your beck and call."

"You're too kind." She retorts with a pretty eye roll. One that has me picturing all the ways I could make her do that exact same motion. "Do you use me as an out?"

"When I need you, I will use you." I mewl. Watching her brain whir, eyes darting across the smugness laden upon my skin. Fingers taut against the cotton of her shirt hem, twisting the material into knots.

"What you need is to go to bed." She grumbles, frustration riddling her furrowed brow.

"Then take me to bed." I purr, pushing her boundaries as far as I possibly can. Watching her squirm under my thumb. Every hiccup, hitched breath, and squeeze of her thighs doesn't go unnoticed.

"Alright then." She says defiantly. Rising from her seat, she holds out her hand for me. To help me stand. I shrug off all of my excess layers of blankets, placing my cold hand in hers and pulling myself to my feet. "Do you need me to dress you, too?" I tower over her a good eight inches, and even more just below the waistband.

"Undress, preferably." I tease.

"Is there something you want to say to me, Leon?" She asks, eyes shifting down my body and back up slowly.

My mouth dries out, wondering how far I'm willing to push what's gotten me in hot shit before. But she's not backing down. How far is she willing to let me go before reeling me back in? But when I take too long to respond, she continues.

"I'm not going to fuck you while you've got the flu."

"It's just a sinus infection." I counter with a shrug. "Are you saying you'll fuck me when I'm healthy?"

"If you think you can pull off this amount of confidence without the drugs, yes." She says, realizing we're still holding hands. Mine are significantly warmer now.

Oh, my little firestorm. You don't know what you've awoken in me.

"But for now, bed." She says sternly.

"Will you come check on me tomorrow?" I tease as she drags me into my bedroom. Not exactly the way I had originally imagined it, but that can be fixed another time.

She rolls her eyes, straightening out the pile of comforter and sheets, tucking back one side for me to climb into. "You're insufferable." She crows, corners of her mouth twisted into a smirk.

"Are you *staying* until tomorrow?" I ask, a little more seriously.

"Not a chance, big guy." She teases. I sit on the side of the bed, and she comes to stand in front of me. Close enough for me to wrap my arms around.

An overwhelming sense of Déjà vu befalls me. Like we've been here before. But I know we haven't.

She smiles down at me, like she feels it, too. Before leaning down and placing the tiniest kiss on my forehead. A blush I didn't know I was capable of dusts my ears.

"I can't let my *boyfriend* be sick and not take care of him." She teases, ruffling my already tousled hair. "Knock if you need me." She raps her knuckles on the wall that joins our rooms, walking toward the door. "I'm taking your keys so I can lock your door. And so you don't take a midnight joyride GTA style."

"My hero." I chuckle, not caring if she robbed me blind. Everything in this apartment, in this world, is hers if she so wanted it to be.

"Get some rest, Leon." She instructs over her shoulder.

I will be doing no such thing, not until I ease the need she's dredged up. Not until I've satisfied myself only after she's done pleasing herself.

It doesn't take her long after returning to her apartment to climb into bed. The near silent buzz of her vibrator against her clit has her releasing muffled moans. My mind runs wild at the images it projects. Back arched, teasing a nipple with one hand, commanding the toy with the other. Those full, pink lips parted, releasing the most seductive noises. Doing her very best to not be heard. I deny myself the release I so desperately seek until I hear her climax.

I slept like a fucking baby. Like I'd never slept a day in my life. The release was enough to knock me out. I awoke with the sun shining through the window, bright and early and slightly able to breathe through my nose.

The sinus infection is waning, thank all the Gods that may or may not exist, on day five of meds. But I feel like a new, changed man now. Well, I feel well enough to not want to bed-rot for the entire day. Something awoke inside of me with my newfound health.

Must have been River's visit.

I'm itching to go to the gym. I haven't been well enough to go since getting sick and I'm ready to get back to my regular routines. Gym, work, home, River.

Changing into something more gym appropriate and throwing on shoes, I reach for my keys as I head for the door. Only I come up empty.

Right. River took them.

Trotting back to the bedroom, I knock on our wall. Loud enough for her to hear, even if she is asleep. Unless she sleeps like the dead. In the silence, I wait for a response. But silence only stilled further.

I knock again, louder this time. Wait.

Still nothing.

Fucking hell, River.

Guess I have to take matters into my own hands. Grabbing a couple of paper clips from the desk drawer, I make my way over to her apartment. I knock again, just for good measure. Maybe she didn't hear me the first two times.

When she doesn't answer again, I kneel down on one knee, angling the already bent paper clips into the lock. Twisting, pulling, pushing until the lock clicks.

Turning the knob, the door gives way two inches or so.

The sliding deadbolt catches.

"River?" I yell into the nearly quiet space.

Muffled noises come from within the apartment. Barely there, barely audible. But I hear her. Almost an apparition of the woman I'm searching for.

From the limited view inside, I can't see much of anything but the wall closest to the door and a little of the living room. Trying to come up with a plan to get this deadbolt off.

A shadow floods my vision, shoving the door back. Pain shoots through my nose, ricocheting down my sinuses and into my temples as I stumble backwards into the hallway. Clutching my now bloody and still slightly congested face. Wood and metal slamming against each other ring through my ears, near deafening.

Anger courses through me. Rage. I saw red in lethal shades. No one is getting between me and my girl.

Ever.

Shouldering into the soft spot right where the chain held, the door gave way easily. Revealing exactly *who* was to blame. A short, uncannily Chris stands widely just a few feet inside the threshold.

My focus on him doesn't linger when my eyes fall upon River. Tied and gagged to one of the island chairs in the corner of the living room. Tears stream down her puffy, beautiful face. Her eyes hollowed. Pleading. Filled with shock and pain. Begging for an end.

She barely recognizes me. Not an ounce of familiarity stares back. And my heart nearly breaks.

What happened to you, River?

Another blow to my jaw cracks through the room. Sending more pain splintering through me once again. Sending me flying back into the wall. Righting myself, palming the sore spot on my jaw, I turn to face the problem.

"You've always gotten in my way, Kang." Chris drones, clenching and unclenching his fist as if the impact it had on my jaw hurt him more than it did me. His mouth is uncannily large, filled with pointy, glistening teeth. "I was just enjoying my breakfast. She tastes just as delicious as you'd expect."

My vision narrows on River once more. She's barely dressed in a baggy t-shirt, pulled high on her hips. Clearly stretched from a struggle. Completely bare from the waist down.

Ankles tied open to the legs of the chair. Arms bound in thick, coarse rope behind her back. Mouth gagged with some sort of cloth restraint. Tiny cuts, like cat scratches, litter her arms, legs, throat, face, stomach. Any exposed skin contained those cuts. Especially around her knees.

But it was the sickly look of her face. A gray hollowness that swallowed her whole, almost as gray as thick, heavy fog. Tears wet her cheeks. Hair messed in every direction.

I make a step towards her, to what's mine. To intervene with whatever the hell happened here. To right what this fucker has wronged. Blood boils beneath my skin, thinking about that slimeball touching her, hurting her. Toying with her. He steps toward me, almost blocking me from her.

"What did you do to her?" I demand, instantly forgetting about all the pain that once coursed through me. Replaced with blinding rage of a man who's going to kill anyone who dares hurt what's mine.

"You thought that you could save her from me? That I wouldn't even bother getting a taste of *her?*" He twirls a chunk of red hair around his fingers before putting it up to his nostril. Sniffing long and deep, moaning at her scent. "It's hard resisting the temptation of the Old Gods."

I lunge for him, unphased by the nonsense he's spewing. Fists fighting air as he steps quickly away, laughing. A laugh that grates on my last fucking nerve, that sounds like five voices at once. I try again, but he steps back further. Taunting me. Backing himself into River's room. Into a corner.

"Your girl tastes like a wet dream." He teases, continuing this sick waltz we're doing.

I feel like I'm getting nowhere. I'm fast, but he's somehow faster. Like he knows my moves before I make them. My fists never connect where they should.

As we're one step into River's bedroom, trapping him between me and the bathroom, the door slams closed by itself. Lights flicker, like they do when the power's about to go out.

Except it's a sunny day outside.

"You think you can win?" He asks, still twirling the hair between his grubby fingers. "You have no idea what you're up against, boy."

"Try me." I taunt. "Fight me."

"I don't need to."

A blood curdling yet muffled scream erupts from behind me. Whipping around, I try to open the door, but it's sealed shut, unbudging. The screams continue for a second longer, ringing throughout my ears as I search for a way to get to her.

"What the hell are you doing to her?" I bark, moments before my forehead comes in contact with the wooden door.

"What you've been too chicken shit to do for months." He hisses, inches away from my face. Pinning me to the door with my arm behind my back.

"Don't you say another fucking word." I threaten, adrenaline coursing through me. He's unbelievably strong, but the panic and anger running rampant are a deadly combo. I throw him off of me with a sharp shoulder check.

He falls backward but rolls onto his feet. Further into the room. I descend on him before he has any idea where the fists are coming from. A punch to the jaw, the gut, groin, anywhere I can hit, I swing. Pushing him further and farther into the room and into the bathroom.

River's screams quiet.

"I should kill you." I growl.

He just chuckles, brushing blood off his bottom lip. Gripping the bathroom door to keep from slipping into the room, he has nowhere to go from here. Reaching, grabbing for him, he grabs me in return. Sending punches, knees, anything he can at me.

I don't feel an ounce of it.

Focusing on getting him a step into the bathroom, hard tile the perfect material to bash his head into, he's wailing on me. Blood spews from my nose, my mouth, places that should feel pain don't.

With a fistful of white hair, I move from under his reign to slam his temple into the counter. Only stopping short when I see the reflection in the mirror. Not mine.

Chris's.

Gray, hollowed skin like Rivers, but paper thin and cracking. Void, black holes for eyes. A long, pointed and crooked nose. A too wide, too many teeth, mouth turned down in shock.

Unlike anything I've ever seen. The stuff made of nightmares. Things they only show in horror movies.

Unhuman.

Unhuman.

Before my eyes, Chris and the being in the mirror disintegrate into rubble leaving nothing in my fist but ash. A perfect ash line from the sink to the floor where the *thing* used to be.

I don't – can't – dwell on it too long. Running out of the room, I force open the bedroom door with ease and slide on my knees to River, still tied to her chair. Working to remove her restraints, gag first, then arms and legs. She doesn't speak. Just sobs quietly and breathlessly.

The scratches that littered her skin vanished. The hollowness that plagues her cleared. Almost as if it never happened.

Once she's free, she falls into my arms. I catch her instantly, fixing her shirt to cover her exposed bottom. Pulling her onto my lap. Stroking her hair, she sobs into me feverishly.

There are no words, no explanation for what I saw back there. The evil that reared its ugly head. Impossible things, beings, monsters. Nothing could calm my erratic heart, the panic and adrenaline coursing through me. But she doesn't need to know what I bore witness to.

She had her own slew of horrors.

"I got you." I breathe over and over again into her hair. Body shaking violently underneath me. "I got you, angel."

CHAPTER 11

River

It was already devoid of light outside when I came to. The darkness of night had settled around my wholly altered world, like a blindfold had been set back over my eyes. As if I could somehow unsee the horrors from the light. In my body's self-preservation, I slept for what felt like an eternity. Hard and unmoving in the cocoon I'd been wrapped up into. An eternity that only lasted fifteen hours.

And not in my apartment, but in Leon's.

He had held me so tight; I almost couldn't breathe. His arms around me are the only anchor I had left in this world. There was an aching that radiated off of him, too. One that screamed into the void. That sunk its hooks into me and swore vengeance for that *thing* that hurt me.

Almost killed me in my own apartment.

Thinking about setting foot back into my apartment pulls me to the brink of projectile vomiting all over Leon's immaculately clean home.

The home that now shelters me, welcomes me like a sanctuary. The same white linen bed that beckoned me in my dream the first night here, now warmed by my body heat. Pillows stained with the tears that wouldn't stop falling.

Leon, the ever attentive man he is, took up a post beside my bed. Holding my hand. Brushing his fingers through my hair. The occasional kiss on the forehead. Never leaving my side.

When I'd awoken, I'd practically been a different person.

I'd become mute. No words came to me or left me. I can't manifest them into existence, to express to Leon how thankful I am that he saved me. To tell him about all the wretched things that *monster* did to me. Things that no one should have the physical capabilities to do.

All emotions have left me. As empty as a cloudy night sky in the country. There is no distinction between them, it's all numbness under my skin. Everything I used to feel so deeply, now washed away with the tides.

Even as I look at Leon, nothing that I once felt for him washes over me. Not as all-consumingly as it once had. Though, I can still feel it simmering deep within me. Like a slumbering beast beneath a dark, eerie mountain.

My limbs can barely drag me from the bed to the couch, where Leon sits, staring at the door. Almost like he's daring someone, anyone, to enter it. A bloodied and bruised face lay below smoldering fire glistening in his eyes. I barely recognize him.

His eyes fall upon me. Softening instantly into the man I know. The man that made my heart soar into the stratosphere. I can't bear to think about how I can't bring myself to smile back at him. To give him some reassurance that I know he needs. To tell him that I'm okay.

Lie to him for his own sake.

"Hey, angel." He coos, springing to his feet. Gliding to my side in easy motions. Strong arms cascade around me, pulling me into an even stronger, chiseled torso. "How are you? Did you sleep okay? Can I get you something?"

His questions fall from his mouth in rapid succession. But I make no move to answer them. I can't answer them. Lifting my chin to look at him, his eyes scan my body, my soul. And somehow completely understanding.

"Let's get you something to eat." He guides me to the living room where he sets me down gently on the couch.

"I made us some Beef Stroganoff with carrots and smashed potatoes."

The smell of the aforementioned food wafts into my nose. My mouth waters instantly. Stomach howling for food. I hadn't eaten in almost thirty-six hours. The corners of my mouth twitch upward with a hint of a smile as Leon brings over two bowls, going back to the kitchen for drinks and a platter of smashed potatoes.

Two tall glasses of water are set down on marble coasters. One for each of us. A spoon is plunged into both bowls. My stomach screams for nourishment.

Yet, I can't move an inch to pick up the glass. Or the spoon. Or even a potato. Leon's eyes watch me attentively, studying my movements. Or lack thereof. Cogs turn in his head, brow creased with frustration.

"I'm here if you want to talk about it." He offers quietly.

I know you are, I want to say. We're both silent for another moment. He eats his food. I stare at mine. Leon reaches for a potato. Plucking it from the plate between two long, shaky fingers. Bringing the thin, crispy root vegetable close to me.

"Try it." He nearly begs, bringing it closer. Nearly touching my lips. I open my mouth, an exuberant force to do so, and bite down.

Flavor explodes over my tongue. Rosemary, thyme, garlic, olive oil, and so many others that my brain has a hard time distinguishing.

My eyes must have given Leon some indication of enjoyment because a relaxed smile slips over his clearly tired face. His hand doesn't move until I've taken the last bite of potato. Then he says, "I took a lot of cooking classes in my early twenties." He pauses, eyes my hand as it reaches for a carrot. "This was one of the first meals I learned how to cook without fucking it up." A breathy chuckle escapes him.

I'm honored, I think.

"I'd always thought if I didn't go into music that I'd have

loved to have been a private chef."

I didn't know you worked in music.

"Music's always been my first love. The thing I can do to keep myself grounded. Even when my world turns upside down."

Does your world get turned upside often? Do you get woken up in the middle of the night by someone letting themselves into your apartment? Do they tie you up like a hog at the county fair just to defile you, rape you, burn you, cut you? Do you look at that same person and see something inhuman?

My eyes grow cold. Glassy.

"My best friend, Elio." He says with worry in his mahogany eyes. "We were as thick as thieves."

Were?

"He was the first friend I ever made in second grade. He was the new kid, and a raging nerd. Mrs. Duggen paired us up for some kind of science experiment and we became fast friends. We hung out all the time, picked each other for all the projects, the whole thing."

I'd love to see pictures of little kid Leon.

"We were inseparable. I even convinced my parents to let him join us on our annual family vacations. And I think they only said yes so that I could have someone to keep me entertained." His eyes grew immeasurably sorrowful. "We got into some serious trouble on a cruise to the Bahamas. Something to do with beating some drunk guys in cornhole."

You can play cornhole?

"We ditched senior prom to have a LAN party with a bunch of guys from other schools. You know, since junior prom consisted of my date drinking too much spiked punch, throwing up all over me, and then ditching me for Jerry Spellman, the captain of the football team."

What an asshole.

"We had plans to be each other's best men. To be the Godparents to each other's kids. To have family vacations. Our wives would be friends and so would our kids. We had this idea of our lives all laid out."

That's what I had always wanted Nancy and I to be.

His bottom lip quivers. My hand reaches for him, the only thing that doesn't feel as daunting as a Herculean trial. Leaning into my touch, he kisses the palm of my hand.

"After we'd argued over something so stupid – over the fact that we both liked the same girl. He'd stormed off mad as hell. I didn't hear from him for the rest of the weekend."

No one's worth risking a friendship like that.

I return my hand to my lap.

"His mom called me early the next week to let me know that Elio had died from a fentanyl overdose."

Oh, my god. I'm so sorry.

"She still blames me for it. Even to this day." His shoulders hunch. "And I quickly realized I didn't even like Jenny all that much. Not enough to ruin my friendship over. To lose my best friend over." Tears well into his eyes. I stop myself from scooting close to him.

Up close, his face is almost flawless. No wrinkles or lines crease the supple skin. His brown eyes trained on me like a sniper. The *clink* of the spoon in the bowl rattles throughout the now silent apartment. His hands raised midair, almost waiting for a signal.

"I haven't really cared about anyone since Elio." He says. His eyes scan over every inch of my body. A breath hitches in my throat at his ogling.

Even though I know Leon would never hurt me, I can't shake the creepy crawlies that coat my skin. The image of Boyle's pitch black eyes floods my vision. Too many teeth.

I force myself to breathe. *Inhale. Exhale.*

Leon did not hurt me. Leon is my safe space.

Invisible hands caressing my body. Vile touches that cause my nervous system to revolt. Pain pinpricks under my skin, where the cuts once resided. Screaming rings in my own ears as grief and loss and anger and unbridled rage wash over me all at once.

Like a dam had been broken.
"Until you." He says.
My world and all its turmoil stills.
"Me?"

CHAPTER 12

Leon

Her eyes shine with pain. Agony. I had hoped that my ramblings about Elio had been enough of a distraction to keep the nightmares at bay. I hadn't any idea what she'd gone through. Just the aftermath that I'd bear witness to.

She hasn't said a word. Not made a sound. But her eyes are distant. Almost like a stranger standing in my own apartment. River was barely recognizable and it's breaking me. My heart twists and wretches in my chest at the thought that I've lost her. Not physically, but mentally. Emotionally. She's nowhere to be found. And I'm desperate to do anything to bring her back.

Watching her succumb to the torment roiling under the surface, I blurt out the first thing I thought that could bring her back to me.

"Until you."

"Me?"

A single word. Barely above a whisper. If I hadn't seen her lips move, I would have sworn I dreamt it.

But she's looking at me like a deer in headlights. I'm regretting ever uttering those words. But I meant them. I meant so much more than what I said.

"Why me?" She asks in the lingering silence. Voice stronger, more defiant than before. "What's so fucking special about me?" Flames erupt in her once muted eyes. Fury masking the pain.

I can't explain to her how I feel this cosmic pull

toward her. How from the moment I first saw her, there was something about her that drew me in. That I'd vowed almost immediately that I wouldn't let anything happen to her, even though I didn't even know her at all.

Especially not how I'd claimed her as my own.

"Why, Leon?" She asks again, gripping her spoon so tightly that her knuckles begin turning white. "Why did this happen to *me?*"

"I don't know, angel."

"Then, why am I so special?" She asks, venom spewing from her words. "What makes *me* so special?"

"Everything." I say before I lose the courage to do so.

"Excuse me?"

"Everything about you is special, River." The words fall from my mouth with ease, like they'd been waiting to be said for a lifetime. "From the way you carry yourself, to your kindness, to your free spirit. You're a once in a lifetime kind of person." *You're my person.*

"I'm not." She demands, almost like she could hear my thoughts. "I'm not anything special." Her lip quivers. I reach my hand out to her, but she immediately slinks away. "Don't." She snaps. "Don't touch me." She stands, fists curled at her sides.

"Angel," I coo, standing with her. She shakes her head, warning me not to come closer. "Baby." I say, raising my arms to her.

"I am not your baby. I'm not your fucking angel."

I knew she didn't mean it.

"River, look at me." Her eyes snap to my face. "With everything I am, I will never hurt you." I take a gentle step forward. She doesn't move. "I can't lose you."

"Don't guilt me into that." She snaps, shaking my fingers off her arm. "You don't get to say that to me. Not after what I went through."

She tries to walk around me. My hands grasp the air as she evades my touch. Stomping quickly to the front door. I'm right behind her. Trying to make sense of what's going on in her head. What I can do to help her. What I did wrong.

Everything I said – did – runs through my mind at lightning speeds. Each word crystal clear in my head. I can't pinpoint exactly what set her off.

With her back to me, right in front of the door, she halts. The world stops for just a second as I watch her reach for the door. A shaky hand grasps the cold metal. And she holds it for a moment. Then drops her head, hand falling back to her side.

In slow motion, she falls to her knees. Racing to catch her before she hits the floor, I scoop her up into my arms.

"I can't do this." She mumbles, head hung so low I could barely see through the curtain of red hair that hid her face. I sweep it behind her ear, lifting her chin. "I can't go back there."

Cradling her shaking body in my arms, I rock the both of us. Lulling and shushing her sobs. Unable to think of a single thing to say that could ease the aching within her. The same aching that's ripping through me somehow.

She had asked me why she's so special. Why I'd latched onto her and couldn't let go. And the truth of the matter was that I don't have any inkling of an idea. I didn't lie when I said all of those things about her. I could never lie to her about how important she is to me.

And the more I get to know her, the more reasons I have to protect her. To hold her. To call her mine. I couldn't tell you why she's been a magnet, but I'm so incredibly grateful that she is. That the universe or God or whatever cosmic alignment had to happen to bring her to me. She's given me something to live for. I know that's a lot to put on one person, and maybe I'll never mention it to her, but I'll be forever grateful to her for bringing me back to life.

"Let me handle it." I say, offering her any sort of solution for her agony. Her eyes look up at me, tears swelling and falling in rapid succession.

"How?"

"You can stay here. With me. We'll make it work." I offer,

not really knowing how we'd make it work. Not knowing if we'd be able to move past this. Not knowing why I'm so willing to accept her into my life. In every facet.

"I can't do that." She shakes her head. "I can't go back there. I can't live here. What if someone comes looking for me? I can't get you involved."

"Hey, hey, hey." I say. "I've got you. I'm not going to let anyone hurt you." She searches my face for something, then nods. "You're more than welcome to stay here with me."

"What about you?" She asks worriedly.

"What about me?" I ask with a slight grin. "I told you. We'll make it work. *I'll* make this work. If it's what you need."

"I can't ask you to do this."

"I'd burn the entire world down for you." I admit, cradling her face in my palm. There's a flicker of fear in her eyes. "I'd do anything you asked. Just say the word and I'd do it."

"Why?" She asks, bringing her hand up to grasp my wrist. I expect her to pull me away, but she doesn't. Though, her grip is strong enough to hurt.

"Because there's something about you that my soul can't let go of." I say without thinking through my words. "And it terrifies me not knowing why. But it's you. And I can't stop it. I don't *want* to stop it."

Her grip tightens. Lip quivering. "You feel it, too?" I nod. I knew what she meant. And it's like a weight was lifted from my tired, achy shoulders. "I thought I was crazy."

"Me, too." I chuckle, nearly breathless at the beauty before me. Barely a smile paints her lips, but it's there. "We don't have to do anything, be anything, you don't want. But just know that I'll be here for you. For everything."

She nods as worry lifts from her murky eyes. "Same to you." She breathes, leaning into my chest. "You sure you're okay if I stay here for a little while?"

"Stay here forever," *my love.* "As long as you want. What's mine is yours now."

"And what's mine is yours." She exhales, breath ghosting down my arm. Something in my head, my heart, goes taunt like a string being pulled tight.

Our eyes meet. I could have sworn we both felt it.

CHAPTER 13

River

Days were hard.

Nights were harder.

I'd almost quit my job the first time Mark Borkowski asked me on a date. I'd turned him down, as politely and professionally as I could. And he took it about as well as you'd expect. Which wasn't well at all.

He was fucking relentless. But I was angry. I was – am – furious at everything in this world. Rage and spite and this *thing* in my chest that beats so feverishly for Leon were the only things keeping me going. I could hold my own against him. He was nothing but a pesky fly for about two weeks after the incident. Then, suddenly his comments grew lewder. His flirting turned to harassment. His actions became intolerable.

I didn't – couldn't – tell Leon about it. I had failed to protect myself against Boyle. The world felt heavier, like my load to bear was significantly more. And I bear the weight of being a failure. Of being a burden to Leon. There were days where everything was excruciating. I wasn't about to lean on Leon for constant conflict resolution.

Especially not after he'd confessed that he'd burn the world for me. I couldn't give him the fuel and matches along with a target. As much as I wish I could watch Mark burn for the shit he's been saying to me – about me. I couldn't have a potential second body on my hands.

Even though I still don't know where the first body went. I never saw Boyle leave. Never saw a body in the apartment. Leon wouldn't let me go into the bathroom, but I caught a glimpse of it. There was no body there either. It's almost like he vanished into thin air. And that terrifies me more than seeing a dead man in my apartment.

I never got the closure of making sure he was good and dead. Never got the chance to spit on his grave for what he did.

There's been some distance, time, between me and what happened. Though, I know I'll need a lot more of it behind me to feel even remotely okay. I couldn't shake the constant need to look over my shoulder. The feeling of someone, some unseen force following me. Like there are eyes watching my every move.

Eyes that aren't Leons. Though, I keep telling him he's going to get sick of my face with how much he stares at me. Sometimes with a gentle smile. Most of the time, with worry. Like he's studying each pore in case one day he won't get the chance to see them anymore. Or that he's also making sure I'm still here. That my corpse isn't walking around without my wretched soul attached to it.

He's stuck to me like a helicopter parent. Insisting on driving me to and from work. Accompanying me to the grocery store. He's even insisted on going with me to get my nails and hair done this week. He even asked if he could come to the very private elopement.

I told him no. Skylar said he could come to the reception. So we compromised. He'll drive me to the elopement and wait in the car like a stalker until we're done.

If he knew about Mark, he'd go off the deep end.

But he's been so sweet, so accommodating.

He called a guy he knew to forge documents to get my name off my lease so that no one could track me to an address. Hired a different guy to wipe as much of my personal information off the internet as possible.

I didn't even know you could do that.

Almost all of my belongings are in a storage unit in Leon's name in Macon. So far away from here that I feel like I've lost parts of myself again. But then I remember what happened and I forget the need to pick up that silly hobby. Because the pain, the PTSD is so strong that it's completely debilitating. I forget about wanting to do anything at all.

I try to put on a happy face. If not for myself, then for Leon. Especially after everything he's done. Everything he's sacrificed. He doesn't deserve to bear the weight of my failures.

But some days are harder than others.

Some nights are harder than others.

I know he deserves more than my broken body and soul. Especially since he's patient and kind. He cooks me dinners and we watch TV together. He holds my hand as I fall asleep, claiming that he wants me to know he's always there. He doesn't push me for sex, even though I know he wants it.

I tell myself it's okay if he's getting it somewhere else. That I don't care if he does everything I wish I could do with him with someone else. We're not dating, I tell myself. I have no stake to claim. I can't assume he'd wait around for me either. I'm so far beyond fucked up that I shouldn't even think about sex right now.

Except, I do. I think about it when I wake up in the middle of the night and his body's pressed against mine and all I can imagine is how much I want his fingers inside of me. How desperate I am to feel his mouth. All the ways I would let him defile me. I tell myself I shouldn't be thinking this way. That I shouldn't want that after what Boyle did to me.

But I can't stop it. Not when I told him I'd preferred to sleep with him as a coping mechanism. So he didn't have to sleep on the couch like he'd offered. Which is all true. But not the entire story.

My entire body craves him in some unholy way. I think about all the gentle caresses, the acts of service, how our bodies fit together like he's been the one thing I've always been missing from this life.

And I swallow it all. I force it all down beneath the surface in hopes that it'll pass like a storm heading down stream. And I swear my heart nearly explodes at the thought of hurting him. That everything I do hurts him, upsets him.

That's why I can't tell him about Mark.

I can't see him upset again.

I tried my hand at making dinner tonight. With Leon's supervision of course. He's a much more extravagant chef than I will ever be, but it's been a good day. And I thought I would return the favor.

Blackened salmon with lemon orzo.

It was edible.

Leon, however, had performed a Tony-worthy scene like it was the best meal he's ever eaten. I couldn't tell if he was faking it to boost my ego and encourage me to keep trying. Or if he'd simply forgotten the bulgogi masterpiece he'd made a few days ago.

I guess a win's a win. Especially considering I hardly can stomach food anymore. I usually don't make it more than a few bites in before I feel the need to vomit. So I save all of my leftovers for work.

We'd taken up to watching my comfort show. I've seen all the episodes a thousand times. I know the plot inside and out. It's predictable. It's comfortable.

Just like the way I'm nestled into the corner of Leon's couch – our couch? – with my knees pulled up to my chest. A blanket thrown around me to hide the wringing of my hands from anxiety. Sitting a safe distance away in hopes that I'll eventually convince myself that I don't want him desperately.

"Who's this guy again?" Leon asks, breaking the silence.

"Joe Mantegna." I state, feeling the effects of the evening sunset befall upon me. Like some stickier, nauseating version of sundowning.

My phone lights up from its place on the couch between us. I glance down at the message and sigh. Heavily. Piquing a curious look from Leon. I shrug out of the cocoon and swipe away the notification out of frustration.

"What's wrong?" He asks, furrowed eyebrows accentuating his puzzled look. Masking his usual stoic concern.

"Oh, it's nothing." I half-lie. It really was nothing for him to be concerned about.

"River," He scolds, all focus lost on the show.

"Leon," I pipe back, not at all in the mood to deal with whatever he was about to say.

"What's wrong?" He asks again, more sternly.

"It's nothing to write home about." I say, rolling my eyes. "Why do you want to know so badly?" I ask, readjusting myself back under my blanket.

"I feel entitled to know." He quips with a half-smile. One I would love to ogle at if he weren't grating on my last nerve about the subject.

"You're insufferable." I say lightly, splattering an equaled grin onto my tired face.

"Yeah, and you're still in my apartment. So, I must not be *that* bad." He counters with a smirk. "If it's nothing bad, then just tell me, angel."

Angel. The main pet name he's chosen for me. The one that sounds so sickeningly sweet dancing off his tongue. He knows how to get his way. That's for sure.

"Fine," I concede.

He sits up in his seat, ready to listen to whatever I was going to tell him, no matter the magnitude.

"So, I have this coworker, Mark." I start, watching his eyes rove over my face with uncertainty. "You know what? Never mind." I stop, not wanting to talk about it still.

"Just tell me."

"It's stupid and honestly none of your business." I quip.

"Anything involving you is my business." He replies sternly. All the air in my lungs is expelled instantly at the command in his voice. The possessiveness that resides in his words. "*You* are my business." He reiterates.

"He's just been relentlessly asking me out for weeks."

"Do I have to-" he starts, ice dripping from his words.

"No." I snap. "You do not have to get involved. You wanted to know what I was upset about. So, I told you. If I wanted your involvement, I would have asked for it."

After a pause, he says, "Alright." His body sinks a little further back into the couch. "Do you not like him?"

"No!" I nearly shout, involuntarily. "Why would I?"

"It was just a question." He states, returning back to a less hostile version of himself. "You and I aren't together. You can do whatever you want."

"I know that." I retorted. "Same to you."

Silence surrounds us, except for the voices from the TV. I pick at the skin around my fingers, my blood heating behind my cheeks. A wave of undisclosed pain wafting through me.

"Why don't you want to date him?" He asks softly after a moment.

Because he's been a Grade A douchebag since the moment I met him? Because the idea of dating anyone besides you is repulsive. Because if I fucked anyone else, I'd only think about you.

"Is he bothering you?" He asks through clenched teeth.

"Will you kill him if I say yes?" I ask dryly.

"I'll consider it."

"Then no."

He sighs deeply. "Fine. No, I won't kill him."

"Then yes. In a sense." I say. He makes no move to reply, no muscles churn besides his chest rising and falling. Almost like if he moves, he'll unleash a whole beast he won't be able to control. "It's nothing like Boyle. He just doesn't take no for an answer. It's nothing I haven't been able to handle before."

"Before?" He snaps.

Jesus Christ. "Yes, Leon. Men are pigs. Relentless fucking pigs. And I've dealt with them my whole life. They're a plague."

"I'm asking nicely, little firestorm." Another pet name. One for when I'm being extra uncooperative. "Is there anything I can do to make this problem . . . disappear?"

"Do you have any suggestions?" I ask, turning to face him. To see the turmoil on his face.

"Well, the faking dating arrangement can be reinstated." He offers.

"Oh, so sorry. I didn't know you'd called that off." I snap, instantly regretting the hatefulness I'd spewed. "Do you think that'd work?"

"Are you in the market to date?" He asks, swerving the conversation. A wave of panic washes over me quickly.

I can't tell him the truth.

I can't lie to him.

"Depends on who's asking." I say coyly, avoiding the question, panic settling into my bloodstream.

"I am." He replies with a toothy grin, suddenly enjoying watching me squirm under his thumb. "What would you tell me?" I try to steady my breathing under his watchful eye. I cultivate a reply as quickly as I can. One that won't incriminate me to the fullest extent.

"I'd say that I'd take that knowledge to the grave." I say defiantly. Sitting up a hair straighter, my chin jutting forward. He hums to himself, a pensive look on his beautiful, lethal face.

"And what would I have to do to get you to spill your guts, little firestorm?" He asks, gaze trained on me like a predator with his prey. A deadly smile slithers over his lips.

"What are you willing to pay for it?" I ask with a raised eyebrow. "For all I know, you're just trying to get in my pants." He laughs darkly, rattling my bones. Eyes lingering on me with a look I can't place.

"You know, angel, you've got some wicked attitude tonight. What's gotten into you?" He asks, voice low and deliberate. Sultry and seductive. Eyes deepening with each word, each utter of the pet name.

"What?" I asked, breath hitching in my throat.

"You're giving me a run for my money." He croons. "And I'd have to say that I've been exceptionally patient with you, little firestorm." He grins, shaking his head.

"What does that have to do with anything?" I ask.

"I think I should be able to name any price in the book and you'd have to honor it." He slides a hair closer, resting his arm on the back of the couch. "I think you like the chase. Being chased. And you're running fast." His hand brushes my cheek. "But, angel, I'm faster."

He closes the distance between us, faster than I can stand and get away. Pinning me down to the couch by my throat. A whimper escapes from deep within me.

"Do you trust me?" He asks, hovering over me. Even though the very essence of my being is screaming at me, demanding that this is wrong, I nod.

"My price, angel?" He breathes, chest rising and falling confidently. The silence that surrounds us is deadly. Heart racing, I cling to what is about to be. "Run."

He lets go of me and my feet fly out from under me. He cackles from behind, rapidly closing in on me as I run for the door. Turning the handle, I fling it open to reveal the dull hallway. The dingy tannish yellow walls, the cracks in the tile. The emptiness. The door slams shut again.

"Not fast enough." He growls, locking the door. Spinning me around and throwing me against it. My heart pounds in my chest as his hand roams up my body from my waist to my collarbone. "Maybe one day I'll set you free so I can catch you *properly.*" His lips graze the shell of my ear.

"And what does any of this have to do with M-"

"Don't you dare utter another man's name from that pretty little mouth of yours, my little firestorm." He growls. "If you know what's good for you."

"You're so sure of yourself." I say less confidently that I had originally intended. He's making a puddle of me, and he knows it.

"Do you trust me?" He asks again, as if the first time was a test. I gulp, nodding again. "Then give me your phone."

"What? Why?" I ask, clutching my phone in my fingers. Not realizing I had grabbed it in my mad dash to the door. He doesn't utter a word, just looks at me expectantly.

"To tell *him* that if he wants you then he'll have to get through me." The back of his index finger strokes the side of my face. "Now. Give me your phone."

"What are you going to do?" I ask breathlessly.

"Showing him how taken you are." He says punctually.

"Doing what exactly?" I ask. "Kissing? Fucking?"

He raises a single eyebrow. Almost as a challenge. I'm immediately overwhelmed by how the desire to do exactly both of those things. How overwhelmingly intoxicating he is. I squirm out of his grip, slinking further into the apartment. He stalks after me, the devil in his pitch black eyes.

"Okay, I take it back." I surrender, holding my hands up.

He lurches forward, reaching for my phone. As his fingers graze my skin, the butterflies burst in my stomach looking at the grin staring back at me.

He knows exactly what he's doing to me.

"Oh, angel." He sighs. "It's so cute that you think you've got a choice."

Clutching my phone to my chest, I take another step back. He mocks my step, right arm bent at his side, extended towards me. He walks toward me with confident strides, a crooked smile on his face. That cunning smirk grows wider with each passing step. I step back further. He's hot on my heels.

"Do you want me?" His voice is low, each syllable makes my legs weaker. "To be your out?"

I want him to be so much more than an out, but I can't say that. I need him in a way that's concerning to my health. I gulp against the dryness in my mouth.

"Not if that's all I'm going to be to you." I snap. My measly threat elicits a chuckle out of him.

"Oh, my little firestorm. Is that all you think of me?" He asks. I nod defiantly. The world feels as though it's spinning in slow motion. He *tsks*. "Well, I guess I'll have to show you just how serious I am."

Arm still extended; he motions for me to give him the phone. I don't bother fighting him on it, entranced by the power exuding from him. Right down to his core.

"Do you want to share with the class your foolproof plan?" I ask through the tightness in my chest. I definitely didn't see my night going this way.

"Of course." He says coyly, making his final stride to close the gap between us, leaving not an inch between us. "I'm sorry you ever doubted my commitment." I give him a puzzled look. He continues before I have time to ask. "Do you want to do this or not?" He asks with a thick eyebrow raised to the top of his forehead.

I nod as his hands slide to my waist, pulling me close to him. He nestles me in front of him, bringing his arms around my wait and clasping them in front of my belly button. Leaning his chin on my shoulder, he cocks his head to the side. I tilt my head as well, watching as he angles the camera to take the picture.

"Act like you like me, little firestorm." He growls in my ear. My heart thunders in my chest as I nestle into him. His lips find my neck just as the flash explodes across my vision.

Once my vision returns, I stare at the picture. The essence of beauty kissing my neck seductively. Everything I've ever wanted, captured in time. For some fucking fake ruse.

"Go on. Send it to him." I demand, less daring than I had originally intended. He smirks, arms still wrapped around me. Dark eyes peering down at me, watching me with precision. Studying my features, how my body reacts to him.

"You're going to be alright, angel." He chuckles. Not a question, but a factual statement.

"We'll see how tomorrow goes." I say.

"My offer still stands." He jokes darkly.

"What? To kill him?" I ask with a breathless laugh.

He nods. "I keep good on my word."

"Is that the only thing you're good at?" I jokingly ask.

"Wouldn't you like to know." A mischievous grin

plastered on his otherworldly features.

"That is kind of why I asked." I retort as flirtatiously as I can muster. An eerie silence slips between the two of us as his back straightens, stepping away. Completely unrecognizable.

Another wave of unsurmountable pain washes over me.

CHAPTER 14

Leon

Nothing prepared me for how enraged I am at some guy I don't know. So angry I feel it seething in every breath I take, every beat of my heart. Blood boiling underneath my skin at the sound of another man's name on her lips. At the idea of him even making her uncomfortable. Of him doing worse.

I can't think, can't breathe thinking how I need to find a way to make her mine. To find a way to profess my undying and all-consuming feelings for her. All I wanted to do was claim her as my own. Body, mind, soul. Physical, mental, emotional. Nothing brings me even close to being at ease.

And she's so perfect. So insanely perfect. And I'm on the verge of internal combustion any time I look into her eyes. Ones that were once so full of life. I used to bask in their light.

Sometimes I wonder if this is all my fault. If all of this ruin surrounding us – her – is something I caused. That I shouldn't have laid claim to her in front of Boyle. Maybe he saw it as a challenge. Maybe he wouldn't have been interested in her had I not put a target on her back.

I don't let myself sit in that fog too long. Not when there are bigger fish to fry. Not when I'm trying to rebuild my little firestorm. My sweet angel.

There isn't anything pressing at work, so I decided to take the day off. To try and mend the bridge I'd squandered yesterday. Say I'm sorry for her not being able to trust me.

And to keep my mind off going up to her work and plucking that low lying bastard off the face of the Earth.

I shoot her a quick text. *'I'm cooking tonight.'*

'You cook every night.' She retorts back almost instantly.

'I don't see you complaining.' I say.

'Never said I was.' She says with an eye roll I can feel miles away. *'What are you planning, oh Great Chef?'*

'You if you keep that attitude up.' I say, imagining the heat that floods her cheeks, her thighs. The way she squeezes them together when she's flustered.

'Is that a threat or a promise?'

'Both.'

'Okay, big guy.' She retorts.

'Would you prefer homemade ramen?'

'I am merely a bystander in whatever it is you're doing.' She teases. *'I like my ramen like I like my men.'*

'Hot?' I ask before she can reply.

'Can't argue with that.'

'And I like my ramen like I like my women.' I paused, waiting for her to read the message. *'Spicy.'*

'Ramen sounds yummy.' She says.

'You won't be disappointed, my little firestorm.'

I've got a few hours until I go pick her up. The anxiety and lack of control slowly creep up my spine. I've got too much time on my hands. I need a distraction.

My only escapism over the years has been music.

Normally, I don't pitch personal songs to the label period. Let alone for new artists. But the song I wrote for her on the night we first met needed to be heard. I needed to get that song out in the world. And the track releases tonight at midnight.

I should do something fun, right? Do something that will impress her? Throw her a surprise launch party for her song? She deserves it. She deserves all the credit. My muse. I want to hear all about her day at work. Even the coworker situation. I need to know how he took the fall. And if it hurt him like he hurt her. Or if some concussive maintenance is needed.

Grabbing pillows, blankets, spare sheets, I toss them all into the living room with a hefty throw. And begin assembling a very rickety pillow fort. Throwing our bed pillows on the couch for extra comfort.

I don't want her to be uncomfortable in the slightest. She's my angel. My little firestorm. If she's comfy, she'll stay longer. There's nothing I wouldn't do to keep her around.

Once the blanket fort is a fraction more structurally sound than my mental health, I give myself a mental pat on the back before throwing myself into digging out some string lights and other things that I know would make her love the space even more. Fairy lights, candles, fall scented room spray, ambient music playing from the TV.

She'll love it.

I speed over to pick her up from work before I'm too late. Having gotten lost in the thrum of dressing up the place. The drive isn't too far, even in Atlanta traffic. Before I know it, before anxiety and anger have completely ruined my day, I pull up to the front of her building.

Standing as still as a statue on the sidewalk is the most beautiful girl I've ever seen. She's wearing a cream button up with flowy black slacks and chunky heels. Her hair is down and curled. The light makeup on her face only accentuated her features.

"Hey," I call, motioning for her to get into the car. She makes no move to look at me. "Angel?" I called again.

Her eyes locked on something across the street, the parking garage. I follow her gaze, looking at a man staring directly at her. Except, it wasn't a man at all.

It was another of whatever the hell Boyle was. Its reflection in the window revealed exactly what I'd seen that night in the bathroom.

Same sickly looking human figure. Same black holes for eyes. Same too many teeth bared at me. The creature makes no move towards me, or River, but I know it's got her locked in its sights.

"River Celeste, get in the car. Right. Now." I demand, trying to get her attention.

"I can't move." She mutters. Sobs.

I spring from the car, feet pounding the pavement. Closing in on her before that thing across the street can make a move. Guiding her near frozen body into the vehicle. A chill slithers down my spine. Like a cold, metal talon threatening to sever my own ability to move. To breathe.

Forcing myself to overcome that unnatural feeling, to be stronger and more cunning than the literal ice forming in my bones. I throw myself into the car, speeding off. After a mile or two of absolute silence, River lets out a long breath. Nearly collapsing into her seat.

"What the fuck was that?" She asks in a near whisper.

"What did you see?" I counter.

"Nothing."

"No, tell me." I fight the need to eye roll.

"I'm being serious, Leon." She says, chest rising and falling rapidly. "I didn't see anything. I was blind. I couldn't see anything more than vague shapes."

"What?"

"I was standing on the sidewalk, waiting for you and wondering why you were late. I got a cold chill and then my vision went blurry. And it kept getting worse. Until all there was left was my heartbeat pounding in my ears and fuzzy lights and shadows." She gulps audibly. "When I heard your voice calling my name, my vision came back, but it felt like there were a million pounds of weights holding me to that very spot."

Another wave of silence rushes over us. My head is completely empty of all the thoughts I'd once had. All the things I had wanted to share and talk about with her have completely vanished.

But it was her hand pulling mine from my lap that brought me back to reality. Her delicate fingers weaving through mine. A soft, knowing look draped over her face. Color slowly returns to its normal rosy tint.

She's faced monsters. Horrible, disgusting creatures time and time again. Yet, she still finds it in herself to comfort me. To put her own feelings aside and think of my own.

And I am not enough. I will never be enough. Not nearly enough of a man, a good man, to bask in the glory of a woman as selfless as she is. I will never be enough of the man she needs. And I know that I shouldn't bother trying.

But with *everything I am,* she is *it.* In my blood, my bones. My heart and soul. All that I am, all that I will ever be. She is the end and the beginning. The light and the darkness. The sun, the moon, and all the stars. There is nothing in existence that she is *not.*

Nothing could pry me away from her. Not hell or high water. Not heaven or all its angels. I'd give anything, *anything,* to protect her. To safeguard her like a precious gem.

"When I was younger," she says, idly looking out the passenger window. My thumb stroking the side of her hand, a signal to keep going. "Whenever I'd sleep on my stomach, I'd always have the hardest time waking up."

I hum curiously.

"I used to call it sleep paralysis because I didn't know what it really was." She continues. "I still don't. I would fight and fight and fight to wake up. I'd have a full blown panic attack trying to force my eyes open. I was awake, though. In my head. I knew I was awake, but I couldn't force my body to move, to open my eyes. It felt like I was dying." She squeezes my hand.

"That's what it felt like? Like dying?"

She hums in agreement. "I imagine that's what suffocation feels like." Her eyes turn to me, more vibrant than they were before. "Until I heard your voice, I thought I was dying then, too."

The whole way home, I was wondering if my stupid little pillow fort would be enough. If it even survived. If it meant anything to her that I'd done it. If it was all in poor taste after our second run in with whatever the hell those things are.

But she stands mouth agape in the foyer ogling at the creation I had slaved over designing. The most color in her face as I'd seen in weeks.

"Do you like it?" I ask when the silence becomes a little too much to bear.

"You did this for me?" She asks, a layer of complete disbelief resting in her words. Her now bare feet shuffle her forward to inspect the building code of our evening abode. I follow her dutifully.

"I did." I say, resting a hand on her lower back, guiding her further into the space. "I wanted to do something to cheer you up." Turning around, she flings her arms around my neck. Standing on her tippy toes, she plants a kiss on my cheek.

"Thank you." She says with specks of tears threatening to well in her eyes. Quickly turning away from me to wipe the evidence away. I pretend I don't notice them.

"I'd hoped to entertain a beautiful lady with homemade ramen and a continuation of her favorite TV show. If she'll have me, of course." I tease, moving to the kitchen and collecting pots from the cabinet for tonight's meal.

"Looks comfy enough for royalty." She says, following me to the kitchen and planting herself in a barstool to watch. Just like she does every night. "Just like you."

"I'm definitely not royalty." I say.

"Then why are you listed in my phone as Prince Leon?" She teases, reminding me of the shenanigans I'd gotten up to when I'd put my number in her phone a while back. "What about that, huh?"

"A guy can dream."

"Keep dreaming, *my prince*." She coos sweetly.

"Mm, I like the sound of that." I tease. She rolls her eyes at me but doesn't say anything past that. So I continue. "How was work? Did that guy behave?"

"I didn't see him."

"No?" I ask.

"Scout's honor." She puts her hand over her heart. "He never replied to me, either." I release a sigh.

"Good. Maybe he got the message."

"It'd be hard not to when you were swallowing me whole in that picture." She laughs nervously.

"I can do much worse, angel." I tease, silencing any snide remarks she thinks about making.

"I'm going to shower." She announces, quickly rising from her seat.

"Make sure it's a cold one."

She sticks her tongue out at me. I give her a wink and her pace increases.

Dinner's ready by the time she returns.

Freshly showered, smelling of green apples and oranges. An easy smile on those delectably full lips.

I lay out an array of pork belly, green onions, soft-boiled eggs, baby Bok choy, bean sprouts, radishes, mushrooms, and snap peas. She comes to meet me in the kitchen.

"Hey," I stop her before she can sit down. She gives me a raised eyebrow but meets my extended hand with hers.

"Hey to you, too." She says. I pull her close, slow dancing to no music at all. "What's got you in such a good mood?" Placing one hand on her hip, the other holding her hand at shoulder height, we sway together. No words come to me for an explanation. Only that I'm perfectly content to be here with her. Forever.

"If I'd have known you in high school, I definitely would have taken you to prom." I whisper against the shell of her ear.

"You definitely didn't know me in high school. And be glad you didn't." She quips. "Full emo. No fucks given. Worshipped a flat iron."

"And you, my little firestorm, didn't get the displeasure of knowing me in high school. I used to have braces, no muscles, and an affinity for Linkin Park."

"Oh, my god. No way!" She squeals. "You were scene?!"

"Hey, watch it. My fringe was top notch." I scold. She giggles, sparks flying through her golden eyes.

"Maybe I would have been in love with you back then."

"Who's saying you can't fall in love with me now?" I ask, putting feelers out for any form of reciprocation. She gives me a grin but doesn't reply. Whether I struck a nerve or not, she doesn't let on. "Come on. Let's eat."

We eat our meal in relatively comfortable silence. I swap our usual water for the pear soju that my parents got me for my birthday. She's a perfect enough reason to crack open the bottle. I offer her a shot. She accepts, throwing her head back like a party veteran. Her eyes twinkle as she swallows, enjoying the taste seemingly as much as I do.

She climbs into the blanket fort, snuggling up to a pillow while I clean up the dishes. Carrying the bottle of cold soju, I climb into the fort with her. Passing the drink to her.

The only light illuminating our home for the night is the TV, dimly lighting her silhouette. I nestle her under my arm, where she belongs, throwing a blanket over her exposed legs. Once I'm settled, she encapsulates me in the same blanket.

A tap on my knee catches my attention.

"Thank you. For all of this." Her voice doesn't make it above a whisper. "It's more than I could have ever asked for." I squeeze her shoulder tightly.

"You don't have to thank me, angel." I say, kissing her temple lightly. "You deserve eons more." I want to say so much more. Something profoundly risky and meaningful, but my tongue stops it all. I can feel the words fighting to escape, but they never do.

"I'd disagree but thank you anyway." She nestles into the couch, leaning into me. My index finger traces lines on her shoulder, and she breathes a sigh of relief when the show starts playing. I don't think I'll be able to focus on the show anymore.

CHAPTER 15

River

I didn't mean to fall asleep with my head in his lap. Though, at this point, this was nothing new. I was just rarely the one to initiate physical intimacy. But I had been so comfortable and so *safe* that all the tension I felt melted right off my body.

At some point between episode four and five – and a finished bottle of soju between us – I'd come to this inhibited realization that my life would never be normal again. Not just this uncharted territory that we navigated between the two of us, but this seemingly never ending spiral of mischance.

But on top of everything, all of the ill luck that's changed my life for the worse, I'm still grappling with the never ending swell of emotions I hold for Leon. For the man who puts me before himself. Who has taken me in without question. He'd been the picture of a gentleman.

Last night, it didn't take him long for his arm to move from the back of the couch to directly around my shoulder. And that quickly turned into cuddling, which eventually turned into me falling asleep in his lap. I couldn't help but sink into his warm body. Comfort enveloped his entire being. Comfort, warmth, safety. It was woven into everything he did, everything he was. Everything I craved.

I'd never known what '*home*' is supposed to feel like. Never pretended to have experienced it in childhood. Chased after it in adulthood, yet it always evaded me. But if this is what it's supposed to feel like, then I'd hit the jackpot. I'd won the lottery a million times over.

He'd woke me up before the sun herself shone through the massive windows. Shaking me gently, his voice gravelly in my ear, calling my name. It sounded so sweet, so gentle in the pronunciation of each syllable, that I thought Dream Leon had returned.

It was 5 AM. He offered to move us to the bed, but I didn't bother getting up and neither did he. I nestled back into our blanket. We slept the rest of the morning away. Because this was who we were now. Not together. Not, *not* together.

After a slow morning supplemented by a hangover, we went out for breakfast at a bagel place down the block that he suggested. Which I found to be the only bagel shop so far to satisfy my need to eat an entire block of cream cheese with a side of bagel.

We walked around the neighborhood park for an hour or so, until the Saturday crowds came rolling in, only then did we decide to go back home.

"Are you sure you don't want to come with me to LA?" He asks, reminding me that he would be going out of town for work late next week. His arm thrown around my shoulder, our steps lazy and slow.

"As much as I appreciate the invite, I'll have to decline." I snark. I'd love to spend a weekend away from the nightmares that consume me. Curled up in a hotel room with the most beautiful man I've ever seen on the other side of the country. "Wedding weekend."

"Shit, I forgot. I'll cancel work." He says, pulling out his phone from his pants pocket.

"No the hell you won't." I demand, fingers gripping his wrist to stop him. "You don't have to rearrange your plans."

"I wanted to go with you to the wedding." He confesses.

"You didn't know about these work plans until now?"

"I found out last week, but it honestly slipped my mind. It's no problem to cancel. I promise." He reassures, taking my hand in his.

"What are you even going to LA for?" I ask, harsher than I had intended. "I feel like I don't know anything about what you do for work, anyway."

"Music award show. I'm a music producer, angel. You know this." He laughs lightly.

"Yes, yes, yes. You told me. I've seen the equipment. You so graciously let me play with it once. But you've never shown me any of your music. You're very secretive." I say, hands clamming up against his smooth skin.

"It's not that interesting." He says, as if I would not listen to him read the dictionary if he so chose to do so. The disappointment on my face is evident. "When I get back, I'll show you – tell you whatever you want to know."

I nod solemnly, knowing that he held everything that I am in the palms of his hands. That my life, what little is left of it, belongs to him. That I am not completely broken or dead because of him. His graciousness. His kindness.

But part of me is relieved to have that peace of being alone. To – for the first time since moving in with Leon – be *alone* with myself. To allow myself to surrender to that black hole that's slowly creeping up on me. Threatening to swallow me whole.

Thursday came too soon. I thought I had wanted to be alone, to enjoy the solitude that would come with an empty apartment. But the drive to the airport nearly killed me. Drove me right to the brink of tears at the drop off gate.

He saw my tears before I could wipe them away. Before they could even fall onto my cheeks. A soft smile bewitched his rosy lips. Gentle worry in his eyes.

"Don't cry, angel." He coos, leaning over to plant a kiss on my forehead. "I'll be back Sunday. Or sooner if you need me. Just give me a call." I nod. Unable to trust my voice. I force the sadness, the waterworks, back into my eyes. Forcing an incomplete smile in his direction. "You sure you don't want to come with me?"

HM DAWLEY

I nod. "Yeah, planes scare me." I half-lie. "Besides, someone's got to go to work tomorrow."

"I keep telling you to quit." He jokes, his full cheeks bobbing as he talks lightly.

"Yeah, yeah, yeah. I'm not quite ready to take you up on that just yet." I retorted. He knows I'm proud of the determination I've put into getting where I am, but sometimes I'm not sure I deserve the good that's happened to me. Just the bad.

"Next time I'll plan better and bring you with me." He promises as a car honks behind us, waiting for us to move.

"Yeah, next time." I say guiltily. "Don't miss me too much." I swallow the building emotions, anything I've ever felt for him, down in one swift gulp. I'd never wanted something – someone – more. The endless sea of gratitude and appreciation for him is only supplemented by my admiration for his selflessness.

"I'll miss you like hell, angel. Counting down the hours until I see you again." He replies sweetly.

And as much as I hate to see him leave, I can't hold him here forever. I can't pretend that I have the power to keep him with me. The vow we made, the words we'd shared after Boyle, proclamations of our mutual devotion. It all felt void sitting in the silence, realizing I don't know him as well as I'd like. As well as I think I deserved, considering we share a living space. A bed.

He smiles one last time, stepping out of the car with only a single carry-on suitcase to his person. I wave at him, and he blows me a kiss before disappearing through the glass doors. I wish I had kissed him. Properly.

The drive home was painful. Quiet.

Skylar and Dana wave from their parked car further into the parking lot off the trail. Both looked as lovely as ever, my emotions welled inside me at their beauty. Sky wore a flowy lavender dress with a tiny lavender bouquet. Dana wore

122

a white button up shirt with khaki shorts. Picturesque and in love.

My heart hurt from the fullness.

The officiant, a mutual friend of theirs from back home, saunters over in a black romper, iPad in one hand, a professional camera in the other. Her long, brown hair down to her waist. She looks at me with piqued interest, a crooked smile on her deep red painted lips.

A sense of unease wafts over me as I look into her eyes and smile. Her eyes, as blue as the deep sea, felt devoid of all life. Everything that should shine brightly behind eyes as pretty as hers, completely empty.

The smell of pennies stings the air. *Weird.* I've never smelt pennies before. Always tasted them.

I shake the thoughts, that uncanny feeling from my mind. Telling myself I'm just crazy or that it's just a trauma response. My phone buzzes, startling me. A call from Leon.

"Your lover?" Dana asks curiously, having snuck up on me.

I roll my eyes and answer. "Good evening, Mr. Kang. How can I be of service today?" I ask jokingly.

"Good God, I missed your voice." He breathes. "But don't ever call me Mr. Kang." Butterflies erupt in my stomach, causing my mouth to clamp shut with whatever dumb remarks I could have made.

"How's LA?" I ask, veering the conversation away from how badly I miss him. Or how my body reacted to his command.

"Lackluster without my angel." He coos, and I'm so very thankful I didn't put him on speaker. The group decides to start hiking while I'm on the phone and I trail close behind. "How's home?"

"Lackluster without my prince." I mock, fighting the need to giggle and kick my feet like a little schoolgirl. He laughs nervously, for the first time in a long time.

"My, my, the flattery." He whistles. "Remind me to call you when I'm back at my hotel room if you're going to keep talking to me like that."

"You're so bold now that you're across the country." I joke, losing my footing on a particularly mundane rock. Nearly twisting my ankle. A tiny whimper comes out of my mouth in response to the pain, but I limp through it.

"Make that noise again." He growls.

"Leon, I'm hiking." I complain. The officiant, who I've yet to learn the name of, turns around to look at me with another curious look. "I will hang up on you."

"And if you do, you're in for it when I get home." He threatens as his voice grows husky. "I'll come home right now, firestorm."

"Maybe you shouldn't be talking like that in public." I tease, heat rising to my cheeks. The need for friction between my legs is ever present. "You can definitely give me a call later, though. I'll help you sort out that *problem*."

"I'm holding you to that, angel." He growls. "I'll talk to you soon."

I catch up to the group quickly, feeling slightly embarrassed about my own growing need inside me on someone else's wedding day. The three of them are chit chatting like I was never supposed to be included in the conversation. Or at least Officiant looks at me like she'd rather I weren't there.

Her name is Astra.

Astra, to my surprise, doesn't hate me. Or at least she doesn't act like she wants to kill me in the woods and leave my body for the vultures. Maybe I'm just a hard person to like.

She links her arm with mine as she regales me of how she knows the brides, Dana's childhood friend, and what she does for work, a professional photographer. To say she was enthusiastic when she talks is an understatement. The brides are engrossed in her stories, hanging on her every word.

"So, who were you talking to?" Astra asks when she's run out of fun and interesting life stories to tell.

"That's her boyfriend." Skylar teases.

"Not boyfriend." I clarify with a twinge of pain. "Roommate." A tugging in my chest brings me almost to my knees. Thoughts of what Leon and I *aren't* flood my vision. Everything that we are, there is so much that we aren't.

"Roommates in a one bedroom apartment." Skylar continues, clarifying upon my statement with a sideways glance.

"Sounds like one of you is in denial." Astra comments. "Do you have a picture of him? To show the class?"

Sure I do. All I do is take pictures of Leon. Very non-cinematic shots of him cooking, watching TV, in the car. Whatever mundane things he does, I have a picture of.

So I pulled out my phone to show them one I took a couple weeks ago when we went out for late night ice cream. Sitting in a booth at the back of the parlor, a chocolate cone in his hand, looking directly at the camera (into my soul), a dollop of ice cream on the corner of his mouth. The most angelic photo I have, the way the light reflects in his mahogany eyes.

Everyone oo's and ah's. That tugging in my gut returns.

Astra's eyes narrow. Even though her words blend in with Skylar's and Dana's, there's a skeptical look on her face. Either she can't believe that Leon's with me, or she just doesn't believe that I know him in the first place.

And almost right on cue, he shoots me a text.

'Have fun tonight, little firestorm.'

Astra notices the message, throwing me another look. "Little firestorm?" She asks.

"Is it because of your temper?" Skylar teasingly asks. I nod, not really knowing where he got the nickname from or why it's his go to when he's feeling extra frisky.

Astra pulls Skylar and Dana into another conversation that I clearly wasn't meant to be a part of, given that its subject matter seemed like an inside joke to them. Lingering at the back of our small crowd, I reply to him quickly with two pictures. One of the sunset over the ridge as we cross over, and one of the group in front of me, laughing.

And a single question. *'Isn't it weird how big the world is?'* How vastly expansive the world is and that we somehow found each other.

The elopement was a beautiful, sunset lit endeavor. Heartfelt vows exchanged as the sun crept down over the ridge. Photos were taken and we were on our merry way back down the path. Exhausted and ready for a long, hot bath.

Hiking down was obviously much easier than hiking up. Calves killing me the entire way, I revel in the parking lot in sight. In the AC waiting for me in that swanky BMW Leon's letting me borrow.

Skylar and Dana prance happily ahead of Astra and I, as happy as the summer days are long. Astra leans over to me, a crooked smile over her mouth.

"I'm sorry if I came across as mean earlier." She says, her words holding very little weight. "I didn't know anyone would be joining us."

"It's okay." I say, too tired to care about making false friends. "No hard feelings."

She hums in disagreement. "Well, I didn't say all that." She cranes her neck around. Eyes darting to see if anyone's watching before she leans in closer. "I am saying that you should watch who you show that boyfriend of yours to. People love a celebrity." As her words settle onto me, she saunters away without a second glance back.

As soon as I get home, depression sinks in. The words that Astra had muttered to me so casually. The denial I had been in as I searched his name online when I'd gotten back into *his* car. The shock that skyrocketed my body was immense.

I had failed the first law of womanhood.

Always google your men.

I hadn't bothered to look him up until this point. Partially because I didn't have a reason to. He'd never given me a reason to be skeptical. Partially because I knew I couldn't handle whatever was waiting for me when I looked.

And I should have the moment he told me he was going to an *award show*. Should have put two and two together. Music producer + award show = famous. He's not the sound guy, obviously.

Leon is so ordinary, though. Not in beauty or in brain or even in brawns, but he doesn't radiate celebrity. Fame. *Wealth.*

He was Leon. My Leon. The one who holds my shaking body when I wake from a nightmare. Who cooks me dinners. Drives me around the scenic parts of the county to show me the prettiest homes.

The man that saved me from death. Welcomed me into his life with open arms and zero expectations.

Why would I ever have second guessed any of that?

He had told me to watch and cheer him on from home and I promised him that I would. Even if it now makes me sick to my stomach to even turn on the TV.

Once home, I shower and dress. Nestling myself into a corner of our shared living room to watch the award show.

Part of me wishes to see him walk across my screen, to win that award that I know he's worked hard for. Deserves. The other part wishes that this is all another nightmare. That I'll wake up and he'll be home and a normal person.

But then I see all the A-list celebrities walking the carpet at this event. All the beautifully manufactured people who spend thousands of dollars to look gorgeous. How my frumpy outfits pale in comparison. How *ordinary* I am in comparison. He's always been cut out for the beauty of fame.

Not me. Not at all. It all hits me at once. Everything that I had dammed up inside bubbled up to the surface.

I'm not cut out for this. Not for the competition of

outshining celebrities to win a man who's so far out of my league I can barely see him. I work in risk management. I make enough to get by, not enough to retire after a number one hit. I have no desire to be famous. I can't keep up in a competition that puts you farther ahead the more money you have.

Rhinestones, diamonds, and gold jewelry adorn each celebrity as they strut confidently down the carpet, piling on the pressure to my chest tenfold. I should stop watching, but I can't. My eyes are glued to the screen, still hoping I'd get to see him, even if in my heart it's only to say a one-sided goodbye.

Is this goodbye? I don't want it to be. I don't ever want to say goodbye to him. But the thought of spending another night in his apartment makes me nauseous. The walls close in on me, everything in my vision is completely foreign to me.

If it weren't for being frozen in front of the TV screen, waiting for him to show up, I would have packed my things into my car. Run from what I knew I could never compete with. Let him go. Don't bother holding him down, getting your hopes up.

It's late when the show ends, Mr. Leon Kang nowhere in sight. The overwhelming desire to chuck the remote through the wall is ever present. Even more so when I pull up his socials. All the songs he's got credits for.

He's got all the production credits for my favorite song.

How could he not tell me? He didn't lie about his job title, but he certainly didn't tell me he was world renowned.

As I scroll for what feels like eons through any article published with his name in it, betrayal swells in my chest. Stinging worse than if he had just rejected me all together. All the awards he has to his name, the songwriter and producer credits, the features, the interviews, the *net worth*.

Anxiety builds in my system to the point of eruption. Fight or flight. Severely elevated heart rate. All scream at me to put the phone down. Get off the damn internet, but I can't.

It was like watching a trainwreck unfold before me. I was witnessing my own murder in real time, and I wanted to vomit. I want to take back everything. All this time. All these months.

All the words I said were so painfully real. I laid bare for him nothing but honesty and vulnerability. The tears that I'd shed on him for a woman I no longer could be. I wish I could take it all back. That I could not feel any of what I feel for him.

And I know I can't. I know in the very depths of my being, my soul, that I couldn't swallow up those words again and claim they never happened. For everything that I am resonates with everything that he is.

I just wish he had been honest. Did he not trust me to know he was famous? Did he think that since I didn't know who he was that I wasn't ever going to find out?

Doom scrolling leads to tears that stain the collar of my shirt. I turn the TV off and slink to bed. Knowing full well that I don't think I'll be able to get any amount of meaningful sleep when I'm shacked up in Leon's bed. In a bed that smells like him more than it does me. I'd envisioned myself in it forever. That feels as empty as my stomach. Physical exhaustion breaks me. I want so many answers from him, but I also never want to see him again.

That's a lie. I absolutely want to see him again. It's a natural part of my existence now. His presence in my life is the one thing keeping me grounded most days.

He is seemingly all I have. Had.

Whatever.

As the tears pour into my ears, my phone lights up, illuminating the darkness I've surrounded myself with. His name and our picture pop up and a new wave of resentment and agony crashes down on me like a riptide wave, pulling me under the current of his magnetism.

I don't have the strength to answer. I don't want to explain the shaky voice and the occasional sniffling to a man who couldn't be bothered to tell me the truth about who he is. So, I silence the call.

He calls back. Relentless. Once the call drops, I turn my

phone off. I'll see how I'm feeling in the morning, even though I already know the answer.

Another tug in my stomach nearly causes me to vomit. Except I haven't eaten since before Leon left.

CHAPTER 16

Leon

I thought I was overreacting when she sent me the picture earlier. That something looked off about the woman in the middle, like she wasn't quite all there. But I thought nothing of it since the security alarm clicked off and back on, and the camera showed her entering our apartment. I'd become overbearing. To the point of smothering my little firestorm nearly out.

So I thought backing off would help breathe some oxygen into her. Show her that I trust her. That it's not her that I don't blame her for anything that's going on. I'm going to do whatever I have to do to make sure that she's cared for. Provided for. Safe.

But my hovering knows no limits. No bounds to calling and checking in. Making sure she's still alright. Hearing her voice to sooth the turmoil threatening just underneath my skin.

"What's got you so worked up?" Dante asks, his palm on my shoulder. A tall, broad built rapper with a mouth full of gold. He blended in well with the crowd surrounding us. The school of fish that swim through the sea. One big mass of bodies compacted into a too small venue.

"It's nothing." I lied. If he notices, he doesn't let on. "Would rather be working than partying."

Strobe lights flash, some techno remix of a popular song cuts over the blaring speakers. This after party is bigger than last year's. But the food's still shit.

He laughs heartily. "And that's why you get paid the big bucks." His eyes level with mine, he says, "All work and no play makes for a man with no bitches. Come on, man. Let me show you some of my favorites here tonight."

"I'm good." I nearly snapped.

"With your looks and money, you ought to be the one-"

"Hey, Leon. Hey, Dante." A woman coos as if right on cue. "Nice to see you two again." The woman looks me up and down before her eyes do the same to Dante. Her dress is a swanky piece of gauze that covers absolutely nothing.

Jerica. A well-known pop singer. And my ex. Technically. We dated for a couple of months. I didn't really want to date her anyway, but she was constantly asking me out.

I'd really never had the desire to date anyone. No drive to build a relationship or partnership with anyone. No one intrigued me enough to want to start a life with.

Jerica never believed me. Thought she could change that. Believed that we could be an unstoppable duo, a power couple both in and out of the spotlight. But we never made it farther than a single shotty date, some poor communication, and a string of hateful messages that ended things before they ever started. And a single one night stand.

And all I could do now was picture River wearing her exact dress. The way it would meld to her curves. How I'd take it off of her.

"You boys want to go somewhere a little more private?" She asks us, a hand reaching for each of our arms.

"Count me in." Dante nearly squeals.

"I'll pass." I say, pulling my arm away from her touch.

"Come on, man." Dante repeats. "Live a little."

"No." I demand, the muscles in my jaw flexing hard against my clenched teeth.

"You sure? We had so much fun last year."

"And it was a mistake." I snap. "A mistake that you knew would happen."

"Are you saying, '*I told you so*'?" She condescends.

"I'm saying that what we were wasn't anything more than a damn business transaction. I didn't want to have anything to do with it, but you only saw me for what I could offer your career. You only cared about yourself."

"We're in the business of only caring for ourselves, sugar." She coos. "We take what we want, who we want, for whatever reason we want. And no one bats an eye because that's what we do."

"No. That's what you do."

"Don't act all innocent, Kang." Dante barks, sliding his arm easily around Jerica's shoulder. "You're no stranger to taking what you want."

"I don't know what you're talking about." I snap.

"Don't play dumb." Dante barks. "We all know your reputation precedes you, Kang."

"Let's not forget that beautiful girl you're trying so hard to hide." She says with a wicked grin. Dante's eyes shift from me to her and back. "It'd be a shame if she saw the *real* Leon. The one who never backs down from a fight. Has more underground ties than the dark web."

"How do you-" I try to ask.

"You think you could hide her? From me of all people?" She asks with a cackle. "The world keeps tabs on you, Kang. I, especially, like to know when Killer Kang is up to something. And corrupting a perfectly innocent girl is the kind of news I'd like to prevent."

"You know *nothing*." I snap. "I would never hurt her."

"Does she even know you're here? Rubbing elbows with the lesser folk? That you've been the master of shady deals for as long as you've been in the business?" She asks, eyes deadly.

"Leave her-"

"Poor little River. All alone at home while you're here. Basking in the glory you claim to despise. Enjoying having your cock sucked by everyone looking up at you from your iron-clad pedestal."

"Would you shut-"

"What would little River think about you if she knew the real you, Kang?" She asks, voice dripping with venom.

"It's none of your business."

"Oh, but I think it would make for good reality TV." She leans in close, breath ghosting the shell of my ear. "The biggest story of the year. I can see it now. Leon Kang *finally* gets a girlfriend." Her words are barely audible through the pounding in my ears. "Finally gets a girlfriend and he'll break her, beat her down, drag her to hell right with him."

"Jer. That's enough." Dante tries to intervene.

"No." She snaps at him. "Because once she realizes that you're the worst kind of scum, she'll leave you just like you left me."

"I didn't leave you." I bark. "You were the insufferable bitch who insisted that we *'give it a go'* even though I told you I had no desire to date you or even fuck you. You're the one who got your feelings hurt when what I told you came true."

"Shut your whore mouth." She winces.

"You want to talk about lying down with the hellhounds? How about you keep your conniving ass away from me and my girl."

"Or what, Leon?" She tests, arms crossed over her chest. Deep-seated rage runs rampant through my blood.

"Or I swear to God, it'll be the last thing you ever fucking do." I growl. "I'll make sure that I live up to that reputation you love to throw in my face so much."

Her face pales. So does Dante's.

"Alright, enough." Dante's words were lackluster.

"If you even so much as *think* about my girl, I'll kill you. You hear me?" My voice booms, even over the crowd.

She makes no move to acknowledge what I'd said. To the threat I'd made. But her body is as stiff as a board.

Dante says something that I don't bother listening to as I stalk off. Preferably to a quiet place where I can call a taxi to my hotel. And call my girl.

No amount of long-distance phone calls or text messages will make up for the constant roiling that's coursing through me. How the *fuck* did she know about River. I'd made it a point to keep her as hidden from this life as possible.

For that specific reason.

I need to hear her sugary sweet voice. The velvety words that fall from her pretty pink lips as they calm my senses. How I need her to calm me now that all I can see is red behind my eyes.

Ring, ring, ring.

Nothing. No answer. That's okay. I'll try again. No need to panic just yet. There's nothing to be concerned about.

Ring, ring, ring.

Still nothing. Okay maybe there's something to be a little concerned about. I tried a third time, except this one goes straight to voicemail.

Something's not right.

A pang in my chest nearly knocks the breath out of me. Is she okay? Is she hurt? Sleeping? There has to be a logical explanation for this.

I checked the security camera, even though I told myself I wasn't going to. I don't see her. She's either not there or she's in one of the many blind spots.

I tried once more. Straight to voicemail again. Something is severely wrong. I can feel it.

I need to go see River. I need to make sure she's okay. Making a series of phone calls, all in a flurry, to the people I'm leaving in Los Angeles. I attempt calling River one more time, to no avail. I called a taxi and prayed I would make it to the airport in time.

Time moves painfully slow on the ride to the airport. Waiting in security lines. To board. For departure. It's all a bunch of fucking waiting.

All the while, my mind races. Going over every detail, interaction, and piece of information that could lead me to a logical conclusion meticulously.

Did Jerica somehow get to her? Did she say something to her about me? God, what the fuck am I supposed to do if she's told her something true? Something that River doesn't like but is a hundred percent true.

A woman is sitting next to me on the flight, her focus mainly on the reality TV show she's watching on her iPad. She's the best plane row companion ever. Until about two hours into the flight. She removes her headphones and leans over to my seat. Over the console between us.

"You look tense." She gawks with a cheeky smile. She looks to be mid-thirties at most. Big brown eyes, curly black hair, and flawless skin.

I don't bother answering. I don't have to answer questions from prying strangers. Not when my angel's safety could be on the line.

"Is it a girl?" She persists. Another blank stare. "Tell me, what's got you wound tighter than a two-dollar watch?" She asks. Something compels me to answer, but I remain silent. She hums disapprovingly but doesn't press the issue. She goes back to her show.

Another hour goes by. She leans back over the console.

"Sometimes, there are things in this world that cannot be explained." She says, not necessarily to anyone in particular. "Sometimes, we see things, hear things, experience things that go against all that we know as humans."

"What are you on about now, Cassandra?" A man one row behind us asks.

"Have you ever seen things you couldn't explain? That defies all logic?" She looks directly at me this time. I don't dare say anything. Force the will to speak so far down within me that I can't possibly do anything but swallow my tongue.

She smiles cattily, cheeks blooming under her thick-rimmed glasses. Her long slender fingers spring forward. A single glossy business card perched between her pointer and middle fingers.

My momentary stare at the cardstock grows extensive. Wondering whether or not I should take it. Whether or not she would be of any use in answering the questions that continue to bubble inside me. About Boyle. About the things I've been seeing lately. How come it seems as though I've shifted dimensions?

I take the card without a single word. Shoving it deep within my dress pants pocket.

"Is she bothering you?" The gentleman behind us asks.

I shake my head. "No." The first word I'd uttered since boarding the plane.

"We're just having a friendly conversation." Cassandra answers with a settled look.

Her fingers clutch what looks like a rosary in her opposite hand. Gaze shifts to a near-glassy finish for just a moment before returning with a smile. Her attention falters from me, just as the pilot announces our descent.

The sun peaks over the horizon. Casting orange shades on all that it touches. All I can think about is sharing this moment with her. How she should be by my side, experiencing this with me.

The thought quickly leaves my mind as I sprint out of the taxi and into the building. Readying myself to run up an infinite number of stairs to get to her. But, by some unseen force, I catch the elevator with the maintenance guy at the very last second. He gets off on a lower floor. Leaving me with the ever-increasing panic building in my chest.

The doors swing open, I stumble out of them like a drunken fool getting kicked out of a bar. Tunnel vision surrounds my eyes as they lock on my door. Our door. A desert forms in my mouth. Panic envelops me as I run through the infinite possibility of conflicts.

Is she okay? Did I do something wrong?

What do I even say to her?

Knock, knock, knock.

My knuckles rap on the door, perhaps too quietly. No stirring to be heard on the other side. Is she home?

Why am I knocking on my own door?

Unlocking the door, it catches on the sliding deadbolt. With the door cracked, the patter of soft footsteps make their way to the door. Ones I barely hear through the pounding of my erratic heartbeat. A faint *'shit'* escapes from the other side and my heart sinks farther than I knew possible.

"Hey, angel. Let me in." I greet softly, tears threatening to spring from my eyes at the disappointment. Walls closing in.

"What do you want?" She asks, her voice hoarse and harsh. Deep-set anger in a voice that used to consist of only honeysuckles and sweet nectar.

"Are you okay?" I ask, pushing past the clear disdain in her words. Trying to find the root cause. What I did wrong. What happened while I was away.

"Go away." She demands through clenched teeth.

"No." I insist, rattling the chain. She pushes against the door, trying to close it but quickly gives up. Her upper body strength is no match for me. "Let me in." I demand.

"Why should I?" She asks. "Why can't you just sit outside in the hallway until *I'm* ready for you to come inside? Huh? Why is everything always on your terms?"

"Angel,"

"Don't." She snaps. "Don't call me that."

"River Celeste," I push, deepening my voice to be more commanding, but falling flat when I feel a sharp pang in my chest. "Open the door."

"Or what?" She challenges me.

Without a second thought, I shoulder the door right in the soft spot of the chain. It gives way easily, falling off the wall, and clanking against the metal of the door. She squeaks. Hand clutching her mouth, she jumps back at my forced entry.

"Get out!" She points toward the hallway. I push inside anyway. Her nose and eyes are blister red. I move to touch her, but she slinks back like a wounded cat, wrapping her blanket tighter to her body. "Don't touch me!"

"What is it?" I ask. "What's wrong?" My hands reach for her, eyes scanning her body for something.. "Are you hurt?"

"No." She huffs. "Not physically."

"Then tell me what's wrong, angel."

"I don't want you in this *fucking* apartment, that's what!" The conviction in her words stings more than I allow myself to show. Strings begin unraveling in my head. If I don't keep my composure, I know things could get ugly.

"Why?" I ask, stepping closer, arms still outstretched. "What have I done?"

"It's what you didn't do, Leon." Tears fall down her cheek. I need her to let me fix this. To let me right my wrongs. Atone for my sins. Whatever they may be.

"Is it because I went away this weekend?"

"No! Well, yes, but no."

"Then what is it? Please, just tell me." I'm pleading to any God that's listening to give me an ounce of clarity over here.

"You didn't think I could handle knowing?"

"Knowing what?" I ask. She sighs exasperatedly, turning her back and walking further into her apartment toward our bedroom. I follow after her quickly, scared I'll miss something. Anything.

A piercing white screen positioned haphazardly in the middle of the bed illuminated the room to a blinding degree. Focusing on the screen, I catch a glimpse of myself staring back. A biography and a shitty picture of me on some tabloid website.

And on her phone, a text message from an unknown number saying 'Be careful who you take to bed, Little River. Make sure it's someone you won't mind if they stab you in the back.'

Fuck.

She knows.

I never wanted it to get this far. To not tell her who I am.

I was so caught up on how she would feel about it all. I never wanted her to be with me for any other reason than because she liked who she saw at home, not the one I put out to the public. The real me, the one only she gets to see, is the one I refuse to let the public see. Because if the world could see how vulnerable I can be, it would eat me alive. I have a part to play. The stoic, asshole producer that does his job and goes home. Someone who gets exactly what he wants and has no problem doing whatever it is that may be to achieve that. I don't want the world to mistake my vulnerability for naivety.

And despite everything, although there are two of me that I have to grapple with, I am but one person who wakes up every day and decides which life is worth living.

If either life is truly worth living.

For the longest time, that answer was no. I kept marching on for God knows why. Endured years of scrutiny, agony, depression, suicidal ideation, and isolation. All for it to seem meaningless. To not know if walking this Earth was a thing I should continue doing.

And then, suddenly, she comes along. And with her, a new purpose. A heart that finally feels alive. I've found a reason to thaw it out of its cold, dark prison. All the years of depriving myself of who I am seem completely worth it when I look at her. The world fades away the moment I look into those golden eyes. I can forget about everything. The stress of my job. The pressure I put on myself to be the best at what I do without rest. The nagging desire to cease existing.

She is my reason to live, even when I don't deserve to.

She is the light that shines on the snow in the middle of winter. Blindingly brilliant, captivating to the heart. A beacon of beauty and warmth in a frozen tundra. Her presence is a constant reminder that there are things worth living for.

When I look at River, I see the future I had once thought I would never live to see. All the major milestones that you're supposed to have with her by my side. Growing old, being happy. None of that existed before her.

None of it will exist after her.

Her eyes bore holes into my skull. A seething, bloodshot rage exudes from her very being. Insurmountable guilt that cracks over me like a wave against a rocky shore.

Oh, God, I've fucked up greater than ever before. On the one thing that matters to me.

"Are you going to say anything?!" She asks tensely, jaw clenched so tightly.

"Let me explain." The words I utter are an intangible plea. "Please." Gesturing for the two of us to sit down. The room is filled with silence. No movement. Not even a whisper of a breath lingers in the air between us. "Please." Arms crossed over her chest tightly, tears staining her red cheeks. "I'm sorry. Please come here and let me explain."

She huffs, perching on the edge of the bed as far away from me as she can possibly get. I sink into the plush bed, feeling the cave of our bodies pulling us toward each other despite her resistance.

Once I began talking, I couldn't stop. "I know you're mad at me, and you have every right to be. It was never my intention to hide this from you. You- I'm sorry if I betrayed your trust."

"Why didn't you tell me?" She asks calmly, refusing to look at me. "Why would you lie to me?"

"I didn't lie to you." I hold back the venom my voice threatens to have. "I didn't tell you because-" The words slip through my fingers as I silently beg her to look at me. To listen to me. Acknowledge my existence. Our chests rise and fall in tandem. "I wanted to tell you."

"Then why didn't you?"

"I couldn't."

"Couldn't?" She spews, anger laced in each syllable. Clear disbelief written across her beautiful face. "Did someone hold a gun to your head and force you to keep it a secret?"

"No."

"No?" Her eyebrows spring upward, eyes finally clipping

me. Instant regret washes over me. "Then enlighten me, Leon. Tell me exactly what happened that took precedence over the trust you so desperately wanted out of me."

"I didn't want it to scare you."

"Scare me?" She repeats astonished.

I hum a vague response.

"I was scared when Boyle broke into my apartment and tried to kill me. I was scared when he was raping me." The reality of what she went through sinks in. She'd never spoken of what all he did to her. "You being a multimillionaire celebrity doesn't scare me in the fucking slightest. What scares me is your willingness to keep secrets from me when you know *so much* about me. I so willingly moved in with you and I don't even know who the hell you are." Her fingers grip the sleeves of her hoodie with white knuckles. "I trusted you with my life. Trusted you with everything I am. *And you ruined it.*"

"Angel," I say, reaching for her. She slinks away, tears swelling and falling in those broken eyes.

'Finally gets a girlfriend and he'll break her, beat her down, drag her to hell right with him.'

"And what's with the cryptic message?" She asks. "Who the hell was that from? What the fuck does it mean?"

The number on the message. "I'm so sorry. It's my ex, Jerica. She-"

"The singer?" She asks. I nod. "Oh, I'm going to be sick."

"River,"

"How does she know about me?"

"She has her intel."

"Intel?" She asks. "She has people keeping tabs on you? On me? Why? We're not together. We've never slept together. She has nothing to worry about." A pang sweeps through my chest at her dismissal of what we are. Of what we aren't.

"She's angry." I defend. "About how things ended."

"Why?"

"She was in it for a marketing scheme. I wasn't really in it at all." I say, trying to spare her the more gruesome details.

A loose sigh slips from her full lips. "Great. First the money and fame. Now the crazy ex-girlfriend. Next, you're going to tell me you've got a secret family that you went to visit while you were across the country at that damn award show."

"River, I-"

"Congratulations on your win, by the way. *Elevator Music* was my favorite song. But you knew that already. Didn't you?"

"Was?" I ask. Surprised. That is – was her favorite. I'd never heard her listen to it. I didn't even know she'd heard of it. Couldn't explain the magnitude of emotions that burst inside of my chest. *She likes my music. Music that she directly inspired.* My heart squeezes, so tightly I thought it would explode from the pressure.

Her face falls, eyes swooping over me. Searching. Fingers grasping the fabric at her chest. Well-manicured lavender nails contrast against her oversized black hoodie.

"Was?" I ask again. Unable to move past this news.

"Is."

"You said 'was'."

"Why does it matter?" She asks quietly.

"Because-" *That song's about you, angel.* "It just does."

She hums, wiping away the streams that cascade from her eyes to her neck. "Are you ever going to tell me why you didn't want me to know who you really are?" Her voice is almost an inaudible whisper, tired. There's no way I can forgive myself for this.

"The person I am at work, online, in the spotlight, is a very different person than the one I want to be with you." I answer, trying and failing once again to get my hands on her. "That is not who I am deep down."

"That's bullshit." She scoffs. "You are Leon Kang, aren't you? Who has over 300 song writing credits and a 40-million-dollar net worth? Whose birthday is August 18th, 1993. Born and raised right here in the seventh richest neighborhood in

Atlanta, Georgia? The stoic, mysterious, and *dangerous* Leon Kang who the whole world is terrified of and swoons over at the same time. The pictures on the internet have a striking resemblance to the traitor sitting right next to me."

"What do you want me to say, River? That I did in fact lie to you? That I didn't think you could handle the 'real' me? That I don't trust you to know about my work?" Anger swells deep inside of me, threatening to crash down on River if I don't control myself.

"You always want me to trust you. Yet, you can't even be open and honest with me about who the fuck you are. You're a celebrity. You do celebrity things. You fuck celebrity people! The least you could have done is tell me *'Hey, just letting you know I'm famous. Hope that doesn't scare you.'*" She matches my anger with pure venom. Straight from the tap.

"And how do you think that would end for me, huh? If I go flaunting the fame and money, don't you think that'll turn out poorly? That people would take that as an opportunity to try and use me? I'm not opening myself up to that."

"How am I supposed to trust you when you don't trust me with a very vital part of yourself?" Defeated. She's giving up.

"But I do trust you, angel." I coo, moving to her, on my knees in front of her. Begging for this nightmare to end. "More than anyone." Hands cling to the soft black fabric around her waist.

"Then why wouldn't you tell me?" She asks, bottom lip quivering heavily. "What if I had gone with you this weekend and gotten thrown into it? What if I had seen Jerica in person? Was I supposed to just have looked like a fool for being so confused and dumbfounded?"

"No, of course not. We would have had the talk. I would have told you. I was going to."

"When?"

"I don't know." I admit. She rolls her eyes but doesn't say anything. "Angel, you're the only one I trust with the 'real' me.

Celebrity me isn't the real me. This one is. You're the only one who gets this me. I didn't - I didn't want to scare you. I didn't want to put any pressure on you to fit into that side of me. A side that I wish I could escape from." As the words tumble from my mouth, I make no attempt to stop them. I need her to understand why I didn't tell her.

"Why me?" She asks softly, fresh tears threatening to fall from her exhausted eyes. "What's so special about me?"

The same question she asked after Boyle. Only this time I had a different – better – answer.

"From the first moment I saw your brilliant smile, I knew that you'd be trouble for me." My voice shakes under the weight of the declaration. "You're kind, sweet, and funny." She lets out a puff of air, almost a laugh. Indiscriminate of whether it was disbelief or actual laughter. "My days before you were bleak." *I didn't have anything to live for.* "But with you, I feel like I've found a new outlook on life." *I've found something worth living for. Something keeping me tethered to this Earth. There's no desire to jump off the top of this God damn roof.*

Gentle fingers caress my jaw, and I lean into their touch. Silence lingers in the air between us, our eyes lock onto each other. Not daring to say another word. Daring to say everything.

"Of course I trust you, my little firestorm." I reassure her. Watching her bottom lip quiver as the tears slide down her red cheeks. Her touch is more demanding. "I trust you with every fiber of my being. With the most sacred parts of myself. And I'm so sorry that I made you think that I didn't." I stand, pulling her with me. Her arms snake around my waist, grasping feverishly.

My little firestorm. My blaze in the darkness. My guiding light, a beacon in the never ending night.

My angel. My salvation.

Mine. A voice whispers in my head. In my soul. *Mine.*

Intertwined, I can't tell where my soul ends and her soul begins. Our bodies, souls, all the atoms of our makeup swirl together from the beginning of time until the end. She may not be my first of many things, but I have every intention of making her my last. Because without her, I am *nothing.*

"I'm sorry." She murmurs into my chest.

"Hey," I whisper, pulling back just enough to see her face. That beautiful, tired, puffy face. "It's okay. It's hard finding out your fake boyfriend is an international superstar." I joke. Her shoulders shake lightly, but she reburies her face deep in my chest. "Are we good?"

She looks up at me briefly, just long enough to nod and say "yeah," before hiding herself away again. "I thought you weren't supposed to be back for a few more days." She inquires, her voice muffled from my now wrinkled dress shirt.

I chuckled at her revelation. "I caught a Red Eye."

"Why?" She asks, pulling back again.

"Because you didn't answer my phone calls." I say with a smirk. Her eyes grow to the size of dinner plates. "If you don't know this by now, little firestorm, you never disobey me. Don't send me to voicemail on purpose again."

"You came all this way because I sent you to voicemail?" She asks in disbelief, the smallest spark returning to her voice.

"Mhm. You weren't answering my phone calls. I thought you were dead." I tease.

"Clearly not dead." She retorts, gesturing to herself.

I hum. "I think I'll have to give a full exam to make sure."

"And what does-" She asks as my hands roam around her body. Waist, hips, chest, neck. Anywhere my hands can reach. Lips linger inches from mine.

"Next time, don't scare me like that." I growl, hands holding her face and jaw. "Or you'll really be in trouble.

"Oh, is that so?" She asks with a laugh. The rising sun crests through the window, drawing lines over her skin. I could kiss her. Right now. Push her against the wall. Slide my hands down her pants. Mark her skin wherever my mouth touched. Fuck her into oblivion. As an acceptance of her apology. It'd be so easy to take her.

Her breath lingers on my skin. "I'm sorry. Again." She whispers, dropping her eyes. "For overreacting. For making you fly back home."

"Thank you." I say, confusion flickering in her eyes. "For giving me a reason to come home early."

"Why did you go if you didn't want to stay?" She asks.

"I do love getting recognition for my hard work." I say.

"Egotistical much?" She murmurs with a hushed laugh.

"Not. One. Bit." I say chest swelling with a sense of familiarity that I love infinitely. The hominess. Her.

"You're such an August Leo."

"What's that?"

"Your Zodiac sign?" She counters, eyes wide.

"Oh." I say embarrassedly.

She shakes her head with a grin on her face. "Don't worry, I'll teach you."

"Is that all you're willing to teach me?" I ask slyly.

"What do you *want* me to teach you?" She asks, amusement swirling through her words she utters.

"Whatever you want." I give her a smirk, wanting to give in to what I've wanted to do since we met.

Mine. The voice whispers again. *All mine.*

CHAPTER 17

River

The evening sun dances over his tan skin through my blurry vision. His already soft features are only softer in the peace he's found in REM sleep. Soft snores escaping his open lips.

Guilt sinks over me. A sticky mixture of content and guilt linger on my chest like the side effects of cold medicine. A reminder of earlier. Of the carnage I'd caused. I shouldn't have done that to him. He didn't deserve the hell I gave him.

He's a celebrity. Famous. Wealthy.

Perfect. A whisper of a voice sings in my head.

He is perfect. Just not for those reasons. Because he's caring, kind, the only person I feel I can be myself around. Unmasked, unshackled from who I should be. He's a good cook and an even better gentleman.

My eyes trace the curves of his body, each hill and valley accentuated by the fancy and well-fitted clothes that were left over from the night before, his body warm and inviting. This is a view I could drink in for the rest of my life.

One I'd dreamt about before.

My phone rings from on the nightstand. Forcing me to extract myself from the immaculate view.

Nancy. I slip out of bed, rushing to the living room.

"Hey," I whisper when out of Leon's earshot.

"Hey," Nancy replies. "Why are we whispering?" Nancy

asks, mocking my tone.

"Leon's sleeping." I say too quickly. Instantly regretting letting those words escape my mouth.

"WHAT?!" She squeals, shooting up octaves.

"I'm sure the whole neighborhood could hear that, Nance." I gripe with an eye roll.

"You mean to tell me there's a gorgeous, *scrumptious* man in your bed and you're on the phone with me? Go! Go! Don't let me stand in the way of you and a good time!" She instructs.

Then I remember. That I haven't spoken with her since I last saw her. That I haven't told her about anything that's gone down. That I live with Leon now. That we share a bed. That we've done this shindig all out of order, but that he's quite possibly the best thing that's ever happened to me. That he saved my life. In more ways than one.

And I'm not going to.

Not that I'm embarrassed about it. I've just got this sinking feeling that I can't quite place. That speaking about it will ruin it all. A nagging feeling creeps over me. That I should be careful of who's listening. As if the walls have ears.

I can hear a symphony of voices in the background. "What are you up to?" I ask, changing the subject.

"Brian and I are at a charity hockey game for his little cousin." Bleh, Brian. The sheer thought of him leaves a sour taste in my mouth.

"Sounds like a whole lot of fun." I say, unable to make myself sound interested. My mood soured at the mention of her lover.

"Besides taking a very scrumptious man to bed, what have you been up to?" She asks, almost as a formality. No interest in her own voice. Much like my own.

"Oh, you know. Nothing much." I remark, eliciting a scoff out of her. "Was there a reason you wanted to call me?"

"Well, yeah. I need to know if you're coming to my birthday party." She says a slight shift in her tone.

"Your birthday isn't for another two months." I replied.

"I like to plan."

"Since when?" I ask skeptically, eyes falling on the dimming apartment. The natural light fading into dusk once again.

"Since now." She snips. "Can't a girl try and get her life together?" She asks.

"I'm not saying that. I'm just shocked that you're trying to plan anything at all. I'm the planner. You're the go-with-the-flow."

"Yeah, River, well people change." She snaps, voice like ice shards straight to the chest. "Maybe you should try it."

"Excuse me?"

"Nothing. I've got to go." She murmurs. "I'll assume you're coming." The line goes dead before I have a chance to answer. Taking the phone from my ear, a gentle touch falls on my shoulder, startling me.

I turn around to see Leon, sleepy-eyed with pillow creases on the side of his face, standing close behind me. Even through the tiredness that becomes him, his gentleness exudes comfort. The sight of him instantly eases the turmoil that's begun bubbling in my chest.

"What's wrong?" He asks in a deep, gravelly voice that has my insides doing somersaults.

"Oh, nothing. It's nothing."

"No, it's clearly something." He clocks with a skeptically raised eyebrow. Though, the tone of his voice is vastly more erotic than pure curiosity. A malicious grin grows over his full lips.

"No, it's not." I say, diverting my eyes from his watchful gaze. Becoming putty in his hands instantly.

"Yes, there is." He growls deeply, the sound reverberating in my chest. "Do you want to tell me, or do I need to pull it out of you?" He asks, bridging the small gap between our bodies. His hands grasping at my waist, slipping underneath my shirt as if he'd done this a million times. As if he had laid claim to it. Large, calloused hands caress the supple skin of my hips.

"Leon, it's-" My words falter at the harshness of the touch. Fingers digging in roughly. My whole world begins exploding behind my eyes.

"Angel," he commands. "It'd be wise of you to use your words. *Or I'll make sure there's none left in that pretty little head of yours.*" A devilish grin overtakes him, eyes darkening as my face reveals the emotions I'm experiencing.

Desire dances in my eyes. Practically begging for him to do his worst. One of his hands dips to the small of my back, and the other remains steady on my hip, holding me in place.

"Say it." He growls in my ear. I know what he means.

"No." I object defiantly. He cackles grimly.

"My little firestorm, it's impolite to disobey."

"I'm in the habit of doing that. Aren't I?" I ask.

He leans in close, warm breath ghosting over my skin. "It's a very naughty habit you have, *mon amour.*" He chuckles.

Mon amour. French was never my language of choice. Wouldn't even begin to know what he called me. But it sounded sinful dripping off his tongue the way I want to be. The way everything in me is screaming to let him do *anything* to me.

A long, slender finger draws a single, spine-tingling line from my ear down to my collarbone. Lust boils in his molten eyes as he stares down at me, stealing all the air in my lungs as I stare back at him defiantly. Holding what little ground I had. Enjoying the chase even when neither of us were running.

"Is there a punishment involved?" I ask. His grip on my waist tightens threateningly. The answer to my question.

"You have to use your words." He demands, his free hand moving down to my ass, grabbing a handful roughly. My breath hitches in my throat. Hungry lips close in on my throat, and my pulse point under his teeth. "Tell me what I want to hear."

A whimper escapes my throat involuntarily, driving

him to the brink of insanity. "Take what you want." I offer with much less confidence than I had intended.

Pulling away, eyes filled with nothing but white-hot desire, he leans into me closely. Our faces and bodies are inches apart from one another. I can feel his length, every inch of him through last night's clothes.

"Once I start, angel, I won't stop." I whimper again as his finger presses into the bruise already forming on my neck. An unwavering, twisted smirk lingers on his face. He wants me to cave to him. No, he knows I will.

Tension sizzles in the air between the words we've both left unsaid. He makes no move to elaborate on what it is I'm getting myself into, and in turn, I make no move to give the green light.

"Angel," He coos, a hand rises to my lower back. His demands ghost the shell of my ear seductively. Luring me into temptation. Every touch, word, and breath from this man is sending my body over the edge. Desperate to feel him surround me, swallow me whole in any way humanly possible.

My veins pulse with a need I've never felt before. This wasn't just being horny or needing to get laid. This was something deeper and darker than that. Something almost primal.

"What's the matter? Cat got your tongue?" He teases. "Do you need some help finding it?" One hand firm on my lower back, the other travels along the waistband of my shorts, fingers teasing me the lower they travel. Denying me the satisfaction that I crave. Until I cave.

A forced moan leaves my throat as his teasing fingers connect with my bundle of nerves. The sensation and satisfaction are almost enough to have me screaming already. I roll my hips into his palm, trying to create more friction. A deep chuckle escapes from his throat.

"Look at you. Dripping and depraved and so gorgeous."

I hum as his fingers work slow, painful circles around my aching clit. Intentionally punishing me for the lack of words, I know. His eyes zero in on my reaction to his touch.

"How about those words now?" He smirks, never taking his eyes off my face.

"Leon, I-" I whisper.

"What, angel?" He asks.

"I need you." I say, just as he slips his fingers deeper.

He hums approvingly, sinking his teeth into my pulse point hungrily like he couldn't hold himself back any longer. Not now, after I'd given him what he wanted. My hands find purchase in his tousled hair, gripping tightly as he claims me.

"Do you know how long I've dreamt about this?" He asks in between carving bruises into my skin with his hungry mouth. The soon purple and red marks his signature against my pale skin. I pull his hair tighter the harsher he nips. He groans expletives into each mark. Quickening his pace around my clit as he stares me down, watching intently as my body bends to his will.

"Leon," I moan into his lips as they come crashing down onto mine. Fireworks explode across my body as he feverishly, hungrily, kisses me. I roll my hips hard against the strong grip pinning me in place.

He chuckles deeply against my mouth. "Yes, angel?" I whimper under the pleasure, the pressure of him. "Words, like we talked about."

Plunging two of his fingers deep inside again, a gasp escapes me. "Don't stop. Please, don't stop." The only words I can muster through the stars sparking in my veins. Behind my eyes.

"Wouldn't dream of it." He pants recklessly.

My hands move to undo the buttons on his shirt as he pushes me toward the couch, fingers still pumping in and out. With the black button-up open, I finally get a total view of the hardened muscles underneath. He looks like all the wet dreams I've had for months. Yet even better.

The back of my legs meet the upholstery, and he pushes me down, following me closely, keeping his hungry lips on me.

He drops his hands from my body, moving them to hook his fingers into my shorts, sliding them off my body with ease.

"Fuck me, angel. All this for me?" Dropping to his knees, he ogles my half-naked body like a work of art. As if it were the finest painting he's ever had the pleasure of viewing.

"Yes, baby." I say, sinking into the couch. He holds my legs open, nipping up my thighs tantalizingly slowly until he reaches my slit. Pausing briefly to look up at me, expectantly. "Please." I beg, lacing my fingers through his hair again as he dives into me, drinking in every ounce.

Drawing shapes, signing his name in me with his skilled tongue. Flicking and sucking in all the right ways. Stars flood my vision. Throwing my head back, a loud moan escapes my lips as he slips in his fingers alongside his tongue, filling me to the brim.

"You taste even better than I had imagined, mon amour." He groans as he comes up for air, mouth slack-jawed and glistening. His hands steady my shaky legs as he dives back in for more with a hunger so needy and primal.

Tongue and fingers work in tandem to bring me to the brink of explosive bliss. There is nothing else in the world but him, his motions inside me, devouring me. Fingers grip his hair, the couch cushions, anything I can get my hands on as I squirm under his iron grip.

Kneeling before me, between my legs. He moans into my bundle of nerves, sending shockwaves through me. On the precipice of my release.

He pulls back. An involuntary pouty whimper escapes my slacked jaw. He chuckles, moving to stand and unbutton his pants. I reach for him, running my hand along his bulge, feeling his rock-hard cock twitch under my touch. He releases a guttural groan in response.

I pull his pants down, revealing *all* of him. The thickness and length have me saying prayers to gods I don't believe in. Precum dripping from his tip, veins popping and spiraling down and around. My mouth salivates as I grip his cock.

He tangles his fingers in my hair, pushing my head towards his cock. I give in willingly, ready to taste him. As my mouth closes around his cock, he lets out a moan that ripples through the apartment when my teeth graze over him.

His hands pull at my hair, tiling my head up. "Look at me, angel. I want to see you take all of me like a good girl." He demands with fire in his eyes. Whimpering, I keep my eyes on him as I move up and down his cock, swirling my tongue and pushing past my usual gag point to take as much of him as I possibly could. Reveling in his reactions, bending him to my will until he's barely able to stand. Right to the point where I can feel his climax building, ready to pull back and deny him when his grip tightens, and he forces my head to stay down. To keep sucking until he's bone dry.

"That's it, angel. Taking me so well. I knew you could do it." His voice shakes as he releases into my mouth, cum coating my throat and tongue. Lapping up every drop.

Swallowing him down, he pulls me from my seating position, quickly swapping, sitting down, and bringing me with him. Straddling his lap, he lines up his cock to my entrance. I sink onto him, feeling my walls stretch around his still-quivering cock. I focus on my movements, being guided by him with his hands on my hips yet again while his mouth suckles on my hard nipples.

Gripping the back of the couch for stability, I look down at him, a wave of pleasure washes over me as his teeth sink into my skin so ravenously, drawing blood. Crying out in pleasure from the pain.

"That's right. I know you can take it." He groans, thrusts growing sloppy. "You're not going to cum unless I say so."

I nod. "Yes, baby." He moans, sucking harder, flicking his tongue around my raw nipple. I pant, throwing my head back as he picks up speed.

"Fuck," He groans, digging his fingers into my ass.

Fucking me even better than I had imagined he would.

I force my hips through a few more movements before he slams me down deep onto his cock, holding me there while he releases inside me again. A shiver travels up my spine at the sensation of him releasing his load. I attempt to remove myself from him, but he pins me down again.

"I told you, you come when I say so. I'm not done with you." My core tightens at his words. The command within them. His cock is still hard, thrusting deep inside me. Deeper than I knew possible. Hands grab my ass, slapping hard enough to elicit a whine out of me.

Pumping in and out of me, holding me down. On the brink of release. "Please, baby. Please let me cum." I beg, desperate to find release.

Instead, he removed me from his lap before quickly turning me over with my face pressed into the couch and my ass in the air. He reinserts himself, my pussy dripping his cum down my thighs.

"Look at you, begging for me." He growls, slamming in and out of me with fingers digging into my hips. "You know how long I've been thinking about bending you over and fucking your brains out on this very couch?" A hand comes around, fingers circling my clit. Taking me over the edge.

I hum out of brain-dead curiosity, the pressure building inside of me almost overtaking all my senses.

"Since the moment I first laid eyes on you." He growls, taking the rest of my body and soul with each motion. Claiming what was his. What has always been his.

I scream his name as my release washes over me powerfully. Slack-jawed and fucked raw with stars bursting behind my eyelids with each blink. He stills inside of me, hands gripping my body with a fervor I'd never experienced before.

"Fuck," he hisses, sliding out of me. He falls back onto the couch gracefully. Too much grace for someone who's spent and flushed. I join him, throwing my legs over his. A satisfied grin perches itself across his raw lips, and he leans over to plant a kiss on my lips, thumb tracing the curvature of my bottom lip. "Fuck me, you're even better than I imagined."

I grow shy suddenly. "You, too." The embarrassing words escape me before I can stop them. He chuckles, taking my free hand in his. Playing with my fingers while the other hand traces lines on the inside of my thigh.

His touches were gentle. Nothing of the ravenous man from before. No trace to be had of the person I'd let take me. Left in his wake, though, was the devil himself. Otherworldly handsome, promised a life of fame and fortune, willing to grant me all of my deepest desires. Wrapped in such a perfect package. I wouldn't have believed he was real had he not fucked me senseless.

"Is there a problem, *angel*?" He asks, a soft smirk dancing on his face. Leading my hand up to his mouth, he plants the gentlest kiss on my knuckles. "Was it too much for you?"

"No!" I say quickly, embarrassed that I'd made it seem as much. "No, not at all." My abrupt answer has his cheeks blooming and a smile reaching his eyes.

The world halted for just the briefest of moments as I stared into those enormous brown eyes. They held all the cosmos. The beginning and end of the universe. From the Big Bang to the Heat Wave. The turtle that the world sits on. And I am putty in his hands. Willing to be anything he wants of me.

"Good." He says. "Because I'd hate to give this up." His eyes flash to me, a thin layer of jovialness veiling something I couldn't quite pinpoint. His eyes are delicate yet trained on my features. Searching for something.

He could search until we'd have to build an arc and have a staff meeting with Noah himself before he found anything wrong with me at this very moment.

He pulls me into a kiss, a slow, deep kiss that speaks where we both lack the words to express the things we so desperately want to say. I kiss him back with the same passion, mimicking my desires. Expressing the overwhelming feelings building in my chest. Everything I want to say but can't.

His lips turn upward. "Angel," He breathes into my lips, barely far enough apart for the word to sound like anything tangible. "You're mine." My breath catches in my throat at the very real words he's uttered. "Mine." Without a second though, I nod. Incapable of trusting my voice or knowing what to say to such a claim. "And I'm yours." He breathes into my skin. "Without question." Another promise. An oath.

We sit in comfortable silence for a moment, leaning my body into his. I forget that I hadn't returned the vows, but there were no signs of his discontent. Curling his arm around my shoulders, he plants a firm kiss on the top of my head.

"Do you want to tell me what upset you earlier?" He asks, cutting through the silence like a blade through an unsuspecting body. I look up at him in confusion.

"Oh, I just-" I stammer. "Nancy called. She invited me to her birthday party, which isn't for a couple of months, but I don't want to go." I explained poorly.

"Why don't you want to go?" He asks, thumb rubbing softly against my bare shoulder.

"She's been acting weird lately. Almost like being my friend is an inconvenience." I explained poorly yet again.

"How long," he asks, "has she been acting that way?"

"Oh, I don't know. Five months or so." I say. "At first, I thought it was because her mom was getting worse. Because she's dying of stomach cancer. But now I'm not sure." The words hang heavy in the air around me, as if the first time uttering my displeasure with Nancy will somehow reach her. Like it made the impending doom draw nearer.

"So don't go." He shrugs nonchalantly.

"I have to. She already assumes I'll be there."

"Tell her we're busy."

"We?" I ask with a cocked eyebrow.

"Yes, we. You. And Me. We." He explains, causing me to chuckle at his neanderthal description of the word.

"And what will *we* be busy doing?" I challenge.

"Each other." He smirks as a blush blooms across my

cheeks, eyes roaming down my naked body. "You know what, angel. You better cancel your plans for the rest of your life because I've got more exquisite things in mind for you."

"My, my, the flattery." Lackluster sarcasm drips from my words. "You probably say that to all the girls you fuck."

He *tsks*. "I've never wanted to run away with someone more. And it's taking everything in me not to."

"Some people would consider that kidnapping."

"It's only kidnapping if you don't go willingly."

"And you're so sure I will?" I ask skeptically, knowing as well as he did that I would follow him into Hell if he so wished me to.

"I think you and I both know that you don't get a choice in the matter, mon amour." He coos, running the back of his index finger along my jawline. Shyness creeps over me hastily. "Would you wish me to go with you then?" He asks. "I felt bad about not accompanying you to the wedding."

"Well, lucky for you, the reception is tomorrow. So you can still go." I tease. "But Nancy lives back in our hometown. It's an eight hour drive one way. And the closest airport is a two hour drive away. You'd either be stuck in a car with me for sixteen hours or more since I usually have to stop and pee every five miles. Or you'd be stuck with me for an even longer time period for my anxious airport escapades." I joke.

"Honestly, it sounds like a dream." He says. I roll my eyes.

"Do you really want to be stuck at Nancy's party with a bunch of people you don't know? I thought you hated parties." I say skeptically, eyeing him for any signs of change.

"I'd go to the ends of the Earth if you wanted me to, angel." He coos sweetly. "Besides, I'd miss you, and I'm never letting you out of my sight ever again." He says sweetly.

"Never?" I ask, my fingernails scratching lightly at the base of his neck. "Not even to use the bathroom?" He hums out a 'no', nipping at my exposed neck. I squeal in surprise, ducking fruitlessly to avoid his attack. "We're just friends, Leon." I tease.

"Angel, friends don't know how each other tastes." He says, swiping his thumb over my bottom lip. "I'd give you a higher status than that."

"And what would that be?"

"My queen." He says, wonder swirling in those deep brown eyes. Wonder and something else.

"Why 'queen'?"

"Because, *my little firestorm,* I do not kneel for anyone. I do not answer to anyone. But you. I will bend to your every will. Your every mercy. Defend your honor until my last dying breath."

All the air escapes my lungs at once. Any thought I had or could have had vanishes. Leaving me with nothing but his declaration hanging in the air between us. The possibilities and everything that's implied within them.

"Leon, that's-" I can't find the words to say.

"I'm sorry. Was that too much?" He asks, not an ounce of regret hanging in his steadfast gaze. "I meant every word."

"Well, I certainly wasn't expecting it." I say. His fingers go back to tracing shapes into my thigh. "It's a very . . . powerful – world changing thing to say to someone who you just screwed their brains out." He winces, and I realize my words came out all wrong. "I'm not upset by it. I am taken aback, though. Wasn't exactly expecting a 'you're my queen and I'll kill anyone who touches you' vow today."

He laughs a deep, hearty laugh. Paired with a smile that reaches his eyes. Relief washing over his gorgeous features. "For a second there I was worried I'd ruined everything."

"Not a chance, baby." I tease, laying down on the couch fully, pulling him with me. He lies on top of me, nearly crushing my lungs. Head resting on my bare chest, hands around my waist.

"I'm being serious, though. I would love to visit your hometown." He murmurs into my skin.

"That sounds like a horrible idea." I laugh. "There's

nothing to do out there. It's nothing but trees and hillbillies. Hillbillies that think the frogs are gay and that giving whiskey to babies is not giving them alcohol poisoning."

"You'd be there. That's at least one thing to do. Many times." He smirks. "Besides. I love trees."

"You look like the type." I smirk.

"What's that supposed to mean?" He asks, offended.

"You look like the kind of guy who likes nature."

"Did you not just hike Stone Mountain?" He asks with a raised eyebrow.

"I did that against my will. For love, Leon. FOR. LOVE." I say. He laughs, holding up a hand in surrender. "Besides, I can't ask you to go with me. I can't inconvenience you like that."

"You could never inconvenience me." He coos. "I'd love to go. If you'll let me, I can get us a hotel room, have some fun, go to the pool."

"You're thinking about fucking me in a hotel room, aren't you?" I ask through a chuckle.

"And you aren't?" He counters with a smirk.

"Well, I am now."

"You expect me to not be horny when I have you?" He asks, blush creeping over my cheeks again. "You can't deprive me of an entire weekend away from you now that I have you."

"This isn't for another couple of months anyway, you know." I say.

"I know." He quips. "You'll let me come then?" He asks.

"Only if you drive." I compromise. Overwhelming joy springs over his face, a shit-eating grin on his lips.

"Your wish is my command, mon amour."

CHAPTER 18

Leon

I've never been one to be nervous. Especially not for someone else's wedding. Having been to plenty of weddings of big shot celebrities that call me a friend, but I barely call an acquaintance. They meant little to me in the way of enjoyment. Just an obligation.

Making a good impression also has never been on top of my To-Do list. Never had the desire to brown nose anyone or care what others had to think of me. Happily, content being the stoic asshole that everyone eventually grew to dislike. I must admit that I love living rent free in other people's minds. Simply by existing.

Of course, that was until River, my angel, came along. And now my palms grow clammy at the thought of impressing her friends. Of dressing nice enough to impress her. Constantly wondering and worrying about her thoughts, what she thinks, hoping I won't be a complete disappointment.

Or embarrassment.

My angel's got me wrapped around her slender fingers like a hell hound to the devil.

She spent all morning regaling me on who all will be in attendance that she knows about. How she knows the brides. Her favorite memory of Skylar from college. The cryptic things that Astra had said during the elopement ceremony.

It was hard to hide the excitement blooming under my skin when I learned that Astra would be in attendance. Preparing to revel in the enjoyment of watching her face fall when I dared show my face on River's arm. I had half a mind to put my grandma's engagement on her, to make a grand show of things.

"Absolutely not, Leon." Angel had demanded, though her gaze flitted to the bare ring finger on her left hand. *"I'm not going to have you make a scene at someone else's wedding. It's impolite."*

"Astra's impolite. Thinking I wouldn't ruin everyone's fun just for her snide comments." I retorted, eliciting an eye roll and smirk from her place on the couch. Still draped in no more than a baggy shirt that reached her mid-thigh. She's on the way to driving me absolutely mad.

"I'm not wearing your grandma's precious wedding set anyway. You've got to save that for your future wife." She chuckles. A joke she makes frequently. That there's someone out there for me that isn't her.

Whether she's phishing for me to admit she's it for me, or if she genuinely believes that this is temporary, I'm unsure. But admitting out loud to her that she's the only one I'd ever give that ring to terrifies me. Openly verbalizing my feelings and the vast oceans of emotions that I hold for her is about as easy as pulling teeth with your fingers and no Novocain.

As much as those thoughts terrified me, I had no earthly idea if she felt the same way. Or even if she wanted to hear how unhealthily obsessed with her that I am. That I would kill and be killed for her. That I would rather die than be without her. That she's the woman I'm going to marry. I just know it.

That's too much for her to bear.

So all I could say was, *"You can wear them any time."* Her eyes widened and her jaw slacked ever so slightly under the smirk she carried. Rose blush bloomed over her full cheeks, and it took *everything* in me not to dust my thumb over one. To feel the heat that radiated from them.

Now, it's almost time for us to leave, for her to make her grand reveal of the dress she had hid from me since she picked it up from the tailor's on her way home Friday.

Talk about making a big show out of things.

The theme of the reception was backyard fantasy. I've not the slightest idea what she meant by that, but she instructed me on what to wear and how to style my mop of hair. My comment about getting it cut didn't go over very well. She huffed and said she preferred it longer. And those words combined with her fingers massaging the mouse into my locks nearly had me proposing again. Standing in between my legs, looking down at me with concentration laced eyes, slicking my hair back in a way that would easily fit with the ceremony theme.

She picked out black slacks, black dress shoes, and a deep purple button up that I had no knowledge of owning. Instructed me to roll the sleeves up to my elbows. *"Like a dream."* She had commented as I did a slow spin for her, arms held out in almost a questioning manner. Begging for approval.

"Angel?" I ask through the bathroom door. "Are you almost ready to go?" She hums sweetly before the faint clicking of heels on tile crescendo to the door.

"The question is," she says, just on the other side. "Are *you* ready?"

"Born ready, mon amour." I coo. Mon amour, my disguised confession. If she knows what it means, she's never let on. The door swings open slowly. Painfully slowly.

My vision floods as I drink in her beauty. Otherworldly, radiant beauty. Her pale skin is a stark yet stunning contrast to the colors swirling in her dress. Rich purples hug, curve, and billow from her figure. Tight in the bodice, flowing from her hips down to the floor. A perfect pool around her feet. Gold chains drape from her shoulders, connected at the front and back as a sort of decorative armor. A gold septum ring hangs delicately from her nose, paired with an assortment of earrings like constellations on her ears, all gold and celestial motifs.

"We match." She grins sparkling ear to sparkling ear.

"You look *absolutely divine*." I say, not bothering to stop myself as my hands move to her hips instinctively. Soft, supple fabric dancing on my fingertips as I pull her into a kiss. A warm, appreciative kiss that seems to catch her off guard.

It's not the first time we've kissed, but the small peck from months ago and the kisses during and after sex weren't this. They hadn't carried the words I needed to say to her, to breathe into her.

"We're going to be late if you keep looking at me like that." She giggles, lacing her hand into mine like I'd been made for her to do just that.

The party wasn't super lavish like I'd been accustomed to, which was a lovely change of pace. The end of the cul-de-sac had been decorated, all the neighbors pitching in, showing their sense of community for such a special occasion. Fairy lights dusted the ground with sprays of light as the sun seeped below the tree line.

Everyone was friendly. Even Dana's mom. Who hasn't caught me perusing the beverage table when she came to speak to River about how the season of love will come for everyone, and that Dawson was also still looking for his forever person.

"Oh, I'm sure he'll find someone." She said politely with a small dip of her head, jumping as I nudged her arm. "Mrs. Florence, this is Leon. My-"

"Boyfriend. Pleasure." I say, slipping a champagne flute into her hand before extending said hand to the older woman. Eyes wide, flitting between the two of us. She doesn't accept my handshake.

"Well, I'll be, sugar." She crows. "I didn't know a girl like you could bag a man like him." Her words echo as she hastily makes herself busy doing anything but being caught up in the mess that I'd started making.

"That went well." River breathes under a strong sip of champagne. "Does she know her son's gay?"

"Probably not, but she definitely knows you're taken now." I smirk, my arm sinking around her waist, where it'd been since we got out of the car with the exception of getting drinks and going to the bathroom.

She flashes me a knowing look, holding back her laughter as she looks around for someone in particular. Unsure of who it could be since it feels like we've spoken to everyone here at least twice. Ready to steal her away for a moment of solitude, our moment alone is quickly interrupted by three jovial women swarming her quickly.

Two women are dressed in white. The brides, I assume, wrap her in their vice grip hugs. Squeals shrill into the air as they get swept away, chit chatting and laughing fondly over something I can't hear.

A third lingers behind, an unmovable stare trained on me. A smile I knew all too well cursed her too big lips. She'd be conventionally attractive to the naked eye. Eyes that weren't cursed to see the ugly, poisoned truth.

A cold shiver slivers its way up my spine, the same manner that happened just a few weeks ago. She takes a step towards me, and all I can see are the claws, the teeth, the veiled grey skin. She could look so normal had I not been looking at a soulless monster.

"You humans are so easy to scare." She chuckles lowly, her features shifting behind the veil, nearly hiding all of her hideousness. Leaving behind only the faint lingering bitter aftertaste of blood in my nose. The tang of pennies. "I've heard a lot about you, Leon Kang. You're pretty famous."

"What are you?" I ask sharply. The air is loose in my lungs.

"You're lucky you claimed the girl when you did. She is destined to meet an untimely fate." Her words grew cryptic, rage simmering just below the surface.

"What the fuck does that mean?" I pry, fists forming at my sides. "What are you talking about? I'll kill you if you hurt her." My threats feel empty in the face of something like her.

"Land your plane, Earhart." She crows. "I'm not her enemy. Not yours either."

"Then why won't you answer my questions?" I press.

"Because it's funny watching you, of all people, squirm." She laughs like she's just told the funniest joke in a century. She meets my raised eyebrow with mischief. "Even if I wanted to tell you, help you. I can't. Forbidden to intervene with someone's fate." Her nonchalant nature is very off putting for the subject matter.

"Why?" I ask angrily. All my patience exits expeditiously.

She shrugs. "That's the order of things. Even Reapers can't change what's already been set in motion."

"Reapers?" My mouth grows drier by the second.

She hums. "Everything that will ever be, has already been mapped out in the stars. All our days are numbered. Everything we'll ever do is predetermined. Fighting it will do no one any good." Her words grow somber, like the idea that our miserable destinies are set in stone. No matter how much she wished it weren't that way.

River glides back over to me, a thick smile laced over her beautiful features. With one hard look at me, it falters. The creature, woman, I haven't caught her name, so I lean in quickly and say, "Don't tell her." She darts away before River makes it across the room.

"What did Astra say to you that made you look like you saw a ghost?" She laughs emptily, walking delicately with eggshells under her feet.

Astra. It makes sense now. The blurry picture, the veil she held even in photographs. Her power. "She's just mad you look better than everyone here." I lie, placing a kiss on her forehead, a knot forming and tugging in my gut.

"I doubt she said that. Look at her. Peak beauty."

"I'd strongly disagree." I force a smile on my lips as I tilt her head up to look at her. Long and hard. Like it might be the last time I'll ever see her.

PART TWO: THE VILLAGE

CHAPTER 19

River

The wedding reception came and went.

It was a beautiful mixture of lavish and cozy. Purples and gold still lay fresh in my mind, fantasy themes and hominess. They were in love beyond any combination of words the English lexicon can string together. Lots of pictures were taken. So much so my eyes stung from the copious amount of flashes strobing in each direction. Catered by a small, family-owned food truck that served Cajun seafood and the best shrimp and grits in Georgia. And at the end of the night, all the fancy clothes were discarded in the entryway of the apartment the moment we crossed the threshold. The sex was phenomenal, the man before me even more so.

Halloween came and went.

Traditionally my favorite holiday. The mid-fall vibes, scary movies, decorating, carving pumpkins. We did it all. Leon stopped at no expense to go above and beyond. Always the gentleman. Leon's company had an A-list masquerade ball on Halloween night. I wasn't privy to going, but Leon *insisted* that the purple fantasy dress make another appearance. So I obliged. He had someone he knew custom make an angelic/celestial mask to match. He wore a suit that probably cost him more than my college tuition. But he was drop-dead gorgeous. And he smirked at me the whole night. Knowing just how worked up I was getting watching the hottest man alive wearing a mask.

Who knew we were such party people?

Who knew I had a thing for masks?

Thanksgiving came and went. My least favorite holiday growing up. A childhood filled with football, Black Friday shopping, and the world's blandest food. As I got older, I tried to host Friendsgiving but quickly realized I 1) didn't have a lot of friends and 2) couldn't cook. But this year was different. This year I tried to have a good time, enjoying learning to make a tiny feast that Leon and I slaved over for days to perfect. I was only allowed to make the deviled eggs and desserts unsupervised. We still have leftovers in the freezer. Leon babbled about some kind of white bean chili that he'd love to make with the turkey.

Somewhere along the way, Leon got my sewing machine out of storage and took me fabric shopping. I don't have much of a stash if anything, since I've never had room for crafting outside of a single project. I bought everything I needed to make a baby quilt for a coworker of mine and a lap quilt for his grandma, as a sign of good faith. And hopefully a good impression for his grandmother. Lavender and honeybees, two of her favorite things, in a line by Moda Fabrics. The stars couldn't have aligned more.

He hasn't told her about us, yet. Says that the moment the declaration enters her ears, she'll either be on a plane to see us or wouldn't stop begging us to come to her. He has plans to tell her when we visit for New Year's. Which is still a wild idea to me. Being introduced to his family whom he talks so sparsely about. He visits her each New Year, to celebrate that she's still here. And now I'm an official part of that tradition, he says.

My hand-me-down Baby Lock is older than I am. Unsure if the yellow tinge is from age or its original color. It's always been that way, for as long as I've had it. I bought it second-hand from a housekeeper at the hotel I worked at in high school. She was a part-time tailor and made all her grandchildren's clothes. She had saved up enough money to buy a new machine my senior year, so I bought it from her even though she had offered to give it to me for free. The only thing wrong with it is the bobbin sensor is broken. But I'm a pro at bobbin chicken now.

I spent so many days in between the wedding and today hunched on a bar stool, over the cutting mat, behind the sewing machine, making sure this quilt was as perfect as I could get it before it was gifted to such a monumental woman. Each stitch is made with love and lots of curse words. The baby blanket only took me a weekend to hammer out. Start to finish.

Today, like most days, is a struggle to get out of bed. The fading sun never returned. Bringing out the worst in me. The darkness I had repressed when things were brighter.

Today is rough. Barely being able to bring myself to sit in a barstool for a cup of coffee made with love and three sugars by the world's cutest barista.

"Good morning, angel." Leon coos with a coffee-scented kiss. Chipper. He's always chipper. Though, everyone says he's not. He's just this way with me.

"Morning." I groan through strained vocal cords. "If it was a good morning, I would be a stay-at-home trophy wife." An attempt to make myself laugh. To feel something other than this impending doom. The road trip, the darkness. We're going home tonight. I can't imagine anything worse than this and the PTSD combined.

"I can change that." He smirks, mischief dancing in the vast seas of his eyes. A roll of my own doesn't cover up the butterflies swarming through my abdomen. A delicate hand caresses my chin, pulling my gaze to his.

"Is that what you want?" I ask genuinely. Did he want me as a wife? As a 'trophy wife'? Someone who contributes nothing to this relationship. I certainly don't want to mooch. Don't want to sit around and do nothing all day for the rest of my life.

He hums. "I want you. And I want you to be happy."

How grossly too kind. That *a man like him* could be so fond of *a girl like me*. Those words still haunt me in the quiet of my brain. Right when I think I can get used to it all, that I deserve him, those words flood me like a town ill-equipped for a storm. Trapped in my own house. No one is coming to save me.

I want to ask him why he's so willing to marry me. To throw that ring on my finger and get the government involved in our affairs. Tell me why I'm the one he fancies over someone prettier, more exciting, more talented, what have you.

I'm not blind. I see the way he looks at me. I feel the soft touches. How he holds me in spaces no one can see but us. How he protects me and takes care of me with no question. He's not afraid to show me off, but only if I want to be. No one makes my heart flutter more.

There's just a nagging feeling in the back of my mind. One that pulls at this knot in my stomach, reminding me that this could all go away. That something could happen. Anything could happen.

"Wouldn't it be the talk of the town back home if Weird Girl River got married to a famous music producer after barely five months?" I chuckle. Thinking vividly about how I'd be called a gold digger, a slut, anything to get under my skin. Because who wouldn't love to make fun of the foster care kid for doing well for themselves? For finding happiness?

"My grandpa proposed to my grandma after eleven days." He indulges, something I hadn't previously known. "He used to always tell me growing up that 'when you know, you know'. And I thought that was the biggest crock of bullshit I'd ever heard." He laughs lightly, still standing next to me, like I'll fade away if he gets too far. "But he's right."

I scoff. Not because I don't believe him, but because I don't want to believe him. To admit what *I know* would be to admit that I feel so greatly and deeply for him that it'll be as though our souls are fusing. That once I confess aloud how I'd rather burn at the stake than be without him for the rest of my measly, puny, minute life, there would be no going back.

"I'm sure your grandma was just that pretty." I divert

the impending demise under my skin elsewhere. Willing it away from a moment I'm desperately trying to savor. He notices, though I don't know how.

"Maybe I should have proposed to you ten days after we met." He chuckles, a genuine smile eclipsing his full lips.

"What exactly were your thoughts about me after ten days, Sir?" I ask with a raised eyebrow. It couldn't have been much more than a passing thought to him at that time. We'd barely spoken twice. I was just a stranger to him, but because I'd dreamt of him, it felt as though I'd known him for a million lifetimes. That the atoms that make up our souls were once one during the Big Bang.

I can't say that to him.

"Pure filth." He chuckles, scrunching his nose.

"Nothing's changed." I roll my eyes again as if the thoughts weren't swirling through my head. As if sharing a bed with him was ever an issue.

"Call out today. Let's spend the day together." He offers. It sounds lovely, but I can't. My shift starts in an hour. "At least let me drive you. I miss doing that." He whines, pouting his bottom lip.

"Leon, please." I nearly beg, holding in the waterworks that threaten to expose me of how deeply traumatized I am. I'm sure the beat color of my nose is giving me away, tingling just below the surface. "It's one day. Then you'll get to chauffeur me around and spend all your waking moments with me. You'll get sick of me, you know."

"The only thing I'm getting sick of is looking at the back of your head as you leave me." The pout is in full swing. "But the rest of you gives one hell of a view." I lightly smack him on the arm, unable to produce words for the cheesiness he's spouted. "What?" He asks with the biggest shit-eating grin.

There's a word on the tip of my tongue that threatens to slip out. To present itself. To terrify me into oblivion. I quickly swallow it up. Shoving the boisterous, bubbly feelings down.

I can't say that either.

"I'm going to be late," is all I can say.

"Be safe, please. I'll be waiting for you." He smirks, peppering kisses across my neck and jaw, carving his way to my lips with expert precision. Causing airy giggles to escape my throat, trapped in the four walls that guard us.

"Don't ever stop waiting for me, pretty boy."

"I've waited my entire life for you, angel." He says, softly kissing my lips before and after the sentence. A smirk dances on his lips, one filled with obsession and possession. "What's a few more hours?"

What, indeed.

CHAPTER 20

Leon

I've been doing research. In any span of free time I acquire, I throw myself into finding out what the hell those things are. What the hell Astra is and why she somehow seems different. What I can do to keep River safe.

There is a surprising lack of helpful information riddling the internet about grey-looking voids-for-eyes, potentially magical creatures. Monsters. Beings. None of the words fit the atrocities I've witnessed. Continue to witness.

When I turn around, I see things out of the corner of my eye. Things that I know other people don't witness. Shadows dancing where they shouldn't be. Howling noises in the dead of night that are neither human nor animal. Glimpses of Boyle-like monsters in reflections of passing windows or convenience store mirrors. Just as soon as my brain catches up with what it's thought it's seen, it disappears.

Noises, creaks in the floorboards, jolts of wind, or flashes of light send me into a frenzy. Because what if I lose her for good? What if I'm not vigilant enough to keep her safe? Damn it all to hell. Forget about me. The only thoughts that race through my mind daily are what if I don't do enough? What if my inadequacies aren't enough to save her when it matters? I won against Boyle, but what if there are things out there that can do eons worse than he could? How can I fight and win against things unseen and unknown?

I've exhausted all of my efforts. Unable to come up with any answers. Growing more frustrated and paranoid with each close encounter with the creepy kind. I called the lady from the Red Eye. The one that somehow knew.

Cassandra the Seer, she calls herself.

She'd set up a meeting today while River was at work. I would have canceled the meeting if River had wanted to stay home with me, but I knew she wouldn't bite. Knew she'd go to work like she does every day and come home to me each evening.

Knock, knock, knock.

Three soft raps on the replaced metal door. Heavier steel that would hopefully hold better than the wooden ones I'd smashed through. Twice.

Behind the door is the vaguely familiar face of the dark-skinned woman who seems all-knowing. Who, unlike Astra, seems to be willing to help me. Her hair's pulled back in knotless braids, a sage green bandana acting as a hairband. She wears a loose, flowy dress and carries a large canvas tote bag. Very hippie dippy looking, but I hold my tongue.

"Good morning," I greet, flashing her as warm of a smile as I can muster. Peopling has never been my strong suit, especially when I don't have my angel to ground me. To remind me that I can play nicely. I just don't like to. Forget how to.

"Good morning!" Cassandra chirps, slipping through the threshold and into the foyer of our small apartment still littered with a nearly completed quilting project and the reminders that I now care more about having a good time with River than keeping a house that looks like no one lives in it. "I see love lives here." She comments, eyes sweeping over the mingled personalities that are reflected all around us.

Love. I'd thought about the word, the implications, its impact on the space it resides in. Dwelling on it made my heart swell to the point of near explosion. Not something I want to address with a stranger. Not that I'm opposed to the idea that I'm in love with River. The idea just terrifies the fuck out of me.

But it would make sense. To love her. It would be easy to say it with each breath I take. That I love her. It would make sense to say that, feel it in my soul before I marry her. To admit to myself that I'm capable of loving someone, River, the way that she deserves to be loved. That I deserve it in return.

"Would you like to come in and sit?" I offer condescendingly. Remembering River telling me how to greet a guest, but she never told me that I couldn't be an ass about it. Not that we ever have any company anyway. "Can I get you some water? Tea? Coffee?"

"Coffee would be splendid. Thank you." She says, moseying over to the couch and settling into the crook, her bag becoming amorphous as the weight disperses. She instructs me how she likes her coffee, and with the mug in my hand, I join her on the couch. Ready for her to cure all my problems.

"So," I trail off, unsure of where to go from here. "Where do we start?"

"Well, you called me. Tell me what ails you, my child." She coos before a sip of the steamy liquid. "What troubles have you been facing?"

So, I told her. Going over in as grave of detail as I can about the entire Boyle situation. How he seemed here but not all here, weak and strong, ordinary and powerful, full of magic, turned to ash. I tell her about the second creature at River's work. How he paralyzed her, blinded her, tried to sink his talons into me. All of the little things that I've witnessed and can't explain. Hoping for some insight. I leave Astra out, though. While she's not something I can pinpoint right this second, she doesn't seem to pose an impending threat to River, which is my main concern. Only concern.

Cassandra hums along to my stories, scribbling notes down on a yellow legal pad. Sharpie pen flying across the lined paper during parts she deems important. When I've run out of things to say, I sit patiently as her pen stills and she gets a glassy look in her eyes akin to the thousand-yard stare, but yet somehow calmer. Like she's welcoming the distance into her.

The apartment gets colder, a chill running up my spine, and I wonder if I've forgotten to set the thermostat correctly.

If the changing seasons outside these paper-thin walls are leaking in somewhere.

She pulls out a journal from her bag. Leatherbound and well-worn. Undoing the binding and flap, scribbles in what look like a foreign language sprawl across once empty pages. Drawings of symbols and figures litter the margins beside lengthy paragraphs on tan pages. Uncertain if she'd handmade her paper, or if they were aged from time and wear.

"I see." She finally says, clarity resuming in her near-pitch-black eyes. "Well, there's good news and bad news, son." *Son.* She couldn't be much older than I am.

"Good news first." I say a squeak in my voice at the endless possibilities of what the bad news could be.

"Good news is," She starts, leaning her elbows on her knees, extending the journal to me. As if I can understand what lies before me. "It seems like we're dealing with Changelings. Which, thankfully, are very rudimentary creatures. And you seem to have a knack for defeating them." Her words are smooth as their weight settles on my shoulders. Tapping the end of her pen on a particular picture on the left page.

A side view of a humanoid figure with a deep hunchback, sagging features, a mouth with too many teeth, and voids for eyes.

"Changelings?" I ask, nausea and disbelief hitting me simultaneously. "What even is a changeling?" I study the picture until she pulls the journal away. The voids burned into my brain. Images of Boyle's true form in River's bathroom mirror flash across my vision.

It takes everything in me to hold in the contents of my stomach as the nausea becomes overwhelmingly pungent in my throat.

A puzzled, near shell-shocked look flashes over her previously collected demeanor. A surge of panic flashes through me at her sudden change. "You don't know? You can see through the Veil, and you don't know?"

"I mean, that's why I called you, isn't it? Because I see these things, and shit keeps happening, and I don't know what the fuck is going on."

"Oh, okay." She condescended, recentering herself with an inhaled breath to hold in the patience that was quickly waning, stuffing her journal back in her bag. "I guess we have to start with the bad news, then."

Great. Just what I wanted to hear.

"Go on." I usher. "Start with the Veil thingy."

"Thingy?" Cassandra reiterates. I nod exasperatedly. "The Veil," she says, "is like a magical glamour that's cast on all magical creatures."

"Hold on." I interrupt. "Who casts this magical border? Is it like a constant, natural thing that just happens or does each creature have to cast his own?"

"You are insufferable." She scoffs. "I don't know what this River character sees in you." I shrug, mostly agreeing with her. "The Veil itself is as old as creation. From the beginning of time and the formation of all the creatures, to protect the harmony that the Old Gods intended."

"Old Gods?"

"We're getting ahead of ourselves." Cassandra sighs. "There are creatures, other beings, who exist under the Veil. To protect themselves. To protect the humans above. Humans do not have the innate power to see through to the other side, except when they become exposed to a creature's true power and form. Then, the Veil is lifted."

"Why?"

"Some say that when you peer into a creature's magic, their magic peers back. Planting the tiniest drop of it into you. Once the Veil is removed, it cannot be replaced." She explains. "You saw through the Veil to Boyles' power. It seems as though your girlfriend did not. That's why she cannot see what you can."

"This all sounds like a bunch of whack-a-doo shit."

"You wanted my help, Mr. Kang."

"*Don't* call me that." I snap, fists clenched in my lap.

"Look, it's not my fault that you don't like the information that I've given you. You don't get to act like a child because you can't handle your big boy feelings." She snaps back. "You looked into the unspeakable. I can choose not to help you."

"How much do you charge for spewing bullshit?"

"I am not charging you a cent, am I?" She asks, patience running thinner than the smile on her lips.

"I just assumed you would-" I say, embarrassed at the assumption I'd made. The money stuffed in my pocket weighs as heavily as the 'truth' she's trying to tell me. The truth I heavily want to ignore.

"You called me because you're seeing through the Veil. I'm simply telling you what you're already experiencing. The only thing scaring you is reality, son."

"How is that possible, though?" I ask, diverting the conversation elsewhere. "That there are things out there that we can't see until we're face to face with them. And God forbid we survive. We're stuck seeing them forever, for what they are. And they get to walk amongst us like they're our equal?" The words tumble out of my mouth in rapid succession.

She sighs heavily. "Humans are the lesser creatures." She says sharply. "Far too many humans have never honed their magic, deny it altogether. Entire generations and bloodlines lose their magic if left dormant. You cannot consider them the superior species when they can't even-" Her words fall short.

"'*They*'?" I repeat, as if she's not a living, breathing human sitting in front of me. "What do you mean 'they'?" Red flags wave inside my head. Something's not right here.

"It was an honest mistake." She says but makes no move to correct further. "Just a matter of phrasing."

I don't believe her, but she's sitting right in front of me. No forced glamour or Veil in the way of what she is. At least none my *human* eyes can see.

Was she somehow more powerful than Astra, who could nearly completely shield her true form from me? Did she have to work extra hard to hide her true form? This has sparked more questions than answers.

"Are you sure you've never been exposed to things below the Veil before?" She asks, dragging my increasingly paranoid thoughts from their precipice.

"Certain. Not until a few weeks ago. I don't even believe in ghosts."

"Well, you should start."

"Ghosts are real, too?" I ask skeptically. Cassandra nods with a twisted smirk. "Seriously?"

"I cannot believe someone as skeptical as you managed to peer through the Veil." She scoffs, shaking her head with a pitiful laugh. "And you knew how to kill a Changeling?"

"I didn't do it on purpose." I say. "I mean, I meant to kill him, yes. But I didn't think he'd disintegrate in the bathroom. Didn't know they had a fear of bathrooms."

"Mirrors, you-" She stops herself short of whatever insult she was planning to spew. I don't fight the chuckle at her irritation. "Changelings can only be killed by seeing their true image in a pure silver mirror or by fire. Burned at the stake, preferably."

"These apartments have pure silver mirrors?" I ask astonishedly.

"I would assume that they're safeguards against outside Changelings. They're very territorial creatures. That, or the mirrors were original. They made things different back in the day." Cassandra explains, taking in the age of the apartment. Humming at the ill-constructed repairs hiding the water damage and holes in the walls from previous tenants.

"So how will I know if I encounter another *Changeling* or if it's something else?" I ask, hoping to never run into anything else ever again. But knowing that my life somehow never works out that way.

"My sweet child," She coos condescendingly. "You don't.

You just have to hope that they aren't actively trying to kill you. That's the only time what they are *really* matters to a human like you."

A human like me.

Cassandra grew sick of me quickly, but she answered all of my questions. Explained everything in as best detail as she could. And I did give her the two thousand dollars I had withdrawn for her services. She suddenly liked me a lot more after the wad of cash hit the bottom of her purse.

All I want to do is tell River. To share the new information that I had acquired. To show her that I'm better equipped to deal with whatever it is that's coming our way. That she's safe with me.

But I know I can't. If she's not yet exposed to the things lurking beyond the Veil, then I won't be the one to open that can of shitty worms. If she's blissfully unaware of everything, then it means I did my job in protecting her. That I fought hard enough to save her.

'Don't tell her.' Astra's words ring sharp in my ears. Don't tell her about her fate. Or the monsters. Or the Veil.

I also know that part of my more immediate job is to pack the car and get all her favorite road trip snacks, which she had made me a list of on her lunch break, but I had already memorized everything she'd ever once said she liked. Like a creep, yes, I know. Sue me.

And as I'm sitting on the couch waiting for her to come home, my leg bounces a million miles a minute. My phone lights up with a call from the lovely lady herself.

"Hey, angel." I say, stifling the overwhelming feeling building in my chest.

"Hey," She replies, the single word barely audible through clenched teeth.

"Everything alright?" I ask, obviously concerned, rising to my feet. Immediately wondering if I did something wrong or if someone required a can of whoop ass.

"You, my darling sweet summer child, have about two minutes to get down to the parking lot or you're going to be bailing me out of jail for vehicular manslaughter." She says seething. "I know you have the funds, so your pick, lover boy."

"What the hell is going on?" I ask though I'm already on the move to the bedroom. To the twin daggers I have stored under my nightstand.

"Mark's following me." River's voice grows ragged as if acknowledging the problem made it real. The anger and rage fade quickly from her words. Transforming into panic and helplessness. Something I've heard too many times from the screams she exalts in the dead of night. "I've gone in every wrong direction, taken every right turn imaginable, and I can't lose him. He's driving erratically and almost made me crash into a semi." She quickly becomes a shell of the woman who threatened vehicular manslaughter. A parallel to the one I pulled from her apartment. "I need you."

I'm running before I even know where I'm going. A tightening in my gut is the only sign of which way to go. Down, down, down. The dark-washed concrete stairs are no match for the unstoppable force of a possessed man.

"I'm coming, angel. Stay with me." The words leave my throat in what sounds like a growl, unable to contain the rage that's replacing the blood in my veins. The stairwell is lit with harsh lighting that shines so crimson behind my eyes. So much so that it's almost blinding.

When the stairs come to an end, I come barreling out of the stairwell and into the parking lot. Phone to my ear, two daggers in my opposite hand. I've been timing myself; it's been one minute and forty-four seconds. I see River's car pull up to the stop light just down the street, a black car with 110% tinted windows is behind her.

I talked to her the whole time. Telling her to stay with me, to focus on me. Focus on getting back to me. That I've got her. I've always got her. It kills me to have to wait for her to come to me. Where she belongs. Where I can protect her.

"I can see you." She sighs with relief, flooring the gas as much as her little car can as she takes off with the green light.

"Go to your parking spot, mon amour. But drive him by me first." I instruct, insisting to myself that I can be calm and rational about this, but knowing damn well I would rather see the inside of this guy's intestines than let him walk away.

It's been a while since I've gotten well acquainted with the insides of some fucking asshole like that.

"What are you going to do?" River asks In a voice filled with soul-crushing defeat, juxtaposed by fear coursing through the nervous system. Vision clouded with something no one as pure as she should ever have to experience.

The darkness chases the sunset, engulfing the world in a dusty twilight as time slows to a crawl. With each passing breath, my erratic heartbeat is an echoing reminder of the ever-pressing mortality of it all. Of us. Of her.

"Stay in your car." I demand. "I've got you."

Repeated words. Time and time again I've uttered those three words to her. A vow. A testament to my devotion. A proclamation of the innate yearning in my soul to protect what's always been mine. Words I've been saying both in my head and out loud in an attempt to give her some peace of mind.

To say I love her in the only way I know how.

With one last hurrah, pedal to the metal, the little red Corolla comes barreling closer. Passing by me at the speed of light, she makes a near-perfect pit car maneuver. The car spins on its rear tires, leaving black streaks behind on the pavement as she turns down a different row. She makes it into her spot, hyperventilating and mumbling something about me looking possessed.

I don't bother stifling the laugh that escapes my throat as I step in front of the blacked-out car. Twirling the daggers in my hand, I say, "Je t'aime, mon ange. Je reviens pour toi." I hang up before she has time to ask questions or protest my abrupt departure. I hear her gasp as Mark slams on his brakes, nearly missing me. The heat from the engine propels itself around an immovable force.

A Hellcat Demon. How ironic and tragic.

Pale hands slam against the steering wheel, leaving slimy residue in their wake. Laying on the horn briefly before the driver makes a rather dramatic exit out of the severely overpriced hunk of plastic.

I'm sure people say the same thing about my car.

"You and I both know that those won't do you any good." A scratchy voice booms over the roaring in my ears. A pointed, distant stare lingers on my daggers, still twirling between my fingers. A twisted smile laces its way across my face at the realization. The confirmation. *Changeling.*

"I don't need them to kill you." I reply confidently. Primal nature settles on my shoulders like I'd done this a thousand times. Like it coursed through my blood. "But I like toying with my victims. Like to watch them suffer."

"Is that all that little cunt is to you? Your next victim?" He asks, his voice sounding as if it exists in all corners of the world. Rage runs through my veins. Rage, and fear. Fear that I wasn't equipped to handle this. To kill him. "Going to fuck her into the ground and then leave her for the rest of us to feast upon?"

The fear dissipates quickly with Mark's last comment. Because I'd tear him into little bits just for that comment alone. I'd find a way to let the anger I've been simmering my whole life overtake me. Wouldn't bother stopping myself from becoming a monster if it meant getting the job done. If it relieved some of the pain in my chest.

"You should shut the fuck up if you knew what was good for you." I threaten, not that my threats sound solid at all. My voice felt hollow in my throat. Sounding almost foreign as I squeaked out the pathetic words.

A rustling noise crackles through the air in the direction River's gone. Our gazes lock on to the noise to see

River standing just on the other side of a small bush at the end of the row. She's holding herself, arms wrapped tightly around her torso. Her golden eyes flicker between us, sizing up the situation I'd willingly thrown myself into.

I quickly return my attention to the fucker I'm itching to gut. To recenter me for my purpose. Not wanting to give Mark any more advantage than he already had. "And keep my girl's name out of your mouth." I snap, harsher this time. The words bite through the chilling air.

"I was just making sure my favorite coworker got home safely. I had hardly believed she was dating someone when she told me all those months ago. I had to come to see for myself. I didn't expect it to be someone so *vile*."

His teeth gleamed with black saliva, a nasty side effect that I hadn't seen from Boyle. I wasn't sure if he was sick, poisonous, or just gross, but red flags waved in my mind that if I wanted to live, I should avoid it.

Though, if I had wanted to make sure I lived, I wouldn't have started picking fights with *monsters.* But to be fair, they started picking fights with my girl first.

"You know I'm not letting you leave." I say, mulling on the words as they come out, tasting the sweet venom infused into them, savoring the feeling as they roll around on my tongue before striking their prey.

"Oh, really? Because I'm almost certain you wouldn't hurt your poor girlfriend now, would you?" He asks as River lets out a blood-curdling scream. I twirl around to see her clutching her head, crumpled on her knees. Turning back to Mark, his smile grows tenfold, teeth accentuating the too-large gap.

Wasting no time, I dive for him. Forcing the sound of River's unmitigated wails out of my system. Fighting against the urge to run to her instead.

River barely breathes in between screams. Blood-curdling, pain-induced cries that shatter my ears, my bones, my heart. All of me needs to – demands to – go to her. To help her. But I know the only way to save her is to rid this world of this vitriol.

"Leave her alone, you *monster.*" I hiss as my fist grabs a tight handful of Mark's shirt, pushing him against the car. Both daggers pierce greasy skin, and deep black blood oozes from the open pinpoints.

River stops screaming. Just for a moment.

"You're going to have to call me a lot worse to make me reconsider." He mocks with a laugh, face squished against the window. I push the tip of one of the daggers deeper into his skin and he hisses. Saliva drips from the corners of his lips, smearing and sizzling on the glass. "The look on her pretty little face while I mind fuck her. Expose her to all the horrors she can handle, and then go deeper. To ancient horrors that'll certainly break her fragile little mind. Her terror's going to taste so *fucking divine.*"

"Don't you dare touch her." I bark, tightening my grip on his shirt and slicing down the grey skin of his cheek. He winces and the blade cuts deeper with his struggle.

"I don't have to." He laughs, a smirk on his gray and spit-riddled lips. "What do you think I'm doing to her *right now*?" My head spins, my vision lagging as River comes into view, contorted, floating in the air. Her mouth is wide open, but no noise leaves her. "No one can see her, either."

I hadn't turned my head. It was all in my head. I couldn't be certain it was a real image or an illusion. A trick to break me down. I hated to admit that it was working.

"Let her go." I demand. My grip tightening on the handles of my blades. "*Now.*"

"Make me, *lover boy.*" Mark chuckles. "You want her back, take her from my cold, dead hands. If there's anything left of her at that point."

"I will." I growl through clenched teeth. His eyes grow wide as one dagger sinks deep into his throat and he yelps out in pain as I tighten my grip on him, pinning him harder against the side of his car. Sagging face pinned against the window.

"You think you can kill me as easily as you did Chris?" He asks, muffled words seeping out into the world from all directions. The dagger doesn't hinder his ability to speak at all. His body squirms against my grip, against the dagger piercing his windpipe, unable to free himself and protesting the entire time. Seemingly mostly annoyed by the inconvenience of my physical strength.

One thing that Changelings don't possess is any large amount of physical strength. And I prided myself on just how physically fit I am.

My eyes flash to where River is. Or more like where she should be. Not in the sky. Not on the ground. Nowhere to be seen. Part of me is relieved. Maybe she ran far away from the danger. Part of me is terrified. Hoping she didn't get sucked into a portal to Hell. Because if monsters exist, I'll believe that portals to Hell exist.

"You want to make a big spectacle in the middle of your apartment complex parking lot? Do you want people to see you *kill* an innocent man? I don't look suspicious to anyone here but you, my friend." He chuckles, the sound almost demonic in nature. Something straight out of The Exorcist.

"I don't care if the entire world watches me rip your very being apart." I seethe. "You aren't going to like how painful your death is going to be. Because you fucked with the wrong man. You don't get to scare *my girl* and live to tell the tale."

"Kill me all you want. She'll still die in the end." He spits back, nearly hitting me in the eye. Anger fills my veins, swelling my very being with the need to kill. To drain his body of blood and burn the remains.

"Not if I have anything to say about it." I sneer. Flipping his head around, forcing himself to look in the side mirror of the car. I can just hope that there's silver in the mirror. Enough to end him. After a second of pinning him down, after nothing happens, I remove the dagger from his throat. He begins to chuckle wildly. Knowing my plan has failed me.

"You're going to have to do better than that, lover boy."

He snickers, catching me off guard and pushing me backward, sending me tumbling onto the pavement. Quickly, almost too quickly, he stalks over to me, peering down before I can even correct myself.

Slimy hands grasp the collar of my shirt, hoisting me up into a similar position I had pinned Mark in just moments before. Daggers fall out of my hands on impact.

Fist after fist connects with my jaw, my nose, my cheek. Punch after punch is thrown into me with full force that it feels as though I'll pass out from the pain alone. Blood fills my mouth, the taste of pennies, iron and salt, washes over my tongue and drains out the sides of my mouth and down my lungs.

Nothing could take the fight out of me. Not when it comes to River. Not when I just realized I love her. Not when I don't know how much time she has left. Not when I don't know if I'll even survive a *measly* changeling.

If I can't survive this, I don't deserve to.

River screams again, this time she sounds closer, but my eyes are focused on Mark as his fist comes raining down on my jaw repeatedly. Her cries are instantly silent, sounding more startled than in pain and terrorized.

My fists flying to make contact with him seem fruitless. I was so tired. Pain flows from each contact of Mark's fist. I am bloodied and my bruising knuckles send weakening punches his way, regardless of my fading strength. He lands a few hefty punches to my jaw and abdomen. A fight I surely wasn't going to win without a mirror or a flamethrower.

"Hey!" River yells, her voice angelic through the hell raining down on me. Mark turns to look at her, confusion dousing his gray features. "You're not done torturing me, are you?"

"What the fuck?" Mark mumbles, pausing just long enough for me to catch a glimpse of the blurry item in her hands. I scramble out of his grip while he's distracted. Scurrying to my angel as quickly as my tired body can manage.

"I think it's my turn to play." She smirks wickedly, tossing the glass bottle. A lit flame at the spout. The bottle cracks against the pavement at Mark's feet. The flame erupts wherever it touches.

Mark wails, frantically trying to put out the fire that's rapidly spreading over him, around him. A fire that can't be put out. Flames engulf not only him but his car. Certainly, the car fire would attract attention. Certainly, that'll kill him.

River comes around to me, and I drag her away from the scene. Her hands are delicate in mine, tears welling in her powerful eyes. Shudders fill her tense shoulders. She pulls me towards the lobby doors when she sees me lingering, staring at the blazing fire, concern fills the air around us. My hands shake with rage and relief.

She killed him.

And I failed her.

CHAPTER 21
River

Nothing could have prepared me for the terror that coursed through my veins when I realized that Mark was following me home. At first, I didn't notice him in a new Hellcat, completely different from the boxy pickup truck I've seen him driving for months now. I always made it a point to leave with a group and avoid him as much as possible. Even though it's been over two or three months since the wall-punching incident, I was still weary of being caught alone with him.

I spent the better part of a half hour taking wrong turns and side streets in an attempt to lose him. When he caught on to what I was doing and became belligerent, I didn't know what else to do. I didn't want to stop driving, the infinite possibilities of horror that unfolded in my mind nearly paralyzed me. I couldn't imagine a scenario that ended in a clean getaway, and graphic images flashed in my mind.

I was ready to fight, even if it was the last fight I ever had. I couldn't let that asshole win in any capacity, so I formed plan after plan in hopes that I could strategize my way out, but every iteration kept coming up with me bloodied, bruised, and left for dead.

So, I called Leon. I didn't want to ask for help. I couldn't imagine what he could do that I couldn't, but the chances of my demise shrunk with a witness. I could take him, I just needed someone to back me up.

I just needed Leon.

But the way his voice rang through the phone, the

guttural instinct, the confidence, the reassurance. It broke me down to my deepest core. The cracks in my armor caved heavily, similar to his footsteps down the concrete stairwell as he ran to my rescue. His reassuring words, the calmness of his voice like the lull of the ocean at midnight. All the uncertainty left my body the moment I saw him leaning against the trunk of his car. He was the one thing that grounded me in that moment. I took one look at him and knew that no matter what, he'd always be there for me. No questions asked.

As the tears streamed down my face, my blurry eyes glued on him as I watched the whole scene unfold at lightning speed. Sureness and rage were the only things looming behind his dark eyes. The man I knew, who was gentle and kind, wasn't there anymore, replaced by something much more primal.

I would have thought he was possessed.

But then I began to feel the things that Boyle had done to me resurfacing. The sting of metal in my mouth. Phantom slices over my skin that wracked my brain into screaming and screaming until my throat grew sore. My vision bottomed out only to return to the sight of Mark beating the absolute piss out of Leon. And Leon looked closer to death than I had ever expected to see him.

Oh, God.

I had brought this upon him. This wrath that he didn't deserve. He tried to protect me, but I put him in harm's way. So, I had to buck up. Fight fists with fire. The only weapon I could come up with was a homemade Molotov cocktail made from a partial bottle of vodka that had been hidden under my seat, an old scarf I meant to donate a long time ago, and a lighter stuffed in the center console that was there from my pot smoking days.

I wasn't even sure that it would work. Having no clue how to make an actual Molotov, only my vague knowledge from TV shows and the internet. I didn't know what else to do. But it worked. And thankfully, Leon was able to see my plan and leap out of the way.

His demeanor wasn't guarded like I had imagined it would be. He took my hand as I led him back into the complex, his arms finding solace around my shoulders in the elevator, his smile slowly returning the moment we were alone together.

Now, he stands in our bathroom, bloodied, and shirtless, staring at me with the softest doe eyes I've ever seen. Completely different from the ones who had been so willing to protect me just moments ago. We stood watching the limp body burn for only a moment before I dragged him back upstairs to clean him up, to talk through what had just happened.

I'm perched on the vanity counter in front of him, reigning in my undeniable attraction to the chiseled physique before me. Running a bloody washcloth over his features daintily, wiping away the evidence, wincing through the touch. I wish I could kiss his pain away, dotting his skin like sun-kissed freckles, but I don't want to cause any irritation.

One of his clean shirts lies on the back of the toilet, I had pulled it wrinkled from a pile of laundry we've been avoiding folding for about a week now.

I move my attention to his knuckles, his shaky hand rests in mine as the warm water rids his skin of his unwavering loyalty, and the desire to press his tanned skin up to my lips is ever present, like I can heal his wounds as an inept thank you for being my hero. My prince.

My gaze is focused on the scrapes on his otherwise perfect hands, unaware of how cautiously he's looking down at me until our eyes meet once I'm done. I set the washcloth in the sink and return to him with a smile that only stems from my appreciation and adoration of the relationship blossoming around us. No matter where our branches grow, our roots will remain bound into each other in an unmovable proclamation of devotion.

His fingers wrap around my chin, gently lifting my head. Sitting on this counter is the first time I've been at eye level with him standing. The light hits his face, casting shadows in the dimples of his cheeks.

"You're worried about me." He chuckles, his fingers moving to cup my cheek, the gentleness of his touch sends shivers over my skin.

My hand comes up to find purchase around his wrist. "Am I not supposed to?" I ask, watching the light dance in his watchful eyes.

"I never said not to." He flashes his stark white teeth.

"Are you worried about me?" I whisper, the weight of my words almost too heavy to bear. A witty comment flashes across his face. He doesn't say it, but the look that follows answers where his words fail. We share the silence that surrounds us, his hand moving from my cheek to my neck. The electricity flowing from his fingertips raises goosebumps on my arms.

"Thank you for saving me." He whispers in return after a moment of prolonged stillness. I lean in, placing the softest peck on his non-injured cheek. His skin is soft and warm, the singular constant in my life these days. He smiles and plants a firm kiss on my lips, wincing ever so slightly.

"I'd say you saved me." I say, avoiding his gaze. "I didn't know what else to do. I'm sorry I put you in that situation." The words rush out of me rapidly, guilt riddling my joints.

"Shh, don't be sorry." He reassures me. "I'm glad you called me, angel." He wraps his arms around my waist, hands resting on my lower back he takes a step forward, standing between my legs. "I'm sorry I failed you."

"What?" I ask harshly, unsure what he means. "You didn't fail me. What are you talking about?"

"*You* killed him. I wasn't the one who saved you. You saved me. And I failed you, but I won't do it again. I swear."

"You didn't fail me, Leon." I nearly wept at his exhausted admission. "You came to my rescue. You come to my rescue every time I call. I couldn't let him hurt you anymore. I had to do something." His eyes were wide, gazing at me with a culmination of emotions I couldn't pinpoint.

There were a million things I wanted to tell him. How I had no idea that the cocktail would be successful. How I had just so happened to have a mostly empty bottle of vodka still stowed away under the seat because I was too lazy to ever fish it out after it had fallen during a post-college move.

How I'd never been so elated to see someone burn to death. Or that I had seen this creature inside of Boyle all those months ago and now I see them everywhere. I wouldn't have had so many nightmares had I not kept seeing these *monsters.*

And I had heard him call Mark a monster, just like I knew he was. The too-big mouth, pale gray skin, empty eyes. Was Leon calling Mark a monster for following me, or had Leon seen him for what he truly was?

I rest my head on his shoulder, unable to form any sense of my internal monologue. Not wanting to further ruin Leon's day with my crazy talk. We stay like this for a moment too brief.

"I hope I didn't scare you." His words are muffled through my shirt, nestled in the crook of my neck. His lips press against my collarbone as he talks, a sensation that I've grown quite fond of.

"You could never scare me, Leon." I say, running my nails along his shoulder blades. His arms squeeze me tightly, reminding me just how strong he is. "Never."

He lets out a breathy laugh and untangles our limbs. The emptiness lingers with the smell of pennies and Hermes cologne.

"Shall we hit the road?" He asks.

"Am I going to need to find a new job?" I ask as he slips the clean shirt on. Leon guides me out into the living room with our conjoined hands.

"I'll take good care of you, angel." He smirks at me over his shoulder, winking as he does so.

"You better." I tease with a well-worn smile.

CHAPTER 22

Leon

This trip is going to be one for the books and we haven't even left the state yet. Between the karaoke sessions, the silly trivia games, and the debriefing of who I'll encounter in Virginia, this is the happiest I've seen her in a long time. All the while, my hand stays firmly planted on her thigh.

I'm honestly surprised she's this jovial after what we both endured earlier.

The backlight of the car illuminates her perfect features, capturing only the major hills and valleys of her body as she snuggles into the seat with her knees against the center console, facing me. Both her arms engulf one of mine as if to claim a piece of me that wasn't my heart. My fingertips brush up and down her leg, drawing incomprehensible shapes into the denim of her jeans. Even the moon can see her sleepy smile from its place in the stars.

We stop somewhere around Charlotte, North Carolina for a late dinner of chicken nuggets, fries, and sodas bigger than our heads. She offers to pay but I decline, and she makes a joke about how it's high time I start taking care of her.

She reminds me of stories from her college years, how she got a full ride to her university despite "what happened to [her] in [her] childhood." Whatever that means.

She asks me about my childhood, and I tell her that it was just me and my grandma most of my life. I tell her more about Elio and some of the shit we used to get up to. About how my parents weren't around much and how only my grandmother came to my taekwondo matches. How my grandmother tried her best to raise me to be kind and respectful. The gut-wrenching day that she got diagnosed with dementia. We had to decide then and there that it would be best to move her back to her hometown with my uncle, her only son.

She sits back and listens intently, careful not to interrupt any of my stories. When I've said all I could say, she squeezes my hand gently, almost as if to say thank you for sharing.

As we pass into Virginia, she grows antsy, and the calm and happiness that once existed within her is rapidly replaced with restlessness. Leg bouncing, fidgeting, and nervous ticks. I try to keep my hands on her at all times, giving her any kind of reassurance that I've got her. We've got this. There are still almost three hours until we arrive at our hotel, and her armor seems to be disintegrating with each passing mile. I squeeze her hand, one that causes her eyes to look in my direction.

There's so much I wish I could say to her. So many things that I wish I could put into words that would bring some sense of comfort. The things I wish I could say to ease the pain behind her eyes. She's helped me more in the last few months than I think I'll ever be able to repay.

Maybe that's why my hands always long to find her. They don't just miss her. They *need* to speak to her. A language all their own. One I'm still learning. I'm not sure she even understands, but maybe if I keep speaking it, we'll learn together. Maybe I'll spend the rest of my life trying to make it up to her, to show her how special she is, how priceless I view our time together, and how she occupies the space in my mind even when she's not around.

The words of both Astra and Mark linger around me. The prophecy of her death. Of our short time together. I have to find a way to stop it. I don't give a damn about fate. What kind of life to live if I just accept that she's meant to die, and I have to sit back and accept it?

"You're awfully quiet." I say, my thumb rubbing the top of her hand. A very hypocritical statement, I know. She hums gently but makes no move to further the conversation until I nudge her. She's breaking my heart.

"Am I a coward?" She asks, the self-doubt ever present in her voice. I ask her what for.

"What?"

"Because I'm scared."

"Why are you scared?"

"I haven't seen them since I graduated high school."

"Who?"

"My foster parents."

"*What?*" I ask, dumbfounded at this new information. A stark revelation that I truly don't know her as well as I'd like to think I do.

"I guess I have to tell you now, huh?" A nervous laugh escapes into the air surrounding the both of us in a level of tension I haven't felt from her before. "When I was twelve, I was taken from my parents and placed into foster care. My bio-parents were charged with child neglect and went to prison. I lived with the Cohens right up until the state checks stopped coming. Then, I lived with Nancy until I graduated and moved away for college. My parents both died in a car accident shortly after my eighteenth birthday after they got out of jail. I haven't seen the Cohens since that summer, and I'm scared I'll run into them. There's only like 500 people in this town." Her words are vulnerable and scared, just like they were pleading on the phone earlier.

"Did they hurt you?" I ask sternly. She doesn't answer, shrouding the car in silence. Thinking that these people who were entrusted to keep her safe had harmed her lit a fury inside of me that I couldn't simmer. The pitiful look in her eyes is giving me a million reasons to start my career as an arsonist. "Did they *hurt* you?"

"Their oldest son-" Her voice breaks, delicate fingers

HM DAWLEY

grip my forearm in an attempt to ground herself from what she's preparing herself to say. "He liked to watch me when I changed. Would sneak into the bathroom while I showered. Came into my room and jack off while I slept."

Dear god, what the fuck.

"What's his name?" I asked through clenched teeth.

"He never touched me." She pleads, tears welling in her voice. The pain is nearly too much to bear. For the both of us.

"Just tell me his name, River." I hadn't used her government name in so long that it felt like acid on my tongue. Like I hadn't meant to say it, yet I said it with such voracity that I was certain she'd slink away from me.

"Please don't do this. I don't want to cause any trouble." She pleaded, her nails digging into my skin.

"What's his name?" I demand, fist clenched around the steering wheel, trying to redirect the growing fury.

"Brian." She breathes. I spent a moment mulling over the name, Brian Cohen. The name rings some sort of bell, but I can't pinpoint the source. My face must have contorted into something vicious because she asks, "What is it?" She studies the silence that lingers between us. Her tears recede, even if it was minimal.

"Nothing. Just memorizing the name of my mortal enemy." I retort, eliciting a huffed laugh from her.

"Okay, Almost Batman. You're about 960 million and two dead parents short, but I can respect the grind."

"I've got the money; you've got the dead parents. We're a perfect duo." I riposte. We laugh at the jokes, but when the dust settles, we're both silent. The only noise that surrounds us is the wind around the car and the barely audible song playing on the radio.

The rest of the ride is half-comfortably quiet. The whole time, I'm plotting what I would do to this Brian dude if I ever got the displeasure of meeting him. All the ways I could make his life an absolute living hell. At some point, she falls asleep, curled up in her reclined seat. Her tiny snores are the cutest thing I've ever heard, reminding me to breathe through all the rage building inside of me.

We pull up to the resort, a looming brick building with a white dome and white pillars nestled in the woods. The property lights expand in all directions, illuminating different areas and activities that were closed at 2 AM. I park the car, and the jolt of the car wakes River. I climb out of the car and sprint around to the passenger side to open her door. I extend a hand to help her out and she expresses her sleepy gratitude. I retrieve our bags from the backseat before we make our way into the main lobby.

She quickly sobers up as her eyes dart around the hotel lobby. Panic overtakes her eyes once again. She leans in and says, "What the fuck are we doing here?" I don't intend to answer the rhetorical question, but we reach the front desk before she has time to ask again.

The receptionist greets us warmly and we return the formalities. "What can I do for you tonight?" The receptionist was a tiny woman, no more than 4'11 and 90 pounds soaking wet. She can't be more than 20 years old with a very goth persona. Her badge says Ginger.

"One standard king room, please." River says before I have any opportunity to form a sentence, let alone speak. I squeeze her elbow. She looks at me with confusion as Ginger asks some clarifying questions.

"What's your finest room?" I ask, feeling the public stoic look harden over my face. Ginger is taken aback by the question, mumbling to herself while she looks at availability.

"We have our Luxury President's Suite available. This room is our most luxurious, premier room on the property, sir."

"Tonight, and tomorrow night available?" I ask. She nods. "Perfect. We'll take it." I glance over at River, whose jaw is scraping the floor. I can't stifle a laugh at her bewilderment. Ginger gives us the total and I pay. Ginger and River have near identical looks of disorientation, though River looks like she's going to hurl in the nearby gold trash can. Ginger processes our room keys and gives us a rundown of all there is to do at the resort, and I ask what time the pools close. She says that they're open 24/7, but there's only a lifeguard from 10 to 7. I thank her for her time and service and drag my lovely companion toward the elevators.

"I could kill you." She mumbles, intentionally beating me to the elevator button.

"You wouldn't." I laugh.

"I could."

"Why, then?"

"You just spent SIX THOUSAND DOLLARS ON A HOTEL ROOM!" She whisper-yells. "Are you out of your ever-loving mind?!" *For you, always.* "And you have a Black Card?!"

"We all have our secrets, angel. My net worth *apparently* isn't one of them." I tease, wrinkling my nose at her. She rolls her eyes, and we get on the newly opened elevator. I press the tenth-floor button, and we glide up to the clouds. She huffs, a dusting of blush wafting over her cheeks again. "What is it?"

"What?" She asks, eyes avoiding me. I tucked my thumb and index finger around her chin, forcing her eyes on me. Without having to ask again, she continues. "I used to work here in high school. This place was overpriced ten years ago, I knew it was going to be more expensive now. You didn't need to pay for a room we'll barely be in at all." Her eyes held a sense of guilt that I was beginning to understand. The pieces of her history paint the picture of abuse and neglect at the hands of the people who were supposed to take care of her. Even if she doesn't know it herself, her past is still haunting her in drastic ways. I feel for her.

"I don't know about you, but I plan on being in this room *quite a bit.* Besides, I like spoiling you." I shrug as the elevator dings, opening up to a small foyer with a singular door on the adjacent side. We step lightly onto the plush carpet. I move to open the door, but her hand clasps around my elbow. As I gaze down at her, I panic. *Did I say too much?*

"Sorry, I'm just not used to all of this." She gestures vaguely around the room. "The *'luxury'* treatment. The expensive rooms in fancy hotels. Being chauffeured around my dinky hometown by a rich man who drives an expensive car and wears expensive clothes, who also lives in a relatively shitty apartment complex. I'm just getting whiplash, is all."

I nod, somewhat understanding where she's coming from, but not entirely. Most people would be ecstatic to get their very own rich husband.

"I just want to make you comfortable. You deserve it." I say as I usher us into the room, taking in all of the plush carpet, white marble, and high-end art that littered the nearly 1,500-square-foot penthouse, and for a moment, I understood her confusion. In my everyday life, I don't live that lavishly. The car and parts of my wardrobe, sure, but I try to blend in normally, I buy groceries and cook for myself. I don't go to high-end restaurants to eat gold-dusted caviar. I enjoy the barely eight hundred square feet of my apartment and not being surrounded by other rich people. I like being reminded I'm human.

"I'm sorry if I've made you uncomfortable with all of this. That was never my intention." I apologize, gazing longingly at the most beautiful woman I've ever seen gliding her fingers over a particular painting in the foyer.

"What are your intentions?" She asks. The question hangs in the air as we stand face to face, and I wonder what kind of show I really am putting on for her. I intend to spend eternity treating this goddess-like royalty. To show my appreciation for her being in my life. Her persistent sunshine is the only thing that keeps me going some days. I want to make her feel the way she makes me feel.

But I can't say that, can I?

I can't confess that there's a building volcano in my chest and I don't know if it'll turn into love or heartbreak or both. I don't know if I would want to go back to being strangers if it came down to it. If my Friday nights return to being filled with late nights in the studio to drown out the violent voices in my head. I would desperately miss the laughter that swims in our apartment where we're curled up under a blanket on my couch watching a show that I didn't think I would be that into.

I won't forget how supple her skin feels underneath my touch or the taste of her that lingers in my mouth like sweet candy. I can't lay my feelings on the line, on the slim chance that she'll understand, because what happens if she doesn't? Will she find it weird and creepy if I confess to her in the first place? Surely, she wouldn't want to be friends with someone who fell in love with her after only a couple of months.

I'm in love with her. I've been avoiding those words, because if I acknowledge them, then they're real. Then, suddenly, my world could collapse around me. I can't lose her to some words, but I love her. *I'm in love with her.*

God, I'm so in love with her. My heart has never been so full. I look into her eyes and see a future, our future. It's crystal clear. A wedding in Vegas. A honeymoon in the Bahamas. A cozy home in a cul-de-sac with a fenced yard. Big Christmas trees that we make a tradition to decorate each year. Flowers bouquets that I pick from our very own garden weekly, just because.

But it's so much more than the big moments. It's the small ones, too. It's waking up next to her, feeling her body, and kissing her forehead as the sun crests over the horizon. It's hearing her sing in the shower in the morning before work, packing her lunches, kissing her goodbye knowing for certain that she'll always come back to me. There's supposed to be certainty in our future, like the North Star, always guiding me home.

But there's also uncertainty. Looming in the shadows. Her supposed demise. *My* demise. I can't live without her. I can't, I can't, I can't. I love her. I love her. I love her.

"To have a good time with you." I say with a smirk, avoiding the internal turmoil. She rolls her eyes and gives me a cheesy grin, but I sense she isn't happy with my answer.

"Smartass." She mumbles, but she doesn't press it any further. She grabs her bag and heads in the direction of the bathroom.

I gathered the clothes from my suitcase for a much-needed shower. As I'm doing so, I hear the soft pad of footfalls enter the room and then abruptly stop. I turn around to see the blush rise to her full cheeks at the sight of me in just my boxers. Like this woman hasn't seen me naked before, let alone in underwear. I chuckle involuntarily.

"Don't act like you haven't seen me naked before." I snark. She climbs into bed and she's sitting cross-legged with a smirk on her face as she eyes me up and down.

"It's one of my favorite sights." She sighs, resting her elbows on her thighs, grinning at me from ear to ear.

"Is that so, angel?" I ask, moving towards her. She tosses her phone on the bedside table, drool pooling in the corners of her agape mouth. "I was going to let you get some rest, but I think you've gotten yourself worked up." I tease, taking her hand in mine and rubbing it along my growing cock. She fights back a gasp at the abruptness but doesn't pull away.

"Do you need me to help you with that?" She asks, looking up at me with wide, glistening eyes. My hands search her body, roaming over the hills and valleys of her silhouette. She's aching to be touched, and who am I to deny her?

"Please, angel." I beg, my tone dark and intentional. She palms my hardening cock through my boxers, moving to the edge of the bed. She tugs at my cock, releasing it from its constraints before spitting on it. She rubbed in the saliva with a couple of pressured strokes, enjoying the moans I release from pleasure. My hands find her hair, their favorite place to be, gripping close to the scalp and forcing her head down on my cock. She opens her mouth obediently, taking me in as her tongue swirls and laps up the precum that seeps onto her velvet tongue.

She moves her hand into her shorts, fingering herself while sucking my cock like the *good girl* she is. I can feel myself wanting to cum from her luscious mouth. I pull her back by her hair, throwing her down onto the bed, ripping off her shorts before her back can hit the mattress. "My god, angel." I groan, lapping up her wetness, hearing her gasps as my tongue licks and sucks. My hands grip her thighs hard enough to surely leave bruises, keeping her legs spread apart so I can see all of her begging for me. She arches her back, fingers laced into the bedsheets, her legs begging to be set free. She's always so sensitive and always dripping for me, it's completely unfair that I can't have her for every meal.

"Oh, baby." She whines as my tongue flicks around her hardened clit, pulsating with every stroke. I throw her legs over my shoulders, sliding two fingers inside of her, wishing I could swim in her orgasm as it comes crashing down around me. I lap at her cum like a thirsty bastard, her legs shaking violently as she screams out obscenities.

I'm so ravenous for her, I can't wait for her to come down. I keep lapping at her until I feel my cock pulsing, aching to be inside her tight pussy. Flipping her over and pulling her to the edge of the bed, I pin her arms behind her back and line up my cock at her entrance. Her legs shake harder as I thrust myself inside her, both of us releasing primal moans, her pussy soaking my cock, taking all of me as I slam into her repeatedly.

"Look at me. Let me see you." I demand. She turns her head so I can see the pleasure on her perfect little face as I fuck her just like she needs to be. Her slack-jawed look paired with her dripping pussy make me almost lose it. "Fuck me, angel. You're so perfect. And all for me."

"Yes, baby. All for you." She groans. My thrusts grow sloppy at the sounds that leave her fucked lips. She knows that calling me baby will always send me over the edge. I keep fucking her, hard and rhythmic thrusts as she's moaning out obscenities once again. With one final thrust, slamming as far into her as I can, I shoot my load, coming all over her perfect little pussy. After she's taken every last drop, I ease out of her, pulling her up onto the bed. I slip us both under the blanket, wrapping her in my arms, drinking in how beautiful she looks all fucked out.

My hands trace her body gently, still feeling her muscles vibrate from how hard she came. She looks up at me with big doe eyes and a smile.

"You're so cute." She laughs, leaning weakly over to plant a kiss on my lips. I brush a piece of hair out of her eyes as she tilts her head toward me.

"I'd say you're cuter, angel."

"I disagree." She retorts, but all I can do is chuckle.

"Get some sleep."

"Make me."

"I think I just did." I tease. She rolls her eyes and snuggles closer into my chest. We lay in relative silence for a few moments, and I'm almost certain she's asleep until she says something.

"Have you ever been in love?" She asks, a heaviness in her voice that I can't quite place. I panicked for just a moment, not ready to give up my words yet, but the tone she took didn't sound like she's phishing for something.

"Yeah," I sigh, feeling this thousand-pound weight lifted off my chest. I didn't admit it, but I did, in a roundabout way.

"What was she like?" She pushes. "Assuming it's a girl, of course. I don't want to judge if-"

"She's lovely." I reply. She hums solemnly before I get a chance to continue, a light snore echoing where her hum ends. I can't help but smile and sigh in relief that I don't have to explain. She probably didn't catch my answer either. "She's the most beautiful woman in the world." I whisper, pulling the sheets up around her chin. "She's an amazing woman." I pause, making sure to keep the tears in and my voice low so as not to wake her. "I love her endlessly." She snuggles into my chest where we fit together. I drift off to sleep with my love in my arms. Where I intend to keep her for as long as I can.

CHAPTER 23

River

As the morning sun crests over my still sleepy eyes, a new sensation washes over me, one I can't quite put my finger on. At least, not until the consciousness comes back to me. Strong, muscular arms have snaked their way around my still-bare waist. Fingertips graze my stomach underneath the shirt that never got discarded. The clock on the wall says six fifty-nine, and I'm reminded of another Florence Cromwell poem I read once.

The sun will lay across your skin, a kiss from Mother Nature.
As she too understands the beauty of you.
The breath held desperately will puff through my nose,
as I grip your fingertips.
Through it all, the vast changes of seasons,
I'll still hold you, nose to nose,
my hand will tightly wring through yours.
The birds, the squirrels, the flower beds,
and even the wind will cease all function.
For even they will understand my pure
and unrequited love for you.

When I was little, I perceived love very differently than I do now. I think we all do. We become cynical after everyone seemingly lets us down. When you're young, you give your friends cool rocks you find on the playground. The older you get, the more you start bargaining with things of higher value to appease people who don't deserve the discount.

But this? This is different. We are a planetary force, with an undeniable gravitational pull, and I'm uncertain if we'll collide catastrophically, or rotate in harmony.

There's a deep-seated ache in my muscles that stems from the physical exhaustion of yesterday's endeavors, most of which I haven't bothered unpacking. Fear has the most excruciating toll on the body, and I'd venture to say that I experienced it in excess. I don't particularly like showing weakness, as I feel it isn't becoming of me, but Leon brings such a sense of stability and comfort that it's almost involuntary.

I enjoyed our trip up here, despite having debilitating anxiety for half of the ride up here. I got to hear his reason why he's so grumpy on the outside, and I get it now. He'd built castle walls and a moat around what remained of his heart. Everyone has disappointed him, and I somehow feel inclined to take his heart into my hands and warm it.

I adore him in all the childlike ways you adore your best friend and all the best ways you adore your lover. There isn't a part of him that I've seen so far that I didn't want to wash my hands in, but I can't help but think we're moving so fast. Or maybe I'm just used to traditionally slow relationships. Though, if he keeps looking at me like I hung his constellations, I'd say yes to running away and getting married before the words even left his lips cold.

But maybe it's all a fruitless endeavor. Maybe we're destined for now and not forever. If so, will the poetry he writes if this all goes wrong elicit the same guttural reactions ten (twenty, fifty?) years later, the same way it pulls me to the brink of my existence in the moment? Or will our happy ending only be told as folklore to children? The kind of love to be yearned for by teenage girls? Will I survive this if I'm swept away by the current?

Would we find each other again if we're reincarnated? Will we in other universes feel the same way as I do right now? Will I recognize him through space in time? Do I get the privilege of experiencing this love in every lifetime?

Love. I do love him, that much is certain. I love him like the sun loves the moon. I can't put stock in anything in this life but my love for him.

Before we were close, my eyes could find him in any crowd, and it was like a yearning in my soul. A desperation to be near him, to speak with him, even if just for a moment. There's always been a pull to him that I've never been able to explain. We somehow always managed to find each other, no matter where we were. No matter that we were strangers. No matter that he didn't know I dreamt of him, yet he was always familiar. Comfortable. Warm. Strong. Like home.

I used to be a big flirt on purpose. I liked how I could flirt my way in and out of all types of situations with people of any gender, but whatever spell he cast on me has disabled all cognitive function and I turn into a babbling mess with no coherent thoughts.

I remember the delicacy at which he plucked a small piece of lint off my cheek, how it felt like my heart ceased to function and so did time. It was just us, and that's when it all went downhill. I may have been able to fight off the feelings had he not been such a duality with his unapproachable façade that was intimidating and hot as hell. Half the time I was worried I was doing more harm than good when I would call out to him or say hello, but somewhere along the way, I could see the icy exterior thawing, revealing more of his true personality. The twinkle in his eyes whenever he laughed made it all worth it.

I've always been good at reading people, having studied behavior my whole life. Confident in my ability to strike up a conversation with just about anyone, enjoying being a stranger you feel comfortable talking to. Revel in knowing that I've left the conversation having easily pulled information from someone and that they didn't even get my name. However, my homebody tendencies have always hindered my ability to make and keep friends.

That, and my inability to see the good in anyone.

Maybe it's because I hated the pity parties that seemed to follow me anytime I would tell someone what had happened to me as a kid. I hated it then. I still hate it. I hate being perceived for what happened to me rather than the person I am. I don't like being seen as anything but able to handle whatever situation I'm in.

When I was twelve, the night that I was taken from my parents, I remember sitting in the social worker's office in the middle of the night. She gave me animal crackers and grape juice and told me she'd stay with me until they found a placement for me. I begged her to tell me why she took me from my parents, but she never caved. She never told me what happened that night, just that I wasn't safe there. I remember the pity in her eyes as she looked at my unwashed rat's nest of hair, my stained and dirty clothes were all the confirmation she needed that she was doing a good job.

But that was normal for me. I was used to wearing hand-me-downs from the neighborhood kids and eating food from the food pantry that mostly consisted of top ramen, mixed fruit, and beans. I was used to the bullying that happened regularly by kids who saw any signs of weakness and ran with it. The teachers looked at me with the same pity in their eyes as that social worker did, and I grew to despise it. I grew bitter on the inside, but no one got to see that.

I had a part to play. The little girl inside of me asked what we did to deserve all of that, a near stranger on the outside who laughed in the face of danger. We didn't deserve what happened to us. I so desperately wish I could be the one sitting in that social worker's office to talk with her. I would tell that scared little girl that not everything that happens to us is our fault. Bad things happen, and we can't explain it, but things will get better. That she'll work a million times harder to give herself the opportunities that others were handed on silver platters. That she'll spend her whole life running from the boogeyman, but that she's strong. I'd encourage her to stand up for herself more and never let people talk shit about her without giving them a reason.

That twelve-year-old little girl deserves a fucking apology. She deserves so much more than the life she was forced to live. The psychological abuse, the sexual abuse, the bullying, the attempted suicide at sixteen. It all pales in comparison to the complete loss of her innocence. She didn't know what was going on. She thought all the things that she experienced were normal. That she deserved everything that happened. She looked at the mess her parents left, the devastation that surrounded her when the dust settled, and was forced to grow up in the blink of an eye.

One minute, you're playing in the creek down the hill from the trailer park without a care in the world. Next, you're planning your future before you get your first period. You spend all your library time taking career aptitude tests and studying for tests with the fury of a thousand suns because you can't bear the idea of being stuck in that godforsaken hell hole reliving the worst days of your life surrounded by the people who made your life a living hell.

Through it all, I always had Nancy. She's been nice to me since our kindergarten hopscotch days. She snuck clothes she outgrew to me whenever I would stay the night. Always under the guise of *'I can't wear them anymore and I know you can because you're smaller than me.'* She was always taller and curvier than me. I was plump, still am, but her clothes always had a worn comfort about them, and her laundry always smelled like lavender.

I know moving out of state was a point of contention in our friendship. She probably curses my name often for leaving her all alone in a town we both swore to leave, but I never thought that she would fill my absence with Brian Cohen. He makes me nauseous just thinking about him. I don't know what good she sees in him, but I know what she doesn't see.

She doesn't see the years of torture he put me through.

She didn't know that I would find him standing over my bed while I slept, that he would try to take pictures of me in the shower, or that he would jack off over my dirty clothes whenever he thought I wasn't home. This lasted until I moved out at eighteen. Which just so happened to be the year his younger sister, Angie turned twelve.

He had a new focus then. A bond he had been grooming her whole life. I could see the pattern and it made me angry and sick to my stomach. I saw little me in the confusion in her eyes. The way his comments made her severely uncomfortable, but no one ever believed he was capable of doing any harm. It was my duty to protect her because no one protected me.

I took her aside one night and I told her he did the same thing to me. That if he made her uncomfortable, she had the right to stand up for herself. If she ever needed someone, to call me. That was the last thing I said to her before I had to leave. The confidence returned to her, and I felt like I had done my part.

That was until, of course, I saw the news reports about a month later. I was working in this exact hotel and my manager, Cody, had the news running in his office, and I could faintly hear it from the front desk.

Twelve-year-old girl's body found in stream.

At first, I didn't think anything of it, it was tragic, but I didn't put two and two together.

The body of Angelica Cohen was recovered from the stream in the early morning hours, just thirteen days after her disappearance.

The news coverage had interviewed the family, the parents yelling, screaming, and crying to catch their baby's killer, recanting the story of how she was taken from their home through the window. *It has to be someone we know, and we won't stop until we find this sick son of a bitch and throw him under the jail.*

The police never considered Brian a suspect, but I had

my suspicions. I came to the funeral, like most of town, and I cried for the first time in six years.

Did I do this to her? Did I warn her to stand up for herself and did she pay the price?

She'd be twenty-two now, almost twenty-three. She should be out partying, drinking, having fun with her friends, dating, and going to college if she wanted to. Not dead in the ground somewhere in bum-fuck nowhere. She always said she wanted to be an astronaut, and while I know that was just the imagination of a go-getter kid, I like to imagine that she was serious. That the little girl went on to work for NASA. That in another universe, she gets the justice and the life she deserves.

It's seven fifteen, and the sun peaks over the horizon just a little more than before. Backlighting the mountains that surround us. I attempt to wiggle free from Leon's iron grip, but it only makes the vice tighter. I let out a half-frustrated sigh and rotated in his arms. Turning to face the sleeping prince.

His eyes, heavy and barely open, linger on my face like he's seeing me for the first time. Like he's never woken up to the sight of me before. I have half a mind to say something snarky, but I stop myself. Allowing myself this moment of tranquility. He has no idea how much this means to me. How much *he* means to me or how indebted I am to him.

That I love him.

Perhaps one day I'll be able to roll over like this and kiss his nose and tell him just how in love I am with him. But today's not it. Today's the day for laying my head on his chest, wrapping my arms around his bare waist, and drinking in the quiet time. It's been go, go, go for what feels like fifteen years. And for the first time since then, I can finally breathe.

A nagging, almost acidic feeling swirls in the back of my throat. Anxiety builds in the pit of my stomach with each passing second. Something's going to go wrong today. I can feel it shake my bones like a warning sign.

A death rattle.

Leon hums quizzically, bringing the arm that was once

wrapped around my waist up my spine, allowing his forearm to run parallel with it as his hands find purchase in my hair. As his fingers trace stars into the base of my skull and an ache settles over my body as the nerves ramp up, all I can hear are his words from yesterday. *'I've got you.'*

"Good morning." He says the base in his voice echoing through my ribcage. "How'd you sleep, angel?"

"Good morning to you, too." I comment, raising my head from his chest to kiss his swollen lips. "I slept heavenly. You?"

"Like a baby." He flashes me a pearly smile, and the conversation falters. We stare at each other and I'm unable to think of a single thing to say when Leon interrupts. "Hey, what was with that question last night?"

"What question?" I ask, knitting my eyebrows together.

"You don't remember?" He asks, surprised.

I shake my head no. "The last thing I remember was you making a smart-ass comment about making me go to sleep." I say, trying my damnedest to jog my memory on what he's talking about. "What? Did I ask something outlandish?" I ask, pulling away from him to sit up. Thoroughly perplexed.

"Oh no, if you don't remember, then you don't get to know." He teases, trying to pull me back down gently. He's not trying, because he's strong enough to take me down without any issue.

"No! Tell me!" I plead. He sits up next to me, the blanket falling off his chest and pooling around his hips.

"Nah, I don't think I will." He smirks as he hops out of bed and sprints towards the bathroom. Cackling the whole way. Butt ass naked.

I climb out of bed and stretch out the stiffness accumulating in my muscles. I throw my shorts back on and wander around the suite, taking in the finer details. Spending some time looking over the paintings in each room, the ornate ceilings, and the marble fireplace in the living room before I come across a binder full of resort activities, restaurants, and room service menus. I picked out a couple of items for the both of us before calling and placing our order for breakfast.

I meander out onto our balcony. The icy December wind nips through my thin clothes, burning my skin. The dull gray of the mountainside is beginning to liven up with the incoming sun rays. The cold, wood railing pierces my fingertips, and the sharp air enters my nose.

I wasn't out on the balcony long before the sliding door rustled behind me and out popped just the head of a very handsome man scowling at me.

"You'll catch a cold!" Leon calls from the crack in the door, wearing nothing but a towel around his waist. His mop of hair soaking wet. When our eyes meet, he opens the door and ushers me inside, shivering as the air pierces his exposed skin.

"If you didn't get me sick that one time, then I don't think a little mountain air is going to kill me." I tease, hooking my fingers into his loosely tied towel. He slinks back with a tiny yelp, and I cackle maniacally.

"I didn't try hard enough. I'll keep it in mind to spit down your throat next time I'm sick." He snips, taking my hands in his to warm them up.

"Why wait?" I tease, with a wink. A bewildered look flashes over his eyes, but before he can reply, there's a knock on the door. "Perfect! Breakfast!"

"You got room service?" He asks, following me to get to the door, his arms folded over his chest.

"Is that a problem, Mister I-Like-to-Spoil-You?" I ask with a quirk of my eyebrow at him and his unexpected attitude.

"Only if you didn't get me anything." He pouts. Trailing behind, he stands a few feet back while I grab the door, suddenly self-conscious of his naked body. It makes me giggle, because how can he be self-conscious? He's smoking.

"Well lucky for you, I did." I answer, wheeling the cart in from the hallway, stopping just long enough to lift the lids of both plates. One plate had two over-easy eggs, sausage patties, and hashbrowns while the other had a stack of strawberry cheesecake pancakes with fresh-cut strawberries and whipped cream.

"Then no problem here." He says, practically drooling.

"Are you eating breakfast naked?" I retort, pulling the lids back on the plates.

"If you're up for it." He smirks and I roll my eyes. "What? You don't like the view?" He asks, raising his arms and giving me a spin. Halfway through, his towel comes loose, and he flashes me. He yells and runs off into the next room. I can't contain my laughter as I end up doubled over. He's yelling obscenities and pouting very loudly. After I pick myself off the floor, I take the plates over to the little breakfast nook in the living room.

He returns a moment later dressed to the nines. Fresh black slacks that accentuate his legs and ass. A tight black button-up shirt with the sleeves rolled up to the elbows. I give him a whistle, catcalling him as he blushes and hides his face.

"Don't be shy! I've never seen you this snazzy!" I tease.

"You've seen me naked." He retorts, his ears flushed red.

"Yes, and you're smoking. This-" I wave my fork up and down his body. "Is also insanely hot, you know."

"Is that why you wanted a strip tease after the award show?" He asks, sitting down across from me at the table.

"What can I say, you look good with and without clothes. You can't expect me to contain myself when you look so scrumptious." I compliment him, reveling in his shyness. "We're going to a birthday party, you know. Not a wedding."

"I have to impress your friend's friends." He says, digging into his breakfast.

"And you're going to show up your girlfriend. I didn't pack anything nearly as fancy." I whine.

"Lucky for you, I like spoiling you." He says with a mischievous look in his eyes.

"What are you planning?" I ask skeptically.

"You'll see."

CHAPTER 24

Leon

After breakfast, I finished getting ready while River took a shower. I took a minute to admire the us-sized dent in the covers before making up the bed. This felt normal and welcomed, something I'd sell my soul to have it last forever.

The bathroom quiets as the shower flutters off. I can't help myself from stealing a long, breathtaking look at her when she comes into view. A towel wrapped around her body, shoulder-length hair dripping water down her collarbone. I can feel the drool pooling in the corners of my agape mouth. She notices my stare, releasing an airy giggle.

"Like what you see, lover boy? She teases with a wink.

"Always," I swoon, moving close to her, my hands instantly finding the curves in her waist. She blushes when I wink back at her, swooping in to give her a feverish kiss that I know will leave her a little hot and bothered before I slip out of the room, giving her a bit of privacy.

Once she's ready, she comes to find me. She's dressed in the brown plaid pants, cropped army green ribbed sweater, and chunky boots I'd packed for her. Dainty gold jewelry adorns her ears, neck, and fingers. Her damp hair curls at the ends naturally. *When did she get a nose ring?* All this time I've spent studying the lines of her face, I never once noticed a septum piercing.

"Is this new?" I ask.

"No, I wear a spacer or tuck it in. I'm not allowed to have it for work." She sighs. I take a moment to look at how the simple gold ring sits on her face. The contrast it brings to her freckled cheeks.

"Tragic." I say. She looks at me with confusion. "It suits you." *There it is.* A crimson blush floods her cheeks, her eyes now avoiding mine, inspecting the very interesting floor. "You look gorgeous, per usual."

"Thank you." She whispers shyly.

"Shall we?" I asked, holding out my bent elbow for her to link her arm through. She flashes a faint smile and takes my arm in hers.

I guide us to the car arm in arm, watching her reactions to everyone we pass. Her eyes constantly scan the faces of everyone we encounter. Her muscles are stiff to the touch. I keep my cool, hardened exterior returning. She makes no move to distance herself from me, easing the restlessness building within me.

The drive to Nancy's house was no more than ten minutes, but it was the longest ten minutes I've ever experienced. There was an air of anxiety that we both carried around today. I want to make a good impression on her friends, but I also want to be there for her and make sure she's taken care of.

Turning down the long, paved driveway, the GPS says we have arrived at our destination. As we pull up to the massive house, I can see a figure standing in the bay window, an older woman with her nose turned up. The house was red brick with white columns, similar to the resort. I park the car on the side of the house with a paved parking pad, and we get out. I offer her my hand, but she declines, wiping her hands on the front of her pants. I give her a reassuring smile and follow her lead as we make our way up to the front door.

Knock, knock, knock.

She raps her knuckles on the red metal door, looking over her shoulder with apologetic eyes. From the other side, someone shouts something incoherent before footsteps quickly approach.

The door swings open wide, revealing a tall, blonde woman and a much shorter, stout, and balding man. The woman squeals and wraps River in a strong hug. My mask slips back over my face, much to my chagrin. I want to be approachable and friendly with her friends. But something feels wrong.

I can taste pennies.

Why the fuck can I taste pennies.

"Come in, come in!" The woman says, ushering River inside before I have a chance to grab her, missing her wrist and pulling on her sleeve instead. She reaches back, fear swelling in her gold eyes, and I grab her fingertips before she's pulled away. I follow them inside.

"Nancy, this is Leon. My boyfriend. Leon, this is Nancy." River introduces. A panicked look she can't hide on her face.

"Pleasure to meet you, Leon." Nancy quips, turning to face me head-on for the first time. I expected black pits for eyes and too many teeth, but she looked fine.

She looked human.

"And this is Nancy's fiancé." River interjects before I can find something wrong with her. My focus turned to the short man, his stature and arrogance of a man who was at least a foot taller.

"Brian," the man says and extends his hand. Studying his face, his features are too uncanny, but he isn't a Changeling. Something is wrong, but I can't pinpoint the source. My body tense as I shake his hand firmly, a tight smile forming across my lips.

"Cohen?" I ask. River snaps her head towards me, a larger fear in her eyes than before. Nancy looks between the three of us with solitary confusion.

"Yeah," Brian confirms. "How'd you know?"

"I've heard a lot about you." I say, retracting my hand. A feeling of repulsion, of treachery seeping into my pores.

"All good things I hope." He laughs cockily, eyes flickering between the three of us.

"I think you and I both know there's nothing good to say about-" River flashes me a warning glance, but Nancy's already talking over me to prevent me from finishing my sentence.

"Is he treating you well? Keeping you company in my absence?" Nancy asks, throwing a sharp glance in my direction even though she's clearly not talking *to* me.

"He's the best." River replies before I can interject. Her eyes look at me with a sense of fondness. "Couldn't ask for anyone better."

Nancy hums (disapprovingly?). "Good to hear." She says.

"Do you need any help setting up?" River asks, feeling the weight of Nancy's disapproval hang in the air. Nancy pulls River into the kitchen to work on snacks. I hang back in the hallway with Brian, keeping one eye on him and one eye on my girl.

"So," Brian asks, "what do you do for work?" He's trying his damnedest to peer around me and into the kitchen. A skeevy and very punch-able look on his face. I take a step in front of his line of sight.

"Music production." I huff exasperatedly. "You?"

"Car sales." He boasts with a crooked smirk. I hum unenthusiastically, not giving him the attention that he so desperately craves. "Is producing music lucrative?" His tone insinuates that my job is superior to his. He's probably thinking I'm some kind of unknown artist with twelve terrible songs on SoundCloud. And for all I care, he can keep thinking that. This little gnat isn't worth wasting my time.

"It is when you're good at your job." I reply, catching a glimpse of the elderly woman I had seen earlier. She had made her way into the kitchen with River and Nancy. An angry look on her wrinkled face. I can hear Nancy and the woman arguing about the amount of food being served at the party. Nancy quips back, saying there's going to be thirty-plus people.

Great. More people to impress.

"And are you good at your job?" Brian asks skeptically. I shrug, he doesn't deserve anything more than to rot in a ditch.

"Are you good at yours?" I quip, leaning against the wall beside the door, arms crossed over my chest. He stumbles through a handful of syllables that sound like absolutely nothing while a satisfied smirk settles on my face. A gentle hand touches my shoulder. My head snaps to see River peering up at me. "Everything alright, angel?" She nods toward the arguing pair in the kitchen.

"Just like how I remember it." She says, her fingertips reaching for my hand through my crossed-armed stance. "You okay in here?" I notice that she's not addressed him once, she won't even look at him, but all those years of pain are written across her face with neon colors.

"Never better." I remark, uncurling my arm to wrap around her waist. "Brian and I were just comparing salaries." I snark, hearing Brian huff. She exhales a sharp 'HA' before throwing her hand over her mouth and leaning into me. My fingertips graze bare skin at the dip of her back, sending a shiver up her spine that only I'm privy to.

"He wouldn't give me a number." Brian whines. We both cut our eyes at him to see him sulking. "Music production. What? Are you some kind of underground rapper?" River and I both laugh sharply. Furthering Brian's sulking.

"Put your micro-penis back in your pants, Cohen." River snaps. "You're only going to get your feelings hurt if you find out." Brian scoffs, opening his mouth to protest, but she's already on him like vultures to roadkill. "Do you ever *fucking* listen?" She whisper-yells.

"And what are you doing with your life, little sis?" He asks, eliciting a darkness in her eyes that sends pin pricks over my skin, causing my shoulders to straighten and the need to step in between them grows. But she's a grown woman. She can handle herself. I know she can.

"*Don't.* Call me 'little sis'." She snarls, clenching her fists behind her back.

"My apologies. I should have just assumed that you've turned to selling yourself for rent money. You know you can always call Brother Brian for money if you need it, sweetheart."

"What I do is none of your fucking business." She fires back. "And what are you doing? Hm? Still jerking off across the street from the middle school?" Her words cut through the air like knives.

"Shut your *whore* mouth." Brian's words ripple with anger, pointing a nubby, shaking finger in her direction.

"You can call me a whore all you want, but you can never call me a pedophile. Can't say the same for you." She yells back across the hallway, the argument escalating quickly. "I bet I could call you a murderer, too."

"What are you fucking talking about?" Brian snips, not daring to take a step closer, but his anger boiling all of his tainted blood.

"Angie." River says. "I know you fucking killed her."

"You're fucking delusional!" He barks. "I'd never kill her. I'd never laid a hand on her. And I never laid a hand on you." He spits his last words so quickly that he doesn't realize what he's just admitted to. River's face falls, any malice previously existing on her gorgeous features now ceasing to exist.

"You fucking admitted it." She whispers, exhaling a shaky breath around her words.

"No. No, I didn't." Brian defends,

"Yes, you fucking did." She demands, revelations crossing her face. Her fingernails dig into my forearm with force. "You miserable, washed-up, peaked in high school, balding motherfucker." I smirk at Brian, proud of my angel for holding her own in the face of the sleaze ball who hurt her.

"Dude, you're just going to let her talk to me that way?" Brian squeaks, looking at me like I'm supposed to help him. Like I wouldn't enjoy seeing his brains underneath my tire treads.

I laugh darkly. "I don't think you understand that you don't want me to get involved, Baldy."

"Are you fucking serious, man? Control your bitch ass girlfriend." Before he could continue. Before I have a chance to lunge for his throat, River launches herself at him.

With a fistful of his shirt collar in one hand and her other arm at his throat, she hisses her words through clenched teeth. "It's so comforting to see you're still the same misogynistic coward you've always been." Fear flashes over his face. "I may not have fought back when we were kids, but I swear on my dead parents' grave that I'll end you right where we both stand before I let you control me with fear."

Her chest rises and falls heavily. The air is as still as a warm summer night. Tension lingering where uncertainty lay. I watched the two of them with anxious curiosity, willing to step in when needed, but happy to let my angel defend her honor in any way she wanted. She's willing to fight back against this piece of shit scum. My heart swells with pride.

"If you think you're going to get away with any more shit, then you're fucking mistaken because I'll make sure no one can find your rotting, disgusting body before I let you ruin any more of my life. Are we *fucking* clear?"

A gasp escapes from the doorway beside me. I hadn't heard Nancy approach, or I would have said something, or taken her ass out. Whichever was needed. "River! Get off of him!" Nancy yells, running into the hallway. "What the fuck is wrong with you?!"

"Yeah, what the fuck, River?!" Brian screams, eliciting a pathetic response from Nancy. River lets go of him and I immediately throw my arm around her shoulder. Nancy fixes Brian's collar before turning back to River.

"Do you care to explain yourself?" Nancy asks with a motherly scolding tone. River has more darkness in her eyes than I've ever seen before. "What the hell is your problem? You always do this shit!"

"Do what?" River huffs, folding her arms over her chest. Nancy scowls at her like a naughty child she can't stand being around. Nancy turns up her nose at River, a clear act of disgust.

"You ruin everything. Make everything about yourself and ruin everyone's day. Without fail. I don't know why you even bother to show up anywhere." Nancy reprimands, crocodile tears welling in her eyes. Her voice doesn't convey the same emotions.

"It looks like this new scumbag boyfriend of yours is a rather bad influence." Brian remarks. However, River has no problem lunging for him again. Nancy steps in between them. I smile wickedly at Brian, pulling River back under my arm.

"No, she's always been this way." Nancy spits. "Always been the worst fucking person to be around. So self-centered, you couldn't put your hatred for my fiancé on the back burner for one goddamn night!" With each word Nancy spews, waves of shock fall over River's face.

"Language!" A feeble voice calls from the kitchen.

"Whatever, Nance." River hisses, escaping my arms and pushing past Nancy and Brian.

She makes a B-lining for the back door. I follow hot on her heels. She pushes the sliding door open and runs onto the porch into the freezing December air, taking a seat on the steps leading out into the fenced-in backyard. Shutting the door behind me, I sit next to her. She leans her head on the railing, arms folded on her knees. Her eyes don't meet mine, but the maroon color of her nose and the moisture on her cheeks tell me everything I need to know. I moved to rub her back gently with the palm of my hand.

"Am I that insufferable?" She asks softly, breath fogging around her mouth with each exhale.

"Of course not, angel." I coo, turning her body so her head is on my shoulder. "If anyone's insufferable, it's those two loony bin residents."

She half-chuckles at my comment, then says, "If she hates me so much, why did she invite me here?" Her words fall pitifully around us, and my heart is breaking at the sight before me. Her red bottom lip quivers uncontrollably as I hold onto her tightly, fighting everything in me to contain the need for vengeance. She needs me here, right now, more than I need to give those fuckers a taste of the underside of my boot.

"I don't know, angel." I say. "We can go if you want. You don't have to stay here." Silence lingers for a short moment before she pulls back. I brush the tears away from her cheeks with my thumb and she returns her gratitude with a soft smile.

"I'm sorry." She mumbles softly. "I'm sorry for bringing you here. For stirring up drama. That you had to drive me eight hours for this... this bullshit." Tears rack through her body, swelling her chest with deep sorrow.

"There's nothing to be sorry for." I say, rubbing her shoulders. "You didn't do anything wrong, mon amour." My calloused thumbs rub over the saltwater rivers flowing down the mountains of her cheeks, the icy air nipping at the warm liquid before it even has a chance to settle.

"I knew we should have just stayed at home." She sniffles. "I knew this was a bad idea."

"Hey, hey, hey. Look at me." I command, pulling at her chin. She looks up at me with scarlet eyes. "This isn't your fault."

"She hates me, Leon. You don't say that kind of shit to someone unless you hate them." She pleads, but not with me, with some higher deity that betrayed her.

"I don't think she hates you. I think she hates me and the fact that you're a little kickass firecracker she can't control anymore." I joke, breathing a sigh of relief when her shoulders shake with a tiny laugh.

"Is it weird that if she does hate you, that makes me want you more." She teases, scrunching her nose cutely.

"Does it look like I'm complaining about that one?" I ask rhetorically, pulling her into a small kiss. She kisses me back a little more vividly than I expected her to. Her touch reminds me why I'm here. Why I would stay and surround myself with people I don't know for a woman who's breaking my love's heart. I'm doing it all for River.

And I'd do it a million times over if she asked me to.

"Why is Nancy with Brian in the first place?" I ask, the

mountain wind whistling through the trees that surround the McMansion of a house.

"He's the first guy she was ever with after high school." She replies, but that's not the answer I'm looking for and she knows it. There's a long, pregnant pause, her eyes falling to the ground below us before she says, "She doesn't know."

"What? What do you mean she doesn't know?" I ask skeptically. Her eyes sink further away from my gaze. "Angel, talk to me. Why doesn't she know what he's done to you?" I ask firmly, completely shocked and trying to reel it in.

"I didn't tell her." She mumbles, barely audible.

"What do you mean you never told her?" I reiterate, my heart feeling as though someone's taken it in between vice grips and tightens hard.

"She wouldn't have ever believed me. Not when we were kids and definitely not now. She'll just think I'm making it all up for attention. Because I'm such a spiteful, bitter person and everything has to be about me." The anger and defeat in her voice battle with the sarcasm and aloofness of her snarky comments.

"Did you tell anyone?" She shakes her head 'no' first. Then nods 'yes'. "Who?"

She sighs. "Brian's little sister, Angie. He started doing the same things to her that he did to me, and I told her to stand up for herself. And because of me, she turned up dead." She says, "But no one else. I didn't – couldn't – tell anyone else."

"Best friends don't date their friend's abusers." I sigh. She sniffles and shrugs her shoulders, now shaking from the cold onslaught we're facing. Severely underdressed for the weather. Georgia is somehow much warmer. "What does she see in him anyway?"

She chuckles lightly. "I ask myself the same thing." We both laugh and sit in the silence that follows. The party's starting, and people chatter inside the house. Her head hangs close to her chest.

"Hey," I say, moving her chin to look into her eyes again.

I can't help it. She has the most gorgeous features I've ever seen. "You know I've got you. Always."

She nods and says, "Thank you." My hands cup her scalding hot face, pulling her into another kiss. Her lips smile against mine. "You sure do love doing that, don't you?" She teases, pulling me back in. Her lips taste like strawberries.

"As if you don't." I retort with an eye roll and a lip bite. "Do you want to ditch the party?" I ask, desperately hoping she'll say yes.

"And miss ruining Nancy's day *and* showing you off? Not a fucking chance." She says, standing up and pulling me up too. My hands find her lower back, and I kiss her one more time, lingering over her rosy skin. There's something about kissing her that I haven't quite gotten over. It makes my head swim.

We walk over the door, but just as I'm about to pull the handle, she stops me, looking up with sincerity in her eyes.

"Thanks, again, for always being my knight in shining armor. My prince charming." She says, placing the softest peck on my cheek. I flash her a grin paired with a wink and pull her inside into the warmth of the house. There are maybe twenty voices spread throughout the expansive house.

We intermingle with the party. River casually talks with people she hadn't seen in over a decade. Most of the reactions are surprise mixed with intrigue. She can strike up a conversation with anyone yet turn around and shit talk or stick her tongue out in a gagging motion.

"I admire your ability to be two-faced." I whisper to her, handing a cup of lemon ginger punch right as she finishes conversing with a woman wearing an ugly Christmas sweater.

"If they can do it, so can I." She shrugs, taking a sip of the punch. "I'm liking my odds so far. Only four people told me they thought I was dead. And only one of those thought I would have killed myself by now."

"Well, I'm glad you're still here." I say, admiring her in the dim kitchen lighting.

I'm glad I get to experience these things with you, angel.

"Hey, River, can we talk?" Nancy asks from the other side of the island. "Alone."

"What do you want?" River counters without moving an inch from her spot, plucking a grape from the bowl on the counter. Never breaking eye contact.

"Look, I'm sorry about earlier. I didn't mean what I said. Can we just talk like adults about this?" Nancy begs. Though, River seems like she couldn't care less. *My girl.*

"What? So you can accuse me of ruining your birthday *again*? If you want to say something, you can tell me here." River scoffs, crossing her arms over her chest. Staring down her latest opponent.

"Can we please just have this conversation in private." Nancy pleads, her voice breaking.

"Why should I leave the party you so desperately wanted me to be at? I'm having a wonderful time." River says with malicious niceties.

"Oh, I'm so glad you're having a good time." Nancy scoffs. "Whatever, we can talk later. Enjoy the party, love birds." Her sentiments are hollow, but River accepts it, turning, and moving from the kitchen.

As we enter the den, she greets another handful of people who look like they've seen a ghost. All of which she greets with a smile, silently taking a tally of who all say they thought she had died at some point.

My hand stays on her waist as she introduces me to each one as her boyfriend. I return the pleasantries as best as I can, swimming in how confidently she's showing me off. So giddy in fact, that most of the asshole exterior is tucked away. At least for now. Until we'll inevitably have to deal with Dumb Ass and Dumber Ass.

My cheeks hurt with how much I've been smiling.

"Are you enjoying yourself, baby?" She asks when we've finally found a moment to ourselves. Putting her arms around my waist when it's just the two of us nestled into a corner of the living room.

"I'm enjoying you." I grin. She giggles through the kiss, the bubbles escaping into my mouth.

"Who knew you were so sweet on me." She teases.

CHAPTER 25

River

The party eventually dies down.

At some point between the sun setting and the wolves howling, all other guests peeled out of the driveway like bats out of Hell. It felt like I missed the memo on why we all needed to leave before the sun fully set, and I was prepared to leave with the best of them. But Nancy said she wanted to talk, and as much as she pisses me off, lately I feel somewhat obligated to hear her out.

Nancy and I sit on her childhood bed facing each other, her back on the headboard and me by the footboard. Neither of us committed to being the first to break the silence. Both of us are entirely too headstrong for our own good.

Leon had commented before I willingly locked myself in a room with Nancy. He'd mumbled it into my hair as he held me so tightly that I thought I was going to suffocate. Something about calling him if I needed reinforcements. That nothing in this world could keep him from me.

My heart simultaneously melted and froze. On one hand, the sentiment was nothing short of something I expected him to say. He was, by all accounts, incredibly protective of me.

But there's been this nagging feeling in the back of my mind that I can't shake ever since yesterday morning. There's *something* off here, with this place. Something I can't see or touch, but it's there. Lingering in the room like stale air.

The taste of copper is strong in the back of my throat.

The hairs on my arms stand up with the force of whatever it is that disturbs this place as my mind wanders into the view outside of Nancy's window. The woods.

A deep, thick forest filled with memories of my childhood. Wildlife. Crickets and deer. There were times when we'd spend all day roaming the wooded area around the property. Sometimes we'd wander so far that Mr. Jenkins would catch us on his trail camera and call her mom to come get us because we'd 'clearly lost our way'.

But we never once got lost. We had string and invasive Spanish moss to guide us back the way we'd come. We had our imaginations and intuition. While hers was never on track, mine never failed me.

All those days spent playing in the forest, they were like a second home to me. They were the only ones who knew my secrets. They held my favorite climbing trees, sitting trees, and berry bushes. Nothing could have taken that away from me.

Except tonight, those woods look terrifying.

They look as though they hold an evil far older than human civilization. The monsters that roam the Earth now reside in the shadows of those thick evergreens. If I weren't so sure I was just being paranoid, I could have sworn that the trees were staring back at me.

Nancy coughs, jolting me out violently out of my trance. She looks at me with bubbling anger. Her near-silver blue eyes pierce my soul with a fervor I can't shake. Judgmental eyes roam across the expanse of my face, scanning for any anomalies. Searching for a reason, a justification to hate me. To dump me like she dumped Jerry McAllen. Left his ass on the side of the road after he said he didn't like her dog. It's certainly a power move until it happens to you.

I want nothing more than to tell her what Brian did to me, but I know nothing I say will change her mind. She loves him. She thinks she's going to marry him and have his babies. She made up her mind when she sided with him and not me. Not that she needs to side with me for any reason. I don't care if she dislikes Leon. Truly don't care if she hates his guts. But she may not have known *everything* he did to me all those years ago, but she knew good and well that he was a terrible, awful person. He always has been.

"Can I ask *why* you jumped Brian?" She asks, her voice barely above a whisper, eyes falling to the nails she's picking at in her lap. She winces, but only briefly.

"You know he knows how to provoke me. Please don't act like this is the first time I've ever lashed out at him. He was my foster brother. He knows how to get under my skin and he's good at it." I defend, probably harsher than I needed to.

Her bedroom was once painted pink and green with lace curtains. Now a barren hellscape of white, like a padded room.

We used to lay in this room, on the floor by this very window on hot summer nights and talk about everything from crushes to colleges to pregnancy scares. I remember one time in our senior year, sitting right under the windowsill, authoring an English paper, where she told me not to tell anyone, but she thought she was pregnant, and she didn't know who the baby daddy was. She ended up not being pregnant, but the trauma will always remain.

In seventh grade, I confessed to her that I had a crush on Rosie, a girl in our class. She had just moved to town, and she was really, *really* pretty. Nancy told me that people would look at me funny if I went around saying I liked girls. I didn't get what she meant because people already looked at me funny for a plethora of other reasons far less controversial than being a queer teenager in a small mountain town in the mid-2000s.

The hallway bathroom is where she did her makeup for homecoming. I always sat with her to keep her company, because it was the only thing I could do since I couldn't go. She offered to buy my ticket, but it was always more than that. It was the fact that I didn't have a date to go with or anything nice to wear. I wasn't about to ask her to pay for a ticket to an event where I would just get laughed at.

The backyard was where we would go to practice her

cheer routines. We would go for late-night swims in the pool when her parents were asleep. The countless nights I just laid on a pool float, staring up at the unpolluted sky counting the stars, wondering where in the hell life would take me.

The echoes of girlhood are ingrained into the core of this house. Once filled with laughter, singing, and dancing, now there's not even a single conversation going on. There's no life. There's no happiness. It's depressing here.

"You've always been out to get him." She snips, transporting me back to being a kid and being scolded by my mom for drawing on the trailer walls in my closet. "He's a good man, River." It sounds like she's trying to convince herself of her statement more than me.

"What makes you think he's such a good person?" I ask as gently as I can muster in the face of someone so wrong yet so loud about it.

"He's never done anything to you." She demands, a fisted hand at her side. "You're the one that ruins everything and then runs away." Her words sting like they're filled with bitter hatred and venom.

She's supposed to be my best friend. She's been on my side since we were six. Why is she all of a sudden turning against me? Why does it feel like nothing I have to say matters? What's so special about this hateful, bitter creep that she's willing to lay down her life for?

"Please tell me how he's a good person, Nance." I nearly beg. When she doesn't answer my pleas, I answer for her. "He was a huge bully growing up. He's still a bully now. He's misogynistic, incapable of taking care of himself, is thirty-five, and still lives with his mother." She stops me before I can continue.

"If you had been around, you would know his dad left his mom after Angie died. He had to take care of his mother. He was all she had. Some of us have familial responsibilities." She explains pointedly. "You wouldn't know anything about that, would you."

Ouch.

I chew on my words, what I want to say to her versus what I will say. How if I said some shit like that to her for no fucking reason, I'd be buried in the backyard so fast.

To say that I have no sense of familial responsibility is just plain rude, but somehow so true. I don't know what it's like to have to give up anything for someone.

I didn't grow up having people to fight for me. No one stood in my corner of the octagon. I didn't have that sense of community or blood ties. I was lucky if I had food on the table or running water to brush my teeth with at night. And when I was in foster care, I was lucky if I had a moment where I didn't have to worry about my privacy. The Cohens didn't love me. My parents didn't care about me.

It wasn't until recently that I truly felt what it was like to have someone always in your corner. It wasn't until Leon that I even knew what it felt like to have a person look at me like I wasn't a burden. With soft eyes and no hatred in his heart. And maybe I'm jumping the gun. Maybe I'm projecting. But how Leon treats me is how you should treat someone you love.

You stand in their fucking corner.

"You're right." I agree, tears welling in my eyes at the clear lack of respect for our youth. "I don't know anything about having a family." I snap, having had enough of all the blame being placed on me. "I'm an *orphan*. I wish I had grown up with two parents who loved me, even if it was as fucked up as yours. Maybe if the whole town hadn't hated me, or if my life wasn't so fucking cursed. Maybe you should have thought about me for once. Maybe I would have stayed around longer."

My words sting as they exit my mouth. Years of forced silence boiled over all at once. Hitting their mark. Nancy's face falls in shock.

"You know that's not what I meant, Riv." She hisses.

"Then when the fuck did you mean? Did you think that I would pity your poor fucking soul for staying around to help your abusive mother? Do you think I would ever want to stay stuck in this fucking town filled with washed-up has-beens who cannot fathom a life outside of their small town? Do you think that maybe if the hand I was dealt looked a little more like yours, I may get where you're coming from? I got a shit pot, Nance. I've been beaten with the ugly stick for as long as I can remember, and you have the fucking audacity to turn this around on me?"

"I thought we were family is all." She whimpers.

"We were. You were all I had for so long." I say, sniffles chase the tears away that form in my rage. "But you've been pushing me away from the moment I left. You have no idea how terrifying the real world is when you have no one on your side."

"You never came back!" She screams.

"I didn't want to!" My lungs are on the verge of collapsing. "I wanted nothing to do with this place from the first time someone laughed at me about my matted hair. Dreamed of getting the hell out of here and never looking back. And I came back for you. It's not my fault you never left."

"You know I can't leave." She winces again.

"Yes, yes, yes. Mommy dearest is in desperate need of a hospice nurse." I mock. "It was always my plan to get out of here. It was yours too until your mom got cancer. I don't even know why you're taking care of her anyway. You've always said you hate her."

"I don't hate her!" She snaps, the fury in her eyes returning from where they had gone distant. "Don't you ever talk about my mom like that. She's always had my best interest at heart."

"You don't believe that." I deny, crossing my arms over my chest. "Do you?" The conviction in her stare says otherwise. She hangs her head low as she rubs her stomach and winces. "Are you okay?"

"Yeah, yeah. I'm fine. Just ate something bad." She grumbles. Pain causes Nancy to tense her whole body and jolt her breathing, face twists up in immeasurable discomfort as she grasps her stomach.

"Are you sure?" I ask skeptically with a raised brow.

She shoots me a menacing look as the pain settles. My concern is a touchy subject. "I said I'm fine. Do you ever back down?" She grumbles. I roll my eyes, unable to reason with her.

"What's wrong with you? You've been at my throat all fucking day." I ask. "You've honestly been at my fucking throat since I asked you to help me move. You could have just said no to me if you dislike being around me that much."

"Nothing's wrong with me. I just think the way you act around Brian is very childish and I don't think he deserves the treatment you dish out to him." She says, counting her breaths as another wave hits her so hard she nearly doubles over.

"So, what's with the pain?" I ask, keeping a close eye on her. Something sounds off in her voice, but I can't place it.

"Nothing. I told you it must have been something I ate."
She's lying.

It's the inflection in her voice, one that I'm all too familiar with. She involuntarily pitches her voice higher than normal.

It's the same way she would lie to her mom about losing a sweater when she really gave it to me. Or when she would say she was going to the mall with me but would actually go to her high school boyfriend's house. I've heard it a million times.

Why does she think that I won't notice she's lying now?

"Please don't lie to me, Nance." I plead, placing a gentle hand on her knee. She peers into my eyes, and we both witness the collapse of our friendship. All while she's covering something up. Keeping secrets and telling lies.

Fear dwells deep in her eyes. A fear so primal yet so foreign that I've seen before. During a time of cataclysmic turmoil. She's always been brave, always had her life together, always ten steps ahead of any problem at hand, but this was pure terror, and she knew I knew.

"I'm not lying!" She shrieks, her voice quivering as it

rises in volume.

"Well, something's clearly wrong, Nance." I gesture to her body with my hand. "Do you need to go to the hospital? Can I get you something?" I might as well be pleading with a solid brick wall to let me in. Sitting in front of a total stranger, in a room so unfamiliar to me that I'm clawing at my skin to leave. This was a bad idea. I should just go.

But I can't bring my feet to move out from under me.

"No, you can't do anything! You've never been able to do a damn thing in your whole life. You just run and run and run from all of your fucking problems. You make it impossible for people to like you. Your self-absorbed ego is so fragile that I wouldn't be surprised if you were just using Leon for his money! Taking the opportunity while you can? Or is it because he knows you're desperate?" Her words send ice through my veins, my breathing becoming frantic as the anger takes over yet again. Tears pinprick at my nose and eyes, threatening to break any composure I thought I had.

"You can talk shit about me all you want, but don't you dare bring Leon into this. You have no right to talk about him. You don't even fucking know him." I spit my words through clenched teeth.

"I don't know him, but I don't fucking know you either." She barks. "You've been so secretive about everything our whole lives. You never gossip, you never told me anything. I did all the talking! Do you know how hard it is to be your friend? You never went out to parties or hung out with anyone besides me. You were so fucking depressing." She winces through another round of pain, this one seeming worse than the last. But I didn't care at this point. I reveled in the instant karma.

"Did you ever stop to think about why I never brought up anything about myself? Or why I never went to parties? It's because I was the town freak! Everyone either pitied me for what happened with my parents, or they were making fun of me for it. I was poor. I didn't have money for nice things. People have been making fun of me long before I got put into foster care." The rage, red hot and burning to the touch, building inside of me felt like a volcano ready to erupt. My repressed trauma threatens to break down the walls I spent years building.

And through it all, through all the harshness of her words, I still wanted to understand why. Why would she say all of this to me now? Why have the floodgates collapsed today? Why am I the verbal punching bag? What have I done wrong? What have I ever done to her to warrant any of this? Why now?

"You act like everyone fucking hated you! You hated yourself. You caused all of your problems. You've always been a run-away-from-your-problem kind of girl, and you still are, and I feel so incredibly sorry for you. Have you ever thought about how your actions have affected everyone else?" Her words send piercing daggers through my skin. One after another, their sharp blades sink into my flesh, coating themselves in blood before pulling back so that the open wounds could bleed adequately.

"I just wanted a life where people didn't look at me with pity in their eyes." I defend, though it is useless. My head falls like my spinal cord has been severed. I don't have it in me to keep fighting. Exhaustion sweeps over me like a sleep agent, too tired to keep up this losing battle.

Nancy scoffs, shifting to her feet, and readying herself to leave the room. These feelings have been pent up for quite some time. I had no idea.

As she goes to move toward the door, a puddle of some liquid gushes from her, like she peed on herself.

She stares at the now-soaked hardwood beneath her feet. "No, no, no, no, no, no! This can't be happening!" She shrieks. I jumped to my feet, though I had no plan on how to help her. Or even if she wanted my help.

"What the fuck?" I ask frantically, stepping around her to grab a pile of towels from the linen closet just outside the hallway. "What's going on, Nancy?"

I haven't used her government name in almost two

decades. Always claimed to hate it. But the woman staring back at me is a near stranger.

"Shit!" She curses under her breath, wiping herself clean with a fluffy white towel that looked like it cost a fortune. Smearing blood and mystery liquid onto the stark fabric. Another wave of pain hits, knocking her to the floor. "It's not time. I'm not due for another two months," She wails through clenched teeth and fists around towels.

Anger replaces her fear. Whatever was happening, it was happening right now, and it was enough to make her furious.

"Due for what?!" I ask, confused, holding out additional towels and throwing some on the floor to soak up the bodily fluid. "Nancy?"

"Don't act dumb now." She barks, annoyed at my question. My lack of knowledge of her current health status. "I'm having a baby. Right. *Now.*"

"YOU'RE PREGNANT?!" I holler, loud enough to wake the neighbors and alert whatever is lurking in the woods across the house. "Since when are you pregnant?!"

"Now's not the time, River! You have to help me!" She waddles, legs spread in discomfort, toward the door. Grabbing her shoulders, I help her walk. Shouldering the brunt of her weight in an attempt to alleviate some of her pain and pressure.

Even though she's been the biggest asshole on the planet and I'm certain our friendship will never recover from the words she's spewed at me, I'm not leaving her. I'm not making it a point to prove her right.

As we walk down the stairs, I'm helping her breathe, the same way they show in movies. I don't know if it's right, but it's what we're doing. She's having a fucking baby?!

How could this be happening?! What kind of fucking weekend am I having right now? First Mark, then Brian, then this? And after the words that Nancy had the gall to spew at me, I'm supposed to be happy for her?

241

I should be. This is something she's always wanted.

When we were kids, we had talked a lot about if we ever wanted kids and she'd always expressed that she'd want me to be the godmother to her babies. I agreed back then, but that thought is long gone now. We may never speak again after today. My best friend has become a total stranger. There's no way I would say yes if she asked me to be this kid's god mom.

As we make it down the big, curving staircase, I call out to Leon, clear panic laced in my voice. He comes sprinting from the living room, alarm in his big boba eyes as he takes in the sitcom scene unfolding before him.

"We need to leave right now. We're having a baby!" I announce. Leon takes the towels from me and grabs my bag as another wave hits Nancy hard on the landing. Leon heads for the door.

"NO!" She bellows, almost in slow motion as Leon's hand reaches for the knob. "We can't go outside!" A tight grip on the banister and widened eyes are all Leon needs to pause long enough to reconsider.

"What? Why?" Leon asks. His confusion knits his brows higher and higher.

"We can't go outside." She repeats. "It's too dark."

"*Too* dark?" He reiterates with a scoff. "It's nighttime."

"Exactly! You don't go outside at night." Nancy pleas through another contraction. "I'll have this baby in Mom's jacuzzi tub. It's big enough."

"Nancy, you're not thinking straight. Let's get you to the hospital. To someone who can deliver your baby." I bargain, panic-stricken at the thought of the mere thought of delivering a baby in a bathtub. She's out of her fucking mind.

"No, Riv. We *can't* go outside!" She grabs my arm with the fury of a thousand suns. With fear and terror swimming in her silvery-blue eyes. Eyes I know her baby has.

"Why not?" Leon asks, frustratedly shoving his hands in his pockets. "Give me one good reason we can't go outside, or I swear to God, I'll open this door and throw your ass out on the lawn." My hand clasps over my mouth, half-shocked Leon would say such a thing. Half-not.

Leon Kang is the king of holding grudges.

"You city folks wouldn't believe me if I told you, but you just have to trust me." Nancy's eyes are begging us – me – to listen to her. Hear her out.

I was inclined to. What if she knew about the things that lurked in the dark. The monsters that go bump in the night. The magical creatures who can't be stopped. What if she knew? What if they were here, in my hometown?

"Hear her out, Leon." I nudge, pleading with my eyes at him to listen. To have the chance to hear her reasoning. It would be a good chance to finally tell him about the things I've been seeing. The nightmares that live right outside the door don't seem so far-fetched when others corroborate your story.

Leon gestures for Nancy to get on with her explanation, hand perched on the doorknob. Fingers ready to grip and turn at any sign of trouble.

"There are things in the woods now. Monsters. Things that only come out at night and make your skin crawl. There have been so many missing tourists in the last year. Authorities say it's an increase in bear and wolf population, but everyone who lives here knows. We hear things. See things we can't explain."

"What kind of monsters?" I ask, maybe too eagerly.

"I don't know. Some people say that there are these troll-looking creatures that hide in the forest near the lake. Or these too tall, lanky no-faced beasts that wander the streets avoiding the light. Or the people that look like people you know until they don't."

Leon's face falls, barely enough for anyone to notice. Except I do. I see the subtle realization cascade over his face. But whatever he's feeling, I can't place it outside of realization.

"You have to believe me." Nancy whispers to me. "This isn't the same place we grew up in. There are things out there that want to kill you. That will hunt you down for sport. No one knows where they came from or why they're here, but we only *survive* by staying inside."

I'm not crazy. I'm not crazy. I'm not crazy.

I nod, pushing back the tears swelling in my eyes. "I believe you, Nance." I say softly, relief washing over her face. As if my response had been the one thing tethering her to this very room. Leon leans a large, tan hand to the door. My heart skips a beat as he latches the deadbolt and turns to face us. Me.

Something beckoned me to him. A force I can't explain. A phantom hand on my back pushes me to him and I don't deny it. So he comes to me instead. Like he felt it, too.

"Thank you, thank you, thank you." Nancy gushes, waddling off down the hallway, leaving Leon and me alone for a brief moment.

"Since when is she pregnant?" Leon asks, resting a gentle hand on my waist.

I can't tell him what she said to me in her bedroom. The vitriol still sticks to the roof of my mouth. How when we *are* allowed to walk out of this house come sunrise, there will be no returning. To say that kind of shit to your best friend of over twenty years, to hide your pregnancy? There's no way I could ever trust her again.

If I tell him all of this now, he'll certainly throw her out to the monsters. He won't even hesitate.

"Since about seven months ago, according to her. Since about five minutes ago for me." I quip, gripping the material of his shirt gathered at his waist. Pushing out all the turmoil spinning through my head.

"Are you okay?" He asks, moving a bit of hair from my neck to place a gentle kiss just under my ear. I nod, forcing a smile through my fading façade.

Nancy approaches us, breathing through another round of contractions. "Where's Brian." She asks, grimacing with each step. Leon and I let go of each other to move to either side of her, putting her arms over each of our shoulders.

"Now is not the time. You can call him later." I replied.

"No, he was supposed to be here! He was just here before we went upstairs. Where did he go? I need Brian with me." She explains in a panicked hurry.

I feel bad for her, believing in magical monsters but not in the fact that her baby daddy's a bad fucking person. Having a baby with a pedophile. I feel responsible somehow. Maybe I should have told her all those years ago. Maybe none of this would be happening right now if I had dared to speak up back then.

But look where it got Angie.

"Do you really want Brian here?" I demand harshly, guiding her to her mother's giant jacuzzi tub. She takes a moment to ponder what she wants. If she never made a single decision before or after this, she's going to make this one. We're stuck in this fucking house. Might as well have a damn baby.

"No." She winces again, spitting the word through her clenched jaw. Stopping and waiting for her to catch her breath, Leon and I share a look.

He knows that I'm holding something back from him. He's just as good, if not better, at reading people as I am, and he *knows*.

"But what choice do I have?" Nancy asks solemnly.

It takes everything in me to give a goddamn fuck right now and push down all the negativity and hesitation I feel for what was once our friendship so that she can feel comfortable. I've been doing that shit my whole life, it seems. I've been putting her on a pedestal for so long. Maybe I wasn't looking at the evidence right in front of me.

"You have all the choices in the world, Nance. It's your baby." I say, the hollowness sharp in my voice.

"Will you stay with me?" She asks, her cry so small and fragile, and I'm back to being thirteen again.

All the world seems to be against me and the pretty girl from a well-off family is my only safety on this tumultuous ocean. She'd taken me under her wing years prior. She made me feel important and special. But this time the rose-colored glasses have fallen off. I've heard the whispers that sound like screams. The agony that it is to be my friend when it's inconvenient an echo in my heart.

I'm tired of running and I'm tired of fighting. Exhausted from being drawn and quartered, only for the executioner to tell me to get up and walk it off - it's so undeniably unbearable.

"I don't have much choice, do I?" I ask, settling her onto the edge of the tub. Leon rolls up his sleeves to prepare to help Nancy into the tub. "Why did you keep this baby a secret, Nance?" I ask, nose stinging and waterline swelling with the swell of betrayal I wasn't allowed to feel.

"I know how you feel about Brian. I could only imagine how you'd feel about me having his kid." She explains as we maneuver her into the tub. The Tuscan tan bathroom has been untouched since the early 90s.

"That doesn't give you the right to keep this from me." I scold. "You want to bitch and moan about me not being there for you or caring about any of this, but did you ever stop to think that if you had told me you were pregnant, I would do whatever I needed to, to be there for you?"

"Now's not the time to play the blame game, girls." Nancy's mother tsks from just outside the bathroom.

"Is it a boy or a girl?" Leon interjects.

Stunned, Nancy says, "It's a girl." She pauses, looking at me with a mixture of fondness and hatefulness. A combo that would take decades to describe the uncanniness of it. "Brian and I decided on the name Angelica. After Brian's little sister."

My jowls salivate with the need to dispose of any food in my system. "You always wanted to name your baby Iris." I defend with disdain in my voice.

"Here we go." She groans.

"Don't start." I snap. "The last time you talked about having a baby girl, you said you wanted to name it Iris."

"Her."

"What?"

"You called my baby an 'it'. She's a 'her'." She defends. "You always hated the idea of children; I was surprised you ever agreed to be a Godmother."

"Yeah, well you can take back the status since me being in your life is such a goddamn burden." I hissed.

"I wouldn't want you to be her godmother if you were the last person on Earth." She grumbles childishly. A breath passes in silence before Nancy lets out a blood-curdling scream that sends shockwaves through my entire body. Gripping the side of the tub with an iron fist.

"Go lock all the doors and windows. Quickly. The smell of blood will draw them near." Nancy says coming down from an intense wave. "We don't have much time."

CHAPTER 26

Leon

What the fuck, what the fuck, what the absolute fuck?!

"I'll go. I know this place like the back of my hand. Keep watch on her." River says, wringing her hands on a towel by the sink. Cleansing herself of the blood that once stained her ivory skin. "Keep her safe, Leon."

Gripping her elbow as she passes, a look of fear flashes in her eyes. My stomach churns, a swell of an oncoming tsunami ready to give way. "Be careful out there." I say, pulling her into a deep, longing kiss meant to say everything I knew I couldn't possibly come up with the words for.

She nods her head and tips me a pinstriped smile before darting out of the room, around the old woman looming in the hallway and out of sight. The hallway goes on forever as I watch her walk away.

Turning to the very pregnant, very unhappy about being left in a room alone with me Nancy, she quickly adverts her gaze elsewhere. Fumbling while simultaneously trying to wiggle out of her clothes and keep herself covered.

"Do you want some help?" I ask begrudgingly. Nancy grunts something akin to a 'no' and continues struggling against her cloth restraints. With a huff, I go to her, grabbing a handful of fabric at the base of her neck and pulling. Which, in turn, caused Nancy to thrash against my grip.

"I got it, I got it. I fucking got it!" Nancy shouts.

"Clearly, you fucking don't." I retorted.

"I don't need your pity." She says, even though she's

glaring at a large towel on the opposite side of the room. I give it to her, and she mumbles out a very diluted "thanks." She white knuckles the side of the tub again in a wave of pain.

Taking up a post on the edge of the tub, I study the woman who has been so vile to my River. The woman who would choose a pedophile over someone she considered to be her family. And maybe I'm going to Hell for what I'm about to say to her.

"I don't pity you." I tsk, taking in the beige tiles and merlot accents of the dated bathroom. "I despise you."

"Excuse me?"

"You disgust me."

"What is your problem?"

"*Let me finish.*" I demand, turning my burning eyes onto the half-naked woman. Boring holes into the center of her forehead until her mouth clamps shut in both fear and annoyance. "How can you choose your best friend's abuser over her?"

"What are you talking about?" She asks meekly. Without another word, only a pointed stare, she continues. "If you're going to imply something, motherfucker, then just spit it out and say it."

I chuckle at her mixed amalgamation of the two phrases. "River tells me you don't know about the years of abuse that Brian caused her. How you wouldn't have believed her if she told you. Care to explain why that is?"

"Brian never did anything to her. She's spinning you lies like she always does."

I hum disappointedly, enjoying the pain that washes over her sweaty face. "See? She was right. No sooner than I could get the words out of my mouth, you defend Brian like he's the patron saint of lost causes." She scowls at me, tongue ready to fire off some bullshit I'm itching to hear.

"Why are you so quick to believe everything she says?" She asks pointedly, readjusting the towel over her body, shaking with the cold coming in from the open window above the toilet.

Wait. Since when was that open?

"Why are you so opposed to believing her?" I ask, closing the window and double-checking the lock. A pair of piercing yellow eyes flash just on the other side of the window before disappearing into the night.

My heart pounds in my chest, shaken by the sudden onslaught of terror coursing through my cold veins. The house feels too big. River feels too far away.

"You don't know River as well as you think you do." She croons, not bothering to look at me. Not seeing the panic I'm desperately trying to stifle. "She's always made up these grandiose stories about how bad everyone was to her. Big imagination. Bigger hatred for the world."

"Have you ever thought that maybe you don't know her as well as you think you do?" I ask.

"How would I know her less than you? I've known her since we were in kindergarten."

"I don't know, Nance. Maybe because you, much like everyone else in this goddamn town I've met today alone, all seem to look at River like she'd a dead girl walking. Like they're surprised she isn't taking up graveyard space in a cemetery somewhere." I retort, restless hands fidgeting with finding the blemishes in each of the tiles on the wall.

"We all thought she'd be dead by now." Nancy admits, the first real confession.

"'*We*' as in you, too?" I push, turning my hatred to face her head-on. A new fire ignites in my veins. *What's taking River so long?* "If you hated being her friend so much, then why did you string her along all these years? What did you gain from it?" My words cut through the eerie silence that surrounded the house. You could have heard a pin drop in the grass outside. Could hear shuffling feet on the linoleum across the five thousand square feet. But there was nothing. No signs of life outside the echo chamber of this damn bathroom.

"I don't answer to you." She grunts, reaching down to

her cervix. "Shit, shit, shit. I'm like eight centimeters dilated."

"What'd I miss?" River asks, socked feet shuffling quietly into the room, startling the both of us. She takes in the tension in the room, shooting me a weary look, unsure which way to go. To me, or Nancy.

"Your boyfriend interrogating-"

"She's eight centimeters." I interject, pulling River's attention away from Nancy long enough to redirect the conversation. "Her labor's progressing quickly."

She hums and nods, turning back to Nancy. "Your mom followed me around while I locked up. It's kind of creepy to have someone always over your shoulder." She notes with an empty chuckle. Nancy rolls her eyes harshly but doesn't rebut.

"Can I give birth to my baby without you two making comments left and fucking right?" Nancy asked with chattering teeth. The house has become undeniably cold, even with the heat blowing through the vents.

River throws her hands up in an act of aggravated compliance. Pulling scissors and gloves out of her back pockets, she sets them down on the vanity. Daintily, she takes off her jewelry one piece at a time, handing them to me for safekeeping. I carefully put them in my pocket and kiss her on the forehead. She strips herself down to her underwear and bra, slipping on an oversized shirt I don't recognize. The logo on the back is that of an animal rescue group. She completes her ritual by tying her hair back away from her face.

"I stole an old shirt of yours from the donation bag in your closet, so I don't bloody my clothes. Hope you don't mind." She says, clearly not caring if Nancy cares about her choice in thievery. All emotion has escaped River's voice. Not an ounce of empathy in the emotionless stare she uses to slice through the room.

She's terrifying. And so, so hot.

"Do you even know what you're doing?" Nancy snarks, removing the towel from her body upon River's silent command. Those deadly golden eyes.

"No." She states bluntly. "Do you?"

"No." Nancy grumbles.

A dark line runs down the center of Nancy's stomach. A near pitch-black line against her sickly pale skin. Smaller branches vein out from the main line, wrapping their way around her entire torso. Deep purple stains a half-inch splotch.

"Nancy," River whispers with wide, petrified eyes.

"It's fine. It happens." Nancy dismisses River's clear concerns.

"Nancy, is he hurting you?" River asks.

"No! Of course not!" Nancy defends. "It's the baby."

"Is this baby human?" I ask rhetorically. River shoots me a 'shut the hell up' glance, but Nancy's gaze is one of guilt. Almost remorse. She doesn't meet my stare, and River is too busy glaring at me to notice. The purple splotch moves from one spot to another, almost like how you'd see a baby punch its mother's stomach in utero. Except this baby's moving bruises around like it's easy as pie. "Are you bleeding out?"

"Leon, shut up." Nancy insists, shooting me a disgruntled look. I flash her a cheeky smile and waggle my fingers. River leans in to inspect Nancy's stomach. The seemingly alive bruise. One of River's nails pokes at the bulging spot and it recoils. Retreating into Nancy's skin. Nausea wafts over me at the sentience of this *thing*.

BANG, BANG, BANG.

The three of us jump at the startling rush of noise through the wall just on the other side of the window I closed earlier. We exchange confused looks as the salty scent of the ocean wafts into the room, seemingly from nowhere.

"Nancy, there are two things I need from you right now." River demands in a whisper-yell, getting on her knees and leveling with the pregnant lady. "I need you to tell me *what* you know about these monsters." She says eye to eye with a scared-looking Nancy. "And I need you to tell me what the fuck you're about to give birth to."

"I don't know." Nancy pleads, trying to level her

breathing as a wave of contractions swells, making blood pool in the bathtub underneath her. "I don't know." She repeats.

"This baby's coming whether you tell me or not. I need to know what we're dealing with!" Panic floods River's voice as she takes up position, ready to catch this monster baby.

"I don't know!" Nancy wails, her shaky legs straddling the sides of the tub as makeshift stirrups, hands grasping the back of her thighs. Readying herself to push. "I can't do this, I can't do this, I can't do this!"

"You don't have a choice now, girlfriend." River scolds with knitted eyebrows. She glances at me one last time and nods me over. I come to stand beside her, the top of her head barely making it to my waist. "Ready?" She asks me, and I nod. Like she said, we don't have a choice now. This shindig is happening whether we want it to or not.

The silence that builds as we wait for another contraction is groundbreaking. Surrounded by labored breaths and the rustling of leaves outside send shivers up my spine. My fingers linger on the base of River's neck, tracing lines into her supple skin. Goosebumps form under my touch. Ever the sensitive baby, so reactive to my touch.

All I want to do is be alone with my angel. To give her my undivided attention. To have hers. To fulfill all of my teased promises. Instead, we're stuck in this freezing bathroom. Watching the birth of the AntiChrist. Probably.

It all came in a flash.

Nancy built up a scream that nearly shattered the windows. River commands her to push, gloved hands ready to guide this creature out of its mother.

Everything happens all at once.

As soon as Nancy pushed hard one time, the top of the baby's head crowns. A full, thick head of black hair.

Two more pushes and the baby's halfway out. The child's features are that of a normal baby. Wrinkled, alien-like, but nothing out of the ordinary.

One more push and the baby's free. Attached only by

the umbilical cord, silent as a mouse. For a moment, I half expected the baby to be dead. River places the seemingly normal baby on Nancy's bare chest.

Nancy's eyes water and her bottom lip quiver as she looks at her baby. This child that she's just met, but clearly loves. With newly freed hands, River takes two silver clips with old bleach stains and clamps the umbilical cord. Taking the red and black scissors in her dominant hand, she hesitates to cut the cord. Looking up at Nancy, who doesn't have any idea we're still in the room with her.

With a swift snip of the scissors, mother and baby are disconnected. And as if right on cue, the baby makes its first noise. A cry unlike any I'd ever heard.

It wasn't a cry at all.

It was a song.

A melody. A near-perfect operatic voice that called to some primitive part of me to run away screaming. To throw it outside with the monsters. Because it was one.

The taste of pennies stings in my mouth.

CHAPTER 27

River

Oh, sweet mother of Jesus. What the actual fuck did Nancy give birth to.

This kid has to be some sort of a siren or something with the way you would expect it to open its mouth and scream-cry, but all it does is sing fucking opera or some shit. Or at least the siren equivalent to opera. Very enchanting if it wasn't so goddamn creepy. Nancy doesn't even seem to notice the abnormal sounds of her child in the same way that Leon and I do. And I'm not inclined to ask what the hell that's all about.

I've heard that women are supposed to have an afterbirth or whatever it's called when they have to push out their placenta. I keep encouraging her to push again, but it's like Nancy doesn't even hear me anymore.

It's like she doesn't hear anything.

The iron smell of blood floods my senses as Nancy stands from the tub, completely naked, dripping blood down her legs, and attempts to leave the bathroom with the baby in her arms. Without a single word.

"Where are you going?" I ask fruitlessly, quickly climbing to my feet to follow her bloody footprints. As soon as she steps over the threshold and into the hallway, a booming voice shakes the house, rattling my bones. Stopping me dead in my tracks.

"WHERE'S MY BABY?!" The voice calls. Disembodied. All-encompassing. Uncanny. The windows rattle in their frames. Leon runs to me, grabbing my arm in the frenzy.

The smell of iron fills my nose, my mouth, my lungs.

A tug on my stomach.

For just a moment, the world is eerily still. No wind whipping around the house. No noise anywhere to indicate any sign of life. I even held my breath in anticipation of what may come.

Blood stained my hands through the gloves, my borrowed shirt, my legs, the freezing tiles, down the hall, and out of sight. The air is so sharp and pungent that I'd have assumed I was transported into a butcher's meat freezer. Leon and I wait for something to happen. For the tension to break. For an explanation of our erratic heartbeats.

Filth covered my body, but also my soul. How could I stay and help Nancy give birth to that *monster?* Why wouldn't I just take my chances outside with the darkness and what looms inside it? What is even lurking in those woods?

Could we make a run for it back to the hotel? Would they even let us back in if the whole town is locked down after sundown?

The mental exhaustion settles over me quickly, sharp pain lacing its way down my neck and spine. The adrenaline, the guilt, the anxiety, the anger, it's all too much. Leon calls out to me, willing to be back from my disassociated state, but I don't know if I can take a single step from where I'm standing. The cold tile warming underneath my feet the longer I stand unwavering. I don't know what specifically is paralyzing me. Can't pinpoint exactly what held me firmly in place.

"Let's get you cleaned up." His voice booms in my ear. Not that he was yelling, but it echoed in the quiet. Leon's strong, comforting hands tug gently at the bloodied shirt's hem, sliding it easily over my head. He then proceeds to help me remove my bra and underwear.

Unbased embarrassment rakes over my skin as his eyes flow up and down my body. Not seductively. Not like he wanted to ravish me here and now but searching. Looking for something, anything wrong. Big boba eyes seize mine. Calloused hands engulf my face, pulling my gaze to him solidly.

Then, he speaks. "You are *the most gorgeous* woman I've ever laid my eyes on." His words are soft, similar to his smile. His hands follow my jawline down my neck and to my shoulders, the way you run your fingers over a real crystal glass before filling it with ungodly expensive wine. He studies me carefully, making his own set of assumptions about my comfort, though he doesn't say anything. I can see it in his eyes, it's written all over his face.

I attempt to give him a warm, comforting smile, but I can't force it into my eyes, and he can see that they're lackluster.

He moves behind me, turning us to both face the mirror over the sink where I take in my unsightly body covered in someone else's blood and fluids. He kisses me behind my ear before turning away to turn on the shower. The icy air nips at my exposed skin, pecking goosebumps up through the surface.

It doesn't take long for the steam to penetrate the air, warming my achingly cold appendages. For a moment, I let the warmth consume me. Drawing my eyelids closed, sleep washes over me. Even though it wasn't anywhere near midnight, my usual bedtime. Exhaustion settles over my entire being. I might very well crawl into that shower and sleep forever.

Leon chuckles lightly, the warm exhale ghosts over my skin as he continues his barrage of kisses up my neck. I hadn't noticed his return. "Come on, angel." He ushers me over to the shower. The open glass door lets droplets of hot water spray onto my bare skin.

I step in, seemingly having forgotten how to breathe at the sight of Leon, naked and skin gleaming from the moisture in the air. Words escaped me, and you'd have thought I didn't know any language at all. My suspected arrhythmia kicks in.

I hum, keeping my eyes away from my reflection in the slowly fogging mirror. The dull overhead lights cast our complexations in yellow and tan hues. He leans in to kiss me again, lips supple and soft as they linger wherever they touch. Sending shivers down my spine.

His hands move up and down my body and I lose myself in their ability to hold me together, even when I'm just a pile of rubble in his hands. If being in love with Leon Kang was a crime, I'd plead guilty every time. No questions asked.

"I'm sorry I got us stuck here." I apologize, running my wet fingers through his thick, black hair.

He hums thoughtfully, a sly smirk coaxing up the corner of his perfect lips. "Certainly, this is not ideal. Not exactly how I wanted to spend my evening, but I think we can make do." He teases, still kissing stars up and down my neck. "I say let's take advantage of this mansion."

"If I wasn't terrified out of my mind about everything right now, I'd be *very* down for whatever you have in mind, lover boy." I retorted. A smile blooms as I turn his head to steal a kiss from those full, wet lips.

"You sure I can't take your mind off things right now?" He asks, raising and waggling a sole eyebrow, smirking when my cheeks blister with blush.

"I can be persuaded." Before I can gain my bearings, Leon spins me around, pushing me up against the tiled shower wall. One strong hand grips my hip while the other slides around to my needy, aching pussy. He slides a finger over my folds, taking in my wetness, and chuckles darkly. Bringing his coated finger up to his mouth, he licks it clean and goes back in for more.

He takes his time stroking me, circling my clit with precision and deep satisfaction as he drinks in each moan that escapes my lips. I'd never been very vocal during sex until Leon. His touch is electric against my skin. The need to be quiet only heightens the pleasure. His hand comes up to cup my mouth, to keep me quiet from our potential listeners.

Leon's thick, hard cock presses against my ass. Throbbing with each of my reactions. I'm pinned completely, helpless against Leon's strength. At his mercy. I ride the high of his expert fingers, need building and building and building until I can't take it anymore.

"Don't come until I say so." Leon growls lowly in my ear, feeling my pussy clench around his fingers. Removing his hand from my mouth, he positions my hips upward to angle himself at my entrance, quickly pulling my hips down and sinking me on his cock.

With the return of his hand over my mouth, he pounds into me hard while his fingers still circle my clit. I bite down on my lip to keep from crying out from the swell of pleasure.

"You think you deserve to come tonight, angel?" He asks darkly, breathing rhythmically in time with his thrusts. Each one pushes further and further into me until it's almost too much to take. I nod my head and utter a muffled 'yes' that gets lost in his hand swallowing my face.

He moves his hand to my neck, squeezing the sides as he does so. Freeing my mouth to speak but restricting my ability to speak all the same. I beg, *beg,* him to let me come. Overstimulation threatens to take over.

"If you come now, you know the punishments." He croons with a wicked smile on his face. Eyeing me with a predatory look. I nod again, knowing just what would happen if I disobeyed him. The brat in me desperately wants to. And as his fingers will my climax to fruition, stars bloom behind my eyes. A chuckle escapes from deep within his throat at my disobedience.

As my orgasm crashes over me, Leon pulls out of me, leaving me empty and aching for his cock. Gripping the back of my head by my hair, he throws me down to my knees. With shaky limbs, I reach up and start stroking him, causing a moan to echo off the walls and reverberate my ears, into my bones.

Leon pushes my head towards his cock, dripping with precum and covered in my orgasm. I open my mouth, salivating at the thought of drinking in his cum. Stroking my tongue over him, I revel in how undone he's coming with my touch, my mouth.

He guides my head with an iron grip on my hair. The sting of the pain feels heavenly under his strength. I take in as much of him as I can, gagging as he pushes further into my mouth. His orgasm builds with each stroke, each lap of my tongue.

He picks up the pace rapidly and sloppily until he stops abruptly, shooting warm, thick strokes of cum into the back of my throat. I drink him in, careful not to miss a drop. With spit still leaking from my mouth, he pulls me up and kisses me. His eyes are wild with desire, nearly pitch black.

With the tension eased in my shoulders and my body still recovering from such a hard orgasm, Leon has to help me finish showering. Which isn't entirely something unusual, he's done it before, but this time it feels more sensual. I get lost in the feeling of his hands massaging shampoo into my hair and how the expensive shower gel moisturizes my skin.

Inside this shower, with Leon and the warm water, I'm certain nothing can get me. No monsters, or monster babies, or mothers to monster babies can harm me. And if it weren't for my pruning fingers, I could have – would have – stayed in here forever.

CHAPTER 28

Leon

I did my best to clean the blood off the floor. However, our little detour in the shower may have allowed it to set a little longer than maybe it should have. No matter, because I made do with the cleaning supplies tucked away under the kitchen sink while River busied herself trying to find Nancy in this maze of a fucking house.

This place apparently has two kitchens. One upstairs, and one in the basement. Which is where River and I found Nancy. Baby slung over one shoulder, sound asleep, frying what looked like a very lean steak or roast. The smell is unlike anything I'd encountered before.

I was weary of the baby. River and I both heard the thing sing the song of its people, whoever they may be. There's nothing normal about that baby.

"Hey, Nancy." River says apprehensively, cautiously approaching the woman and her demon spawn. When Nancy turns around to acknowledge us, River continues. "How are you doing?"

"Oh, Riv! Can you believe this baby is all mine?" Nancy coos, proceeding to babble to the sleeping babe.

"Looks just like you." River lies, cutting her eyes at me. "Did you pick out a name?" The dim lights of the downstairs kitchen lighting up only the worst features of everyone here. Giving Nancy the look of someone telling ghost stories over a campfire.

"She named herself. She told me her name is Dinah."

Nancy says, flipping the searing mystery meat, and adding a dash of salt and pepper on the already cooked side. God, someone give this woman some seasonings and one good cooking lesson.

"Oh, that's a lovely name." River agrees. Nancy nods and River asks, "Have you cleaned up? Do you need to shower or need us to do anything?"

"No, I'm good. I'm just going to have dinner and then admire my precious angel baby." Nancy replies.

"What *are* you having for dinner?" I ask, still eyeing the pan before her. The smell coating the inside of my nose in a rancid way.

"This?" She points to the meat. "It's my placenta."

Oh, dear God. Get me out of here.

River covers her mouth and nose with her hand, holding back the vomit threatening to come up from her mildly weak stomach. I'm honestly surprised it took her this long in the night to almost vomit.

"Well, we'll leave you to your dinner. If you need us, we'll be upstairs." I say, hurriedly ushering River away from this cannibalistic bullshit going on down here.

Once upstairs, River collapses onto the couch, covering her eyes, breathing labored but measured. *'I'm working on it.'* She'd said to me the first few times I'd encountered her weak stomach. It was usually coupled with an awkward chuckle and a handful of antacid tablets. More than you're supposed to take at once.

I left her to raid cabinets in search of something that could help ease her queasiness. Coming up short of anything but chewable Pepto-Bismol. Rushing back to her, I tilt her head up and pop the tablets in her mouth.

"Chew." I instruct. She does, wincing at the very pink, bubble-gummy taste of the medicine. I leave her one more time to pillage the fridge for anything to drink. A ginger ale preferably, but again, finding a half-assed substitution. A Coke. I crack the mini can when I return. She turns up her nose again.

"Drink." I insist.

"You're so bossy tonight." She quips but obeys orders.

"It's because I care." I tease, sitting down on the coffee table in front of her.

"You could have saved so much money on the hotel if you'd known we'd be stuck here anyway." River jokes, trying to alleviate the tension I know she feels about my spending habits.

"Eh, I'm not worried about it." I shrug. "I may or may not have other surprises up my sleeve." I confess.

"Is it that you're going to murder me?" She asks with a half-smile around another sip of teeth-rotting Coke.

"Damn, you fooled my plan." I chuckle, brushing her hair out of her face. "No, I'm not going to kill you, angel. But I do intend on making the most of tonight. Even if we are in shark-infested waters."

"Uh-huh. What might you have in mind, lover boy?" She asks, big golden eyes peering into my very soul with hesitant mischief.

"That good time I wanted." I quip, pulling out my phone and searching for the playlist I've been cultivating specifically for my angel. Music starts playing throughout the room, a surprised look dances across River's face. "I had this whole big plan of having a pool date with champagne and chocolate-covered strawberries back at the hotel where I played this playlist for you. Unfortunately, like many things in life, it doesn't always take you where you want. But it takes you where you need to go. And I'd follow you to the very ends of the Earth, River Celeste." I toss my phone onto the couch, pulling her up onto her feet and wrapping my arms around her. As the first song plays, we sway slowly to the beat. "I want to celebrate us."

She pulls back to look at me skeptically. "We've got our whole lives to celebrate." She says with an eye roll.

"And I won't take a single *second* of you for granted. Promise." Moisture wells in my eyes, and my heart swells just like my tear ducts. There's this ticking time bomb and I don't know when it'll go off. I guess no one ever does, but you never think it'll end soon.

Maybe everyone's just saying these things to scare me. To make my feelings weaker. An attempt at a coupe. And perhaps instead of enjoying her at a normal human pace, I fell in love at lightning speed because I knew. *I knew.* Unlike the rest of the world who gets to relish their partner in blissful ignorance of their impending demise, I didn't get that luxury.

But, if I'm honest, I much rather like the pace of loving her. Of being in love with such an extraordinary woman. To love her with everything I have, and it still not be enough to express how genuinely in love I am.

Because loving River is like breathing. She is the oxygen I need. Like I was born to do nothing else but love her. No other accomplishment could compare to being loved by her.

"You're scaring me, Leon." She says as I lean in to silence her with a kiss. Her hands cup my jaw, fingers moving to intertwine into my hair.

"I don't mean to, mon amour." I apologize, blinking the tears away. "You just mean *everything* to me. And I wanted to say thank you for the – the man you've made me. For giving me a reason to keep going. I don't know if I'd be here without you."

"Of course you wouldn't be stuck in a random stranger's house without me." She jokes until the realization settles over her. "Oh. Oh, Leon."

"I had nothing to live for until you walked into my life. So, thank you. A million times. To the edge of the galaxies. It's all thanks to you."

Her full bottom lip quivers heavily, and she wants to break free of my grip, but I hold her tight. As tightly as I can. The song ends and a more upbeat tempo begins. She wipes her eyes on her sleeve.

"Leon, I- you're so much more than I deserve. You're extraordinary."

"I'll be anything for you." I breathe into her skin.

Drinking in her clean, fresh scent. Not her normal smell, but it has her undertones. I'd never forget her.

"Just be you." She pleads, giving me a peck on my lips before pulling away. "Is this just your normal playlist?" She asks skeptically, not recognizing the song playing.

"No, I've been curating a playlist for you since the day I met you." I confess, unleashing all the waterworks she'd been holding back. "Oh, oh no. Did I say something wrong? Oh, angel, I'm so-" I plead. I can't upset her. I love her so much.

"Shut up!" She says, sniffling and smacking my chest lightly. "You're the sweetest man alive and I hate you for it." I'm trying to contain my overwhelming desire to sob.

"You don't mean that." I laugh nervously, taking her hands in mine. "About being sweet. I know you hate me." I say with a wink.

"Of course I mean it." Her bottom lip quivers pitifully. She reaches down, grabbing her half-empty Coke can, holding it up for a toast.

"To Leon Kang, the greatest man I've ever known." She toasts with a fond smile and eyes made of pure gold.

"I'd like to thank God, the Academy, and my wonderful, beautiful, amazing, selfless, kind, and caring girlfriend for this award." I add with a smirk as she hands me the can and I take a swig of the drink. "To River Celeste, my reason for living."

The love of my life.

She takes the can from my hand, holding it up. "I'd like to thank my boyfriend, who always pulls me from the darkness. My light at the end of this once dreary tunnel. My North Star." She drinks the rest of the soda with one sip.

Our laughs and banter echo through the room while my phone continues to play the finely curated playlist decorating months of how I've felt about her and all the songs I've associated with her.

We raid the pantry, cooking whatever we can throw together into a semblance of a decent meal. I justified it by clipping a one hundred dollar bill to the refrigerator with a note, but only for River's sake. These people don't deserve the shit stains I'd leave in the toilet bowl.

Three hours goes by in the blink of an eye. We find and finish off a bottle of expensive-looking wine before deciding to call it a night on the very last song of the playlist.

We walked to our room, or *a* room that we randomly picked that had a big bed and nice, fluffy pillows. Purple bedding, curtains, and rug line the expanse of the room. The adjoining bathroom, while small given the size of the house, was also decked out in purple décor, towels, and bathmats.

Hand in hand, we try to contain our buzzed giggling so as not to wake anyone. The tiredness and bubbles make mundane things suddenly stand-up comedy worthy.

I love her. I love her. I love her.

CHAPTER 29

River

I thought I'd fall asleep instantly, given the drunkenness and tiredness surrounding my very essence. But here I am, staring at the darkness that surrounds us with a clock that keeps ticking along.

Tick, tick, tick.

Leon snores softly behind me, but I'm unable to lull my aching body to sleep, growing restless by the minute. I slip out of his arms without waking him, which is a feat in and of itself, and traverse to the living room through the dim nightlights that line the hallways.

Scrolling aimlessly on social media, catching up on the posts I've missed from the last couple of days. I eventually ran out of things to look at on my following page, so I moved to the explore page. I picked a post that looked interesting.

Ever since I did that deep dive on Leon, my explore page has been filled with nothing *but* Leon out at events and posing with celebrities for promotional pictures. I saved a lot of the pictures of him because, duh, he's hot, but this one staring at me looks different. This one looks familiar.

Oh shit. This one has me in it.

Producer Leon Kang was spotted in a remote resort with a mystery girl.

The image is of us leaving the resort earlier this morning. The same hardened demeanor on his face, staring directly at the camera, but my head is turned away, hiding my face. I'm exceptionally hesitant to open the comments. I know how dedicated fans can be to their favorite celebrities. I've seen what some of them write about him.

I can't do this.

My breath hitches in my throat as adrenaline courses through my body. Curiosity gets the better of me, I open the comments.

'*OMG NO!*'

Oh, this is going to be a wonderful fucking ride. My chest has a thousand-pound weight sitting on it already.

'*But that's my boyfriend.*' '*Who's he with?*'
'*HE'S SO FINE OMFG*' '*When will it be my turn?!*'
'*Ew, he can do better!!*' '*SO HAPPY FOR HIM!!!*'
'*God gave him everything but my number.*'
'*Alpha Leon once again!*' '*Give me back my man!*'
'*He wrecks me every day.*'
'*I never knew I would fall for eyebrows so bad.*'
'*I'm dizzy and trembling right now.*'
'*He KNOWS how fine he is god damn.*'
'*God, I am not this strong.*' '*How lucky is she?!*'

It's almost like watching a trainwreck in real-time. I couldn't take my eyes off of it. It could have been worse, though, but that post came out thirty-two minutes ago.

And now seems as good of a time as any to have an existential crisis about dating a celebrity.

What was I thinking? Of course, there's going to be paparazzi every-fucking-where. Why would I think that rural Virginia would be any different? Oh, good question, River. Maybe because it's RURAL FUCKING VIRGINIA! How the fuck was he tracked out here? Who was it? Who did we pass by that took a picture this morning? How long is it going to take before people find out who I am?

I fly to my profile to change my profile picture to a sunset picture I took a while ago and make my profile private. I do the same with all my socials.

I don't want to be famous. I don't want people following

me around. I am barely coping with the attention that Leon's giving me. I don't want Leon to have to deal with the onslaught of anxiety attacks I'd have whenever we'd step outside, knowing that people might recognize me. I don't know how he does it.

Salt streams swell and fall onto my phone screen. A beacon in the darkness I've surrounded myself in once again. The same darkness that I confessed to Leon he pulls me out of. How can I love him if I'm only giving him a broken version of myself?

I'm tired of crying. It's so fucking exhausting. My head hurts. I need Excedrin and caffeine. I find the tried and true medicine cabinet in the kitchen, plucking a bottle of ibuprofen and acetaminophen off the top shelf and taking two of each. Dry swallowing the pills, much to my discomfort.

I take my time perusing the snacks in the pantry. They had everything you could ever want to eat and drink, which was surprising considering this used to be a heavily disordered eating house. I go into the fridge and grab a soda and water, knowing that I'll get another headache if I'm dehydrated from all the soda that I use to curb the exhaustion migraine. I snag a bag of chips and a mini-Oreos cup, plopping back down on the couch.

Knock, knock, knock.

My entire body freezes in anticipation. Adrenaline fires off all my nerve endings, speeding up my heartbeat, and flooding my skin with pin pricks and heat. *What the fuck was that?*

KNOCK, KNOCK, KNOCK.

It grew closer. I don't know how. I don't know from where, but the noise surrounds me. Almost like it was right next to me. As if I had put my ear right against the wall that was being knocked on. Trying to wrangle in my erratic breathing and heartbeat was useless. If a monster was out of me, it already knew I was here.

I'm sure it could smell the fear wafting off my clammy

skin. Could taste the perspiration on my forehead. Rejoice in the goosebumps and hairs standing on end.

KNOCK, KNOCK, KNOCK.

It was everywhere. Right next to me. Far away, above, below. Loud enough to rattle my ribcage, the windows, the handles on doors.

Holding my breath, I count until the ringing begins in my ears and then exhale. Inhale. Exhale. Focus on something tangible. Focus, River. Focus.

I should have dead-sprinted back to my room. Threw myself under the covers. Let Leon's arms surround me. Find comfort in him like I always do. But this isn't a movie. There are no definitive rules these monsters have to follow, but Leon always felt like he had a plan for anything.

He enjoyed a good fight. Jerica had sent me videos from Leon's underground boxing days. She talked and talked and talked into the echo chamber that was those damn messages about how he's not just an asshole because of his looks. That he's dangerous. That his family are hitmen. His parents work for the CIA. That *he* used to be a hitman. Blah, blah, blah.

I don't think I ever believed her. Not until I saw the sparks fly in his eyes two days ago. She never deterred me from loving him. If anything, she made it worse, because who doesn't love a man who could win a fight?

What sounds like nails rapping on the window freezes whatever train of thought I could form. Any plans of escape. *Tap, tap, tap.* Pause. *Tap, tap, tap.* They continued, moving along the window, almost as if looking for a sweet spot.

Suddenly, it grew deathly silent and dark. Darker than a black hole. There wasn't even the sound of any appliances running. Then, out of the darkness, a familiar voice echoes from the other side of the drawn curtains behind me. "River, please let me in."

The blood pumping through my veins roars in my ears.

Don't answer. Don't answer. Don't answer. Don't make a sound. Don't let it know you heard it. Don't answer.

When I was a kid, my grandmother believed in all the wild superstitions. She said it was because of her native heritage. She grew up in the mountains. She used to tell me that if I didn't learn anything else in this life, I should know two things.

1. Don't answer any call from the woods. Day or night.
2. Don't whistle at night.

I took both of those things with the tiniest grain of salt imaginable. Never bothered to care about a bunch of old lady superstitions. But with everything that's happened in the last few months, I just know that woman is rolling in her grave, itching to say, 'I told you so.'

"River, I know you're in there. Please, just let me in." The voice echoes around me. Circling its prey, closing in. All the air leaves my lungs rapidly. I recognize that voice. Underneath the layers of inhumanity, I hear it. I know that voice.

It haunts my dreams. Even still.

"River, it's so cold out here." The voice pleads. *Tap, tap, tap.* Its fingernails knock on the glass, and I pray it holds. I pray to Gods I don't believe in, to any God listening. If there even is a god, or multiple, out there listening.

Don't let that glass break. Don't let it in. *Don't do this to me. Don't do this to me. Don't do this to me.*

Silent tears fall from my blurry eyes, having left my glasses back in our room. I'd been navigating without them, staring at my phone without them. I can see if I squint, but only up close. Frozen with fear in my spot, there was no chance of me returning to my protector. Not until the monsters are gone. Not until sunrise.

Will my heart give out before then? It's barely midnight. The sun won't make its return back to me for hours. Would I rot on this couch before she comes back? Would the locks on all the doors suddenly unlock like they did for Boyle? Am I even as safe as I assume I am inside these four walls?

"River," The voice – that fucking voice – calls. "I want

to play." I'm hearing shit. That last part sounds like Angie. Begging me to play with her when she was seven or eight.

Angie was always short for her age. She barely came up to my chest at eight. But she used to stand on her tippy toes, pouting and cross-armed until I caved and played with her. Whatever game she wanted. Her games, her rules.

We used to spend countless hours playing outside on the swing set. I would push her until we were both dizzy. Or pull out the worn, very well-loved classic edition of Monopoly that was missing half the pieces. I don't think there was a single game that I didn't go bankrupt. Mostly on purpose.

"I'll make you a deal, little sis." The voice returns to the familiar, stickiness that I've spent years chasing out of my nightmares. "Play my game."

I shake my head as if he could somehow know my answer. Hear my last brain cells rattling around in my noggin.

"If you win, I'll leave you alone. You can go back to that little boy toy of yours, and you can fuck each other's brains out until you're both dead. If I win, well, you'll have to play and see."

I shake my head again. I don't know if I ever stopped shaking it. My muscles shake violently. *No, no, no, no, no.*

"What do you say?" Brian's disembodied voice asks.

No, no, no, no, no. My stomach churns, like an old-timey washing machine and I am the clothes in the drum.

The roaring of my heart fills my ears as I watch the front door handle jiggle, unable to hear it over the adrenaline coursing through me.

Jiggle, jiggle, jiggle.

The metal clatters together against the lock before falling still and silent. Vomit creeps its way up the back of my throat. The pounding in my head increases tenfold. With a *click*, the lock turns against itself. Another *click* and the deadbolt is undone.

Just like that, I've lost my ability to breathe.

"Hello, River." Brian's voice greets. However, no figure

shows itself. The door is still latched. I could make it there before it opens. I could fight him. "Are you ready, darling?"

I stand, unable to control any bodily movement. It's like I'm a bystander in my own skin. I'm me, but I'm just an onlooker as an alien pilots my meat suit.

"What the hell are you doing?" I ask myself. Not just terrified, but furious. *What the fuck is going on with me?*

"River?" I hear Leon call from what seems like miles away. His voice is so distant that I almost thought I was imagining it in the first place.

Yell for him, River. Warn him. No sound escapes my drying throat. My feet stop me ten feet short of the front door. If I could just tell Leon what's going on. He could help. He would help.

"You love him. Don't you?" Brian's voice asks, almost softly. Almost as if he cared. My heart swells, jaw clenched to hold in the tears that threaten to spill. I nod, not knowing if he could see me. Not trusting my voice. Eyes still staring at the unlocked door.

"River, come back to bed." Leon coos sleepily. The tears I tried to suppress fall in thick streaks down my face. My bottom lip quivers heavily. The knot in my stomach deepens.

"You wouldn't want anything to happen to him, would you?" Brian asks.

"Don't you *dare* touch him." The words sound foreign and animalistic as they hit my ears. I don't even recognize myself. "I'll kill you."

"I employ you to try, sugar plum." Brian taunts.

Oh, God. Oh, God. Oh, God. Don't hurt Leon. Please, please, please don't hurt my Leon. Please, please, please, please, please.

"What do you want?" I demand through teeth clenched so hard it sends shockwaves radiating across my jaw. Breathing is excruciating. All of the energy I have left goes into remaining upright. Snot begins brewing in my nose, furthering my inability to fill my lungs properly.

"Play with me, River. Indulge me. You do that, I promise I'll leave your boy toy alone." Brian says like the devil reaching out his hand. *Take my hand.*

"How do I know you won't hurt him?"

Click.

The door unlatches and swings inward, letting in the freezing cold that pierces my nose and chills me to my core. Outside is pitch black, minus the streetlights in the distance. The woods stare at me from within the void, evil and repulsive.

"Come to me, River."

"Or what?" I ask with lackluster defiance, the panic surging through my body is enough to put me on the verge of vomiting.

"Or he dies." He states matter-of-factly, and the tears roll harder, thicker, down my blazing-hot cheeks. The incoming wind nips through my thin clothes, nearly freezing my tears in their tracks.

"Please don't hurt him." I plead, drowning in my fear and terror of what lies just beyond that threshold.

"Then come to me, my darling." Brian's voice coos, and from within the shadows, out steps a man who looks wholy unhuman, yet completely human.

An abnormally tall, thin man emerges from the deepest shadows, just barely enough for me to catch anymore more than a glimpse of his movements. Dressed in dark colors to match the pitch-black night.

That's not Brian.

I will myself to move, to close the door, to deny what was being asked of me. Go back to Leon. Go be with your lover. Run away from here. Drive until these monsters stop chasing you.

Get out of here.

My feet step forward, freezing floorboards sizzle under the heat. Eyes trained on the being in the darkness. Two more steps. Two more steps are all that stand between me and the outside. The darkness.

The woods.

"I'll keep you safe, River." The voice promises. I want to believe him. That nothing will happen to Leon. "I won't hurt your little boy toy. Scout's honor."

I gulp as I take another unwilling step. I can't let anything happen to him. My hands shake violently. Anything I do from here on out could end catastrophically.

I can't risk anything happening to Leon.

"Good girl." Brian coos sickeningly as I take my final step.

"Do you know what game we're going to play tonight, Little River?"

I shake my head. The tall man stalks closer, his eyes glowing vibrant yellow against the pitch black.

"Who's that?" I ask, crazy for even thinking I would receive an explanation at a time like this. "What am I supposed to do?" I ask further, willing an answer from the darkness. Something. Anything.

"Run."

My feet fly out from under me, clinging to my cell phone in one hand, clutching my chest with the other. I barrel off the porch at lightning speed, nearly tripping on the uneven bricks as I do so. My eyes still haven't adjusted to the absence of light surrounding me.

No glasses. No shoes. Barely any clothes. Not a lot going on for me at the moment. Crisp, icy grass prods at my bare feet.

Stay on the pavement. Stay with the light.

Except, the lights are now swarming with creatures. Shadows of different forms are backlit by dim and distant streetlamps. Tall, thin, small, round, muscular, deteriorating. Anything a twisted mind could come up with, and then some. Dozens of things. Monsters.

I am going to die.

Veering off towards the woods, a sharp pain clutches my stomach. I know this is a bad idea. A really terrible, awful idea. But what choice do I have? It's either me or Leon. I can't have them going after him. Not when I can distract them.

The tall White Oaks come tumbling into view. Fast approaching the tree line. The air escaping my lungs doesn't get replenished, and the sharp inhales I take are short and filled with pinpricks throughout my throat and lungs.

As I step into the forest, the darkness gets darker. I hear Brian's cackling laughter in the distance. Twigs snap behind me like I'm being hunted.

I *am* being hunted.

I should have died back in my apartment all those months ago. If Boyle wasn't meant to kill me, then Mark was. But here I am, living on borrowed time. Unwillingly basking in this monster-filled forest like I'm not living in some fucked up fantasy where I'm supposed to be the final girl. But I was *never* meant to be the final girl.

Between my feet pounding the frozen Earth, my erratic heart sending SOS correspondence to outer space, and my very labored breathing, there wasn't a snowball's chance in hell of me hearing anything coming up beside me, around me.

Dead branches and bushes scrape my skin, leaving gashes wherever they touch. Ripping the thin cotton of the pajama pants I had stolen from Nancy's room.

The van comes to a screeching halt, slamming my limp head into the seat in front of me. We've been driving for about twenty minutes or so, in what direction, I don't know.

How far do I run? How long will I have to survive before I ever reach safety and daylight? Will I even have a chance at surviving these monsters? Whatever the hell they are.

Through the pain and exhaustion. The fire set in my lungs. I have never been more driven. Even as I approach the brink of collapse, I push and push and push myself, my body, and my soul to keep running. Keep going.

Because I am a dead man if I stop.

I may as well be a dead man running now. With no end in sight. No light at the end of the proverbial tunnel. Nothing guides me to safety but a pitch-black pit in my stomach as dark as the world around me.

There's no fighting these monsters. There are too many of them. Too many rules that don't make sense for the ones I do know about. Changelings, or so the internet calls them, things like Boyle and Mark, they're easy to kill under the right circumstances. If you know what you're dealing with. But I don't know what exactly I'm dealing with.

The problem is you never know what you're dealing with until you're on the brink of death. Staring the Grim Reaper right in the face is the only time you get clarity. And I'm living on borrowed time.

In the emptiness that engulfs me, it's hard to make out any shapes other than those that are directly in front of me. There's a lingering scent of manure, reminiscent of Mr. Roldan's dairy farm. *Have I run that far already?*

I listen intently to my footsteps, the ones following me. Hunting me. They crunch on the dead grass, dry leaves, and exposed tree roots. Its forest floor hasn't received rain in quite some time, but by the smell in the air, it's coming. If it rains tonight, I might die from exposure before I die from whatever lurks in the darkness.

From nine o'clock, a hand reaches out for me. I yelp involuntarily, trying to skirt out of the way, to keep distance between me and whatever the hell had caught up with me. But I wasn't fast enough. The hand grasps my arm, while another pins my mouth closed.

I wrestle against the sheer strength of my attacker. Thrashing and pulling against the grip that pins me down. Should I scream and alert the others, or should I stay quiet and deal with only one of them?

I choose the latter. Kept my mouth shut but kept fighting. Regardless of how overwhelmingly exhausted I'm becoming.

"Shh, keep quiet." A gravelly voice instructs, pinning me in one quick motion. I'm not so inclined to comply, but before I can think of something to say or do, two big yellow eyes emerge from the darkness at eleven o'clock.

The eyes are the only thing I can see for a long moment. Glowing menacingly, illuminating only the creature's closest features. Pointed, gaunt cheekbones. Graying, fileting skin around the tightest bones.

My teeth dig into my lips under the tight grip over my mouth. Vomit makes its way up my throat. The stranger tenses behind me as the creature stalks closer.

Up close, the figure was much taller and thinner than he seemed from farther away. The man-creature – huffed like a bear as he walked straight toward us. Surely he'll see us, standing nearly right in front of him.

The stranger holding me must think the same thing.

But the tall bear-man-monster keeps walking as if we did not exist at all. As soon as we're clear, the attacker releases me. They turn to vanish without a word, but I grab their arm.

"Why did you help me?" I ask, furrowed brow and tired lungs overtaking any gratitude I felt for the help.

"A 'thank you' will suffice." He – I assume – retorts.

I don't get a good look at him, but from what I can see he looks fairly human. Minus the defined fangs protruding from his mouth. *Vampires are real, too?* His reddish-brown curly hair is cut into a mullet. *Great. Vampires with mullets.* Deep green eyes pointedly staring me down. My eyes struggle to adjust to the darkness, no matter the extent I'm exposed to it.

"Thanks." I mumble, stifling the panic of being faced with a vampire. Grateful for the break to catch my breath. "What do you want in return?" I ask pointedly.

"Nothing." He says annoyedly.

"Why would you help me then?" I ask again, still gripping his arm. Though, he could easily escape if he wanted to. He just shakes his head, huffing out an exasperated chuckle. "People don't just help people for no good reason. So what do you want?"

"For you to survive, little bird."

Little bird? I hadn't heard that name since I was a kid.

"My older brother used to call me that." I snip, my heart swelling with memories of Asher. The few years I remember of him before he went to jail. I was his shadow, and he was my knight in shining armor. No matter how much he hated me. Or how he wanted nothing to do with me.

But I love – loved, I don't know – him more than anything in this world. He always stood up for me when Mom or Dad were going to beat my ass for whatever reason they had at the time. Whether I drew on the walls. Clogged the toilet with flushed toys. The time I said, 'god damn shit kicking motherfucker' and giggled at the direct quote from my father.

I was only in the first grade when he went to jail for selling drugs. I remember that day vividly. It was the Friday before Christmas break, two weeks before his birthday. I got on the bus to go home, and Asher wasn't there. One of the older boys who always picked on me when Asher wasn't looking commented how it was such a shame that I didn't have my brother to protect me anymore.

Asher always had a love of kicking someone's ass. I didn't even need a reason to do it. It was all too fun for him because he'd always win.

Dad was already drunk when I got home. Mom was crying so hard she ended up vomiting. Asher was nowhere to be found. From then on out, Mom and Dad acted as if they never had a son. Refused to acknowledge his birthday. Didn't engage in the conversation when I brought him up.

I gathered up everything I could from his old room before they threw everything in the back of Grandpa Eugene's old pickup and hauled it all to the dumpster. Old clothes, comic books, and the PS Vita he stole from one of my bullies. Whatever I felt was sentimental to me, I hid under my bed so they wouldn't beat me for taking the last remaining semblances of him.

All of those things ended up being lost when I went into foster care. Except for the Metallica shirt I was wearing when Social Services came knocking. I still have that shirt packed away in a bin back in Atlanta.

Asher used to write me letters from jail, even though I could barely read them at first, between being eight and him having the worst handwriting imaginable. I was never allowed to visit him or write him back. I assumed he forgot about me, died in prison, or got out and got the hell out of dodge like I did. I lost any ability to contact him when I was twelve.

I haven't seen him in twenty years.

"Hey, birdie. Long time no see."

My heart stops with a hard squeeze. Tears bloom under my tired eyes. "Asher?"

"Aw, you don't call me Bubba anymore?" Asher throws me a shit-eating grin. Arms crossed over his broad chest. Underneath the hardened, matured exterior lies the same baby-faced teenager. Behind those piercing green eyes, I recognized the boy who used to take me down to the park on Saturdays. Scars litter his skin. 'Battle scars', he used to call them. Even more of them now.

"I haven't seen Bubba in a long time." I half-tease, warm tears falling down my wind-burnt cheeks. "What the hell are you doing out here in the middle of the night?"

"It was hard for me to resist seeing the first Hunt in nearly a decade." He scoffs. "Didn't realize it was you that was on the menu."

"But why are *you* out here? And what the fuck is the 'Hunt'?"

"The Hunt, little bird," He starts, turning to face me with a shit-eating grin. "Was once a yearly tradition that brought all the creatures under the Veil together for one night. To track and hunt down a human that posed the most threat to creature-kind. Guess that you've survived a few too many encounters with us for the higher-ups to think you don't deserve to continue breathing."

So many questions swim through my head. What the hell was the Veil? Why am I the one that poses the most threat to 'creature-kind'? Who the hell are the 'higher-ups' to make *that* decision?

"When I heard it was you, I couldn't just sit by and let you get hurt." Pain laced his words like we were more than two-decade-old strangers. The familiarity was there, but I couldn't bring myself to understand why he would be here now. Why would he risk coming out at night? Even if he is an alleged vampire.

"Can you get me out of here?" I plead, and suddenly I'm eight years old again, needing my bubba to save me. To stop the bullies. To scare away the monsters hiding under my bed.

He shakes his head. "No. I'd be slaughtered if they found out I helped you. They would draw and quarter me if they knew about the glamour, it's no telling how many years my soul would suffer if I tried to get you out of the forest before sunrise. I'm sorry, birdie."

"What are you talking about? There's got to be something you can do to help me. Please."

"I wish I could help you." His answers grow curt.

"Can you at least tell me what to do? Where to go?" I ask. He hums, jaw tensing. Like if he told me any information, his life would be in jeopardy. Or so he says.

"Follow the smell of the pasture until you reach Old Man Roldan's farm. There's an old stablehand's house on a secluded part of the property. Go there and wait until morning. I'll come find you." His instructions are clear, but the map in my head is fuzzy, unable to pinpoint which way to go to get to the farm. How long would it take me to get there? "If you go now, I can distract the next wave."

"No, you should come with me." I argue, a twinge of pain radiating in my heart for him. The idea of losing him a second time.

"Just go, birdie. Fly. Fly far and wide." He turns to walk away, curly hair whipping in the breeze.

"Asher," I called. He turns around only halfway, waiting for me to get on with it. "There's a guy at Nancy's house. His name's Leon. Please, tell him I love him."

He chuckles deeply. "Tell him that yourself. You'll make it through the night. I believe in you, River." And before I can object, he vanishes into the night. The dark swallows him whole.

A howl erupts in the distance, urging me to run. Follow the smell of the pasture. Ignore the ache in my lungs and the dripping wounds on my legs.

The further I ran into this hell hole of a forest, the stronger the stench became. It smells of rotting meat. The way everything in your fridge disintegrates after not having power for a month in the summer with the door wide open. It fills my nose, embedding itself into the hairs, and bringing back the need to hurl. It's not just rotten food. It smells like feces and ammonia, but there's something else underlying that I can't pinpoint. I'm terrified that if I figure out what that last putrid smell is, I might never recover emotionally.

Let's be real. That's a likely possibility regardless of whether I figure out the mystery smell or not.

CHAPTER 30

Leon

The house was sweltering by five a.m. I'm not one to complain about the heat, but this was outrageous. This was the surface of the sun's levels of uninhabitable heat piping through the vents. It was so hot; I had wanted to pack our shit and go back to the hotel room at first light.

When I slunk out of bed, already pissed that River wasn't by my side, my mood didn't improve when I couldn't find her at all. This house was huge, but she had to be in it somewhere.

The front door was wide open, which is probably what tripped the thermostat.

In the kitchen, Nancy and Brian sat at the kitchen table, cooing over their bouncing baby girl. I assumed Brian left the door open when he came in. Whenever he came in.

"Missed you last night, man." I greeted Brian in my passing sweep. "Have either of you seen River?" They shook their heads without further acknowledgment. With a huff, I kept looking.

River had to be here somewhere. All of her belongings lay in our room. Her purse, clothes, glasses. Just not her phone, which makes sense that she would take with her.

I shoot her a quick message. *Morning, angel.*

Nothing. *Fuck.* Okay, okay, okay. Don't freak out.

I'm sure everything's fine. I'm sure she's fine. Curled up somewhere with a book. This house probably has a library or study. She practically grew up here. She knows all the good hiding spots. Knows where to go to get the best peace.

Maybe she couldn't sleep. Yesterday was a lot. I'm not surprised if she busied herself to keep the demons at bay. I just have to find her. And not freak out in the process.

The overcast sky illuminated the world in an unsavory gray. Fog rolling in over the mountain tops like riptide waves. A storm was brewing just behind the clouds, threatening to break at any given moment. Just like myself.

I've been pacing the expansive rooms of this mansion for what feels like years. My restless hands don't find solace in anything they touch. Nothing feels *good* enough.

Something is wrong.

I knew something wasn't right when I woke up and couldn't find her anywhere. Told myself not to panic. Gave her an hour to come find me when she was ready, but she never showed. No amount of calling or texting had her answering her phone. And I didn't hear it ring from anywhere.

To the people haunting this house, I didn't even exist. No one answered me, as if they couldn't see me. I wish I could leave. Pack up our shit and go home. I miss my bed and the woman I love who occupies it.

God fucking dammit, where is she?

The hours tick by. It's noon, but the sun is setting soon with the time change. Where the fuck is she? Why is everyone ignoring me? Should I call someone? Who can I call? Ghostbusters? The Winchesters? Zak Bagans?

Shaun, my nervous Nelly of a manager, calls about twelve-thirty. He had originally wanted me to forgo this entire weekend trip instead of finishing a song for a movie soundtrack. I – as politely as I could – told him to kiss my ass. The song will get done when it's done.

I'm his least favorite client, but I pay well.

"Hey, Shaun. Now's not a good time." I greet. Though, he doesn't hear me because he's yapping a mile a minute. "Whoa, whoa, whoa. Slow down. What the fuck are you talking about?"

"You're not home this weekend are you?" He asks frantically.

"No, why?"

"There was a series of fires set at your apartment complex. The Fire Department ruled it arson, but the news is saying faulty electrical. What apartment number are you again?"

Holy fucking shit. What the fuck is going on? "917."

"That's the apartment with the most damage."

My heart sinks. First, my girlfriend goes missing, then my apartment's set on fire. I don't care about the stuff in it, I can buy more of my things. But River was working on a quilt that she spent weeks on. Some of her most sentimental items were in bins in our closet. Our life was intertwined so beautifully.

Who would want to set it on fire?

The same way River set Mark on fire.

Oh. Well, shit.

"Turn on the news." He instructs, his TV blaring the incident in the background.

Finding a room with a TV was surprisingly hard to do. But once I came to what looked like a game room with a pool table, air hockey, and a flat-screen, I turned on the local news for Atlanta.

But it was on national news, too.

The news feed shows a grainy excuse for a video outside our complex. Several apartments blackened in the aftermath of a midnight blaze. The only scorched window on the ninth floor was the darkest out of all of the burnt dwellings.

"The building manager is calling for a complete demolition of the property with such faulty wiring, but the Fire Marshall says that we may be looking at an arsonist." The news anchor reads.

"We won't know more until the state does a full investigation."

My temper quickly boils to the surface. "Send someone over there to see if anything's salvageable. Send pictures. I need eyes on the ground." It's been a while since I asked for 'eyes on the ground', which is my signal to Shaun that I'm about to get into a whole bunch of shady shit. He knew better than to ask. Just do what he's told and let me handle the illegal shit.

"They're not letting anyone in the building." He counters.

"I'm not asking. Now you either get it together, or I'll call Conklin myself."

"Mr. Kang, I don't know. I-" He stutters, but I cut him off.

"Don't call me that."

"Right, sorry." He apologizes. "I just don't think getting Conklin involved is the best course of action. He's shady."

"Well, I don't know about you, but this looks like a clear attempt on my life. So, I'll handle this however I deem necessary." I'm nearly foaming at the mouth. A deadly combination of unbridled rage and fear. Someone tried to kill me.

Someone went after me and my girl.

Someone's going to die.

"I'll see what I can do, but if I can't make it happen, I'll let you know." He concedes with a sigh.

"And while you're at it, don't forget that I've got enough money to bail myself out of jail, so if you don't fix it the nice way, I'll gladly fix it my way."

"You should see the news in your area." Shaun interrupts.

"Why?" I ask pointedly. I hurriedly flipped through the channels to get to the local news station.

The headline reads *'Atlanta producer in town visiting Hot Springs.'* A picture of River and I leaving the hotel yesterday is displayed in the top right of the screen before it shifts to live coverage of the crowd gathering in the resort parking lot.

"You're here to see Leon Kang?" A middle-aged male news

reporter asks what looks like a teenage girl at the front of the crowd. Police and hotel security are forming a barrier at the entrance, but there aren't enough of them to hold back the weight of this many screaming people.

"I had no idea he was so close to me! I have to meet him!" Says the girl. The embarrassment washes over me like a fever. I can't believe this is happening.

"How did you find out he was here?" The reporter asks.

"There was this guy that leaked his location online and a bunch of us had to go see if he was right." She looks so happy while saying such asinine things.

"Sir, are you okay?" Shaun interrupts my transfixed attention, bringing me back down to the reality of this whole situation.

"No! I'm not even close to being o-fucking-kay! My apartment burned down! My hotel is swarmed with screaming fans. Thank God I'm not there right now. And to top it all off, my girlfriend's missing."

"River's missing?"

"Since this morning. Or sometime last night. We slept over at her friend's house and when I woke up, she was gone." I explain. Though, I don't know why I do. I don't even know where to begin to look for her in a town I don't know where the sun sets at 5 p.m.

"I'll call my friends at the FBI, maybe they can help you up there while I sort out this mess down here." He offers, and for once, I couldn't be more grateful for his willing participation.

"You better get the whole damn FBI, the CIA, the police. Hell, get NASA if they're available. Just get me somebody who can help bring her back to me. I'll deal with the rest of this shit, but I need to find her." It all hits me at once, the reality of her disappearance. Where the hell might she have gone? If she left in the middle of the night.

If she's still alive.

"We'll find her." Shaun comforts.

My hands shake under the weight of everything that's coming down around me. I'm the target of an arsonist, been doxed, River's missing, and I'm completely alone. Soon to be locked in this fucking house for another night, and the only thing I can do is sit and spin on it all.

No. I can't think like that. I *have* to do something. Have to find her if nothing else. I used to track people down for a living. I may be a little rusty, but I can do it. I have to.

The big question. Where the hell is River?

Where the fuck did she go?

I tried calling her again, ears perked for the sound of her ringtone or vibrations. Hoping that she'll just answer me. My phone is unsteady in my clammy, shaky hands. She can't be gone.

I dial her number, holding my breath as I listen intently to the world around me. Almost immediately, I hear a faint ringing in the distance. Racing to the sound, I fling open every door and drawer to find the source. *Come on, where is it?*

The front door swings open with a bang. Her phone sits perfectly outside on the doormat. Screen alight with the first picture we took together.

That night feels eons ago now.

She had changed her lock screen picture a million times, pretty much any time I sent her a new selfie. She changed it to this picture of us just last week before I left for the award show. She said she'd miss me while I was out of town, even though I had offered to bring her along with me. She never changed it back and when I asked why, she said, *'Because every time I look at that picture, I still feel the butterflies dancing around in my stomach.'*

There's always been a pull to her. My head, my heart, the butterflies in my stomach. I try to find that invisible knot in my stomach, the one that tugs whenever I see her and pull. I pull hard. Like trying to echolocate the source of my love.

Staring at her picture willing her back to me, something tugs against that lifeline holding me to her. Answering my call.

Briefly, the memories of that night flood my brain. The first time I felt seen by someone. Her gentle spirit left an unmistakable impression. It was then that I knew she was it for me. I knew then that this was more than just some passing crush. I didn't know then how much I would grow to love her. How she's turned my entire world upside down.

But I'd do it all over again. Every last bit of it.

Because my love for her runs deeper than the Grand Canyon. Wider than the mid-western plains. Vaster than the entire galaxy. She called to me, spoke to me with such ease. It was so easy to love when you felt loved.

I'd like to think she loved – loves – me. That she reciprocates these deep-seated feelings. Even if she never said it, it was written in every action, every stolen glance, every smile. She makes you feel important with that warm smile and sweet disposition.

At one point, I remember thinking I was only infatuated with the version of her I created in my head and that I should probably let that go, but she would always surprise me. She was and is so much more than I could have ever imagined. If I could go back to that night and talk to Leon and tell him how she's going to be the best thing in his life, I'm sure he wouldn't believe me. The butterflies that soared in my body when I wrapped my arms around her waist, those butterflies have never gone away. They're still there with each touch and now my body aches in her absence.

The phone's screen dims, diminishing our photo like the sinking feeling that's growing in my gut. Sitting out in the open, like it was waiting for me to find it.

Why would it be here, like this, and not with her?

I pick it up and stuff it in my pocket. Not knowing what else to do with a phone but no owner. I don't even know if I can get into her phone without her passcode. Am I fucking smart enough to even crack that? Is my IQ high enough for that?

It has to be. River's counting on me.

I take out her phone with a huff, trying to think of what

her code could be. There's got to be something on that phone that can give me any insight as to where she went.

Don't fuck this up, or you'll be locked out forever.

Okay, deep breath, dumbass. I have ten attempts to get this right. Nine incorrect attempts to get into this device before it was completely disabled on the tenth. It's a six-digit number. How hard can this be? It's only a one-in-a-million chance to get it right. Easy fucking peasy. Think about this, Leon. It can't be that hard. You know her, don't you?

Do I know her? I'd like to think I do. I know her favorite color, her middle name, her birthday, her favorite holiday, and her hobbies, but do I know her enough to crack a nearly impossible code? Am I confident in my knowledge of all things River to know what kind of code she'd use?

Fine. Let's start with her birthday. I don't think it'll work, but I'll try it anyway. 020395. Wrong. Shit. I don't know why I thought that would work, she's not vain enough to make it her birthday.

She's also smarter than that.

Okay, maybe this is vain of me, but what about *my* birthday? 081893. Nope. Fuck.

Is it a random number sequence? She looks like a random number combination person. I only have 999,998 other options.

123456. No dice.

112233. Nada.

445566. No.

778899. Nothing. God dammit! I'll try again in a minute. Why is this so much harder than I thought it would be? Why was I ever under the assumption that this was going to be easy?

010101. No. Shit! I'll regroup in five minutes, I guess.

Okay, think, you dense bastard! Three more attempts. Don't fuck this up.

Have I ever seen her unlock her phone with the passcode and not the face ID? Yes. Yes! Friday night in the car.

It was too dark for the face ID to pick up, so she typed in her password. I saw it out of the corner of my eye. It started with number one.

121212. Nope. Oh, okay. Never mind. I'll be here for another fifteen minutes. Thinking about my mistakes. My fucking shortcomings.

Think harder, you dumb sack of shit. Was it a pattern? Was it an important number?

135790. Nothing.

Oh, shit. This is it. The last chance. I have to get this right, or the phone is completely useless forever. I'll have to buy her a new one if I don't get this.

Starts with 1. Looks like a random number combination. Looks like a pattern.

159753. Unlocked.

OH, SHIT I DID IT! Hallelujah! Thank you, Jesus Christ. You're a real homie right now.

Wiping the beaded sweat from my brow, I stare at the unlocked phone until the screen darkens, locking again. I put in the code to confirm that I am, in fact, a goddamn magician and near giddy when it unlocks with ease. My first breakthrough since this whole shit show commenced.

Where should I even look first? Messages? Emails? Social Media? No, I should look at her recently opened apps, right? The first app in the lineup shows a picture of the two of us from yesterday morning, clearly taken by someone I had made eye contact with. The same photo plastered across the news earlier. Her face is hidden from view, but there's no denying that that's me. I don't even bother looking at the comments. I already know what they have to say. I can only imagine she meticulously read each one. She was never meant to be subjected to any of this.

I'm reminded of the crowd outside our hotel, how there's a slew of people out there waiting to see me. None of them were invited, but did that matter to them at all? I'm only half-relieved to be here and not dealing with all of that bullshit

HM DAWLEY

down the street.

Did she know about the oncoming mob, though? Is she the one to tip them off? Surely not. She's never made a move like that before, but her disappearance is certainly questionable. No. She wouldn't do that to me. Would she?

Besides, if she were the one to dox, why would it be the hotel we haven't been at since nine a.m. yesterday?

If she wanted to get the hell out of dodge before the mob, she would have taken all of her belongings. There wouldn't be these pieces of her everywhere I look, like dissipating airplane contrails. If she had wanted to vanish on her own terms, there would be no trace of her anywhere.

On her own terms. What? Am I a conspiracy theorist now? Do I really believe she's been kidnapped and that's the reason she's gone? It's more likely that she hit her head and is unconscious somewhere. Right?

Oh, God. What if she is? Is she okay? I have no idea where to even begin to look. Do I risk it and go on a wild fucking goose chase to try and retrace any steps she could have possibly taken? This town isn't massive, but I'd be here all week walking in circles trying to find a needle in a pile of pine needles.

I'm getting way ahead of myself. My mind's running a million miles a minute. I can't get anything done like this. Goddammit! I've gotten so fucking strung out; I can't even think straight. The anger coursing through my veins reminds me just who I used to be. No, who I am. Just because she made me soft, doesn't mean I'm not the same underneath. She just hasn't seen it yet. At this rate, I don't even know if she'll ever want to or get to.

God, I'm so reckless. The one time I let my guard down, this shit happens. I should have been more vigilant. There's no reason I should have ever let this shit happen to me. *Me.* I'm the Leon Kang. People fear me for a reason. I may have been lonely before, but at least my reputation heavily preceded me. No one came after me like this. No one so much as even looked

292

in my general direction before. My days were filled with going to work, going to the gym, and going to bed. Not once did I ever have to think about what was going on around me because no one dared to even think too hard about me. I always thought that was a bad thing, but maybe it was the better solution altogether.

Maybe if I hadn't been running late to work the day we met in the elevator and my eyes never gazed upon her, I wouldn't be here. If I hadn't run into her at all, maybe I would be able to go about my days as if I'm not the most lovesick fucker that's ever graced this God-forsaken Earth. If she hadn't waltzed right into my life so effortlessly, maybe my nights would still be boring and uneventful, but maybe that's not what I want.

In all honesty, I don't think I could imagine my days any differently now. The boring, mundaneness of before seems simple, but now that I've tasted heaven, I don't think I could go back.

The angry, sorry excuse of a 30-year-old man isn't who I want to be anymore. The old bounty hunter isn't who I *am* anymore. Something in me was ignited, something that can't be doused, and why would I want it to be? While life was dull and devoid of any color, it was safe, but I'm tired of being safe. The sheer thought of going back to having dinner alone, listening to the sounds of my thoughts with no end in sight, makes me want to throw myself off the nearest bridge.

I see what I've been missing all this time. I've been missing her late-night conversations and tired giggles, new perspectives and difficult arguments, a deep bond that I truly can't explain, and the most amazing woman I've ever had the pleasure of knowing. No amount of sitting and spinning on how nothing's adding up, how everything feels like it's gone to shit, there's nothing that could ever make me wish for my life to be as devoid as it was before her.

I've spent the majority of my life alone and I assumed it would always be that way. From the minimal social interactions I had as a kid, to being called weird and made fun of for not having but one friend in my teenage years, to being a loner and being the one everyone's afraid of. I've never been someone that people wanted to hang out with, go grab drinks with, invite out to personal parties, what have you. I've drowned my whole personality into being the stick-in-the-mud workaholic who never has any fun because having to be alone is easier than setting yourself up for pain.

I never realized what I was missing. From the moment our eyes met, life felt different. I felt different. It's like I've been having an out-of-body experience this whole time; watching someone else live my life through a TV screen. She smiled at me and opened up a whole new path in my life that I sprinted down gleefully.

She's made me a better person and I want to be a better man for her. There's so much I haven't figured out how to put into words to thank her for the awakening she's bestowed upon me and I'm begging on my knees for the universe to give me one more chance to make it right.

"Sir, I was able to get a few things from your apartment. Not much survived, though." Shaun informs me, after my third call in an hour. I'm trying to find it in me to be patient with him, but the patience hasn't found me yet. I keep telling myself that I'll be cooperative and that things will go smoother if I keep my tongue in cheek, but there will be no guarantees. I've already mouthed off a few times.

It's been an excruciatingly long three hours of sitting and spinning with no one to talk to. No one but the people in the pictures on the walls listen to my grumblings. I've never felt more feral and in need of human connection than I do right now. I'm losing what little sanity I have left with the passage of each painfully quiet second.

"What'd you find?" I ask, sucking on a stale cough drop. Would have preferred a lollipop, but I'm making do. *Like I said, I'm trying to keep myself in check.*

"The fire safe from your closet, and surprisingly, a bin in the farthest part of your apartment that the fire burned the coolest. A black heavy-duty plastic bin with a mixed bag of items."

Oh, thank my lucky stars I put Grandma's rings in the fire safe.

"Thanks." I breathe a small sigh of relief for the important documents and sentimental items that survived the blaze. "Were you able to get in contact with your FBI friend?"

"I did. They said they were deploying some special agents from the CIA. I sent them to your location."

As if right on cue, there's a hearty knock on the door. And I might as well be the only living person in this house with the way no one else seems to notice anything going on around them. Thankfully, I haven't heard that baby sing Phantom of the Opera in almost 24 hours. So, that's a plus.

"Must be them." I comment, hanging up the phone as I reach the front door. Twilight closing in on the mountainside, I can appreciate these people coming before complete darkness. Even if they are just regular government workers who have no idea about what lurks in the woods at night.

Swinging the door open without checking the peephole first, I put on my bravest, hardest mask. Ready to face whoever they'd sent. Just on the other side of the threshold, lit lowly by the porch light that works when it chooses to, stand two agents. One man. One woman. In their mid-fifties, but they don't look their age. They look much younger.

"Oh, Leon." The woman coos, leaning in for a hug.

"Hi, Mom. Dad." I say, halted dead in my tracks.

CHAPTER 31

River

Stingy, bloodshot eyes cling to whatever consciousness remains in my system. A pathetic attempt to grasp at the sands that slipped through my fingers, each desperate and frantic handful falls faster and further through my loose grip. Each blink grows longer and heavier, willing myself into a much-needed slumber that I fight desperately.

The sun dared to kiss the foggy horizon, wishing to witness any and all horrors that lay in wait. Time's presence still peeks through sheer curtains. Because time simply does not stop for horrific tragedies to pass. I envy her, the sun, in her ability to hide, but curse her all the same. For whom was she to watch as all Gods abandoned us on shaky, faulty ground? I wish I could retreat behind a veil of secrecy and escape any fates that lay before me, just as she can do.

Each passing second is filled with gentle reminders of why I have to keep going, to keep fighting. No matter how desperate I am to give up, it pales in comparison to the need to get out and return home safely. I have no idea what's going to happen to me now that my time's running out. All I know is that I will take the full force of whatever is to come.

I'd forced myself to stay awake through the night, which wasn't an easy feat to do once I reached the stable hand's cottage on the far edge of Roldan's property. Once inside the run-down and clearly abandoned cottage, all my body screamed for was to curl up on the dirty floor and go to sleep. But I couldn't. I had to make sure I survived. That I saw whatever attackers were on the hunt.

I don't know if this cottage is magically protected or what, but the monsters swarmed around outside, but didn't – couldn't, I don't know – get in. They howled, scratched, hissed, clawed, and caterwauled all night. But I was safe.

I slept through all of the daylight that the first day had to offer. Sunday, if my memory serves me correctly. The monsters dissipated after the sun rose fully, but there wasn't enough strength in my body to get up off the cold floor and try to navigate back to civilization. There wasn't enough daylight to account for how slow I'd be moving.

It's been two days. It should be Monday now. I think. I'm not sure. Time feels wobbly like it's moving so painfully slow and also exponentially fast at the same time. The nights last eons.

For two whole days, I've been cooped up in this filthy, rundown shack. Tired, hungry, and thirsty. Begging for relief. A hot bath. A gallon of water. Some goddamn Ibuprofen. Any sleep I'd managed to catch wasn't worth a damn.

The monsters come back as soon as the sun sets. And I'm starting to think they'll never go away. I can feel my stomach attempting, and succeeding, to eat itself. I was never much of a hunter or a gatherer as a kid, but the need for food is going to whip me into shape faster than any Girl Scout camp ever could.

Tomorrow, I'll go out and see if there is any food available nearby. See if I can find something to satiate my growing hunger. Maybe find some acceptable drinking water.

I don't know exactly how far Roldan's farm is from Nancy's, but I know that it's got to be a good, long hike. It could take me days to find my way back, and I don't know where I'm going.

If I can just *survive*, like Asher said, maybe someone will come looking for me. Leon must be worried out of his mind. I have to survive. Asher's coming back for me. Leon's looking for me. Some people will miss me. I can't just lie down and give up.

When will they show, though?

Is it bad that I'm worried about not calling out of work? I've got to be losing my fucking mind right now. That should be the *last* thing I'm thinking about.

Of course one of the things I'd be harping on is my work ethic while being confined in a dilapidated cottage in my hometown with no strength to get up and help myself and no one coming to look for me.

I miss my bed. *Our bed.* Leon's arms around me while we sleep. The smell of freshly brewed coffee. Not pissing in a toilet that looks like it will give me typhoid if I touch it and that flushes.

I'm a simple woman. All I want is running water, food, heat, and the love of my life.

I really do miss Leon. I miss a lot of things, but he might be at the top of my list.

A faint voice whispers, "Hey, angel." Low and sultry, the familiar voice reverberates through the air, quickening my pulse in a way I almost forgot was possible. Not of fear, but of relief. I can't see Leon, but I can feel him all around me. The room I occupy is dark, almost nonexistent, with no light to illuminate my path. The darkness goes on for miles, but it's calm.

"Leon!" I yell, but it comes out muffled. Echoed, yet stifled.

"There's my sweet girl." The familiar voice echoes throughout the space, almost close enough that I can touch it.

"Leon, where are you?" I ask, beg. My entire body aches with the need to feel him. To see him.

"I'm everywhere you are mon amour." He coos sweetly. As if right on cue, he appears dressed in all white. A true beacon in the

darkness.

"Where am I?" Anxiety courses through my chest, weighing me down. Tears stream down my face in rapid succession seemingly out of nowhere.

"Don't cry, I'm right here." He reaches out, his hands reaching for me, just out of reach.

"I can't do this." I beg, reaching out desperately to catch him in my fingers. My feet don't move me to him. An impending doom feeling chases me, inches turn to miles as I grasp at a ghost. Exhaustion settles across my soul, creeping its way into my bones. A feeling I've grown so familiar with. My legs collapse where I stand, arms still outstretched towards an oasis.

"You absolutely can do this, angel. I'm rooting for you. You have to come home to me." The words, while whispered so softly and gently, sink into the very essence of my soul.

And as soon as he appears, the vision of him vanishes, leaving only the words that surround me in his wake.

The wailing is getting worse. Tonight, night three, there seem to be droves and droves of things *wailing and moaning* in agony outside. This is what Christians think Hell sounds like.

I hate to admit it, but they might be right.

But, amid my existential crisis on the half-cleaned floor caused by these *things,* it got me thinking. And we all know that's never a good sign.

I wanted to apologize.

I need to tell him I'm sorry for dragging him into this. I shouldn't have allowed this to happen. He was always meant to stay back in Atlanta, making music that I could hear through the walls of my apartment, blissfully unaware of just how hard I would fall for him. I could have been perfectly content admiring him from afar. Maybe our friendship could have blossomed in due time, but I should have stayed my happy ass in my apartment and pined in silence over a man that was - is - clearly out of my league.

He's everything I've ever wanted. Ever since I was a

little girl, all the lists I ever made about who my perfect partner would be consisted of all the things that make up Leon Kang, and yet somehow, he far exceeds all of my wildest dreams.

When I was super young, the list mostly consisted of silly things like 'nice hair', 'funny', and 'likes to eat'. Very normal, generic things.

When I was a teenager, it grew into more philosophical things like 'had to be a feminist', 'supportive of my independence', and 'have similar political and spiritual values as myself'. Of course, always in addition to the pre-established lists.

The older I've gotten, the more things I add to the list. I've been single long enough to be comfortable being single forever. I could go on for days about all the wishes I've accumulated over the years and how Leon fits every last one of them.

Once, while Leon and I were camping out on his – our – couch at a far too late hour, he looked softly into my soul and asked me what living meant to me. It was an odd question, even for how philosophical we were getting at the time.

Amid a completely separate conversation, he threw me one hell of a curveball question. It made me realize that I don't know what I classify as living. I've been in survival mode, fight-or-flight, my whole life. I don't think I've ever given myself the grace to live.

"Well, what does it mean to you, chuckles?" I asked him.

In the quietness that followed my counter question, a wave of sureness washed over his face, just before his answer escaped his lips along with his Citron Vodka-scented breath as it filled the space between us.

"To live is to be loved and to be loved is to be treasured." I chuckled at the expression, unsure what it meant, but liking how it sounded as it rattled around in my devoid-of-all-thoughts head. "I try to define myself by what I spend my time curating because I wouldn't ever want to waste my time on things and people who don't mean anything to me."

"That's a good motto to have." I replied, internally screaming at the top of my lungs because who would say that to just anyone? He said it so surely like he knew I was a safe place to say it.

We're so different.

I'm outgoing and friendly but I don't do it on purpose. People say I'm easy to talk to, a good shoulder to cry on. Always someone willing to lend an ear. I know I talk a lot, but never really about anything important and rarely about myself.

He listens intently to any random thought I have, any garbled concoction of words I throw together at any given time. Always with the loveliest twinkle in his eye, like every minute detail he hears is the most riveting piece of information he's ever heard.

Yet, he's so *feared.* Always stoic and standoffish in public. Where the world can see him. There were plenty of times when I would see him from a distance and want to say hi but second guess myself. He would consistently look pissed or not in the mood to talk, but my innate need to have the smallest conversation with him always trumped my primal instinct to not poke the sleeping bear. Any time my mind would run circles around itself trying to stop the impending doom. He would hear my voice, and his head would spring up from wherever he was looking, zeroing in on my location. A smile always spread to his cheeks and eyes.

He's so selfless. From buying/making dinners, to building pillow forts in his living room like we're children, to protecting me without question. I don't feel like I bring enough to this relationship to constitute all of the selfless acts he's bestowed upon me. I never wanted him to get the impression that I was using him.

As pathetic as it sounds, he's all I have.

CHAPTER 32

Leon

"What are you guys doing here?" I ask, perplexed at their appearance altogether, but now of all times? Here of all places? None of it made any feasible sense.

"We got a call from our supervisor that your manager called the FBI and that you needed our services." Dad says nonchalantly. As if he's talking to a damn coworker about how the weather was over the weekend.

"Okay and what exactly are your services?" I ask, arms folded over my huffing chest. These two were the very last people I ever wanted to see. What kind of expertise could they offer?

"Government services." Dad snips back, fire behind his eyes. A direct copy of my own.

"That's rich." I retort, stomping off to collect my things to leave before the sun sets completely.

"Where are you going?" Mom asks softly, pain laced in her gaze. She always hated how Dad and I never got along but never did anything to take one side or the other.

"Don't worry. I'll be back. Just don't pay any mind to the people who live in this house. And apparently don't go outside after dark." I say, patting her shoulder as I pass, collecting my shoes, jacket, and keys. She nods but says nothing further. A pointed pinstripe of a smile on her thin lips.

When I returned to the house from getting our stuff from our unused hotel suite, two more stuffy FBI agents had joined Mom and Dad. Introductions were minimal. One man named Brice Sinclair, and one older woman named Janice Hames.

Whatever they had been discussing before my entrance, they suddenly became tight-lipped. I guess that's a given for FBI cronies. But I did catch a single word that changed the entire trajectory of my thoughts. *'Magic.'*

What the fuck does the FBI know about magic? Okay, maybe they know more than I do. But why would they think this is a magic-related disappearance?

I asked as much. Everyone in the room has their eyes on me as I stand unwaveringly still, gripping the back of a chair with white knuckles. Waiting for an answer. No one dares to say anything or make a move. They're all waiting for me to react, like I'm a ticking time bomb just waiting to explode, but in all honesty, I feel so empty and hopeless.

Because how the fuck am I supposed to fight magic? I just learned about the Veil and Changelings a few days ago. There's a whole magic system and magical creatures, not just monsters, I don't know about. How in the hell am I going to figure out how to beat whatever or whoever took River?

A pit forming in the depths of my stomach drains all the emotion right out of me. It starts with any amount of optimism I possess, working its way through the rest until I'm left with nothing.

I can't lose River. I just can't.

I can't let Astra be right. I can't let those monsters take her away from me. No matter how hard they try, they can't have her.

I'd dig my way to hell to find her.

"Mr. Kang?" Sinclair asks me.

"Leon. Mr. Kang's that one over there." I say, pointing to Dad.

"I think we need to have a serious conversation, Leon." He turns in his dining room chair and continues. "We need to know exactly what you know."

"Your guess is as good as mine." I shrug. "You'd have better luck throwing darts at a list of topics and having a high school debate over it because I don't know a damn thing."

"Lose the attitude, son." Dad scolds. I flash him a harsh glare, but his eyes aren't even looking at me. Darting everywhere but my general direction.

"You want to find your girlfriend, don't you?" Hames asks with a softened expression, flashing me a gentle smile. I nod, panic gripping my chest so tightly I can't breathe through the wave of pain. "Then let us do our jobs."

I sigh, knowing she's right. Unwilling to accept that anyone in this room could help me save River. I pull out the chair I'm leaning against and take an exasperated seat. "Get on with it then."

Sinclair sets down his papers on the only empty surface on the small dining table, watching me with a sort of thoroughness that makes you uncomfortable once you notice it.

The quaint dining room fills with ear-piercing silence. The sun has set behind the picturesque mountains. Not a peep from the wilderness outside. Nothing from the family downstairs or the old lady haunting the halls. They've completely disappeared.

"You sure you want to do this, Leon?" Mom asks like I have any semblance of a choice in the matter. They need to know. I'm the only one who knows River. Knows even remotely what happened before bed yesterday. I wish I could be more helpful, but I don't know what actually happened to River.

"I've got nothing to hide." I say. "I just want to find her." My voice sounds so foreign to me, soft and pleading with anyone who'll listen to bring my Angel home.

"We're going to do everything we can to find her." Mom reassures, hand reaching across the table to touch my arm. Her hands are ice cold.

"Please, ask me anything." I say, nodding at Sinclair to start.

"Okay, let's get started."

So I told them everything. Sparing no detail.

Everything from Boyle to Mark to Nancy and Brian and their Siren love child to what I know about under the Veil and Changelings. The leaked photos online, the fire in our apartment, the cryptic messages from Astra and Cassandra. The things I've been seeing. The creepiness of this town and how everyone avoids the dark and night like a plague.

The cogs of the FBI machine were turning, and everyone chimed in at least once to add their theories about who/what it could be, what motive was behind all of this bullshit. But I heard none of it. Nothing registered in a language I understood.

Once everyone was satisfied with the amount of information they pulled out of me, Hames came up to me, remorse on her face. "I'm so sorry, sugar." She apologizes, wrapping her arms around my shoulders.

I'm sure she meant well, but the words fell on deaf ears. It means nothing to me how sorry she is. The pity and sympathy won't bring River back to me. Nausea creeps up my stomach and throat, the only sensation in my aching body. I excuse myself to the bathroom.

Alone in the bathroom, I sink against the closed door. This is ridiculous. We should be out looking for her. We're never going to get her back if we keep sitting on our asses speculating where she is or who did this. We need canines and a search party. I can't keep sitting here doing absolutely nothing.

A *pang* in my stomach tells me I need to eat. I haven't had anything since last night. The idea of eating makes the nausea exponentially worse.

Knock, knock, knock.

"Leon, are you okay?" Mom asks from the other side of the door. I've never had it in me to be intentionally mean to her, no matter how infuriating her actions could be.

"About as well as you'd expect." I reply, another wave of nausea wafting over me. "I'll be out in a little while. I just need some space."

"Please don't go outside." She pleads and I roll my eyes.

"I won't." I say. She remains silent for a moment before turning and retreating down the hallway. Leaving me to feel like a kid who'd locked himself in the bathroom after he got in trouble. Which is exactly what I am.

If I had just been more vigilant, kept my eyes on her. Taken her home right after the party. She'd still be here. She'd still be with me. We could have been on our way back to Atlanta.

But then, would we have gotten caught up in the fire? Where are we going to go when we go home? Where am *I* going to go if she doesn't come back to me?

No.

I'm not thinking like that. She's alive. I'm going to get her back. Even if I have to slaughter every living creature that stands in my way on my way to retrieve her. I will get her back. She will come back to me. She has to. I can feel it. She's still alive. I just know she is.

River's purse sits on top of the dresser across the room, staring at me like an aching reminder of its missing owner. The blue leather of the Louis Vuitton bag is soft. I'd bought it for her as an early Christmas present. I had declined to tell her the price, but if she knew she would pitch a fit. Little did she know I'd sell my soul for her happiness. Six thousand isn't much in the grand scheme of things.

The things that aren't packed away in the car for safekeeping are piled neatly in the corner. The items seem so miniscule for such a monumental woman. Someone who I care for so deeply. All that I have remaining of her is a black duffle bag with a handful of clothes, and her purse.

It's infuriating. Someone took her away from me, stole her out from under my nose, and then torched her belongings in a different state. Like they're trying to erase her existence from the face of the planet. They would have to kill me for her to be completely forgotten.

The sleep I'd gotten last night was shit. And by shit, I mean that I didn't sleep a wink at all. I stared at the front door until three a.m. and decided I should *try* to get some sleep. That was a fucking laughable effort. I tossed and turned until all the sheets had come off the bed and the comforter had twisted into an amorphous blob.

Exhaustion eluded me. I'm sure it'll catch up with me eventually, but it hasn't yet. The sun rose behind the thick curtains and drawn blinds. Not a peep from any monsters outside. There was something creepier, more sinister, about knowing that the woods were filled with monsters, and it remained silent than if they had all swarmed.

It's been twenty-four hours since she'd been gone and there was a timer ticking down in my head to forty-eight hours. Like that damn TV show that my grandma used to watch from the kitchen table at full volume.

"Good morning, love birds." I say to Nancy and Brian as they pass me, heading out the door. They don't acknowledge me, as if I'm not even there. Sinclair throws me a quizzical look as they strut out the door with their baby in their arms. "Don't stay out too late!"

The door slams shut behind them.

"Are they always like that?" Sinclair asks.

"Since she had the baby, basically." I snark, wondering where Nancy's mom's hiding now that the new parents are out and about.

"Interesting." He says, nodding. Losing himself in thought.

I go about making breakfast out of what little scraps of food are left in the house. Not daring to forage in the downstairs kitchen. While they might not acknowledge me, they might kill me if they think I stole their baby's food. Not that the baby can eat a cheeseburger, but you never know with these psychopaths.

I scrounge up some eggs, enough ingredients to make pancakes, and a few pieces of mixed fruit from the pantry before they go bad.

There's enough batter to make everyone a small stack that I serve to the sleepy, crusty-eyed people hunched over paper files and laptops. Each person gives a meek 'thank you' except for Dad, who chooses to only acknowledge me with a nod.

I don't bother staying in their dungeon while they analyze any and everything. It'd just heighten my blood pressure, and that's exactly what I don't need right now.

It's still relatively early. The sun threatens to burst from behind the clouds. The town and what I could see beyond it are gorgeous as the pillars of light shine down upon the Earth like some kind of prophetic blessing. The mountainside had turned mostly brown weeks ago. Even still, it was beautiful.

Crisp air whistles through the valley below, and it's here that I understand how people can find religion. Not that I have, but I understand the notion of finding the beacon amidst the horrific. Taking the one good aspect and turning it profound to make sense of all the tragedy and loss that fills the darkest corners of the world.

If River were here, and this was anywhere but her hometown, she would want to snap a picture. She loves sunrises and the wonders that nature has to offer. So I do just that. For her. I take a picture of the beauty that surrounds us, even in such a gut-wrenching moment. I'll show it to her when I see her again. Tell her about this moment and how I only thought of her. She is my beauty in everything horrific. My symbolic light beams stream from the sky. Calling me to her church. To worship a false prophet.

There's only so much time a person can spend cooped up in somebody else's house with nothing to do before he starts going stir-crazy. No amount of trashy TV, stupid phone games, or scrolling online can fill the need to *do something.*

A walk sounds nice. Except, I need to be here when River comes back. I need to be the one to greet her first. Or should I be out in the woods, scavenging for clues to find her and bring her back to safety? Sinclair said that the local police have gathered a search party and will be working until the sun starts to set.

Because no one in this town is out after dark.

And yes, I've seen some shit. I heard some weird shit the night Nancy gave birth. But this just seems a little bit extreme, don't you think?

Deciding to take that walk and get some much-needed fresh air, I pass by the gaggle working in the dining room. There had clearly been an argument just moments prior. The tension is thick, Mom and Dad not daring to look at each other. Sinclair and Hames look at each other wearily.

Rage filled Mom's tired eyes as she stared at me from across the room. A lifetime of hatred swam in them. Years of anger were finally bubbling to the surface. Worry shows on her skin in the form of stress lines and crow's feet. There's an air of separation between the two of them. Dad so clearly avoided something. The disconnect between them wafts out of the room like an unwavering stench, reminding me that most people exist in a state of uncompromising.

Too many people wander through life being content with the compromise of love. They'd rather hang on to the love they're forced to compromise with than sit in the silence of being alone.

There's nothing wrong with waiting for the right person to come along. There's no need to rush into something just because you feel as though you have to. There's everything wrong with being so in love with the idea of love that you can't function without having it attached to your hip, no matter whose shape it may take.

But then it swings so far into uncompromising that you now have two unwavering people at a stalemate because of this lack of maturity and communicativeness. Two people set so far into their concrete ways that it swings them into a completely different ballpark.

I've watched Mom and Dad's uncompromising nature my entire life. Watched it rip apart holidays, birthdays, family vacations, and regular Sunday dinners. Those two could shatter worlds without saying a single word to each other.

Heavy, weighted claustrophobia settles into my chest, masking any sympathy I could have mustered up for them. I do feel bad that they've landlocked themselves into a loveless marriage. It's just not everyone else's problem.

"Excuse me, I need some air." I say to no one in particular as I turn and walk away from the crowd toward the front door. Unsure if anyone even heard me in the first place. It didn't matter.

The unknowingness of it all is becoming entirely too much to bear. There's an ounce of solitude in the fresh mountain air. It's peaceful in an almost eerie way.

Where do I go? I have nothing waiting for me wherever it is. I could traverse my way into town, but there's nothing there for me but more people who have a million questions about shit they're not entitled to know. I could get in my car and drive off the nearest cliff, but that won't solve anything. Surely my soul would find a way to be trapped in this godforsaken town for all eternity.

Be my fucking luck.

What I want most right now is to know that River's alright. I need to know she's alive just as much as I need her in my arms right now. And as much as I want to sit around moping about it, I need answers. I need to be out there hunting for her. She needs me and I don't need to be sitting on my ass feeling sorry for myself right now. I should be doing something productive. Conviction overtakes my stride as I sprint my way down the long, paved driveway and into a rather quiet downtown, a new conviction flowing through me.

I can still feel her with me. I just have to find her.

Muscles and tendons ache with a burning desire to find a resolve. The pavement under my feet echoes the sound of my hasty footsteps. Similar to just days ago when I barreled down the stairs to her aid. Ready to defend her to my dying breath then, willing to do it again now.

I will stop at nothing to get her back. Come hell or high water. Come fire and brimstone. Whatever it takes, I will do it.

CHAPTER 33

Astra

To think that I'll be responsible for the death of not one Grimaldi, but two, is as euphoric as it comes.

God gave me a task.

A mighty, world-changing task that I thought I wouldn't be able to accomplish. But who am I to deny God when his plans need to come to fruition? Who am I to walk with the Creator and devote my life to all he is, just to not accept the task given to me?

If He thought I was capable enough to *give* me the task, then I will do the task. He has given me all the tools, the best training money can buy, and enough confidence to roast a man alive. I could take down armies with my sheer will alone.

But I'll start with the Grimaldi duo.

I'll undo what should have never been. Stop the madness before the madness stops the world. Right what was wronged all those years ago. And next, I'll stop that time traveler once and for all.

Leon, I think that was his name, the mate of the Grimaldi woman. The poor soul had no idea what he was walking into when he fell in love with *her*. I pity him, if only for the notion that he will have to grieve that loss for an eternity.

An untimely, yet necessary loss.

I had warned him to cherish it while he could. I hope he did because the Hunt brought a bountiful feast. A boy and a girl. A brother and a sister. Bound in tainted blood. Destined to die for one another. Remarkably poetic if you ask me.

It was a shame that they were both so gorgeous. Such a waste of energy, of mass conservation. The whole bloodline is befouled. Thankfully, the boy took care of his mother and the grandfather died from old age.

All that's left now is to perform the summoning ritual. To put on display the consequences of messing with destiny. Make an example out of them all.

He will be here soon. To see my work. To see that I am worthy.

Soon, all will be right.

CHAPTER 34

Leon

"How cruel is it that stories had to have plots. That they can't all be filled with fluff and sex." River had once said after her favorite book characters died.

She's never been so right.

The town is eerily quiet.

I reach the bottom of the hill they call Main Street. My breath billowing up and around my face in plumes of hot air. The steep hill will be agony to climb back up. If not because I feel weak from the catastrophes of this weekend, but because they don't make hills like this in Atlanta. This is *literally* some mountain holler shit. My ego is only a little depleted admitting that I'm not built for this bullshit.

"Good morning," says a passing girl with a meek voice. "Are you Leon Kang?" She's short, young, maybe late teens.

"Yes, that's me." There's apprehension in my voice. I'm not sure what to say to her or where this is going. I remember what River told me about being more personable. I wish I could conjure up that energy right now. "Can I help you?"

"I heard about your girlfriend."

"What about it?" I ask.

"That she disappeared." She says with the utmost certainty. "You have a girlfriend, right?" She asks. I don't bother answering. "My dad works with a guy whose son works on the police force and there's a rumor going around that your girlfriend went missing, and they think her brother did it."

"Well, that's just painfully untrue now, isn't it?" Interjects a blonde man with a curly mullet. He's dressed in a classing hard and fast eighties metal band enthusiast attire. Tattoos peak from under his jean jacket around his collar and hands.

"Who are you?" She asks with a cocked expression. I'm sure my face mirrors hers.

"The brother." The man retorts with a sly grin. "And you must be my future brother-in-law." He turns to me, throwing his arm around my shoulder, and gripping it tightly. He smells of tobacco and vanilla. At least six four. A mischievous glint in his vibrant green eyes.

There's no way this fucker is related to River.

But I can see the similarities between them. The same shaped eyes, a dimple on the right cheek, face shape, and nose. She'd never once mentioned that she had a brother. But to be fair, she never mentioned anything family-related. She especially didn't announce that she came from a town of loonies.

The girl's eyes grow wide as she takes in the sheer wall that was this man. There was something uncanny about him, and I know the girl saw it too. He looks perfectly human, but my hair stands on end. The taste of pennies coats the back of my throat.

The man winks at the girl, causing her to turn and sprint down the block without so much as a glance backward. "She'll make for a tasty meal later." He mumbles, sniffing the air she once resided in. "Why don't you and I take a little walk, shall we?" He asks, his grip tightening on my shoulder. Making it unable to escape.

"I'm not going anywhere with you." I scoff, but he drags me along regardless. Like I'm some kid he's being forced to bring along with him. No one looks twice at us.

"It's in your best interest that you do, Leon." He says lowly as if he doesn't want anyone around us to hear what he is saying. "I need your help."

"I don't even know you." I roll my eyes, feet shuffling as we walk further into town, past Christmas-decorated shops and light poles, a sign for Jack's Tree Farm past exit four. Away from the heartbeat of the little mountainside village. "And whatever you need my help with, you can't afford."

"Are you still in the hitman business?" He asks with a smirk. I throw him a skeptical look. *How could he possibly know?* "What? I did my research on you."

"I don't think that's on my resume." I scoff, but he's not buying my denial.

"Doesn't have to be, amigo." He squeezes my shoulder hard. "When you know people all over, it's like playing *'Six Degrees of Kevin Bacon'*. You can make your way back to just about anyone."

"Good to know." I huff, side-eyeing the man, whose name I still don't know.

"The name's Asher." He says. I think this guy can hear my thoughts. "Big brother to your sweet little River. I'm sure she never mentioned me because she hasn't seen me in twenty years." Asher, if that's even his real name, introduces himself, annoyed at the semantics I'm putting him through.

"Hi, Asher." I mock. "Why hasn't River seen you in twenty years?" I ask condescendingly.

"Long story." He shrugs with a tight smirk. "We can discuss that at Christmas when we get our girl back."

"*Our?*"

"She was technically mine first."

"That's weird." I say, shaking my head at this fucker. *How the hell have I gotten myself into this situation? Who even is this guy?*

"Not like that, you dipshit." He retorts with a hearty slap to my shoulder. I hold in my wince. This guy is strong for his stature. It's only halfway impressive. "She's my baby sister. She's your girl. We have the same goal in mind. Protect her."

"Yeah, well I've got it from here. Thanks."

"Clearly, you don't." He scolds, and it stings. He's right, unfortunately. "If you had it under control, you wouldn't have lost her. Your apartment building would have burned down. Now you need to tell me why so many creatures are hunting her."

"How do you know-"

"It's my business to know things." He says, a southern twang escaping with his words. I hadn't noticed the accent before. "I've been keeping tabs on her since I got out of prison. And until you came along, she was fine. So I need to know what the hell happened."

"Woah, woah, woah, man!" I jolt to an unexpected stop, forcing him to stop with me. "What the fuck do you think I have to do with this?"

"What I just said." His eyebrows kiss his hairline. "I didn't stutter. And if I did, you heard it twice."

"I didn't do anything to her." My fists ball up in my pockets. "I would never."

"So who's after her?" Asher asks, voice softening a fraction.

"Changelings is what I'm told." I confess, feeling a weight being lifted off my chest at the conviction. "There's been at least two who have tried to get her."

"No, it's something bigger than that." He shakes his head in disbelief, mulling it over for a second. "Changelings don't have the collective wherewithal to put together a child's lemonade stand. Let alone organize a *Hunt*."

"'*A hunt*'?" I ask as he starts walking again, dragging me along with him. "What the fuck is that?"

"Seriously? You don't know?" He asks. I shake my head 'no'. "Do you know anything?"

"For the sake of my health, let's just assume the answer's no."

"Jesus Christ," He mumbles under his breath. "Alright, fine. A Hunt is when someone, a human, comes in contact with one too many magical creatures and lives to tell the tale. The

Veil is there for a reason and when that magic is threatened, then that human is usually hunted down for sport and killed. Hence, the name."

"She's dead?" I ask, all the blood leaving my face. It's Monday. She's been gone for a long time. She could be long dead by now. God, I'm such a fucking piece of shit. How could I just sit around and let so much time pass and have her stay in danger?

"Okay, cool your jets, my brother in Christ." He sighs. "She's not dead. She's at a cottage one town over. I've been checking on her."

"So why haven't you brought her home?" I ask, furious that this guy has her holed up in a cabin somewhere and is just now telling me. "Take me to her."

"Easy, cowboy." He rubs the bridge of his nose. "There are bigger problems that we have to deal with first before we can get her out of that cottage."

"Like what?" I scoff, anger and rage swelling in my veins.

"Well, firstly, the cottage she's in is a Mage's cottage. It's heavily warded against any and all monsters, so they can track her there, but they can't get in. Not even I can get in." We reach a car in an abandoned Piggly Wiggly parking lot. A nearly pristine '67 Mustang. He motions for me to get in. "Secondly, the Hunt won't end just because you brought her back from the cottage. It won't end unless she's dead or can prove no ill harm to the delicate magic we're forced to uphold."

"'We'?" I ask, sliding into the passenger's seat.

"You are as oblivious as they come." Asher sighs, turning over the cold engine. A loud rumbling escapes from within. The car sounds brand new. "Even River noticed the teeth. She thought I was a vampire, but still." He grins and a clear set of sharp fangs poke out over his lips. "Ghoul."

"Ghoul?" I reiterate with a clueless nod. "What's that?"

His head falls along with his grin. "A much more controlled, palatable, zombie." His head snaps up again, a glint in his green eyes at the clear shock on my face. "Don't worry. I'm not going to eat you. Unless you break River's heart."

"How comforting." I mumble as he pulls the car out of the parking lot and onto the single-lane road leading out of town. "So, tell me what your plan is, hot shot."

The plan was – is – as follows.

When the sun goes down, we sneak into the cottage, sneak her out, *and* take out all the monsters that will be swarming. We've yet to discuss who'll be the one doing the carrying of River and who will be the one taking shots at the monsters.

We have a brief window when the sun goes down for maybe half an hour where those who wish to get the grand prize from River's death are just waking up, making their way to her. Following her scent through those thick woods.

They stretch for miles.

Roldan has at least a hundred acres that butt up against three other farm owners who own the other three-quarters of the county. This cottage is dead center of those woods. Just over the property line of Roldan's farm.

In theory, the plan is straightforward. In practice, we don't know what the hell we're doing or what we're walking into.

"Mr. Kang, we've been looking for you." Sinclair says as I step through the door, nearly two thirty. Sitting there, staring at me like a parent waiting to scold a late-for-curfew teenager. He notices the rigidity in my body language, raising an eyebrow at me. I turned my attention quickly to someone else, anyone else, who might get me out of dealing with his hawk-like watch. "Where've you been, bud?"

"I needed some air." I scoff. His judgment only deepens. "I just went into town. Ran into some people who used to know River."

"Well, do you want to share with the class what you

learned?" My dad asks with a hearty cough, swinging his weight onto the doorframe of the room he just exited.

"I'm good. Thanks." I snip, attempting and failing to contain my eye roll. "You guys make any headway on whatever it is you're solving?"

"We're looking into the disappearance of your girlfriend!" Dad shouts, throwing the coffee mug he clung to. Dark liquid erupts from the ceramic as it shatters against the wall. "And you're out there lollygagging like you don't give a damn!"

"What good am I doing here?" I shout back. "I'm going crazy! I've told you *everything* I know to help you! What more do you want from me? To sit on that fucking couch for another millennium and rot into it with grief? Do you want me to go blow my brains out? Throw myself off the nearest mountain? Please, by all means, tell me what you expect me to do."

Thick, hot tears brew under my lashes. One's I'd yet to let myself shed over anything that's happened. My hands shake so violently at my sides I'm worried they'll fly right off my arms. I don't know if feeling everything all at once is any better than feeling absolutely nothing at all.

"You failed to mention that this was a magically inclined kidnapping. I think you've yet to tell us anything." He responds, nearly breaking the sheet rock as his fist comes flying to meet it.

"What are you talking about?" I ask. "I told you everything I knew about magical monsters."

"We did a sweep for magic, Leon." My mother says softly. "There's heavy magic in this house. Succubus magic."

"What are you saying?"

"It looks like she got lured outside by a succubus." Janice chimes in. "I thought they were extinct, honestly."

"Extinct?" I ask, baffled at the nonchalant tone of everyone in the room. My head spins with the rush of information, the room soon follows. Everyone's faces blur, and I have to grab the wall to steady myself.

"There hasn't been a succubus sighting in almost a century." Sinclair says from somewhere in the room. My eyes are unable to focus on where he is, though. "But there's clear succubus magic here. Strong and prevalent."

"I told you about Nancy's baby. It's cry sounded like an opera song or something you'd expect to hear from a siren, if those are real." I say, desperate to regain my composure.

"Of course sirens are real." Janice confirms with the smallest eye roll I've ever perceived. Like she didn't want to believe that I didn't know what she clearly knew. "Don't recommend going out on the ocean without beeswax. It's an ancient practice, but it's efficient."

"In any matter," Dad refocuses the attention back on him, rubbing his obviously sore fist. "It's clear that you have a lot to learn and it's time you learn a thing or two."

"And what might that be?" I snark, except I'm in no way in any shape to be back talking when the world feels like it's spinning a little too fast.

"You might want to sit down for this, baby." Janice says. Mom comes up to me, her gentle touch guides me to the aforementioned couch that I'd been expected to rot into.

The four of them gather around, an intervention waiting to happen. There's a tightness settling into my chest that grips me back to reality. Four walls that were once so far apart in this massive room seem to be closing in now.

"Do you know why we lived in the neighborhood we did when you were younger? That your mother and I still live even to this day?" Dad asks.

I shake my head 'no'. "I just assumed it was because you guys had too much money to know what to do with."

Janice scoffs, catching me off guard. Dad continues. "Because the community we live in was specifically designed to ward off magical creatures. To protect its people from the things that go bump in the night. It was warded by a mage that's long dead, but she was the strongest of her kind. We see the horrors that those monsters cause every day. Day in and day out. That's our job. We handle these cases and right the wrongs that are caused." There's fear, anger, *pain* in his voice as he talks. Years of pent up secrets spilling out of an emotionless (if you discount anger) man.

"I didn't know you guys even knew about this stuff until yesterday." I say.

"That's how it's supposed to be." Dad says with a sigh. "You were either supposed to follow in our footsteps and join the force or never find out about these horrible, wretched creatures. And I'm sorry it's come down to this."

"What happens now that I *do* know about this?" I ask, the air failing to return to my aching lungs. All eyes on me, pity in each one. What little food sat on my stomach threatens to expel itself. They all exchange knowing, sad looks. "What does it mean?"

"You need to be blessed by a mage." Sinclair says. I expected nonchalant, but his tone is almost panicked.

"Cool, let's go do that." I nearly hopped up from my seat.

"Son," Dad says, and by the tone alone, I know what he's about to say won't be any good news. "The mage that blessed our community was the last known mage we had on file."

"But there's a mage's cottage in the next town over." I blab, immediately regretting letting them in on this information. Knowing they'd never approve of our totally foolproof plan to get River back. "Or so I've heard. From a guy in town."

"There can still be protected dwellings but no living mage." Mom says, rubbing my arm tenderly. "Once a person, place, or object is blessed then that thing is blessed for the entirety of its life. Even if the entire item breaks, the individual pieces of that item are still protected."

I nod, not really knowing what to say. River's in a magical dwelling, sure, but there's no mages to help break this curse? To help rectify this situation? Damn me straight to hell, I couldn't care less about me, but there's no one to save River?

"What about you?" I ask Sinclair. "You're pretty young,

how do you get by without protection?"

His face falls in horror at my question. As if I couldn't put two and two together to see he was the youngest in the room. If the last of the mages had all died out long before he or I were born, then how the hell was he still walking around in his line of work?

"Leon," Dad warns.

"What did you do to get protected?" I ask again, more sternly this time. The once diplomatic, stoic, unreadable man suddenly can't make eye contact. Face flushed of color.

"Just drop it, Leon." Janice says sympathetically.

"What? Why?" My blood pressure begins to rise.

"Some things you don't need to know." Janice mutters, shaking her head.

"Please don't make me say it." Sinclair pleads, tears swelling in his eyes. "No one knows."

What the fuck does that mean?

"So there are alternatives and you're going to keep a tight lip about it when it could save me? Save River?" I bark, jumping off the couch. Fuck, I sound like a cornered dog.

"Son, it's not like that." Mom says. She makes an attempt to say something sympathetic, but I start moving and my ears stop listening. Filled with nothing but the roaring sound of my heartbeat in my ears. I stormed out of the room and into the yard.

Sinclair says something I ignore, I'm too focused. My feet stomp through the pristinely manicured yard and out into the encroaching darkness of the night. Twilight paints the sky a periwinkle and the stars shine brilliantly. A first breath of fresh air, it doesn't register in my collapsing lungs.

I'm going to protect her. Even if it kills me.

CHAPTER 35

River

My eyes fly open at the jingle of keys against the front door.

Fucking hell, who the fuck is that?

This place is a pigsty. Clearly no one's been here in a long time. Years, probably. A thick layer of dust coats every surface, at least a half-inch thick.

The door swings open, and the world outside is as dull and depressing as it is here. Storm clouds and the smell of the countryside rain peek into the door before it's shut, and we're completely forgotten by her once again. The smallest glimpse of the remaining daylight ripped from under my fingertips.

In walks a short, pale woman with long blond hair and ocean blue eyes. She's wearing thick long johns and a burnt orange beanie over her braids. She's carrying an army green duffle bag over one shoulder and a to-go cup of coffee in her right hand. She's very pretty, and I feel like I've seen her before.

She's very clearly not happy to see me.

I quickly try to scramble to my feet. Desperate to put myself in a position of some advantage against the intruder. If I don't trip over my own tired feet, I can grab something to wield as a weapon. Except my body physically doesn't move.

Not an inch. Not a single muscle reacts to the command. *Move, dammit. Move!* My arms, legs, torso, all of it below my neck is completely paralyzed.

Panic begins coursing through my veins, seizing them in its deadly grip. My lungs take too shallow of breaths. I'm fighting against myself, a prisoner in my own skin.

The smell of pennies coats my nose. *Weird.*

The pretty woman throws me a dirty look, like I was a small child she had just put into time out. Quickly, she turns her attention to unloading the stuffed duffle. I watch carefully as she meticulously pulls out its contents. A large ball of twine rope, three metal railroad stakes, a rubber mallet, a revolver, a box cutter, a box of black rubber gloves, a plastic tarp, and a smaller bag that jingles like it contains small glass jars. The same clicking noise as my glass spice jars back home.

She finishes arranging her torture devices and turns to me, a roll of duct tape in her hand I hadn't seen prior. A whimper escapes my desperate throat as she zeroes in on me, ripping off a piece of tape with her teeth.

"Did you really think you could come into my home and bring a bunch of foul breathed beasts with you?" She asks, the smell of coffee rakes over my skin as she inches closer. "You think there wouldn't be a price for your stay?"

I gulp. "I thought this place was abandoned." The comment came out faster than I could swallow it back down. With a wicked grin and a snap of her dirty fingers, the cottage is transformed into something straight from a fairytale.

With it, she also changes into something ethereal. Something otherworldly. From country attire to a full length velvet robe cascading under her fitted corset. Long chestnut brown hair, stick straight flows down to her waist. Eyes so white they were almost an icy blue with deep purple veins spider webbing over the glaciers.

"Astra?" I ask, her features more defined, almost gauntly. "Astra, you have to help me." I plea, begging for the woman we share friends with to listen to my story.

My eyes widen as she lunges for me without any hesitation. Her hand shoots for my neck, hardened fingers and nails digging themselves into the tender flesh of my throat. A whimper of pain escapes my lips as my lungs desperately try to retain what little air they had left.

I wanted to fight. *Needed* to fight back. Whatever was going on, it was overpowering me in a way I'd never encountered before. She was unnaturally strong for such a petite woman. Fingers easily grasped around my lifeline, holding me down, draining me of what little air remained in my lungs right. I knew the force behind her grip would leave bruises, dead or alive. The panic spikes again as my body slowly accepts that I'm inching closer and closer to unconsciousness.

Just when the stars start to fill my vision completely, she tightens her grip as she throws me backwards, sending my head crashing into the wall behind me.

My ears fill with the sound of bone cracking just seconds before the pain spreads from the back of my head to the rest of my body. There's a warm, wet stream oozing from the impact site that trickles slowly through my hair before reaching the base of my neck and pooling into the thin fabric of my shirt.

She mutters something at me that I don't register before storming off toward her pile of torture treasures. My lungs gasp for air desperately, unable to completely rid them of their burning.

I can't force myself to focus on anything other than the ringing in my ears, the pounding in my head, and the air filling my achy, stinging lungs.

I wanted to worry about what she was doing. What the hell she's about to do. But I can't. Even the voices in my head are dead silent through the overwhelming pain pulsing over my skull, down my neck, over my face. Whatever she's planning to do to me, it better kill me because I don't want to live through this. No matter how much I know I should persevere through whatever fresh hell is coming. I don't want to.

Through the excruciating pain radiating everywhere, tears stream down my scraped and cut face. I'm exhausted, my body has nearly completely given out.

"For two nights, you've sought refuge in a dwelling

that's owned by a Mage. You brought hundreds of magical creatures *here* and they've fucked up the wards! You even brought a ghoul! Now I've got to redo the glamours, the protection wards, EVERYTHING because of YOU." She snaps, plucking duct tape and a long knife from within the smaller bag.

"They were going to *kill* me." I whimper, beg. Still prone. Still in excruciating pain that flares with each beat of my heart, every breath I take.

"And rightfully so!" She snaps, waving the knife in my direction. If I could have flinched, I would have. I did internally. "You shouldn't even be here. Walking this Earth, let alone *my forest.*"

"So what? You're just going to hogtie me, throw me outside, and let the monsters have their way with me?" I snap, harsher than I needed to. Harder than I knew better than to.

A powerful hand comes up and slaps me across the face. The lightest of all the abuse thus far, but still leaves stars across my vision. Pain splinters through my nerve endings, leaving me wanting to rip the flesh off my bones.

"Little girl, you're going to wish that were the case. You're going to beg and plead for me to end you that mercifully." Her voice boomed throughout the cottage, and I imagined throughout the forest. Leaves shaking with the force of her rage.

She stomps around, spewing anger laced coffee scented words, grabbing different items from her pile. But the words sound foreign to me. Whatever she's saying is completely lost on me.

That is until a revolver appears in her hand as she's loading a single bullet into the chamber. She gives it a spin and slams it closed.

My whole world stands still in a cold molasses kind of way. Everything around me still moves but the inevitable is yet to come at a fraction of a snail's pace. All the pain that once ailed me has now magically dissipated from my body. My only thought, only reaction, is the frozen adrenaline that courses through my veins.

Frozen in my own body. Frozen in my mind.

A petrified heart attempts to beat its way out of its cage, leaping for freedom in the same way I wish I could.

I'm going to die. I'm going to die. Oh my god, I'm going to die.

The knot forming in the pit of my stomach is wound tighter than a two-dollar watch, ready to break at any second. Panic flushes over my face. Suddenly, I'm burning up in a room that was just ice-cold moments ago. The room becomes a sort of echo chamber of my great demise. All senses heightened to extreme measures to compensate for the inability to do anything. I can't even fight back.

The gun is pointed directly at me. I can almost see clear down the barrel when she decides to move it a hair to the left and pull the trigger.

BANG!

A sharp ringing fills my ears and my lungs gasp for the air they lost as my entire body gets pierced with enough adrenaline to revive a dead horse. I see her lips curl into a menacing, evil smile. There's now a bullet sized hole carved into the wall behind me, only an inch or so from where it would have made clear contact with my skull. Tears steadily fall from my eyes onto the floor where each drop collects its own ecosystem of dirt that swirled around like glitter in a snow globe.

"One thing about messing with a mage, girl, is that we. Never. Miss." She barks, inches from my face yet again, grasping my jaw in her small yet strong hand. "Whatever you think your life is worth, I promise you that it's not. You are nothing but the manure on the bottom of my shit kickers." She spits her words through clenched teeth, seething with insurmountable rage.

"I thought you said you weren't going to kill me so easily, huh?" I ask in a whisper, my voice still in hibernation.

"What happened? You worried I'm more powerful than you'd like me to be?"

She cackles. CACKLES. Like a witch. "Oh, no, little girl. I'm just playing with my food. There's nothing you can do against your paralysis. No one's going to come looking for you. Not even your poor brother can save you." She pauses as the door opens. A tall, almost dog-like creature walks in on its hind legs carrying a body over its shoulder. "What a pity that you thought he could save you."

The rottweiler-hound drops the body at my feet. The strawberry brown curls are matted with blood and forest floor debris. Bound in metal shackles around his hands, feet, and neck.

"Asher?" I weep, tears welling and falling in my eyes.

His eyes flutter open briefly, and a smirk crosses his bloodied lips. "Hey, birdie." He didn't forget about me.

Fuck, he was trying to protect me this whole time?

"What a beautiful family reunion." The Mage crones, prodding Asher with the toe of her boot. "Make it quick, you two. We have business to attend to." She struts off around the corner into another room, leaving us alone with the hound, who seems to be paying keen attention to Asher.

"I'm sorry, birdie." Asher gurgles, bloody saliva dribbling from the corner of his mouth.

"Nothing to be sorry about, Ash." I breathe, focusing all my strength on breaking the paralysis that grips my body and mind so tightly I'm certain I'm on the verge of breaking. I try to wiggle my toes, my fingers. While I feel them move internally, they don't budge.

"Birdie," Asher rasps, inhaling a sharp breath. "I have a confession." He laughs anxiously. I remain quiet, not knowing exactly where he's going with this. "I thought you were dead. Long ago."

"I got the hell out of Dodge." I chuckle breathlessly. Not that anything I said was funny, but I was so scared. So tired. So out of fight.

"I spent my whole sentence thinking about what would happen to you with Mom and Dad. And when I got out, you were nowhere to be found." He coughs wetly. "I thought they had killed you."

"Lucky for you, they only had four years of pushing me around before the state stepped in."

He continues, almost like he didn't hear me. "I went insane. I tore through every wretched soul to try and find you. But I eventually found you. Alive. And I'd never been so relieved."

"I'm sorry I never got the chance to tell you I left town when I graduated." I say, warm tears carving rivers down my dirty cheeks. "I should have found you first. I missed you every day."

"I missed you too, birdie." He says. "But that's not the confession."

"Then what was it?"

"I killed Mom and Dad."

"What?"

"What they did to you after I was gone was despicable. When I found out from Grandpa Jack, I drove back home to kill them. I *reveled* in the life leaving their pathetic little eyes."

No. No, no, no, no, no.

What does he mean he killed Mom and Dad? Impossible. They died in a car accident. There's no way that Asher killed them.

Oh, my God. Did he kill them?

My breath quickens. The walls of my mind begin to close in on themselves. My skin feels too tight. Panic. Rage. Confusion. Fear. Disgust. Gratitude. "You killed them?" My fingers twitch, almost recoiling from the news. The atrocities Asher has confessed to committing.

He nods, not an ounce of regret in his deep green eyes. He'd always been a hothead. Never one to take being told 'no' lightly. A very disturbed child.

"I didn't know what else to do." There was pain, deep-rooted, solemn pain that ached in my chest at his confession. "You were all I had. They separated us, sent me to prison for *weed* of all things. Sent you to live with those fucking *bastards*." He spews his words through clenched teeth, blood drying on his busted lip.

"Did you ever try to find me?" I ask, the hot tears staining the collar of my shirt with their downpour.

"I found you plenty, birdie. You just never recognized me." He says, eyes softening. "I was a security guard on your college campus. A passing stranger in the grocery store. I always kept my distance, but I was always there to watch over you."

The remaining wind escapes my lungs as the memories come flooding back. The familiar eyes. The curly hair. Everywhere I look, I remember seeing him. Most recently, a few weeks ago in a Korean BBQ place Leon and I went to. How was he always there?

"How?" I ask, a shudder aching its way down my spine.

"Does it matter?" He replies with a wet rasp. "I tried to keep you safe. Even from afar, after all this time."

"Why? I always thought you hated me."

"I know. You were a little shit as a kid. But once I got locked up, I realized that you were my kid. I missed you, birdie." He confesses, each breath becoming harder and harder to take.

"I missed you too, Bubba." I say as another wave of saltwater streams down my beat red face. "God, you don't know how bad it got when you left."

He chuckles. "No, but Grandpa Jack told me."

"Mom's Dad?" I ask. He nods. I'd never met the man. I didn't even know he was still living. I'd only heard stories of Grandpa Jack, but he lived out of state. Mom never really spoke about him. Though, if my memory serves me correctly, I don't remember Mom ever having a conversation with me outside of scolding me for something.

I'd only heard what other people had said about Jack. How he was an extremely stubborn man. Headstrong. Only had one daughter whom he ended up not speaking to. The stories always varied on why they weren't on good terms, so I didn't even know who was telling as close to the truth as possible.

"You would've loved him." He hums.

"Why do you say that?"

"You were everything he ever wanted in a daughter. Everything Mom never was. You are strong, smart, resilient."

"I'd love to meet him someday."

"Maybe in the afterlife, birdie. He died not too long after I got out of jail."

"Oh." I say, disappointed that I'd missed out on meeting the only other family member to ever think of me fondly and love me. Outside of Asher, apparently. I clench my fist. The paralysis slowly retreats from my appendages. Warmth returning to each spot that I resume control over.

The Mage stomps back in carrying a handful of potently fresh herbs and some sort of mechanical device that looks akin to a garlic press with way too many moving parts. She slams her things on the table in the corner.

She hums to herself, back turned, but her hound's watchful eye on us still. The need to stretch out my reawakened limbs is ever-present.

"Hey, old hag. Are you going to make good on that promise?" Asher asks the mage. She snaps her head around to him, pure hatred in her eyes.

"The only promise I'm inclined to keep with *your kind* is to kill you." She hisses, abandoning whatever it is she had started working on to get down in Asher's face.

He throws her a bloody smirk, eyes shining with mischief. "Aw, don't go getting sweet on me now. My old lady wouldn't like that very much." He teases, making a kissy face. The hound in the corner snarls, but Asher's gaze never wavers from Astra's.

With one swift motion, she pulls out the revolver from her holster and aims it directly at my temple. Pulling the trigger without any warning. *Click.* Asher's face falls as my entire body floods with another wave of adrenaline-fueled panic. "Not so tough now, are you?" She growls.

"You leave her out of this." He spits. She aims the gun at him next, a malicious grin coating her bluish-pale lips. *Click.* The roaring in my ears is almost too loud to bear.

"Go ahead." He chuckles. She grabs him by the hair, rearing Asher's head up and slamming it down into the floor. The impact of the hardwood against his face spurs up a bloody stain and a disgusting *thwack* coupled with bone breaking.

"You're going to wish you were dead when I get through with you." Her words mimic the threat she made me earlier.

Every inch of my body throbs in icy-hot fear.

"Leave him alone." I spit. "He's not the one you need to worry about." The ache in my lungs seeps into my words "Kill me." My challenges sound like hollow pleas now. "DO IT!"

The mage tosses Asher aside from her once deadly grip on his scalp, allowing him to collapse onto the floor. She pulls a single bullet out of her pocket, loading it into the chamber without a spin.

Pointing the barrel of the gun at Asher one more time. Finger poised and ready to pull the trigger with pitch-black eyes.

I muster up all of my remaining strength, anything I can conjure up. Adrenaline coats my nervous system. The fight or flight or freeze suspending time into slow motion as I throw my achy, tired, hungry, sleep-deprived, weak body at Asher.

My big brother.

My first protector.

BANG!

CHAPTER 36

Leon

There was a brief tug in my chest and a quickened heartbeat. But only for a moment. Only brief enough to feel it, consider its origins, before it dissipates.

I was close to the mage's cottage, the copper smell thick in the air. It couldn't be more than a half-mile hike to the property. The sun had long set. My car is parked behind a bush just off Roldan's property line. Just like we'd talked about.

It was early, but there was still no sign of Asher anywhere. So I moved in without him.

It would have been nice to have someone watch my back. Someone magically inclined would have been advantageous. But I'll make do. I have to. I have to get my River.

The woods were thick, but just up a slight hill (great, another one) amid a small clearing, was a well-lit cottage made of stone nestled amid hundreds of acres of trees. The trees here grew brighter, greener, than those of the magical property. The evergreens were painted vibrant greens, thick with moss and mushrooms.

Just south lies a barely visible dirt road, downhill from where my destination. It leads from the cottage down into the valley where it intersects with another road a couple of miles down. Shrouded in the darkness created by the woods. A howl erupts from upwind. An unnatural, bone-chilling howl that couldn't possibly be made by anything other than a monster lurking in the shadows.

I quicken my pace, desperate to see River, to have her back in my arms. It squeezes my heart, elation buzzing in my veins at how close I am to having her back. God, she better be fucking okay, or everyone will have to pay for this. There better not be a single scratch on her.

The closer I draw to the cottage, the more I hear things rustling in the shadows. Things that my human vision would never be able to see, but their eagerness to get at my girl prevents them from being as quiet as they could be. The game they play, predator and prey, is not nearly as important anymore.

I make it to the edge of the tree line, no more than a hundred feet from the cottage's front door. I can see into the window, seeing a figure with long white hair stomp around in the kitchen.

That's not River. Or Asher. And all the mages are extinct, so who the fuck is that?

I take one step into the clearing, the gun in my hands feeling heavier than I've ever felt it. Another step. I'm completely exposed.

It's okay. I've done plenty worse with less. I've killed people with hiding spots that wouldn't cover a gnat's left ass cheek. That Toronto businessman didn't see it coming and I was standing right in front of him.

Before I was a world-renowned music producer, I paid my bills being a professional hitman. I've never talked about that career path before. Not with anyone that wasn't a paying customer. And I made good money. Most of it is in offshore accounts. The day I retired from the business, I got so many messages from completely random people saying that if I ever wanted to come back to the profession, they would hire me before anyone else.

I suppose I should tell River about all of that. Surely she won't run screaming from me like I'm no better than the monsters in these woods that are out to get her.

I'm maybe ten feet from the cottage when, suddenly, my entire body feels like it's wrapped in hot coals and I'm unable to move. The white-haired woman peers at me from the window, a malicious smile on her face. Her face is uncannily familiar.

She stomps out of view, further into the house. The gun singes my palms. My fingers are locked into place, unable to drop the molten metal.

An excruciatingly long moment passes as I try to free myself from this paralysis. The monsters huffing, howling, and growling grow louder.

Bang!

The sound of a fired round rings throughout the forest. My chest tightens with the adrenaline coursing through me. Senses heightened to new extremes.

What I can only describe as a hellhound comes sprinting out of the cottage on its hind legs. Straight for me. It tackles me to the ground, gnashing its teeth at me. Regaining movement again, I wrestle with the demon dog for a moment before slamming the barrel of my gun to its head and pulling the trigger.

It falls limply on top of me.

Quickly pushing the beast off of me, the gunfire has seemingly awoken any creature residing in the woods. Every beast's nose is filled with the scent of blood and gunpowder.

I don't grant myself the chance to linger. Throwing myself up, I dash inside just as the door snaps shut behind me. Without my doing. *Oh, this is not going to be good.*

I quickly survey my surroundings, taking in the brightness of the room, the white-haired woman staring me down, the two bodies lying on the floor. A woman hunched over a man.

River hunched over Asher.

"You're too late," crones the white-haired woman. "I've fulfilled God's prophecy. It is only a matter of time before all is right in the world again. You are too late." She reiterates her point.

Her words mean nothing. My River is right there. A growing blood stain soaks through her dirty white shirt. She's right there. She's right there. She's right there.

Oh, oh god. She's not breathing. My eyes sting with tears. Hands antsy to kill this woman for what she's done. *Fucking hell! My baby isn't dead. She's **not** dead. She can't be.*

I lunge for the woman. Her features, though gaunt, remind me of Astra, and for a brief moment, I wonder if they're related. They look so similar. It doesn't matter, though. I'm not in the business of caring right now.

She cackles like a witch before disappearing from where she stood in front of me to being behind me. Swiveling, I come face-to-face with the barrel of her gun. The one I'm assuming shot River. *She's not dead.*

"I see you're upset." She held no sympathy. "But I've fulfilled God's orders. We must rejoice!"

"*You killed her!*" The words sting as they leave my tongue. It feels wrong. This is all wrong. *She can't be dead.*

Tears smear my vision. I can't stop looking at her, lying over her brother, unmoving. The water staining my lash lines makes it nearly impossible to see more than a blur of her. My heart squeezes so hard that it sends actual pain radiating throughout my chest, and my lungs feel on the brink of collapse. No air entered them, no matter how desperate I was. My entire body, mind, and soul *ached* catastrophically. There was no end to the pain. No light at the end of the tunnel. Nothing but a dark void staring back at me.

Staring down the barrel of her revolver, part of me – a very large part – wanted nothing more than for her to pull that trigger. Take me out of this world. If she could take her out, then do the same for me. Send me out of this realm so I don't have to live without her.

She's not dead.

I lean into the gun, the end pointing square at my breaking heart. "If you can do it to her, do it to me." I plead through clenched teeth. "Either you do it or I will."

"Don't be dramatic, Leon." She spits. "You barely knew her."

"How the *fuck* would you know?!" I hiss back. "You don't know *anything!*" Tears and snot drip from my eyes and nose. My whole body vibrates with anger and grief. Denial and acceptance. Bargaining my life for hers.

The woman's face and body, all her features change. *Astra.* "It's my business as God's prophet to know everything."

Before she even finishes her sentence, before the breath between us could grow cold, I knock her gun away, knocking it to the floor and kicking it out of reach. Pointing mine in her place. Aiming right for the forehead. My hands shake violently. Not from fear, but from vengeance.

"Killing me won't bring her back." Astra crones, dropping her disguise. "My destiny has been fulfilled. I am not scared as you should be." She lifts her head proudly at what she's accomplished. Like any of her words make an ounce of sense.

"An eye for an eye." I hissed. "Blind world be damned. You deserve to pay for what you've done." My hand steadies a hair. My finger wraps around the trigger, not hesitating as I squeeze. My body tenses for the recoil, ears anticipating the *bang.*

But it never comes.

Not even a *click* from a misfire. As an evil grin spreads over her face, my face falls.

What the fuck happened?!

"If you want to kill me, Leon, then you're going to have to earn it. No weapons. No magic. A simple battle of brains versus brawns. If you win, fairly, then you can kill me. I will die a selfless death. If I win, then you join them." She cuts her eyes at River and Asher. A pile of bodies on her floor that she thought nothing more of than a dead bug under her shoe.

Astra sticks her hand out.

"Fine." I agree, shaking her hand. *I can't believe I'm doing this.* "What are the terms?"

"Never leave yourself open." She grins wickedly, twisting my arm, causing me to yelp out in pain. She's much stronger than she looks. Pinning my arm behind my back, she leans over me and whispers. "Never judge a woman by her size, either."

She throws me further into the room where I catch myself against the wall. Not giving her a second to gain, I spin, readying myself to swing. Fighting, boxing, was never my strong suit, but I had done it for years to keep up my hand-to-hand in case a job ever went south. Not that I ever missed a shot.

I swing at the first opportunity, my fist connects with her jaw, but she barely flinches. We dance around the bodies on the floor for a moment, swinging, dodging, hitting, and missing. It takes everything in me not to look down at River. Not to give up right here and now and let her kill me.

There's this gaping crater-sized hole in my heart. Devoid of all emotion. Nothing but a vast expanse of nothingness. Not even the astronomical pain that radiates over my entire body, not from the physical assault, but from the loss settling over me.

How can she be dead?

Astra gets a good swing in, knocking stars into my vision and my body on the floor. Landing right next to Asher. Mere inches from his pale face. And River. Her face is hidden by her matted hair, but I can see bits and pieces of her features through the once honey-red hair. Purple lips open in surprise and anguish. Gray skin that once was a glowing constellation of freckles and ivory.

I try to turn my head, to look away from my dead bride. The woman I *knew* I would spend the rest of my life with. But I won't budge. The muscles in my neck refuse to relinquish my right to look at the horror scene in front of me. And for a second I thought maybe it was my body not wanting to let go of her. To hold on to her and all her beauty as long as I could.

But the smell of pennies surges my nose, and I knew

Astra broke the terms of our duel.

"Let go of me!" I growl as she cackles.

"No can do, sugar." Astra hums. "You should never make a deal with a Mage." She takes a seat at a table in the corner, her back to the wall. Picking up whatever she had been working on prior, she quickly forgets about our existence.

How the *fuck* am I going to get out of this shit?

CHAPTER 37

River

I've contemplated my death at my own hands for as long as I could think about such things.

I was told by my childhood therapist that normal people don't actually think about the various ways they would off themselves if given the opportunity, but those intrusive thoughts have been a sort of normalcy and comfort for the majority of my life. Given over much of my younger years to fantasizing about the how's, the when's, and the aftermath of the metaphorical blow up.

Through it all, I tried to remain neutral on the outside, because if there's one thing that life's taught me, it's that the people in your life don't actually care about your feelings.

No one would cry at my funeral. Not a soul would bring flowers to place atop my grave. I would enter this world much like I left it. Alone, cold, and grasping for a denied breath until it felt as though the pain would swallow me whole in a merciful attempt at a sacrifice.

I used to look at my sorry excuse of a life and wonder why I was holding on. If there was anything greater and bigger and brighter out there for me, then it was either painfully far away or always just out of reach, but never available for a poor wretched soul like me.

Either way, the contemplation of life's greater meanings

was always filled with dread and despair. I had no desire to run in a rat race I was always destined to lose, but I kept running purely out of spite. My deep-seated hatred for all the wrongdoings in my life fueled a fire so instinctual in me that I felt completely out of control in the trajectory of my own life. Like I was a mere onlooker or moviegoer watching the events unfold before me with no way of stopping them or the visceral reactions that they caused.

The Grim Reaper was not at all what I expected of him. He was wickedly tall, with broad shoulders, a thin waist, and a slender frame. He wore a very gothic vampiric suit, with jewels down the bodice and thin, round-framed glasses. His hair was slicked back messily, but almost intentional. An oval face with somber, pitch-black eyes.

He was beautiful in every aspect of the word. And his aura put me at peace. Much like death is beautiful and peaceful.

As the cold, bony fingers of the grim reaper curl around my chin, he points my head towards a growing beacon of light in the darkness that turns the frigid air around me into a 35mm film of my life. He and I are the only viewers.

"Do you have a name?" I ask the beautiful reaper beside me, wanting a distraction from what lies ahead of me. He does not answer my question. Memories that were once long forgotten play out in front of me on the magical big screen.

Kindergarten recesses filled with giggles, sticky fingers, and handpicked dandelions shoved into pockets to be hand delivered to mommy and daddy at the bus stop.

The car ride to the zoo for the very first time, eagerly looking out the window at the billboards as they passed at lightning speeds with excitement building in my tummy.

The first family reunion at the lake in the summer of '02 when I got so violently sunburnt, I couldn't function, but the laughter always stayed with me.

The short-lived friendship that blossomed between long-distance cousins that lasted only a weekend, but a fondness I swore to hold onto forever. The secrets of girlhood locked away tightly in a brightly painted world where no one had ever forsaken me because the innocence of children will forever outshine all of the horrible, unspeakable things that you go through even at such a young age. You just don't know how to process it yet, so you don't.

The night I realized my brother wasn't ever coming home.

The first time I was left alone for days and days on end, Mom and Dad disappeared to God only knows where, but I was ten and thought I was the coolest girl ever. They couldn't yell at me if they weren't there. The summer I got to spend all by myself with nothing but a stack of paper food stamps and the appetite of an eleven-year-old.

The harshness of the first winter alone in a new home after being ripped away from the only family I had ever known. The severe depression spiral I fell into the moment my life was thrown into a garbage bag by state police and CPS lasted the duration of my stay in foster care. The terror of sleeping in the CPS worker's office that night while they looked for an emergency placement for me.

The humiliation that was to follow me for years to come. The pity that the adults had for me that they quickly grew out of when they saw how 'resilient' I was. Six years of not feeling safe and protected in my own house for fear of someone watching me change, standing over me while I slept, or jerking off in the bathroom with the shower curtain being the only thing between me and my worst nightmares.

All the times I laughed through the pain, scars that littered my thighs that I eventually covered with tattoos, insomnia that filled my adulthood, and my short stint with drugs in college before I quickly realized I didn't like how out of control I felt when I took them just as much as I didn't like being sober.

All of the failed attempts at relationships turned into endless nights of arguing because I didn't know how to be a good girlfriend. Truthfully, I didn't know anything. I didn't know how to communicate my needs and feelings, or prioritize myself or my partner equally, it was always heavy one way or the other. I didn't know what I wanted out of my own life, so how was I to pick the right person who was going in the same direction when I didn't even know which direction I was going in the first place?

I had big plans for myself. I wanted to travel the world, become multilingual, start hobbies, and find the things in life and in myself that would give me purpose. What organizations would I have donated my time and money to? Would I have become a big sister at the Big Brothers Big Sisters in my area? Would I have gotten a host of angels off the angel tree every year to give back to the kids in situations like I've been in? Would I work weekends at the homeless shelter or soup kitchen? Would I have wanted to start my own business doing a passion I found later in life?

I had hoped to have more of my life together by 28. Hell, I don't even have a last will or anyone to leave my tattered pieces to. All I have to my name is the world's smallest simple IRA that has barely had time to accrue any money and a few boxes of things that have become all that I am.

Years of my life have been shoved into boxes of unorganized mess contributed to the late diagnosed ADHD. All the hobbies I hyper-fixated on that ended up getting donated, sold, or packed into doom boxes are the only things that I have to show for the time and money spent on it all. My educational degrees are all packed away with caps and gowns, the failed attempts at modern art are stored in the back of someone else's closet, and the hand embroidery kits were packed away and sold on Facebook Marketplace before I even finished my freshman year of college. I have no pets, though I would have loved a cat to inevitably rot beside me in bed on lazy Sunday mornings.

I wish I could have spent more of my adult years finding out who I wanted to become. More than the trivial things, but subconsciously, who would I have wanted to become? I would have wanted to be less of a people pleaser, someone that would have made younger me proud to have grown into. I would have loved to have had a couple of good friends in my city, where we could grab brunch and talk about current politics. I wish I had allowed myself the space to be imperfect, always the most perfect version of myself was on display, even when no one was looking. It was critically exhausting.

There were so many things that I wanted to be, but I am out of time. I'm angry that the circumstances around my end are what they are. I'm angry at myself for not fighting a better fight, for not 'winning'. But none of that matters because I'm scared and I'm tired and I'm sad.

I didn't realize that death could be so scary, especially after years of ideation. No amount of exhaustion and horror could release me from how genuinely dejected I am that I'm dying. Gut-wrenching grief fills my lungs in a way that feels as though I'm drowning rather than dying of a gunshot wound.

Why am I riddled with grief? What's causing me to feel the pain of losing a loved one when I'm the one being lost? Because wherever I'm going, heaven, hell, purgatory, or the vast expanses of time and space or even a black hole, there won't be a tall, handsome, stoic teddy bear there waiting for me.

Just when I found the person that brings me the most joy, I'm violently ripped away from this lifetime, forever searching the vast expanses of the universe for any iteration of us where I'm allowed to grow old with him, completely uninterrupted.

A love I had spent all my life desiring, dreaming of, manifesting, begging the universe to grant me, was all being washed down the drain like manic hair dye. A bruise left on the body that will fade over time but will remain with the heart forever. A love that was so brief it has to be comical, but so profound that I'd remember it in every lifetime I get to exist in.

And as if right on cue, Leon's there on the big screen.

Looking into his eyes for the very first time, a new feeling tumbled around inside of me, coming to the surface like air bubbles that broke the surface tension of the stagnancy within me. I brushed it off as nerves because how can you look at someone so beautiful and not be?

Being perceived by anyone attractive is hard, but this was something entirely different. He wasn't just looking at me, he was seeing me. In the same way Dream Leon saw me, Real Leon saw me. In the elevator, in the hallway, in the lobby, in the parking lot, in my apartment, in the dark car rides, in the limitless expanse of time and space, he always saw me. Even when I was unsure of everything in this world, even his feelings and intentions, he could look at me with his boba eyes, soft as dew on a spring morning as it settles over the world, and everything would ease.

Leon is the kind of love that you read about in fairytales. The knight in shining armor, the Prince Charming, your Flynn Riders. His love and devotion are so profound that you feel it in every corner of the universe. He'd build bridges, cities, castles, and pillow forts with his bare hands and then burn it all down if it would make you happy. He doesn't move mountains for you, the mountains move on their own out of fear for the hellfire that he'd reign down upon them if they so much as look at you the wrong way. He's the calm and the storm, a strong tidal wave ready to pull you under, a glimpse at heaven on earth.

I've lived more in the limited time I've gotten the opportunity to love him than I have in my whole life. I could watch a thousand movies and write a million novels on the kind of love that I've experienced with him, and no combination or volume of words will ever fully convey the magnitude of emotions that assist in the psychological makeup of us. He's so much more than I could have ever hoped for, and I'll curse this death with my dying breath for not giving us longer.

Maybe I was always destined to love him. No matter

how brief. The strong and steady embrace of love wrapped into thoughtful gestures and peace of mind were always meant to be a part of my story. The unknown is an ever-present source of anxiety, but the touch of a hand is the only cure.

Love is meant to be slow. Love is meant to be cherished and nurtured through every aspect of your being. You wake up with love and fall asleep with a handful more. Love is bundled into simple interactions, from small acts of service to the twinkle that shines in their eyes as they look at you.

Love is gentle. *You* may not be gentle, but love is. It surrounds you in a blanket of certainty, warm and snug and comfortable. Love can exist in big gestures, but when the seas have calmed, if you are not soothed by the lull of the ocean, love is not around.

As the movie of my life continues to play, tears stream down my face as the realization settles into my chilled soul. This is it. This is the part of the movie I've waited all my life to watch. My love story.

The darkened room shimmers with shades of gold and pink as Leon shows up on the screen before me. It's him, but I don't recognize the surroundings. The film is grainy, almost antique-looking.

The streets of an unfamiliar city surround him as he's looking at the camera - at me - with his dopey grin on his face. I glance over at the reaper, who's unmoving from his place next to me, still watching the movie with me. The attire of the people passing in and out of the frame is indicative of a different time, maybe the early 1900s. He kisses my hand and the camera shifts, panning to the same Leon in a different time.

The same scene plays over and over with different periods, showing the love we've been chasing over all of our lifetimes.

Then I saw a teenage boy, maybe fifteen or so, standing outside the gift shop at the Natural Bridge Caverns with an older-looking woman as she took his picture. As the camera flashes, a head turns in the crowd, looking at where the light originated. It's a young girl with honey-auburn hair who moves away from her group to the boy.

"Excuse me! I think you dropped this." The girl says to the boy, holding out a wallet to him awkwardly. Hazel eyes look at the boy, a strange sense of knowing twinkling behind her nervous gaze.

"Thank you." The boy says with a microscopic bow of his head. "I didn't even know I dropped it."

"Thank you, miss." The older lady says with a soft and beautiful smile on her face. She pats the girl on the shoulder.

"I figured. I would have just mailed it back to the address on your ID." The girl smirks, and blush fills the boy's ears. "What are you doing here?" The girl asks.

"My grandma's always wanted to visit here." He says shyness dusting over his tan skin. "You?"

"School field trip." She says. "I'm River."

"Leon." He holds his closed hand out for a fist bump that I reciprocate, a smile spreading over my once terrified face. Some calls for me from the group. Nancy. I turned back to Leon and his grandmother, giving them a brief goodbye.

"I hope you enjoy your trip, Leon!"

I promise to love you in every lifetime.

A phrase that rings through my mind, body, and soul. We were always destined for love, and I promise I'll find you again soon.

CHAPTER 38

Leon

I could feel the invisible string begin to break. The tug in my chest or stomach wasn't just nerves, but the link between her and me. I grasp at it, willing it to return, but the only thing I'm met with is cold emptiness. Nothing could have prepared me for just how gut-wrenching it is to feel the life leave out of someone else's body. It's like watching a movie that leaves you speechless. Where do you go from there? Where do you go when the only thing in this world that ever meant something to you is suddenly ripped away from you in the worst possible way?

All of the oxygen in my lungs is expelled all at once, like the force of a thousand high-speed car crashes you would only pray to not survive.

I can't move, I can't look away from my love.

Oh, my love, my love, my love. My bottom lip trembles violently. *How I've failed you, mon amour. My sweet angel. My little firestorm.*

Okay, okay, okay, Leon. Think. *Think! For once in your life, use that big fucking head for something useful.* There's got to be something I can do to get out of this situation. To kill that fucking bitch for what she's done. Mage be damned. She deserves to die.

That lying, backstabbing, cock sucking, son of a fucking bitch sat there at that fucking wedding and gave me some

349

sad sack excuse about not changing destiny. I don't believe that bullshit for a second. She's been planning this since the beginning. She had to have been. How else would she be here, too? There's not a single doubt, no coincident bullshit.

Unlike the coward mixing magic shampoo potions at the table, I'm not afraid of destiny. I'm certainly not afraid to change it. Because destiny is not a thing we set in stone, but a river that is carved through each action and inaction we take leading up to a moment. We have the choice; the universe simply offers pathways.

"What do you get from keeping me here?" I ask, tremendously small.

"I'm giving you time to grieve before you two part ways for good." She says without turning to face me. "If you wish to be free, just say so, doll."

"I'd very much like to be out of these imaginary shackles." I snip, my temper shorter than my tongue's ability to remain quiet.

"Then you're free to go." She says simply. I sigh, shrugging my shoulders, bracing to push myself up, but my arms are not my own. Or at least they feel as foreign to me as an ancient language.

"I thought you said I was free to go?" I ask with an incessantly loud eye roll. She cackles that high-pitched laugh, and if my limbs worked, I'd be using them to lob her upside her fucking head.

The more likely scenario is that I'm going to work myself up into a brain aneurysm before I even get up off this fucking floor. That fucking bitch is going to get it, though. Just wait until I can use all my appendages.

'You're free to go,' my ass. Okay, okay, okay. Fucking focus you big-headed bitch. Get it together.

Damn everything all to hell. Every last thing in my general vicinity, in the whole world, in the entire galaxy. If I ever break free, I will be personally kicking the ass (specifically) of all the magical creatures and or monsters in existence because it should be illegal to trap someone in their own flesh prison.

Is there a U.N. for magical creatures? Is there someone I can take this up with? Are my parents the right people to bring this issue up with? Would they even know what I'm talking about?

Do *I* even know what I'm talking about?

No. No, I don't. But that doesn't matter. I've got to get out of this. There's got to be a way to break this magic. But I don't know anything about magic. I barely know about changelings and ghosts and succubi, let alone mages and rottweilers with a sense of consciousness.

Speaking of my parents, I wonder what they'd think of this whole thing. I don't want to think about that too long.

River's skin gets bluer and bluer by the minute. And as much as my crazy internal monologue is fueling the fire in my blood, each time my eyes fall on her, I grasp harder at the string that once tied me to my sweet River.

I think about her laugh. Its bubbly and light consistency made anything, *anything,* better. The way her golden eyes shone in the sunlight. The touch of her hand against my skin. Her all-or-nothing disposition. The softness of her lips.

God, my heart hurts.

I turn my head away from her, which feels sacrilegious to do so. *Wait.* I turn it back in the opposite direction. And back. Two more times. *Fuck yeah!* I send mental feelers to the rest of my muscles, testing the waters and limits of what I can and can't do.

All of my extremities tingle with static, and it takes everything in me not to give away my newfound freedom. But before I get up completely, Asher, who I had thought was long dead with River, lets out a whisper of a breath. His eyes flutter open for just a moment.

I halt getting off the floor, for just a moment.

His breathing is borderline nonexistent, but he nods at

me to come closer. I do so with haste.

"Is she-" His voice is barely above a whisper, barely loud enough for the vibrations to resonate in my ears. I nod solemnly, still unwilling to truly admit the truth. "You can save her."

"How?" I ask, mostly defeated, but a single spark of hope races through my veins. No matter how desperate I am.

"Take her down to the crossroads. Make a deal."

"How will that-"

"Just *do it*, fucker. Do it for our girl."

"What about-" My eyes darted to the witch still mixing her bathroom potions at the dining table. If she's aware of what's going on behind her, she makes no move to show it.

"I got her." Asher smirks, dried blood coating his face. "The bitch can't kill what's already dead." I want to laugh. The pebble of hope blossoming inside my chest is the only thing I cling to. "You'll have to run fast." I nod, a new set of tears stinging my eyes. "I'll come find you two when it's over."

I nod again. Unable to form any sense of words to express gratitude. "See you on the other side, brother." It was his turn to nod.

His filthy fingers counted to three, and once he reached it, I sprung up, shoving down every ach, every pain, every discomfort. Reaching for River and scooping up her cold, almost stiff body and cradling her in my arms.

Hopefully not for the last time. And I ran like hell.

I ran and ran and ran. I'd never been a runner. Never claimed to be anything close to the kind of athlete it took to run for personal pleasure. But right now, I could have – would, if I needed to – run circles around the world. If it meant that I had a shot at bringing her back.

There's a bud of hope nestled in the deepest crevice of my abdomen. A blip in the darkness that surrounds me, both inward and outward. It's the tiniest little glimpse of yearning that's keeping me running.

My feet pound the dirt, slipping occasionally on some loose gravel, as I speed like a madman down this seemingly never-ending road. No crossroad in nearly a mile and a half. My destination has to be close.

The problem with this plan – there are many, but this is just the one that concerns me right here right now – is that I don't know what to do when I get to where I'm going. What do I do at the crossroads? Is someone going to be there to greet me with a Cheshire smile to guide me through the entire process?

I don't know. And only a small part of me cares about technicalities. There's not a single thing I'd spare to bring her back to me. *Nothing.*

Coming to a halt at the wide intersection, there's no sign of life anywhere. No natural or man-made noises. Not even the wind whistling through the trees. It's painfully dark, my lungs ache, and my feet and arms are screaming. I kiss River's freezing cold temple before setting her down in the dead center of the crossroad, kneeling beside her.

Inhaling sharply, I say, "I want to make a deal." It's arctic temperatures out here, even with the stagnant air, but there's a colder chill that snakes up my spine. One vertebrae at a time until it reaches my neck. Like an icy talon.

The moments tick by, either excruciatingly slow or insanely fast. I'm more likely to go insane first or die of hypothermia long before I figure out the magic word to make this fucking deal.

"River, baby," I coo, still desperate to will her soul back into her body. "I'm going to make this right. I promise."

The icy talon comes back, snaking its way down my spine.

"Sorry to keep you waiting." A thick, deep voice purrs from behind me, right in my ear. "I'm very busy these days."

Even with my eyes having adjusted to the pitch-black night, there was no seeing the speaker, but the voice put me on edge. Something was wrong. Very, very wrong.

"I want to make a deal. To bring her back." I say, looking in the direction the voice had once come from.

"'*Her*' is a very broad term. Are you talking about the dead bitch in front of you or Marilyn Monroe?"

My first instinct is to mouth off at the disembodied voice about the very *disrespectful* term they're throwing around for the love of my fucking life. But the survival instinct in me, the one that actually would rather have River alive than both of us dead in a cornfield is screaming at me to keep my mouth shut for once.

And for once in my life, I don't say the first thing that slides down the unfiltered channel between my brain and my mouth. I hold it in. For River.

"The 'dead bitch' is my girlfriend." I state, trying to wrangle the tears threatening my eyes about as well as I can wrangle a bundle of cats. *Not very fucking well.* "I'll do whatever I have to. Just please bring her back to me." Hell knows how to make a beggar out of me.

"How awfully tragic." The voice chuckles. "Do you even know what you're doing, young man? Do you know what's at stake?"

I shake my head fervently. "No."

Nightfall blankets everything around me in a sense of uneasiness and uncertainty. Gravel digs into the pads of my hands, and it takes all the willpower I have to not start punching the ground like that would help anything. Maybe the pain in my hands will stop the pain in my chest or the violent shaking of my shoulders as fat tears create a steady stream out of my eyes. The need to tear my heart out of my chest grows with each unsteady breath.

Why couldn't it have been me?

All the love in the world couldn't stop this, but love caused it. I love her and I'll love her until my dying breath, not just until hers. What I would give to trade places with her, to be where she is, to take the beatings and bruises and bullets that she was never supposed to take. I would sell my soul to the devil to have this end differently.

I can't bring myself to my feet, my legs are too unstable to stand and too stubborn to sit. So, I kneel on the rough road, pleading with whatever or whoever will listen, begging for a second chance, for someone to tie the red string that held us together through space and time back to us. A bond I did not know of until just a few minutes ago, but one I would pledge to hunt down until the end of time for as long as our souls exist in the same universe.

I never got the opportunity to tell her just how in love with her I am. I was deprived of the opportunity to profess my undying love to her. I don't get to tell everyone at work that I'm getting married to the most amazing woman on this planet and the next. Or to hear the old men harp on how marriage is a scam, and wives suck and get to revel in the knowledge that we could never hate each other.

I had it all planned out.

I saw our lives mixed together, ready to grow old and mundane, with her by my side. Her spontaneity would have kept me youthful well into my eighties. My joints would crack, and my back would hurt, but my heart would grow ever fonder of the mischief in her brilliant eyes. Her childlike sense of wonder, her affinity for cats, Lego flowers, and the color purple always brought a sense of home to the spaces she existed in. She was warm like a lit candle, the closer you got the warmer she became. She was sassy, funny, and full of life. When I looked at her, I thought I was going to explode from *love*.

From the moment I first laid eyes on her, I knew she was the one. My heart did somersaults in my chest, I just knew she had put a spell on me. The way she even looked beautiful in harsh fluorescent lighting was the only signal I needed to know she would have my heart forever. A rosy blush tinted cheeks and the passing small talk were the only things getting me through some difficult nights. Her bubbly personality burns brighter than looking straight into the sun. I left my apartment just a few minutes later and rushed home early every day just to have a fleeting chance to ask her how her day was. She was an ethereal magnet that I was always destined to be drawn to. Something about her always felt familiar, like home in a way that I've never had before.

Someone once told me to be careful of who feels like home to you when you come from toxic environments because home isn't where you should be, but this was different. This was everything I had wished home would be and then some. It was homemade baked goods and airy laughter in pillow forts, stealing childlike glances to feed my heart's desire to admire the beauty and grace through every moment I was allowed. Home felt the way love is portrayed in rom-coms. It's profound and all-knowing and all-encapsulating. The anxiety that turns your fingertips cold in all the best ways. Constantly checking your phone for a text and staring longingly at a picture of them and willing the universe to make them love you back.

It's the fierce desire to protect her at all costs. Not because she was mine or that she was too fragile to survive on her own but almost instinctual. She was perfect and anyone who thought otherwise would hear from my lawyer. She was worth fighting for. A love so profound it transcends every lifetime is worth fighting for until your last dying breath.

I couldn't have ever imagined a life where I would be happy to see the sun rise and set every day. A world where the rain could never dampen my mood. I lived in such squalor, running day in and day out in a monotonous existence that left me as empty and hollow as the summer days are long. Then she came along and introduced me to a world full of color and enthusiasm. It was hard not to fall in love with not only the new world around me but the woman who had decided that I was worth exploring it with. Her presence in my life was more profound than I had ever anticipated, and I know I'll spend every moment wishing I could have her back.

I never got to sample her heartbeat in a song. I know it's silly, but from the first moment I felt her pace quicken under my touch that first night in my apartment, I knew I wanted to be able to hear it whenever I wanted. I wanted to remind myself of the reason my days will always be a little brighter. It would have become a personal mission of mine to include it in as many songs as I could, my little signature and an ode to my forever muse.

I'll never get to hold her in my arms again or kiss her over every square inch of her body. I swore to myself that I would spend the rest of my life giving her enough kisses to make her sick of me. My hands have ached to be on her, holding her, in some way ever since they first felt her soft skin underneath my palms. I'll never get to watch her age like fine wine or see her experience all that our life together had to offer. I'll never get the chance to sing her to sleep like she'd begged me to do once she found out I could carry a tune. I'll never get to bring her flowers or pick out new furniture with her. She'll never get to hear me tell her I love her. And I do. I love her so much it hurts. I love everything she is and everything she was supposed to become.

River loved this poet, Florence Cromwell, who wrote one of her favorites. I remember the excitement she felt when she first read it, immediately texting me the poem followed by a garbled string of letters and symbols. I was at work, staring off into space trying to find a good muse through the dreary weather.

> I take in the gloomy days,
> Wet pavement and puddles that hold memories of youth.
> A cold that chills the ache in my bones.
> An earthy smell of rainwater and warm inside jokes.
> A fleeting memory of us, a car ride full of blasting music.
> We laugh as the trees hang down above us,
> A gentle touch from nature herself.
> Rain slides down frosted glass, and I remember the way I felt.
> A sunny memory,
> A campfire that sits in my soul
> And leaves a painful taste of smoke in my mouth.
> Memories that I never want to forget,

The nostalgia suffocating me.

I hadn't the slightest idea then that I would be forced to spend the rest of my life living out her favorite poem. Nothing could have prepared me for the idea that the life of the person I love most in this world would one day turn into a pile of things that wouldn't even begin to make up the complexity of her spirit. The physical items she'll leave behind will collect dust in an empty home. I'll be too sentimental to get rid of the only remaining heirlooms of her existence. The things that once were, become the things that will never be. I'll wrangle the ache in my center with the aforementioned suffocating nostalgia by rifling through her things, leaving fleeting tear stains on clothes that no longer smell like her. I'll mourn my loss first, but I'll mourn her losses forever more. The constant reminders of the things she'll never get to experience will eat away at my soul like rust on a neglected childhood bike.

I used to believe that it was better to never love at all than to love and lose it. However, River's shown me that even through this insurmountable pain, I'm so grateful to have known her, no matter how fleeting. It was nothing for someone to say, 'When you know, you know', and I had always laughed at them because how can you tell that someone is the person for you with just a look? But I took one look in her golden hazel eyes and saw a future and I found her just in time.

Just days before, I had contemplated how meaningful my life actually was, who I've surrounded myself with that would actually care if I disappeared. Life felt meaningless and the only thing keeping me going was music but then one day I looked into a stranger's eyes and felt at home. She looked at me with full eyelashes and a timid smile and there was a sense of familiarity in them, like we had met before in this lifetime and another.

It doesn't go without saying that I fell hard and fast for her. She's so immaculately beautiful it's hard not to. Her ever-flowing kindness is a beacon in my morally gray world. I had nothing to live for day to day until her. I thought I had lost her before, but that pales in comparison to now. The fear that overcame me then, I didn't know if I would survive that, but this? This is a million times worse because she's actually gone. That there's no real coming back from the grave with this one.

But I'm trying. For whatever it's worth, I'm trying to save her.

The cold December air whips around me as the wind picks up, icing my tears to my chilled skin. Numb hands have lost all their strength as they continue to dig into the dirt below.

There's a ringing in my ears and a pounding in my head that I can't shake. This feels too real in a way I had never wished to experience.

In all my time spent daydreaming about us, about our future together, I had always hoped that I would die first. I know it's selfish, but the thought of living the rest of my days without her in them to make them bright and bubbly, well I surely didn't want to experience it. But now, all I'm left with is the finite memories and an ache in my chest that I'm not sure will ever go away.

A hand reaches out, gently caressing my shoulder. Turning my head to peer at the darkened figure, hoping that maybe I, too, will be taken by death, I see a tall, shadowed silhouette. And even though the figure doesn't have any distinguishable features, I can tell that it's looking at me with a look of pity.

Pity for the poor, wretched soul.

I'm instantly hit with a pang of hatred. Everyone's going to pity me. I'll carry this loss around like a scarlet letter and its presence will ignite an anger in me that time could never cure. I don't want sympathy, a room full of flowers, or cards that express empty condolences because no one will know how much I love her. She'll always be the dead girlfriend, but 'they only dated for a little while, so I don't know why he's so torn up about it.'

The whispers and sideways glances will be too much to bear. No one will believe me that this will be the death of me. No one will understand when I say that grief doesn't even begin to scratch the surface of emotions that I'll be tormented with for the rest of my willing life. People will ask me when I plan to move on and be shocked when I answer with never. They won't understand that you wait lifetimes upon lifetimes to find a love like River.

The kind of love you nurture and grow and cherish every day. You wake up and suddenly all of your ailments are gone, the sun shines brighter, and there's a pep in your step that wasn't there before. It's a kind of love that never harbors resentment even after a fight because they are your lighthouse and neither of you could help that the shore is a bit rockier than expected. Every choice you make includes them, not because you have to, not because of any obligations, but because love blossoms when fed. You hand-feed it grapes on a picnic blanket in the park on a spring afternoon. You buy the flowers, but she'll love them more if you pick them out of your garden, trim them, and put them in a vase full of water.

Build her the pillow fort. Cook her dinner. Pick up her favorite candy bar at the store when you go. Love will bloom where it's planted, but it will spread like dandelion seeds when cultivated. Relationships are work, love is not. Love should come as easily as water flows because when you love someone, it shouldn't be forced. Maybe I was always destined to love her.

I promise to love you in every lifetime.

"What you're asking for comes at a high price, my friend." The recently bodied, but still a little fuzzy on the constructs, voice says a little more solemnly than before. "And I can't guarantee she hasn't crossed over yet."

I don't dare ask what happens if she has. If her soul has decided to move on.

"Name your price." I grit through clenched teeth and still-shaking shoulders. The being pauses, letting the picked-up wind be the only testament to the wilderness around us.

"Anything."

"Your soul." It says, again, almost somberly. "An equal exchange."

CHAPTER 39

River

I spent forever watching the highlights of Leon and I in every lifetime. Everything from meetings to proposals to childbirth to death. I watched as the film of our lives ran on an endless spool of tape, a sense of warmth cascading over my ethereal form. Leon always looks the same in every iteration of the film, but our lives are always vastly different in ways I can't even begin to describe. Hell, in one lifetime, he was a prince. I knew he had a sense of royalty about him.

I had never wanted children in this lifetime, but seeing Leon hold the cutest baby girl who adores him just as much as I do could have changed my mind in an instant. He always insisted on naming our daughters after flowers. Jasmine, Lily, Iris, Aster, and Dahlia. All our girls from all of our lifetimes were always beautiful, smart, well-mannered babies. He was so good with our girls. We were so full of love and happiness; it radiated wherever we went. He always had a flower garden filled with flowers named after our children. He's never aware that he does it, but he nurtures his flowers in the way he does our love and our kids. He never raises his voice.

If this is what heaven is supposed to be, then by all means, I'll take it. An eternity filled with watching the love that I'll never get to experience to the fullest. All of the things I could have hoped we would become unfolded before me. We were happy. We were in love.

My god, we were so in love that it hurts.

I just want to see Leon one more time. Then I think I can die. I think he's the only thing keeping me here. Something is keeping my spirit here. A tethered cord that has yet to break, and I'd like to think it's him. That the universe is letting me hold out until I can see him just one more time. My ghostly form can kiss his forehead as he kneels over my mortal body, and I know he'll feel my presence. I can tell him I love him finally, and then the reaper beside me can walk me home where I'll spend every lifetime looking for him again.

"Alaric." The reaper finally says. I'm startled by his deep, yet soothing voice.

"What?" I ask instinctually.

"My name is Alaric." He reiterates with the patience of a saint. I wonder if he is.

"That's a pretty name." I compliment, and for just a moment I think he's blushing. But it's a fleeting moment. His stoic demeanor returns without much fuss. Alaric's brow furrows. *Uh oh. That's not a good sign.* "What is it?" I ask.

"Someone's calling you." He asks with a puzzled expression.

"Huh?" I ask. "Who?"

"Do you have any outstanding debts?" He asks. Like a bill collector? I raise an eyebrow at him and for the briefest of moments, I forget that he's not human. "I'll take that as a no."

"But who's calling?" I ask again, a little pushier this time.

"A demon." He says, turning my blood (if I had any) cold. "They say your time's not up yet."

"Why?" I ask. *Damn, I'm full of questions.*

"I don't know. I had specific orders." He hums intrinsically. As if this phenomena didn't occur to him.

"Do I have to go?" I ask, almost sad that I have to leave.

He nods. "I can't go against orders."

"Oh." I mumble. "Well, if it's any solace, I enjoyed your company."

"Thank you, River." He says politely. The hint of blush is back.

"When it's my time, can I have you again?" I ask innocently. I don't even know if reapers work like that. Or if I can request a certain one. Now that I'm a veteran at dying. I should be considered a VIP.

"I will let my supervisor know." Alaric chuckles deeply, reverberating into my bones, if I had any. I'm just a soul.

A pathway opens where the movie theatre screen once sat showing the most beautiful movie I'd ever seen. The pathway is a dirt road, barely illuminated by the inky-black night sky. For the first time since ... Whatever this is, I feel scared. I wasn't scared to die, or cross over, or anything. But going back scares me. Because why am I going back? I'm excited to see Leon, but will he be there when I return?

"Alaric?" He hums out a 'yes?' "Will you walk with me?"

"Of course." Alaric stands, holding out his arm for me to take. Once again, the patience of a saint. His smile is soft, his arm is strong. I feel weak standing, and I don't know why. He can sense my struggle.

"What's happening to my soul?"

"You're returning. You're starting to feel what your physical body feels. It's been quite some time since your soul left your body."

"What does that mean?" I ask, more like a terrified child than an anxious, yet eager almost-transcended soul.

"It means that you may take a little longer to recover, but you will." We walk down the dirt road together, arms linked. Alaric carries a sense of comfort that I'll miss.

Is it weird to say you'll miss your reaper? Is that what he is?

"Is your title 'reaper' or 'grim reaper' or is it something else?" I ask, trying to squeeze in one more question before I go. He chuckles again, his eyes squinting slightly.

"Just reaper." He confirms. "Grim is reserved for the highest-ranked reaper."

"You guys have ranks?" I ask with raised eyebrows.

"We do." He says matter-of-factly. "You're an interesting woman."

"Thanks?" I say. It's my turn to blush.

"In all my years, I've never met someone who asked as many questions as you."

"If you give me a few more minutes, I can think of some more." I joke. We both chuckle. He halts us in the middle of an empty crossroads.

"How about you keep all those questions for the next time you see me?" He compromises. It warms a part of my heart, or where my heart should be. I nod.

"Deal."

"Don't go making deals with just any creature." He warns with a wink. "I don't want to see you until you die of old age." I give him a military salute and he grins. "Are you ready?"

I look at him and then our surroundings. "No."

"You'll be okay." He reassures me. "I wouldn't bring you back if I wasn't sure." I nod again. "Close your eyes." And I do. Putting my full trust in Alaric. He takes us a step forward and then says, "Okay. Open your eyes."

As I do, I take in the same crossroads that lay before us. This time, though, I see a shadow figure hunched over Leon hunched over me. My body. What's left of my mortality.

Alaric and the shadow figure stare at one other for a moment before the shadow says something I don't understand. Alaric nods along to whatever is said before turning to me.

There's almost a familiarity in his eyes when he says, "It's been a pleasure, River Grimaldi. Until we meet again."

Before I can say a single word, both Alaric and the shadow figure disappear. Leaving me standing over my own body and boyfriend. He's crying. Profusely.

Time passes in a weird way that only David Tennant's The Doctor could explain properly.

I let out a sigh of relief at seeing him again, and I

could have sworn he heard me. He looks around confused at something, but quickly drops it to continue focusing on my still lifeless body.

Leon's shaky hands are outstretched and cautious like his touch would cause harm to my already dead body. They're coarse and cold, but still warm against my skin and I can feel it in my spirit. It sends a radiating light through me that warms me to my core.

I stand next to Leon, who's hunkered over my body, staring at me with the saddest eyes I've ever seen. He looks tired and I know he hasn't eaten or slept. He cradles my hand in both of his, making sure to be gentle. A soft kiss is placed on my skin from chapped lips, tears still stain his perfect cheeks.

His breath is warm against my skin as he whispers to me. "Oh, angel. I'm so sorry." *It's okay, baby.* "Please come back to me. I can't lose you. I love you." *I love you too.*

I place my hand on top of his, hoping to feel him from across the veil and I think I almost do. Tears remain steadily falling from his bejeweled eyes, still shimmering through the immense pain I know he's feeling. He squeezes my hand gently as a wave of the world's most pitiful lip quiver rolls over his mouth. I can feel the pain radiating off of him. *It's time.*

CHAPTER 40

Leon

I feel like I've aged an eternity between when we first got here Friday night and now. I was so ready to give up, not on River, but on living. I had no desire to go on without her in my life. She's the love of my life, my guiding light, my anchor. Without her, I don't want to go on. Nothing is tethering me to this shitty existence other than her. When I felt our invisible string snap, I thought there certainly wasn't a way to change it other than to join her on the other side.

Hell really knew how to make a beggar out of me.

I begged and pleaded with her and that demon for as long as I could to pull through this. Do it for me. Do it for our future. I begged the universe to give me one more chance and I promise I won't fuck it up this time. If she makes it out of this, there won't be a day that goes by that I won't spend making it up to her. I'll do everything in my power to make sure she's loved and well taken care of. I promised to love her and cherish her until my last dying breath. And as I sit in the middle of this backwoods crossroad, alone and anxiously waiting for her soul to come back to her body, I find myself making lists of all the things that we're going to do once she's back.

I'll take a year off and we can travel the world, anywhere she wants to go, I'll take her. I'll make sure we go out on dates often, so she knows that I want the world to know she's mine. I want us to get married and grow old, the whole nine. I want to sit her on my lap in my studio and teach her everything I know. I want to hold her every night and kiss her every morning. I want to write sappy notes in cards, ones that she'll store in a keepsake box and read whenever she's feeling sentimental.

I will sing her to sleep every night, even when my voice is harsh and dilapidated from wear. I will be the best version of myself that I have to offer because she deserves it. I will spend the rest of eternity making it up to her, for what I had to do to get her back. I will pay for this for a million lifetimes. Whatever the price, if it means that she'll pull through.

My soul was just the beginning.

"Leon," A raspy, raw voice calls up to me. Looking down at River, I expect nothing to have changed, but I am so wrong. Color has sprung back into her face, her body's warm, and her golden eyes flutter open.

"Hey, angel." I coo, instantly smoothing out her windswept hair. There's an ache that lingers in the back of my throat, and tears stain my eyes again, but this time for all the right reasons.

Big hazel eyes gleam up at me, a small smile on her still slightly blue lips to accompany them. She gives me the tiniest wave with weak arms, causing my heart to soar. I place a gentle kiss on her lips before taking her hand in mine.

"Hey, handsome. Long time no see." She squeaks, her voice raspy and unsure, but it's hers. I'd recognize it anywhere.

"Too long." I say in a hushed tone. I don't know why I'm whispering, but I am. A silence lingers between us. I don't know what to say other than "I love you."

"I love you, too." She breathes with a small smile. My breath hitches in my throat.

She said it back.

"Let's get you home." I say, lifting her into my arms. I don't know where I'm going, but it doesn't matter. I just started walking down the dirt road. Away from the crossroads.

She's back. That's all that matters.

But this is far from over.

EPILOGUE

Leon

I met Asher outside of the one dive bar in town. I left River sound asleep under the watchful eye of my mother and Janice. There wouldn't be a doubt in my mind that she'd be well protected with those two keeping score.

It's been a couple of days since River's return. The first I'd heard from Asher since that night. He called me. I don't know how he got my number. But he called to ask to meet for a drink. To discuss the situation at length.

The dive bar is run by an Orc in disguise. Or glamour. Depending on who asked and who answered. There are only monsters, magical creatures, allowed in, and I fit right in now.

I see Asher, his ashen brown mullet and denim jacket hard to miss. I walk up to him, patting him on the shoulder as a greeting, and sit down beside him. The Orc bartender slides me a beer without me having to ask. I accept it willingly.

"I see you're no worse for wear." I say, taking in how unscathed he looks.

He hums proudly. "She never saw it coming." He grins ear to ear. "She should have. Claiming to be a prophet and shit."

"She had it coming." I agree, trying desperately to fiddle with my newfound abilities. Trying to hide my newly developed *horns*.

"Gnarly." Asher points to them as their glamour slips

off.

"You don't have to hide them here." The Orc bartender says kindly. I smile graciously, though I was just trying to get the magic down right.

"Have you told River about your...?" Asher trails off when he notices I'm shooting daggers at him with my eyes. "Never mind."

"I don't know if I can."

"What? You have to!"

"What if she's mad about it?"

"You're a *demon* now, dude. You can handle your girl being mad at you."

"I certainly cannot." I huff. "She's much scarier."

"Yeah, whatever."

"I do have something to tell you, though." I say. His ears perk up. "I got a promotion."

ACKNOWLEDGEMENTS

To Jay, my husband. I cannot express to you how grateful I am to have such an amazing and supportive person in my corner. Thank you for always supporting me, for listening to my ramblings, and for the endless love you always show me. I love you.

To Bee, my sibling, editor, and first reader. Thank you for never shying away from my crazy ideas, late nights editing, and long plotting sessions. There can never be enough words in any language to express my sincerest gratitude for your limitless excitement. I'm excited to gush over characters with you for eternity.

To Steph and Chris, thank you for always loving me, supporting me, and showing me boundless enthusiasm for my projects. Thank you for nurturing my love for books and writing for as long as I can remember.

To my friends, Grace, Morgan, and Amanda. Words on a page will never suffice in saying how appreciative I am of your constant love and excitement. You have no idea how our friendships have shaped my life for the better.

To my family, near and far. Thank you, each and every one of you, for showing me that the sky's the limit. That there are no boundaries in your imagination. I hope you enjoy the monsters I've created on your behalf.

To the readers. Thank you, thank you, thank you! I truly never thought my stories would make it out into the world, but thanks to you, they will be loved. Take good care of my Leon and River. They'll always hold a special place in my heart, just as you will.

To myself. Hi. This has been a long time coming. I've been writing for as long as I can remember. My imagination has never taken a vacation. While I've written works that will never see the light of the day, I would like to appreciate that this one has. River and Leon (and others to come) deserve to have their stories told. Also, thank you for sticking to a plot for once. We've got a few more books hinging on this one.

ABOUT THE AUTHOR

HM Dawley is an author whose passion for storytelling began at a young age when she first started weaving stories that blended the eerie and the enchanting. A lifelong lover of books, Dawley has always been drawn to tales of the dark and supernatural, particularly those with a touch of romance that transcends the ordinary. When not immersed in the world of mysterious creatures and timeless or forbidden love, Dawley enjoys the company of those closest to her and her cats, who serve as both companions and occasional muses. With a talent for creating immersive, atmospheric worlds, Dawley's stories invite readers to explore the shadows, where passion and danger collide.